PRAISE FOR ALLEN WYLER

"*Deadly Errors* is a wild and satisfying ride. This is an 'up all night' pass into troubled places that only hard-working doctors know about, a turbulent world of trusting patients and imperfect humans struggling with the required image of perfection. Only a gifted surgeon like Allen Wyler could craft such a wild and wonderful best-of-the-breed medical thriller."   —John J. Nance, *New York Times* bestselling
author of *Orbit*

"*Deadly Errors* gave me chills again and again—it's original, insightful, and brilliantly paced—the sort of a thriller that only a doctor could have written. Wyler's sense of the worlds of the hospital and operating room are unsurpassed. You'll feel as if you are right there. This is a tense, taut, very scary book. It will be hard for any reader to put down."
        —Michael Palmer, *New York Times* bestselling author
of *Miracle Cure* and *The Sisterhood*

"Dr. Allen Wyler—who should know what he's talking about—perfectly captures that mystical combination of awe and terror that is the modern hospital. Dr. Wyler's debut novel is both an engrossing thriller and a cautionary tale of the all-too-frequent intersection of high technology and higher greed. It's a message all of us better pay attention to, or face the consequences."
        —Mark Olshaker, author of *Einstein's Brain, Unnatural
Causes,* and *The Edge;* coauthor of *Mindhunter, Jour-
ney into Darkness,* and *The Cases That Haunt Us*

"Just when you thought it was safe to go back and have your tonsils removed, Dr. Wyler writes a fast-paced thriller which reawakens your scariest misgivings about the medical-industrial complex and the profit motive corrupting the art of healing. This is a story told with authority by an insider, an unsettling backstage tour through the labyrinth of that place we have come to both fear and revere—the American hospital."

—Darryl Poniscan, author of *The Last Detail*

"*Deadly Errors* has a fascinating and frightening premise that gives it the potential to be a bestseller in the Robin Cook mold." —William Dietrich, author of *Hadrian's Wall*

"*Deadly Errors* will curl your toes and make you afraid to enter the hospital for even a minor procedure. No one can write operating room scenes like Allen Wyler. You couldn't get any closer to the action if you scrubbed in and held a retractor." —Don Donaldson, author of *Do No Harm* and *In The Blood*

DEAD HEAD

ALLEN WYLER

FORGE®

A TOM DOHERTY ASSOCIATES BOOK
NEW YORK

Copyright © 2007 by Allen Wyler

DEAD HEAD

A Forge Book
Published by Tom Doherty Associates, LLC
175 Fifth Avenue
New York, NY 10010

www.tor.com

Forge® is a registered trademark of Tom Doherty Associates, LLC.

ISBN-13: 978-0-765-35596-6
ISBN-10: 0-765-35596-5

First Edition: February 2007

Printed in the United States of America

0 9 8 7 6 5 4 3 2 1

DEDICATION

To Arthur A. Ward, Jr., for giving me the opportunity to learn the art of neurosurgery.

ACKNOWLEDGMENTS

In no particular order, I thank the following friends who provided informational contributions to this book: Daryl Gardner; Chip Bogosian, MD; Dave Himes; Russell Lonser, MD; Mary Osterbrock; Jim Laing; Jean Pierre Wirz; Rhonda Gardner; Sandra Schneider; and George Brookman. Special thanks to my agent Susan Crawford and to my editor, Natalia Aponte. For the record, the idea for this book originated with Natalia. Finally, thanks to Tom Doherty and Paul Stevens.

DEAD
HEAD

Georgetown Medical Center, Washington, D.C.

The Motorola cell phone/walkie talkie rang a second before a voice came from the tiny speaker. "Georgetown Trauma, this is EMS four. You have a copy?"

The General Surgery Chief Resident fumbled the instrument from her white lab coat pocket, pressed the worn rubber transmit button. "Affirmative, EMS four. Whatcha got?" She stood in front of a chest-high counter of forest green laminate, reviewing chart notes written an hour earlier by her junior resident describing the neurosurgical and orthopedic injuries sustained by a twenty-one-year-old Evel Knievel wannabe with a Harley Hog. Correction: make that an ex-Harley, since, from what the paramedics estimated, the overpowered machine was now a total wreck. On the wall behind the desk, a round military-style clock showed 14.22 hours.

Early afternoon and it had already turned into the day from hell. *What now?* she wondered.

"We're inbound with an unidentified male with massive crush injuries to abdomen, pelvis, and legs. Estimated ETA about two minutes." The siren wail could be heard in the background of the medic's concerned voice.

She sighed with fatigue, but was immediately perked up by the paradoxical adrenaline surge that an impending disaster can trigger. She started clicking through a mental checklist. "Any neurologic injuries?"

"None that we appreciate."

"Blood pressure?"

"Stable so far. But we've got two bags of Ringers running wide open through a couple a 14 intracaths. From the look of his thighs, he could've bled a couple liters into each one, easy. It's nasty."

"Okay. Got it."

The paramedic added, "I assume you'll pass the word on to the trauma officer of the day?"

With her free hand she pulled out a red, broad-tip, magic marker. "I *am* the trauma officer of the day." *Turkey.*

"Roger that. Out."

She dropped the cell phone back into her side pocket, uncapped the marker with her teeth and printed WDF??!!—her shorthand for What Da Fuck—in large block letters diagonally across the page before tossing the notes into the resident's in-box. She called to the charge nurse standing ten feet away folding a white sheet on an empty gurney, "Nora, we have a major crunch inbound. ETA about one minute from now. Is Trauma One cleaned up, ready to go?"

"Just finishing that now."

Starting toward the trauma bay, she mentally reviewed her well-ingrained knowledge of crush injuries: tissue trapped by compressing forces can cause crush injury syndrome. And if the crush is applied to muscle, it can squeeze huge amounts of acid and complex electrolytes—especially potassium—out to the surrounding extracellular space to become trapped in the affected muscles. Then as the crushing force is released, those concentrated toxic chemicals are liberated into the blood-stream and transported to the heart, kidneys, liver, and other vital organs with disastrous results, like cardiac arrest. Not only that, but the decompression can lead to internal hemorrhage and shock. The syndrome's severity is directly related to the amount and location of injury. Bottom line: This inbound patient was probably a setup for a series of horrendous, life-threatening problems. Of course, that scenario assumed the poor guy survived the next several hours. It was her job to make certain he made it through the ER. If he was going to die, it'd be later in ICU. Not here. Not on her watch.

After making sure his blood pressure and airway were stable, they'd need to image all areas—chest, pelvis, legs—looking for fractures. Even if the ribs weren't fractured, because of the high risk of hypovolemic shock from internal bleeding she figured they'd probably need to intubate him. Sooner or later.

"Nora. Better get an X-ray tech to standby. Oh, and call a respiratory therapist, too."

That was the bad news. The good news was the paramedic didn't believe the patient had neurological trauma. So far, at least. This meant there was no need to try to convince a neurosurgery resident to break scrub and come out of surgery to see the patient. Not yet, at least.

She leaned into Room Two and called to her junior resident. He was hunched over suturing up a scalp laceration, "Yo, Hamilton, got us a major thrash on the way in, so get that closed up pronto. I'm going to need you."

He glanced up, his fingers continuing to tie and cinch the double-square surgeon knot while saying. "This is the last one."

She heard the distant siren just before it cut off. A moment later the automatic doors swooshed open and two paramedics rushed in pushing a collapsible gurney, hesitated only long enough for the charge nurse's extended arm to direct them toward the empty trauma bay.

Two nurses, clad in green scrubs, waited next to the receiving gurney, a white plastic transfer board ready. One paramedic dropped the stretcher's side rails while the nurses wedged the plastic board under the patient's right side, making a smooth bridge across the potential gap between gurneys. Pulling on the white "draw sheet" under the victim, they slid him across the slick plastic to the ER gurney.

Transfer complete, the surgery chief resident moved in to begin examining the man while one nurse began exchanging the EMT's EKG leads and blood pressure cuff for their own. The other nurse scooped up the two plastic bags of lactated ringers the medics had dumped onto the sheet between the patient's legs to hang them from a stainless steel IV pole suspended from the ceiling.

The victim appeared to be midtwenties. First impression: Middle Eastern, maybe. Black hair, black mustache, dark skin. Handsome. Blindly pulling the stethoscope from her pocket and uncoiling it, she asked him, "How you doing?" and wondered if he spoke English. An exchange student, maybe?

His glassy eyes moved to her, "Hurts."

"Where are you?" she asked in an attempt to establish his mental status.

"Hurts."

"What's your name?"

This time he didn't respond.

"No neurologic problem, my ass." she muttered.

His T-shirt—which looked like an early seventies tie-dye replica—had been cut up the center by the paramedics to make room for the EKG pads. Quickly, using the stethoscope bell, she listened to both lungs. Strong breathing sounds from both sides. Good. No air escaping into the chest. At least if he had rib fractures they hadn't punctured a lung. Next, the abdomen. It didn't look or feel distended. This time she used the stethoscope diaphragm to listen, but heard no bowel sounds—a finding she'd more or less expected, given the severity of the trauma. But it meant just one more thing the surgeons would have to monitor once he was transferred to the TICU, since he was at such a high risk for a bowel perforation.

She called out to whoever had a free hand, "Get an NG tube and some suction in here, please," thinking: this guy's gut needs to be hooked up to suction as soon as possible. Last thing she needed right now was for him to vomit and aspirate tissue-burning gastric juice and chewed food into his lungs. As if he didn't have enough problems. She stuffed the folded stethoscope into her coat pocket and began to palpate his abdomen again. *Just my luck, he's got a quarter pounder, supersized fries, and a Coke sloshing around in here.*

A phlebotomist materialized on her right. "You called for lab work?"

Fingers prodding, blindly accounting for anatomy she expected to be there—edge of liver, spleen—she answered, "Chem 12, crit, creatinine, myoglobin, type, and cross for at least four units packed cells." She glanced at the trauma nurse across from her. "What'd I forget?"

"Think you got it all. For now, at least."

She called to the phlebotomist, "On second thought, think you better draw an extra red top just in case," before unfastening the man's wide black leather belt and unzipping his denims. Gently, she began to probe for the bony pelvic bridge just above his penis. "Awwww hell's bells!"

"What?"

"Feels like his whole pelvis is gone." She pulled bandage scissors from her coat pocket and started to cut away his jeans. "We need X-ray in here, STAT. Then get Urology down here. No chance in hell we'll be able to snake a Foley in him. Ten to one they're going to have to place a suprapubic instead. Assuming, of course, he lives long enough for them to get here."

CHAPTER

7:01 PM EST, McLean, Virginia

Marci Dillon dropped the portable phone back into the charger, snuffed out the Virginia Slim Menthol Light, took another sip of Kendall Jackson Chardonnay and wondered what the hell to do for dinner. She checked her wristwatch, sighed, and decided to order a pizza. Angela loved pizza. She took another sip before yelling, "Hey, Angie. How about we get some pizza for dinner?"

No answer.

Marci glanced around the granite and stainless steel kitchen, pushed off the counter stool and stepped to the sliding glass door. "Hey, Angie, time for dinner."

No answer.

At the stairs to the second floor now, she called up, "Angie!" wondering how the little sneak could've made it past her without being noticed. When her daughter didn't answer she climbed the stairs and looked in her room. Then she checked the bathroom and her own room. Back down on the first floor she peered in every room in the small condo before running to the backyard again, anxiety fomenting in her gut. "Angie, stop this game you're playing. You're making Mommy very worried and I don't like that."

Next, she checked the carport, the car, even the neighbor's yard. Nothing.

4:01 PM PST, Moscone Convention Center, San Francisco

"In conclusion," Russell clicked the mouse to advance the PowerPoint presentation to the summation slide, "we've shown the ability to use the activity of hundreds of individual neurons in a monkey's brain to manipulate a robotic hand with the same precision as the monkey's own arm. Ladies and gentlemen, what was once science fiction is now reality." He paused to let that important point—the take-home message of the entire presentation—sink in.

"In closing, I thank my colleague, Doctor Gerda Fetz, for her ongoing collaboration on this project." He gave the audience a hint of a bow. "And thank you for listening."

As the 1,500-member audience began an enthusiastic applause, an audiovisual gnome cloistered in the cavernous darkened ballroom brightened the overhead lights. On the massive screen, Russell's slide was replaced by the blue and white logo of the American Association of Neurological Surgeons annual meeting.

To Russell's left, at the corner of the stage, the session moderator leaned forward to adjust the microphone on the small table in front of her. "Thank you, Doctor Lawton, for your very informative and, I think it's fair to say, provocative presentation." After quickly consulting her wristwatch she continued, "Since we are still holding to this afternoon's tight schedule, we have time for a few questions from the audience."

Several eager participants were already queued up at the various microphones placed at strategic locations along the aisles. She pointed to the closest man. Russell recognized Doctor Herman Nofziger, the notorious chairman of Neurosurgery for a prestigious California university.

Smiling, scanning his immediate neighbors in the audience—mostly old cronies, since the old guard tended to cluster together like herd animals—Nofziger cleared his throat before tossing Russell the perfunctory laudation intended to vindicate the stiletto stab wound that would surely follow. "Doctor Lawton, let me first congratulate you on your extremely elegant research."

Nofziger paused. Russell thought, *But . . .*

"But bear with me a moment, Russell," using his first name as if they were old tennis buddies enjoying a courtside, towel-over-the-shoulder mineral water and lime after a hard-fought, but sportsmanlike match, "I have a two-part question for you. First, although your work is, as I just stressed, elegant, how do you see it applied to day-to-day clinical issues? I mean *practical* clinical issues."

Sucking a tooth, Russell tempered his response sufficiently to justify his own philosophical position while at the same time acknowledging his junior-level position in the dog-eat-dog academic hierarchy. "Let me tell you a story about a real patient . . . an unfortunate man who lost both arms in a job-related accident. Researchers at the Rehabilitation Institute of Chicago outfitted him with a kind of bionic arm, which is controlled directly by his thoughts. Now he can do things like simple, basic activities of daily living that he never would've been able to do without that arm. Think about that, and I bet we'd all agree it's worth something.

"We're undertaking very similar work in our lab. If we can refine this technology, we can truly help very disabled people. As I'm sure you know, the first direct brain-computer hookups have already been achieved in paralyzed humans, with," he rocked his outstretched palm back and forth to indicate questionable enthusiasm, "limited success. Just a few years ago the FDA granted Cyberkinetics—a Massachusetts company—approval to implant chips containing hundreds of microelectrodes into the brains of five quadriplegics to evaluate whether their thoughts could control robotic arms. Since then, at least two other research teams have started similar brain-machine experiments in humans." He could feel the enthusiasm buoying his voice, spreading out, infecting the audience. He got this way sometimes, his enthusiasm carrying him to a high. "Those of us working in this area are not trying to make just a mere incremental change for these people. We're shooting for breakthrough."

The professor nodded sagely. "Yes, yes. All those various applications would be obvious to a first-year orthopedic resident," slipping a little neurosurgeon humor into it. "The point, Russell, is do you *really* believe in your heart of hearts that the taxpayers should be dumping such huge amounts of precious research money into this line of exploration, when the end result benefits only a very few people?" He paused with the oratorical aplomb of a seasoned Southern senator. "Ask yourself how many quadriplegics there are compared to, say, the millions of people who suffer back pain?"

"You are hardly the first person to very eloquently emphasize this point of view, Professor," throwing back some of the same insincere praise, "but I don't believe it's a question that can be answered within the time limits allotted for my talk."

Before the exchange could escalate, the moderator leaned into her microphone. "Unfortunately, that's all the time we have for questions. I suggest that the rest of you with questions for Doctor Lawton discuss them with him during the next three days of the meeting." She glanced at a piece of paper on the table in front of her. "The next presentation . . ."

Russell zoned out, concentrating instead on negotiating the narrow, shadowy stairs leading down off the stage. Clear of the bottom stair he stood motionless, grappling with what to do now that the anxiety of standing behind a podium and looking at an intimidating audience had mercifully vanished, leaving him mentally fatigued but exhilarated at his performance. Stay and listen to the remaining afternoon presentations, or wander over to the exhibits and check out displays of new instruments? He quickly scanned the schedule and realized the final two talks—both summarizing results from a national brain tumor chemotherapy protocol—held little interest for him.

The next speaker's amplified voice began droning as the ballroom light dimmed. The audience hushed to listen.

Russell headed to the back of the room where the audience was still in flux, some attendees wandering in, heads swinging back and forth as their dark-adapting eyes searched for a place to sit while others beat a hasty retreat to the exit. He immediately sensed the presence of someone to his right and turned. A female voice whispered, "Doctor Lawton, may I speak with you a moment?"

He nodded. "Sure. Let's step outside."

They stopped about twenty feet from the auditorium door on the fringe of conventioneers streaming by. She was slender, maybe five foot five inches, flawless light brown skin, sparkling almond eyes, luxurious black hair secured into a ponytail. Indian or Pakistani, he suspected. She wore a well-tailored dark brown business suit, a cream-colored silk scarf knotted around a gracefully long, narrow neck.

Smiling, she offered her hand. "Raveena Khan. I do freelance reporting for a number of scientifically oriented publications, *Scientific American* being one."

Impressed, he shook her warm hand, said, "Russell

Lawton," and realized how lame that sounded since she had already addressed him by name.

"Could you possibly spare a few minutes for an interview, or are you rushing off to another important meeting?"

He considered the exhibits again, then realized they wouldn't be going anywhere during the next three days. "No, I have time."

She fumbled in her beige leather purse, came out with a small spiral notebook and a black Cross Pen. "I am absolutely fascinated by your work and its potential to help people. Thus, I would like to ask you a few questions, if I may." She paused, seductively holding direct eye contact. "Doctor Lawton sounds so formal. May I call you Russell?" Without looking at it, she flipped open the notebook.

"Please."

"I couldn't help but wonder if your technique might be applied to patients with locked-in syndrome?"

"Locked-in syndrome?" he repeated softly, with a note of surprise.

"Yes. You know about it, of course? . . . It's a rare—"

He raised his hand, interrupting her explanation. "Sure, I know the syndrome. It's just that it *is* so rare, I'm surprised you know of it. But just to be sure we're talking about the same diagnosis, it's a neurological disorder characterized by complete paralysis of voluntary muscles in all parts of the body, except for those that control eye movement. It can be the result of a head injury, stroke, multiple sclerosis, or drug overdose. The victims are conscious and can think and reason, but they're completely unable to speak or move. Their only possible means of communication is through blinking. Are we talking about the same thing here?"

She smiled. "Most certainly."

"Well then, the answer is yeah, sure. In fact," thinking back to Nofziger's barbed comments, "I've never thought about it in this light, but sure . . . locked-in syndrome is a perfect example of how a brain-robot interface might be applied."

"Yes, but what I am most interested in is, is it possible to use your techniques—microelectrode recording interfaced with computer-based artificial intelligence—to allow a patient with locked-in syndrome to communicate verbally? In other words, to use a patient's brain waves to produce speech?"

Interesting question, especially coming from a science writer. A question he and Gerda had tossed around during their frequent brainstorming sessions. They'd decided although it was theoretically possible, the present state of the art would render it technically extremely difficult to achieve.

"Yes, it's possible. *Theoretically,* that is." He nodded more to himself than her. "Yeah, as a matter of fact, Doctor Fetz and I have kicked the possibility around several times. Kind of."

"Then you've worked out an approach to the problem?"

Well, not exactly the specifics, but in general. "Yes."

She held deep, penetrating eye contact. Was she hitting on him? Naaawwww, not possible, he decided. Still . . .

She said, "You can't believe how fascinating I find this." She finally broke eye contact to glance around. "I'd love to hear more about this, but I don't want to keep you from your meeting." She spread her arms as if it was *his* meeting. "You're being too gracious as it is." She flashed a heart-stopping smile and bore into his eyes again.

"No problem. Besides, there was nothing left this afternoon I was dying to listen to."

"Yes, but I suspect the depth that I wish to talk about will take more than a few minutes." She dropped her eyes, as if preparing to ask a difficult question. "You don't suppose we could go somewhere quieter, do you? It's impossible to even think with all this noise." Her face suddenly brightened, as if tumbling to an idea. "I would love to buy you a drink if you have the time," she stated encouragingly, locking eyes again, teasing him again with the fantasy that her interest resided more in having a drink together than his work. Was she hitting on him?

"I'd be delighted, but the thing is, I'm not very familiar with San Francisco. Did you have some place in mind? Something close by?"

She started toward the exit, her beige pumps clicking against the cement floor. He fell in beside her. She offered offhandedly, "There is this lovely little bar at my hotel. The Stanford Court. Do you know it?"

"No."

"We can catch a cab. It's only a few blocks away. But further than I care to walk in these blasted shoes. In fact, I can't wait to take them off."

He pushed opened one of the large glass doors to the outside, letting her pass, then followed her outside onto the driveway paralleling Howard Street.

She said, "This way," and turned right.

"But the cabs are down there," nodding to his left.

She continued walking away from him. He caught up to her just as a black limo with tinted windows pulled to a stop in the drive-through loading zone. Two men, the driver and a passenger stepped out, both wearing well-tailored dark suits and wraparound sunglasses. The driver stood with one hand on the top of the opened door, the other hand on the car roof, his sunglasses aimed over the roof straight at Russell. Raveena walked to the passenger door, turned to Russell. "They will drive us to my hotel."

Both men struck him as Middle Eastern. Iranian, Turkish, Lebanese, who the hell knew? Black hair, black moustaches, probably somewhere in their midthirties. Russell stopped five feet from the woman, a gut-level premonition screaming at him not to climb in the Lincoln. "Know what . . . I just remembered I'm supposed to meet this guy . . ."

"Get in, Doctor Lawton." The other man opened the rear passenger door.

Russell held up both palms vertically and backed up a step. "Whoa, sorry . . . not interested, bud."

Before he could turn to walk away, the man slid a flat-black handgun with an attached sound suppressor from under his suit coat. He aimed it dead center at Russell's chest. "Doctor Lawton, please do not force me to kill you."

CHAPTER

2

Homestead Apartments, Washington, D.C.

FBI Special Agent Sandra Phillips shut the front door of her one-bedroom utility apartment and kicked off her black flats and ran her hand over hair cropped short enough to reveal the shape of her skull. She wore a tan blazer and skirt and a cream-colored blouse that contrasted with her ebony skin. For one blessed moment she felt the weight of the day lift from her slender five foot-ten inch frame. That's when her cell phone rang. She dug it out of her purse, flipped it open and recognized the number as coming from her boss's cell phone. "Phillips."

"Hate to bother you this late in the day, Sandy, but we just got a tip from security at Georgetown Medical Center. I need you to follow up on it. Seems the medics brought in a severely injured trauma patient the other day. Male. Midtwenties. Middle Eastern ethnicity. With this All-Hands-On-Deck recent terrorist situation we presently have underway, I think it would be particularly prudent if you run over there and nose around a little. See what you can dig up about this kid."

She glanced at the gold-plated Seiko on her left wrist—a graduation present from her brother. Seven thirty-three. "Why tonight? I mean, if he's in the trauma center, he's not going anywhere in the next eight to ten hours, is he? What makes this guy so interesting?"

"That's true, but the thing is, the victim doesn't have insurance. A couple of his friends came in three hours ago and signed a commitment to pay his medical expenses. Then they deposited fifty thousand into an escrow account." He paused a beat. "How many kids in their twenties have that kind of cash lying around?"

"I see." She sighed, wriggled her toes back into the still warm shoes. "What name am I looking for?"

"Mohammed."

"That's it? Mohammed?"

"That's all they could get from him."

Moscone Convention Center, San Francisco

Russell Lawton said, "You got to be kidding. Right?"

Over his left shoulder late afternoon traffic was speeding by on Howard Street. An intermittent flow of one to three conventioneers, each one wearing color-coded plastic ID badges and schlepping dark-blue canvas AANS tote bags, was drifting past on the sidewalk heading back to nearby hotels, oblivious to the small drama playing out here in the passenger loading zone. Russell became acutely aware of car exhaust in the air and fear squeezing his heart. He heard the distinct sound of a helicopter passing overhead.

Frowning, Raveena shook her head. "They are very serious, Doctor Lawton. I advise you to do as they say."

From behind Russell a strong male voice asked, "Is there a problem here?"

Russell turned to see a uniformed SFPD officer approaching from the street. Before he could yell a warning or ask for help, the man with the gun aimed at the officer. Russell heard two thuds in rapid succession, like a fist hitting a pillow. The officer dropped to the pavement with two closely spaced holes in his chest, directly over his heart.

The shooter grabbed Russell by the arm, jammed the silencer into his ribs and started herding him toward the car with the stern command, "Move!"

Russell noticed Raveena climb into the front passenger seat and slam that door. The driver was also back inside now, his door closed, engine revving.

The shooter pushed Russell toward the open back door. "Get in!"

Dumbfounded, unable to see any other option, Russell slid into a backseat smelling of pine air freshener. The shooter followed him in, pulling the door shut behind them. The limo accelerated with a screech of tires. The driver tapped the brakes only long enough for one car to pass before fishtailing the heavy limo onto Howard Street to a chorus of protesting horns and screeching brakes. The driver began accelerating the Lincoln, weaving in and out of traffic.

For a moment no one spoke. Russell heard the man next to him catching his breath in an adrenaline burn and cracking his knuckles one handedly, left thumb bending each finger in succession, *pop pop pop*, before starting over again. Raveena barked a staccato series of words in an unfamiliar language to the driver. He shot back an abrupt answer in the same language.

Heart hammering his chest, Russell gulped a couple deep breaths and turned to peer through the rear window at the fallen cop, but a succession of neighboring buildings already obscured the Moscone Convention Center. The man sitting next to him continued aiming the black silencer at his chest, watching through expensive sunglasses.

"Jesus Christ, you killed him," Russell blurted.

The man aiming the gun at Russell's chest said nothing.

Russell glanced at Raveena, then at the driver. Neither one looked at him, even through the rearview mirror. As if sensing his eyes, the woman adjusted her posture to look over the seat. "Yes. Unfortunate, but necessary. I believe your military refers to such deaths as collateral damage, no?"

"Necessary? Jesus!" He noticed they were approaching a red stoplight at a busy intersection. The car began decelerating.

Russell reached for the door handle and waited for the car to come to a complete stop. The shooter was still aiming the gun at him, but would he shoot? And if he did, what were the chances the bullet would hit something vital? Just as the car seemed about to stop, Russell jerked the handle and threw his shoulder against the door. It didn't budge.

"It's locked," Raveena said as if expecting his reaction.

Russell's lungs seemed incapable of a full breath, his fingertips tingled. "Goddammit let me out of here," he yelled, pounding the flat of his hand against the tinted window in hopes of attracting the attention of the passenger in the car alongside or a pedestrian on the street. None of the people crossing the intersection seemed to notice. Or if they did, they continued on as if they hadn't, maybe thinking he was just another urban crazy.

"Stop it!" A fist slammed into Russell's flank.

Russell's kidney exploded with deep boring pain, doubling him over, filling his throat with nausea and the urge to vomit. He gasped and turned toward his attacker to fend off the next blow, but the man seemed satisfied with the results so far.

"Doctor Lawton, you are not going anywhere but with us. At least for the moment, you are not," Ravenna said.

Russell remained doubled over, clutching his aching flank, forehead a half inch away from the front seat. "What the hell's going on? What do you want from me? I don't have much money if that's what this is about."

"Money?" Raveena emitted a sarcastic grunt. "No, Doctor,

this has nothing to do with money," spitting out the word as if it were distasteful.

"Then what do you want from me? Have I ever done anything to wrong you? Did I take care of someone from your family?" Considering the diseases neurosurgeons deal with—aneurysms, brain tumors, head trauma, back pain—long-term surgical outcomes were often lousy regardless of the quality of medical care rendered. Leaving bitter emotions toward the surgeon.

"You will discover the answer to that question soon enough." Ravenna returned her attention back out the windshield.

Terrorists? Could they be terrorists? he wondered, but immediately rejected the idea as racial stereotyping. Then again . . .

He flashed on the rash of terrorist kidnapping and beheadings triggered by President Bush's ill-advised invasion of Iraq. Was he being kidnapped as a political statement? Naw, that didn't make sense.

A cell phone rang.

Raveena turned in her seat and looked expectantly at the shooter. He awkwardly shifted positions to dig a cell phone from his suit coat pocket while not allowing the gun to waver from Russell's chest. Using only his one hand, he flipped it open and put it to his ear. "Hussein."

Russell logged the name into memory, figuring he needed to try to remember as many small facts as possible.

Hussein smiled, "Yes, yes. Excellent . . . Thank you." He smiled at Russell before saying something to the driver. In turn, the driver said, "Doctor Lawton, you are wondering why we have, shall we say, conscripted you. Yes?"

"I think the word is kidnapped."

The driver waved dismissively. "Semantics . . . only a matter of semantics. You see, we require your assistance on a delicate matter of grave importance to us."

His three captors had accents, Raveena's the slightest. In addition, the driver's carried a hint of British boarding school. Russell cataloged that away, too. "Assistance with what?"

"All in good time, my friend."

"Your friend? Not fucking likely. And as far as assistance, count me out."

"I believe you have no choice. Any refusal to help us will result in your death."

Russell chewed on that for a moment, his mind still trying to assimilate the situation. If they need me, he reasoned, then they can't very well kill me. Can they? But what if they *were* terrorists? In that case, they probably would kill him. Eventually. He thought about the videotapes of hostages— some beheaded, others shot—that surfaced through Al Jazeera. But that was in the Middle East. This was San Francisco. His thoughts flashed to the September 11th hijacked flight that crashed somewhere in Pennsylvania before reaching its intended target, the group of hostages sacrificing themselves for a greater good.

Russell sucked a deep breath, said, "Well then, I guess you'll have to kill me, because it'll be a cold day in hell before I give you any help."

The driver nodded pensively before saying, "You love your little daughter, Angela, yes?"

A block of ice quick-froze the depths of Russell's gut as a dread-filled premonition warned him not to answer. Then he realized: they already knew her name. Another bolt of fear slammed him.

Hussein shifted the gun from one hand to the other and leaned confidently back against the car door.

The driver said, "She is very beautiful, is she not? And only eight years old. It would be a tragedy if something, shall we say, untoward, happened to her, yes?"

Primitive protective parental instinct warned Russell to say nothing.

Hussein nudged him and held up the cell phone, showing Russell it was the kind capable of taking and sending photographs. "This is a picture of your daughter, yes?"

Russell's first reaction was to turn away and not look, fearing what it might show, but concern for his only child overtook him. He reached out, pulled the small glowing screen closer. He gasped. It *was* Angela. A close-up. Her innocent face contorted, tear streaks glistened on her smooth little-girl cheeks.

Russell lunged, hands reaching for Hussein's neck. "Bastard!"

Hussein slammed the gun into Russell's left temple, obscuring his vision with dancing phosphenes. Pain exploded behind both eyes, forcing him to slump back against the leather seat.

The driver said, "As I understand it, your daughter is very claustrophobic." Then, to Raveena: "Claustrophobic . . . that is the proper word for it, is it not?"

Raveena nodded agreement.

Hussein removed his dark glasses, pressing the stems against his chest, folding them without disturbing his aim at Russell. With a smirk he casually slid them into his suit coat pocket.

The driver continued. "You see, Doctor Lawton, we have, as you Americans like to say, the upper hand. We have removed your daughter from your wife's home and are holding her as leverage. The decision is quite simple, actually. Either you help us, or we bury her alive. So there you have it. Her fate is completely in your hands."

CHAPTER

3

STUNNED, RUSSELL SAT staring at the driver's eyes in the rearview mirror as the black Lincoln worked its way through the congested San Francisco rush-hour traffic. Dark brown eyes filled with hatred.

Throat constricted with fear, Russell croaked, "Why are you doing this? What have I ever done to you?"

The driver raised his eyebrows. "You personally? Done to us? Nothing, of course."

"Then why are you doing this? For christsake, she's only a little girl. Eight years old . . . that's all she is." He glanced at Raveena, hoping that a woman with innate maternal instincts would support his plea.

Unlike the eyes that had so easily lured him from the convention center, they were now hard and cold, filling him with self-loathing at being so easily manipulated.

She said, "Your little girl is, as we said previously, leverage. We believe she might provide you with the proper incentive to assist us. You see, you have total control over her young life. If you cooperate fully with us, she lives. However, if you make any attempt to escape or warn anyone about us," she flipped her hand, as if to say, *it's out of my control*, "she will die a horrible death. It is that simple. Do you understand just what is at stake here?"

Again the frigid metallic fist squeezed his heart. Nausea stirred, forcing a surge of bile up his throat. He swallowed, just barely able to keep from vomiting. He tried to silence the anger and confusion consuming his mind and preventing him from thinking clearly. Just like during an unanticipated complication during surgery, panic could drive the surgeon down a destructive path of errors in critical judgment until the situation became unsalvageable. *Think!*

Russell blew out between pursed lips and wiped both palms on his thighs. "Know what I think? I think this is all bullshit. You don't have my daughter. There's no way you could've taken her from home." He shook his head. "No way."

None of his captors said a word.

"And that picture you have . . . that's all bullshit, too."

The driver asked, "And how could that be?"

"Oh man, that's so easy. The way they can alter things now with computers? Anybody with a software program like Adobe Photoshop can diddle a digital photo in about two minutes. So, that picture? All you need to do is send it to your cell phone. Yeah, it's total bullshit. I bet you don't even know where she is. You're just trying to screw with my mind. That's all this is."

"Yes?" The driver's eyebrow cocked in mock surprise. "Is this what you believe? We know a great many things about you and your daughter. You want examples? I will give them to you. Try this: She was staying with your ex-wife during this congress you were attending. Do you want your ex-wife's address? Or is it sufficient if I simply say she lives in McLean, Virginia?"

Russell swallowed.

"And we know the school she attends, the classes she takes. We even know her teacher's name. Shall I tell you? Of course,

I should. Does the name Agnes McKinney mean anything to you?"

Russell's mouth grew dry.

"You see, we removed her from the yard behind your ex-wife's condo. The yard with the swing. She had her Bratz doll, Cloe, with her. Her favorite doll. So let me ask: are you still convinced this is, as you say, bullshit?"

The fist squeezed his heart tighter.

Russell shook his head, more to convince himself than call their bluff. "No. You don't have her. No way, no how."

The driver spoke a few rapids word to Hussein.

Hussein removed his cell phone, handed it to Russell. "Then I suggest you are finding out for yourself. Call your wife if you are not believing us."

Russell snatched the phone from Hussein's hand. "Yeah, damned right I'll call her," thinking that if these fools really *do* have her, it would be great to leave their cell phone number in the phone records for the police to find.

Marci picked up halfway through the first ring. "Yes?"

"Marci. Russell. Let me speak to Angela." No hello, no how you doing. Their strained relationship long past the point of normal civility. But by joint unspoken agreement, they really did attempt to minimize the relentless bickering in front of their only child.

"You son of a bitch!"

"What?"

"You goddamned son of a bitch. What have you done with her?"

"Done with her? What the hell you talking about?"

"You know goddamned well what I'm talking about, you smug bastard. So help me, Russell, I don't know what possessed you to think you can get away with this, but if she isn't back here within an hour—no make that thirty minutes—I'm filing kidnapping charges!"

CHAPTER
4

CONVERSATION CEASED, FILLING the limo interior with muted sounds of engine hum and road noise and Russell's gut-freezing anxiety. *First these assholes, then Marci. Marci . . . Whoa, wait a minute . . .*

"Hey Raveena, Marci put you guys up to this, right?" He felt a rush of relief, believing all this was nothing more than an act. Then again, what about the cop? That wasn't any damned act.

She turned toward him, thin eyebrows knitted. "Marci?"

"Yeah, you know . . . my ex . . . Angela's mother. She hired you guys to make it look like I kidnapped her, right? What with the custody thing . . ."

As he heard his own words, the idea not only sounded ridiculous, but flat-out desperate.

Raveena shot the driver a questioning look before turning face forward again.

Dread squeezed his heart again. "Okay, you guys have made your point," *whatever that is.* "I'll help you, I swear I will. So why don't you just leave my daughter out of this. She's only a little girl. She's done nothing to you. Let her go."

The driver smirked. "Do you really believe us to be that stupid? She is our insurance that you will do nothing to give us away to the authorities."

Russell wanted to backhand the smirk off his mustached upper lip. Instead, he decided the best strategy—for the time being, at least—would be to appear passive and cooperative. In the meantime, he'd watch for an opportunity. Perhaps Hussein would grow careless guarding him.

"What the hell you want from me?" he asked no one in particular.

Raveena shot an impatient look over the seat back. "Did you not hear me the first time? You will learn the answer to that question all in good time. It appears that patience is not a quality you Americans excel at."

"She's only eight years old, for christsake. She hasn't done anything to you. Let her go."

The driver uttered a sarcastic grunt. "Let her go? What does it matter? You Americans think absolutely nothing of killing innocent babies and women with tanks and bombs and rifle fire. Do not dare speak to us of mercy."

Terrorists. He was certain of that now.

For the first time, Russell glanced out the window searching for landmarks in an unfamiliar city. They were on a main street, moving along in stop-and-go traffic. As they passed through an intersection, Russell's eyes caught a street sign. Castro. It was a street he remembered from a previous trip with Marci in happier times. Before she started drinking and taking antidepressants and complaining about his decision to pursue a research career instead of a more lucrative private practice. Before everything went wrong.

He thought back to his psychiatry training. In any hostage situation, military or civilian, the overriding operative dynamic is dominance. A captor must immediately establish dominance over a prisoner, because without it there is no power. *Like not answering my questions.* They're screwing with my mind, he realized. And this small bit of knowledge instilled in him the first tinge of control over the situation.

The limo turned onto Highway 101, passed through the Presidio and headed north across the Golden Gate Bridge. The car interior remained silent.

Forty-five minutes later they passed a white sign announcing: GNOSS FIELD, NAVATO, CALIFORNIA, in simple black letters.

They were entering an airport for small planes, Russell realized, as the car stopped in front of a building with a WARD AIR SERVICE sign above the front door.

After saying something in a foreign language to Hussein and Raveena, the driver turned to Russell. "Now listen to me carefully to avoid any mistakes. The next thing we will do is step out of this car and walk to that jet like nothing out of the ordinary is happening," with a nod toward a white twin-engine Cessna Citation parked about fifty feet away. "We do not know if anybody is watching or not, but we certainly do not wish to raise suspicions. I must warn you . . . if you make any attempt, no matter how slight, to run or call out or do anything to attract attention to us, Hussein is prepared to shoot you. He may not kill you, but he *will* severely injure you. Should that happen, we will be forced to ring up our friends who are looking after your daughter, and well . . . Are you quite clear on these instructions?"

Time to gamble. Russell folded his arms defiantly across his chest. "You made that point earlier. But here's the deal . . . I'm not about to move a muscle to get out of here until I talk with my daughter. Do *you* understand?"

Hussein raised the gun and aimed it point blank at Russell's forehead.

The driver said, "This is quite impossible at the moment." He jerked his thumb at the jet. "Now, if you will kindly step out of the car and walk to the airplane."

A drop of sweat trickled down the side of Russell's chest,

he sucked a deep breath. "NFW. Know what that means? No fucking way. Not until I talk with my daughter."

Hussein glanced at the driver, who nodded almost imperceptibly. Jaws clenched, eyes now narrow slits, he slid the gun under his belt. Without taking his glare off Russell, he jerked a cell phone from his coat pocket and dialed. After exchanging a few sharp words with the person answering, he thrust the phone at Russell's face.

Russell caught it and put it to his ear. "Angela?"

He heard sobbing in the background, a gruff male voice said words he couldn't make out, then a child's shriek.

His heart seemed to constrict. He yelled, "Angela?" into the phone and slapped his free hand against the leather seat. "Can you hear me?"

Then, after a few seconds, "Daddy? Is that you?"

Russell's heart thudded in his chest. They *did* have her. "Honey, are you all right? Have they hurt you?"

"Yes," she wailed.

His heart ached with concern. "What? What have they done to you?"

He heard her shriek again and a banging as if the phone had been dropped.

"Angela?"

The line went dead.

"Angela?" Russell shook the phone and replaced it to his ear. "Honey?"

The connection had been dropped.

"You sonofabitch." He threw the phone at Hussein's head then lunged for him.

Anticipating the reaction, Hussein was already moving his left hand up to ward off the phone. With his right hand he slammed the gun butt into Russell's left temple. The blow caught him full force, twisting his head to the right, plowing his face into the seat, sending him completely off balance. Dazed, he fell onto the seat, his feet still in the footwell.

Another blow came crashing down on the back of his head, stunning him.

Through the mental haze he heard a voice yell. "Stop! Not now, Hussein."

A hand grabbed his hair and roughly jerked up his head, "Sit up!" then let go of him.

Russell pushed himself upright, his head throbbing with the effort. For a moment he sat very still, letting dizziness resolve and his double vision dissolve into one.

The driver said to Russell: "We complied with your demand. Now comply with ours or we will simply put a bullet in your head, call it a day and depart on that airplane. Again, you have complete control of the situation."

Russell shot him a glare. "Complete control, my ass! You are cowards. All of you. An eight-year-old! Jesus."

Gun wedged between the waistband of his pants and white shirt, Hussein buttoned his suit coat to hide it. He opened the door and stepped out onto black asphalt tarmac. "Come, come." He waved Russell on impatiently.

Russell slid across the backseat, stepped out into warm, muggy air and stood on still wobbly legs. Raveena fell in next to him, slipping her arm around his left arm as if they were a couple, and began leading him toward the jet and the door that had been folded down into a stairway, the four of them rapidly moving as a group.

As they neared the jet, the driver hurried ahead and up the stairs. Hussein dropped back to be last in the procession. Russell followed Raveena up into a plush carpeted cabin of six chocolate brown rolled-leather seats; three on each side, with the front four facing each other as a group.

She pointed to the seat diagonally across from the door. "You may sit there, Doctor. And please fasten your seat belt." She settled into a seat behind a small table and crossed her legs.

The driver opened the cockpit door, said something to the

pilot, closed the door, and dropped heavily into the seat directly across from Russell. All this while Hussein retracted the stairs that collapsed into the cabin door and locked it. The engines revved into a whine. The jet began to roll forward.

Moments later the airplane accelerated down the runway and nosed up, abruptly cutting off the wheel noise. The wheels retracted into the wings with a thump.

The driver scanned his partners' faces for some sign before saying to Russell, "Now I will tell you what we want from you. But first, are you all right?"

Russell was tentatively massaging the scalp over his left temple where a small hematoma had developed, each gentle probe producing a stabbing pain. "You're kidding, right?"

"May I get you something?"

"Got any ibuprofen?"

"When we reach altitude, I'll have Raveena look. In the meantime we can talk. May I continue?"

"By all means," he said and moved his fingers to the back of his head where another goose egg was forming.

"You see," he said either oblivious to the sarcasm or not caring, "your research has suddenly become very important to us. Why, you ask? Because there has been a terrible accident involving a man who is extremely crucial to our, mission?" His eyebrows arched. "By all accounts, this man is not going to survive his injuries. And so, we intend to keep his head alive and functioning."

"Keep his head alive?" Russell shook his own head, the rapid movement shooting unexpected pain down his neck. He paused to massage his neck muscles. "Know what I think? I think we have a major language problem here. What are you really trying to tell me? That you want me to treat someone with a bad head injury? If that's the case, you got the wrong neurosurgeon . . . see, trauma really isn't my specialty. I haven't taken care of a bad head crunch since residency."

"No, Doctor," the car driver said. "My name, by the way,

is Ahmed." He offered his hand. Russell shot it a look of disdain.

Ahmed shrugged, "As you wish," and retracted his hand. "Actually, you *heard* me correctly. The problem is you refused to *listen*. But that, you see, is one of the biggest problems with you arrogant Americans. You refuse to listen to people whom you believe to be inferior. This man who is injured . . . it is extremely likely we will have to remove his head from his body to keep his brain alive."

Georgetown Medical Center, Washington, D.C.

Sandra Phillips stood directly in front of the admissions desk, her chest tight with frustration, uncharacteristically at a loss for words. A few beats later she recovered. "Look, ma'am, this is a crucially important investigation. If you haven't noticed, the terrorist threat level is up to orange. We're trying to do everything possible to prevent another attack like the one we just went through with the FAA."

The stone-faced clerk said, "I'm sorry. I really am. But I'm not allowed to give out that type of information to anybody, no matter who they are. It's the law. You should know that."

"Fine! Who is your supervisor?"

Cabin of the Cessna Citation

Mouth gaping, unbelieving, Russell stared at Ahmed a moment, then laughed, figuring this was some sort of translation thing, a word mix-up of sorts, even though Ahmed gave the impression of speaking fluent English. "Absolutely no way! You can't be serious. This has got to be some sort of joke, right?"

Ahmed's eyes narrowed, his nostrils flared. "Bloody hell! Why do you still refuse to listen. Why?" He slapped the table. "Are you intentionally attempting to irritate me? If so, I strongly advise you change your attitude. Your daughter's life is at stake."

Russell flashed on Angela. The last thing he wanted was to piss these bastards off. He held up both hands in surrender. "Hey, hey, calm down. I believe you. It's just that . . ." he chose his next words carefully. "I want to make absolutely sure we're talking about the same thing here . . . that we're not having some kind of weird language disconnect. Understand what I'm saying?"

The others sat motionless in their chairs, their deadly serious eyes staring back at him.

Russell coughed a brief, nervous laugh into his fist and started massaging his forehead. "Okay, let me see if I have this straight. You want to remove the head of someone and keep it alive? Have I got it right?"

Ahmed nodded slowly. "Yes, yes, precisely."

"And you want me to help you do this?"

"Yes."

He let out another nervous laugh. "But that's impossible. It can't be done. Far as I know, it's never been done. And I think I'd know if it had."

Ahmed said, "Tell me why it cannot be done?" in a challenging tone.

"Because . . ." So many reasons flooded Russell's brain, they forced him to pause and reorganize his thoughts. "Oh man!" He licked his lips and wiped his palms again. "There're hundreds of reasons. Hundreds."

"Such as?" Raveena spoke this time.

He searched for a tactful way to educate these crazy people who held his daughter hostage. "Look, I really don't think you have the right person for this. I'm a neurosurgeon . . ." he cut himself off from saying, "not a miracle worker," and replaced it with, "I don't have a clue how to even begin to approach a problem like that. You need a . . ." he threw up a hand in frustration, "a transplant surgeon . . . yeah, that's exactly what you need. What you're talking about is transplant surgery, not neurosurgery. Do you understand what I'm telling you?"

Ahmed said, "I beg to differ. You are precisely the one to help us. No one else is as well equipped to handle the very unique aspects of this problem as you are."

"But what you're asking me to do is impossible. It simply can't be done." Then a major ramification hit him. "Wait a second . . . what are you saying? What's the deal? I mean about Angela. What happens if I try to help you and . . . things . . . don't . . . work out? What then?"

Ahmed said, "Then she dies," offhandedly, without a moment of hesitation.

"No, no!" Russell violently shook his head. "That's not right. You're condemning an innocent—"

Raveena cut in, "Try to understand, Doctor Lawton . . . the issue is simply not negotiable. The truth—sad as it may sound to you—is we care nothing for you or your daughter. She is nothing more to us than a means to force you to help us. We chose you for this task because we believe you are uniquely qualified for this job. Unfortunate for you, maybe, but fortunate for us. Yes? So there you have it. From this moment on your only concern—if you have any desire for you and your daughter to remain alive—should be to focus every ounce of your energy on the task at hand and assist us in resolving a difficult and unfortunate situation." She arched her perfect eyebrows, as if demanding confirmation. "No more attempts to talk us out of this. No more attempts at trying to bargain with us, either. For the sake of you and your daughter. Now answer the question, please."

His rage sucked any reasonable reply from his lips. Instead, he gawked at her unable to garner a coherent thought.

After several seconds Ahmed asked, "Since you seem unable to answer, let me phrase it somewhat differently. Why do you say this is impossible?"

Russell palm-wiped his face, turned away, and sucked in a deep breath. *Focus.* He mashed the heel of his hand against his forehead, the pressure easing the pain from his scalp bruises. Slowly he turned to Ahmed and mumbled, "Jesus, where to start . . . ah . . ."

Suspecting they weren't that medically sophisticated, he decided to keep the explanation as simple as possible, "Okay, first of all, you need a blood supply to keep the tissue alive. How do you suggest we accomplish that?"

Ahmed offered, "A heart-lung machine. Precisely the same as is used to substitute for the heart during open heart surgery."

Russell did a double take. "What? Are you serious?"

"It should work though, shouldn't it?"

"Jesus Christ." He massaged his neck muscles "Yeah, *theoretically.* Maybe. But practically? I doubt it."

"And why is this?"

Russell gave a strained laugh, more from frustration and nervousness than any humor. This kind of why-not questioning—like his daughter relentlessly hammered him with—could be carried to the extreme. "Okay, okay, let me ask you this: Why would you want to? Keep a head alive, I mean."

Ahmed glowered. "This really is not any concern to you."

"Oh, no? I disagree. If you insist on forcing me to do something totally insane and unlikely to work, I think I deserve to understand why."

"What is there to explain? Ahmed has already explained

this. This injured man is very important to us," Raveena
interjected. "We wish to keep his brain alive so that he can
help us."

Ahmed shot her a withering glare and barked a series of
sharp words.

She glared defiantly back at him, but said nothing. After
several beats of eye-contact arm wrestling—without Raveena
backing down—Ahmed returned his attention to Russell.
"Have you ever heard of a man named Chet Fleming?"

Russell glanced out the window. They were leveling off
above the clouds now, the sun dropping toward the horizon
behind them. Russell took this to mean they were probably
heading east. "Mind if I ask where the hell we're going?"

Ahmed said, "The chap Chet Fleming . . . which by the
way is actually a pseudonym for—"

"Ahmed, I have told you many times. The word is not a
pseudonym," Raveena interrupted harshly. "It is a polinym . . .
a special word that was designed to mean public name." She
addressed Russell: "As I am sure you know, pseudonym
means, quite literally, false name. Due to the, ah," she cleared
her throat to emphasize the next point, "*controversial* nature
of Mr. Fleming's interests, he devised what he termed a public name—a name to be reserved for only his published
work. He did this in order to protect his private life. The dis-
tinction is not between true and false, but between public and
private. He chose the name 'Chet' because it was the first
name of the greatest patent attorney-inventor in history. The
name 'Fleming' came from Alexander Fleming, who most
people associate with the discovery of penicillin."

Ahmed flashed Raveena a look of serious irritation before
reaching for the space next to his seat and hoisting a black
leather attaché case onto his lap. Both latches snapped open
simultaneously. "The point that I was trying to make is this:
Chet Fleming was an engineer and patent lawyer. In the late

1970s, for reasons known only to him, he became obsessed with the notion that a few scientists—neurosurgeons like you, not transplant surgeons, I might add—were attempting to develop a life-support system for severed human heads, and that this technological breakthrough had the potential to alter society profoundly. Indeed! A bit grandiose, I freely admit, but that was his opinion, nonetheless. Anyway, hoping to spark a public debate before it was too late, Fleming applied for and was awarded a patent from your government."

Ahmed withdrew a manila folder from the attaché case and handed it to Russell.

The story unearthed a long-buried memory of a bizarre conversation with one of his professors during residency. "You know, I think I remember hearing something about that . . ." Russell mumbled while accepting the folder. He absentmindedly placed it on his knees and held it closed with both hands, while staring blankly out the window. "There was a neurosurgeon who actually did some pretty weird stuff with animals along these very same lines. Way before my time. Maybe clear back in the seventies. White? Was that the guy's name?"

"Look for yourself, Doctor Lawton. This is no figment of my imagination."

Russell's attention snapped back to Ahmed, who was pointing at the folder in his lap. He opened it slowly, almost afraid to look at the contents.

Having never seen an actual patent before, Russell wasn't sure what one should look like. But as far as he could tell the papers he held appeared to be a legitimate copy of one. The document was perhaps ten or eleven pages of two columns each. The title page read simply,

United States Patent [19]   [11] Patent Number:
4,666,425

Fleming	[45] Date of patent: May 19, 1987

[54] A DEVICE FOR PERFUSING AN ANIMAL HEAD.	*Primary examiner—* John D Yasko *Attorney, agent, or firm—* Patrick Kelly

[75] Inventor: Chet
Fleming,
St. Louis, Mo.

"Thought you said he got the patent in the seventies," he flicked his index finger against the page. "This says 1987."

"Ah, very good, you were paying attention. He *applied* for the patent in the late seventies. It was not awarded until 1987."

"Oh." Russell started reading the abstract:

This invention involves a device referred to herein as a "cabinet," which provides a physical and biochemical support for an animal's head which has been "discorporated" (i.e., severed from its body). This device can be used to supply a discorped head with oxygenated blood and nutrients, by means of tubes connected to arteries which pass through the neck. After circulating through the head, the deoxygenated blood returns to . . .

"Okay, so you proved your point. The government issued some wacko this insane patent. So what does that prove?" Appalled, Russell tossed the file at the table, not caring that the folder and papers slid off the edge and fell to the floor. "It doesn't mean sustaining a head is feasible."

Ahmed flashed a condescending smirk. "You think just because I am from a foreign country and not a neurosurgeon, that I know nothing of medicine? Let me assure you, Doctor

Lawton, I know a great deal of medicine," his expression turned proud, raising the corners of his thick black moustache. "I am a general surgeon, having won my doctorate in medicine from the Middlesex Infirmary, London, in fact. I actually served a year of general surgery at the Cleveland Clinic. But I prefer to practice in my homeland. My specialty, if you choose to call it such, is caring of those who are injured in the fight against the infidel."

"I see."

"No, I am convinced you do not see. Certainly, you do not see clearly. Like most Americans, you are a fool, blinded by arrogance. Because you are a physician and a man of science, I imagined that perhaps you might be more tolerant of people who cherish and follow my great religion. But I sense you feel superior to FMGs, as you like to call foreign medical graduates. Allow me to review a bit of history directly relevant to the subject at hand."

Russell figured the man had a definite problem. And this made Russell even more uneasy. Especially since Ahmed impressed him as the group's leader.

"The French," Ahmed began, "were the first to ask the very important question of how long a head could survive without a blood supply. They began experiments in 1795. These experiments were a direct result of introducing the guillotine as a more humane way to execute people. You see . . . followers of Islam are not the only ones to behead criminals."

Russell thought better of the reply he wanted to throw back at him.

"French scientists asked people who were about to be beheaded to continue blinking for as long as they could after being separated from their body. Can you imagine this? Were they crazy?" He barked a laugh. "What would you say if I asked you to do such a thing? If this happened to me, I would bloody well tell them to bugger off. So, of course, all of those experiments were terribly flawed. No?"

Russell blew a frustrated breath between pursed lips. "Get on with it."

"In 1908, Charles Guthrie—who, I add, won a Nobel Prize for his pioneering work in the field of organ transplant—was the first surgeon to master anastomizing vessels together. This was, as I am certain you appreciate, a great contribution to medicine and vascular surgery. Then, this same year he used this skill to graft one dog's head into the side of another dog. In doing so, he was able to record a series of promising movements and basic reflexes such as papillary contraction, nostril twitching, and what he referred to as," he fingered quotation marks, "boiling movements of the tongue. But unfortunately, complications set in after about seven hours and, sadly enough, the dog had to be euthanized.

"After that progress stalled until in the 1950s when a Soviet surgeon named Demikhov minimized the time a severed head could be without oxygen. This was a very crucial step, one he accomplished by using blood-vessel sewing machines." Ahmed nodded to himself, pausing in thought. "Yes, this saved an extraordinary amount of time. He ended up transplanting twenty puppy heads—well actually," with a half shrug, "this is not entirely true, for they were really head-shoulder-lung-and-forelimbs units—onto fully grown dogs. He attempted to determine what they would do and how long they could survive in this state." Another half shrug. "Usually, they lived from two, maybe six days at the longest. But, they all succumbed from severe immune reactions.

"Now we come to the real progress." Ahmed's eyes grew increasingly intent. "It is in the mid-1960s that a neurosurgeon at Case Western Reserve began to experiment with what he called isolated brain preparations."

Russell snapped his fingers. "That's the one I was trying to remember," he said more to himself than the other three. "Robert White."

"What?" Ahmed asked.

Russell glanced up at him. "When I was a resident I heard some stories about what he did. I'm sure it was the same one. Name's White, isn't it. Robert White?"

Ahmed nodded. "You are familiar with this work, then?"

"Just slightly, and only because it was considered so bizarre. No one could believe he really did those things."

"He took a living brain from one animal and hooked it up to another animal's blood supply to keep it alive. But the problem was, these brains were totally without any sensory organs attached." Ahmed paused. "Think about that, my friend."

Now he remembered what struck him as so weird when he first heard about those experiments. "That was the thing, though, wasn't it!" Russell said. "The thing that made those experiments so far out. The isolated brains . . . you wonder what they experienced?" He shuddered at the thought. "I mean, that was about the same time psychologists and the military were doing some serious work on sensory deprivation . . . to figure out, what happens to a person deprived of all sensory stimulation. And they found out, too. They learned that some subjects went totally nuts. They had subjects hallucinating . . . in fact, some went absolutely psychotic."

Ahmed rubbed his temples before continuing. "A living brain with no—absolutely no—sensory input. Yes, it is difficult to imagine what those brains experienced. What they thought!"

The group seemed to be waiting for Ahmed to finish. Russell said, "Go on."

"At first he implanted these brains in the necks or abdomen of the recipient animals. But that was only the first stage of what turned out to be years and years of research. This also corresponded to a time when huge advances were being made in cardiac surgery, especially hypothermia. It was the heart surgeons who finally discovered that by cooling the brain, they could minimize the brain damage that came with the early open-heart procedures.

"That led White to decide that by cooling the brain during the transplant procedure he could slowly increase the time he had between cutting the blood supply from one animal and reestablishing it to another. By doing this, he found it is quite possible to protect and retain most of the organ's normal function."

"Since you seem to be such an expert on this," Russell broke in, forgetting for a moment his initial repulsion at the concept. "Let me ask you something that's always bothered me about White's work. How the hell did he justify those experiments?" He flashed on Nofziger's question a few hours earlier.

Ahmed appeared surprised at the question. "Is it not apparent?"

"Not to me, it isn't."

"He wanted to perfect a technique for keeping entire heads alive on new bodies. But for whom, you ask? The answer is quite simple. Quadriplegics."

"Yeah? I don't buy that. They'd still be quadriplegics. Without the ability to reconnect the spinal cord, you're still a quadriplegic. And believe me, splicing spinal cords together is still a *long* time away. It wasn't even thinkable when White was doing his thing." Russell shook his head, his initial disgust returning. "No, I don't buy it."

Eyebrows raised, Ahmed asked harshly, "May I continue?"

Russell's earlier distain returned along with his fear for Angela's life. "Sorry."

Ahmed frowned, clearly not pleased by the remark.

"Continue," Russell quickly added.

"Encouraged by his initial results, White removed the head of one monkey and transplanted it to another monkey. His operations lasted a bit more than eight hours. He published a report of his pioneering surgery in the July 1971 issue of *Surgery*." Ahmed removed a stack of papers from the attaché case, glanced at it. "Here is a photocopy. The article is titled 'Cephalic Exchange Transplantation in the Monkey.' Do, you wish to see it?"

Russell didn't answer. Ahmed set the copy on the table.

"How White managed to accomplish the surgery is actually quite clever. He proceeded in very methodical stages. He first gave the monkeys tracheostomies and hooked them up to respirators. Next, he cut the two monkeys' necks down to just the spine and the two carotid arteries and jugular veins."

"What about the vertebral arteries?" Russell asked, thinking of the two smaller arteries that travel up the sides of the vertebrae to feed the brain stem and cerebellum.

"Those he sacrificed." Ahmed paused.

Russell nodded for him to continue.

"Then he whittled down the bone on the top of the donor's neck and capped it with a metal plate. He did the same thing on the bottom of the head he detached. The idea was to screw the two plates together once the transplant was finished. Then using long, flexible tubing, he connected the blood supply from the recipient body to the new head." He smiled, as if this were a major victory. "He then sutured the vessels together. You see? Quite canny."

"Canny but insane, if you ask me. Go on."

"Some monkeys lived for only six hours. Others survived as long as three days. Again, most deaths occurred from tissue rejection. An immune response. This is not surprising, actually. Others? They died from the bleeding. But I think that both of these complications can be improved with modern techniques. Do you not agree?"

Russell sat back in the rolled leather chair and considered what he just heard. "Yes, granted it might be *technically* possible to actually accomplish such an operation on a human, but the risks are horrendous. Not simply because the operation has never been done before, but because of all the obvious complications. No, I still don't believe it can be safely done on a human."

Ahmed said, "You have no choice in the matter, Doctor Lawton. The decision is simply not debatable. Regardless of what you believe, this is the task you have been charged with. I believe you understand what happens to you and your daughter if you fail."

Georgetown Medical Center

Sandra Phillips stood outside the automated double doors. Three quarters up the eight-foot high doors a red plastic sign read: TRAUMA INTENSIVE CARE—AUTHORIZED PERSONNEL ONLY. She squared her shoulders and stepped forward to trigger the motion detector that swung the doors open with a hydraulic hiss. Inside, she headed straight for the nurses station, where a lone scrub-clad young woman with a stethoscope draped around her neck sat typing in front of a computer monitor.

Waiting for the nurse or doctor—you couldn't tell the difference anymore with everyone dressed in scrubs—to acknowledge her, Sandra quickly scanned the spreadsheetlike white board on the back wall until her eyes stopped at the name Mohammed. Immediately to the left of the name was a number 625. She assumed this was his room number.

"Please don't tell me you're Special Agent Phillips."

Surprised, Sandra made eye contact with the woman. "Matter of fact, I am."

Standing, the woman said, "We were warned you might try something like this. I don't care if you are FBI, the policy is no visitors. Please leave the area immediately, or I'll be forced to call security."

"Then call security. I'll only be a moment." Sandra spun around and quickly scanned the room numbers in front of her. She saw 625 and bee-lined toward the door. She entered the room, went directly to the bedside and looked down at the man lying on his back, an NG tube through his left nostril, an IV in his left arm. A respirator sat silently beside the bed, its corrugated tube coiled up but ready to use if needed.

She leaned over, touched his shoulder. "Yo, Mohammed!"

He didn't respond.

"Agent Phillips! Leave at once. I've called security and they are on their way up here. If you do not leave immediately, you'll be physically removed."

Sandra straightened up, headed for the door. "Don't worry. I'm going."

Cessna Citation

Ahmed's words, *"I believe you understand what happens to you and your daughter if you fail,"* echoed in Russell's mind as a storm of anger brewed in his chest. Before any of the terrorists could react, Russell was out of his seat, hands gripping Ahmad's neck. "How do you like not being able to breathe, you sonofabitch."

Russell awoke to a throbbing headache and the drone of jet engines. He was back in his seat, seat belt fastened. Ahmed was rubbing his neck. Hussein was massaging his knuckles. Raveena sat there with an expectant look.

Ahmed said to him, "You are not living up to the reputation of being a smart man."

Russell licked his lips and massaged his aching right temple.

"What did you plan on gaining by strangling me? Revenge? A release of frustration? Your daughter's certain death? Think about what you've been told and stop wasting precious time. You should be planning, not fighting."

Heart racing, his hands clamped into fists, Russell turned from Ahmed and saw his reflection in the Plexiglas window. What options did he have? None. Without moving his gaze from the dark sky, he said, "Apparently you've given some serious thought to this, and obviously I haven't. But just off the top of my head, I can see a ton of problems—all very serious ones—that makes this, ah . . . experiment," he waved his hand to dismiss the word as absurdly inadequate, "appear doomed."

He turned to see if his words registered on Ahmed.

Ahmed flashed another condescending smile. "Difficult most assuredly, but certainly not impossible."

"Well, let's talk about that," defaulting to a trusted, knee-jerk interviewing ploy. "If you're going to have any chance of succeeding at this," he caught himself from saying, *insane,* "experiment, your buddy, leader, whatever, he is, is going to need to be in a very sophisticated medical center. And any medical center functioning at that level isn't going to allow what you're proposing without raising some very serious questions. I'm certain you're going to have to submit a proposal to an Institutional Review Board or Ethics Committee. And that could take months to clear."

Ahmed shook his head. "There will be no review board and no questions."

"Oh? And how's that supposed to work?"

"Because no one will know what we are about."

"I don't understand. What you're proposing requires very sophisticated equipment and personnel. Where do you plan to do this?"

Ahmed answered, "I can think of no better place than at the NIH."

"The National Institutes of Health? No way! You've got to be kidding. Right?"

"I am not joking. Why do you keep asking this question?"

Russell laughed out loud. "That's impossible. Talk about having to deal with red tape. That's the Mecca of bureaucracy." He immediately regretted his choice of words.

"Why do you keep saying this is impossible? It is not impossible. I am deadly serious about this."

Another look at Ahmed's grim face and Russell believed him.

"Look, I'm sorry, I didn't mean to upset you . . . it's just that . . . NIH?" He blew out between pursed lips. "That's impossible. That's a federal government building, and it's loaded with federal police; no way you're going to get away with something as bizarre as that." He stopped and thought, *whoa, wait a second; federal cops. That's good. Maybe these fools will get themselves caught.* Next he flashed on Angela and realized if they got caught, she would die.

"To the contrary, Doctor Lawton. You will make certain we succeed. Your laboratory, it is on campus, is it not?"

"Yes, but—"

"So? What better place than that? You will have all your computers, all your equipment. No, there is no better place to do this. It is settled. We will accomplish our task in your laboratory."

"Are you totally insane? It's an animal lab, not a surgery. It's about as unsterile as it gets. Think about what you're saying you want done and then think about the fact I work with monkeys. They're unsanitary little guys . . . picking their butts and wiping their fingers on the walls. Jesus! It's not even close to having the environment you'd need for human surgery." Stopped, then added, "Much less a place for doing what you're suggesting."

"Let me be quite clear with you, Doctor Lawton. We tell you what you can or cannot accomplish and where it will be done. What you do not seem to realize is that I have worked in battlefield conditions for years. I have saved hundreds and hundreds of fighters injured by your military," Ahmed said indignantly, pronouncing the word *mill-a-tree,* like the British. "The conditions I've worked under, they will make your laboratory seem like an extremely sophisticated surgery. In addition, as you will soon discover, it will do perfectly well. You and I will make this happen. There! The issue is settled."

"Impossible . . ." Russell palm-wiped his face again and thought of all the reasons this was a disaster waiting to happen. He decided on a different tack. "Okay, bear with me on a couple points, okay? Now, assuming you use a pump-oxygenator, which by the way is, in itself, going to be a problem . . . I mean, where you going to get one of those machines? Heart-lung machines aren't just lying around for anyone to use, you know."

"That is not my problem. I am certain you will determine an answer. There must be at least one such machine in an institute as sophisticated as the NIH."

Russell hesitated, wondering where to even look for one, then decided not to lose his train of thought. "Fine. Assuming I find one, we're going to have to anticoagulate the blood with heparin. And this means you're going to need a ton of lab work: Crits, electrolytes, clotting factors, the whole enchilada. How do you expect to pull that off?"

He glanced at Raveena and Hussein to see if they were tracking any of this insanity. Raveena was sitting back sipping a bottle of spring water, apparently unimpressed. Hussein was cleaning his nails with a cheap nail clipper.

Ahmed leaned forward, face intense. "Minor details! All of them! Details for which you must find solutions. Quickly, I might add. Think about what you know of medicine. Improvise. You will be surprised how simply being a good physician can transform failure into success in these situations. So much of modern technology is not really absolutely necessary to practice your art."

"Minor details?" Russell blew out another deep breath between pursed lips. "I couldn't disagree more. These are far from minor details. Furthermore, they don't necessarily have a solution. You have absolutely no idea what you're talking about."

"Quite the contrary, Doctor Lawton. I know exactly what I'm talking about. But you see, I am talking . . . how do you say it?" snapping his fingers, "a worst-case scenario? Yes, these are the correct words I believe: worst-case scenario." He smiled with self-satisfaction. "If we are extremely lucky, there will be no need to actually remove this man's head. The best-case scenario would be to simply transfer him to your laboratory until he can finish his task. But actually, to be brutally honest about this, I very much doubt that will be the case. That said, I suggest we begin some very explicit contingency plans to ensure he finishes his task in the event that his body shuts down. Just in case."

A rush of relief hit. "No kidding? Taking this guy's head off isn't a hundred percent for sure?" he asked hopefully.

"Indeed."

"So, let me ask you, what's wrong with this guy?"

"He had an unfortunate accident. Apparently an automobile pinned him against a brick wall, inflicting massive crush injuries to his pelvis and legs. At present, he is showing early signs of myoglobinuria. Am I to believe you are acquainted with the syndrome of myoglobinuria, yes?"

Russell thought back to his general surgery year. "I seem to remember a few things about it."

"In that case, you surely realize the situation. But in the event you do not, let me refresh your memory. If his myoglobinuria becomes severe enough to begin damaging vital organs such as kidney, liver, and heart, he is at risk for total organ failure. Should that happen, his body will die. We cannot let the same thing happen to his brain."

It was a stretch, but Russell pulled some basic facts about myoglobinuria out of his memory bank. It was, he remembered, a serious complication of crush injuries. The chain of events being: The physical force of impact destroys the muscle fiber. Once this happens, a vicious chemical chain reaction develops that literally causes the muscle to dissolve and fall apart. As this happens, myoglobin destroys kidney, heart, and liver cells. Trash these vital organs, and the patient's chance of survival becomes tenuous at best. Occasionally, however, if the myoglobin toxicity is treated soon enough and vigorously enough, the downward spiraling course can be reversed before it reaches the tipping point. But if that fails to work, the patient is a goner, for sure.

Finally, Russell asked, "We're heading east, right? To Bethesda?"

Ahmed nodded. "Yes."

For lack of anything else to say, Russell commented, "My laptop . . . it's still back at the Hilton. I can't work without it. It's still at the hotel."

Raveena, this time: "Not to worry. We packed up all your belongings, and signed you out of the hotel." She smiled. "We even paid your bill. So, you see, everything is taken care of."

Their thoroughness sent a chill through him. "How long have you been planning this? We're only talking about hours, right?"

No one answered him.

Still trying to think of a way to convince them there was no way their detached head survival plan would work, Russell asked, "Have you considered how is this friend of yours going to communicate? The guy has no hands to write with and no vocal cords to speak with."

Raveena. Said, "Remember the conversation when we first met?"

Russell drew a blank.

"About how you thought you can develop a successful brain-computer interface to produce speech from thoughts?"

Russell felt a rush of blood light up his face. A drop of sweat trickled into his right eye. Although *theoretically* possible, designing and implementing the interface would be a Herculean feat.

Russell shook his head. "At the time I thought you were asking if it was possible. I really didn't think you were asking if I could actually do it, and in particular, do it any time soon. I mean, if you think I can throw together that kind of interface in the next week or so, think again. I can't. That's the truth."

Smiling, Ahmed shrugged. "In that case, we have nothing more to discuss. Should I simply ring up my friends and tell them to bury your daughter now? If so, they shall be very accommodating." In the next moment a cell phone appeared in his hand and he was dialing.

CHAPTER

7

"No!" RUSSELL GRABBED for the phone but the seat belt dug into his pelvis, restraining him just short of his target.

Ahmed dangled the phone up and away from Russell's outstretched fingers as if taunting a ravenous dog with a treat. "Then I wish to hear no more words from you concerning why you cannot do this task. We are quite clear on this point? Yes?"

Russell slumped slowly back into the leather and thought about Angela and then fantasized about killing Ahmed, given the opportunity. "Yes."

"Good." As if Russell had suddenly ceased to exist, Ahmed turned to Hussein and began a heated debate in language Russell could not identify. Raveena sat, legs crossed, thumbing through a woman's magazine. End of conversation.

Seething, Russell shifted positions to avoid looking at his captors and peered through the double-pane Plexiglas at the darkening sky. What option did he have other than accommodate their insane, grandiose scheme? Could he possibly do it? Even with Ahmed's surgical experience—whatever that might actually be—he needed additional help. Certainly, he needed Gerda's help for constructing the necessary brain/computer interface.

Damn! Gerda was scheduled for vacation. A two-week trip back to Germany to visit her brother. When? Had she already left? Another wave of anxiety hit. Managing the project without her would be impossible.

Russell turned back to Ahmed, "I need to make a telephone call. May I use your cell phone?"

"Who do you wish to call?"

"The interface . . . the process by which we feed the brain waves into the computer . . . I need help setting that up. There is a colleague I work with—"

"Ahhh, yes. Doctor Fetz," Ahmed said, cutting him off. "How stupid of me. I forgot to broach this rather relevant point. You see, we are quite aware of how vital she is to this project. This is why we have already made arrangements to persuade her to help you."

"Persuade her?"

Another dismissive wave. "In a moment. What worries you so?"

"Well, see, the thing is she's leaving for vacation soon. In fact, she may have left already."

"What is the problem? You will simply tell her to cancel it and remain in Bethesda."

"Well, it might not be that easy. She's been planning this trip for a while. Her family, or what's left of it, still lives in Germany. She hasn't seen her brother for over a year." He caught himself from saying how attached she was to Gerhard. The less Ahmed knew about their personal lives, the better. "She's been looking forward to the trip, so I don't think it's going to be all that easy to convince her to cancel."

"Once again, you are not listening to what I said. Her brother Gerhard? We know all about him. When you call her, suggest she check her e-mail. There will be a message from our . . . colleagues in Germany. They are quite aware of who her brother is, where he is, and his daily schedule. If she refuses to stay in Bethesda and help us, they will kill him. You see, it is really quite simple. Now, is there still a problem?"

Jesus! They knew her brother's name. Russell stared at Ahmed, then Hussein.

Ahmed studied him a moment with the faintest hint of a smirk. "We will be landing in a short while to refuel. You may use my phone then. But remember, Doctor, even if you care little about your colleague's brother, your daughter's life remains at risk."

Russell's ears popped, snapping him back from deep concentration on how to start to manage the task he was threatened with. He realized the Cessna must be losing altitude and glanced through the window at the ground. By now the horizon was gobbled up by blackness. The only way to tell sky from earth was by the widely spaced clusters of lights visible below. Off in the far distance glowed a much wider expanse of lights. A city. "Where are we?"

No answer.

He turned to his captors. They were still engrossed in a heated debate, but now Raveena was throwing in occasional comments.

Fifteen minutes later, the small jet rolled to a stop one hundred feet from a one-story commercial building. A sign across the aluminum siding read EPPLEY AIRFIELD, OMAHA, NEBRASKA, in large black block letters. A red and white Texaco fuel truck pulled up alongside the jet's right wing and stopped as one lone ground crew chocked the Cessna's wheels. Off to his left stretched the main commercial terminal, with several American Airlines jets docked. A smaller low-fare United Airlines plane emblazoned with a giant "Ted" was rolling past, left to right.

"We will wait in the building while they refuel," Ahmed said in a tone that left little room for debate. "If you wish, you may buy something to eat. I am told they have vending machines available."

Russell unbuckled his seat belt, stood and stretched as best he could in the small cabin. "I don't want to wait. Let me have the phone now."

Ahmed handed it to him while Hussein pushed open the door and lowered the stairs. "Remember your daughter," Ahmed warned before nodding for Russell to follow the other two passengers out of the plane.

The terminal's small waiting room smelled faintly of aviation fuel and grease and had a floor of worn green linoleum squares, many of them with chipped and curled-up corners. Russell powered up the phone and glanced around. The four of them were the only souls in the waiting area. The sparse furnishings consisted of a cheesy faux walnut laminate counter enclosing a business area with three deserted Steelcase desks. To his left, two side-by-side vending machines leaned into each other like drunken sailors. One held soft drinks, the other, snacks. A sign on the wall behind the desks read: WELCOME TO OMAHA, HOME OF WARREN BUFFETT. On another wall hung a picture of the president and a large chart for calculating mileage to nearby small landing fields throughout the Midwest. Off in a corner waved an American flag on a listing flagpole.

Not particularly hungry but figuring it was going to be a long night, Russell fed two dollars into one vending machine and punched the Mountain Dew button. After retrieving the chilled can from the machine, he set it on the counter, withdrew a PDA from his suit coat and looked up Gerda's home number. She was most likely asleep, he figured, while listening to her phone ring. A woman of precise and punctual routines, she hit the sheets early, arriving in the lab every morning at 7:30 AM sharp after having sweated exactly forty-five minutes on the elliptical cross-trainer at a nearby health club.

The line picked up, and he recognized her crisp German accent immediately.

"Gerda, Russell. Look, sorry to wake you, but something very important has come up."

"Not to worry. What is it? You are okay? You sound upset."

"I'm fine."

"Are you sure?"

"Yes," he lied again.

Hussein stood next to him, making no attempt to hide that he was listening to Russell's words. Raveena and Ahmed stood by the vending machines, chatting. Raveena was drinking from a can of orange juice while Ahmed worked on a bag of potato chips and a Coke.

"This is a hypothetical question, okay? But how easy do you think it'd be to extrapolate the software that controls the robotic hand to one that could produce synthesized speech?"

He heard two contemplative breaths from the other end of the line, then: "We are talking about expressive speech, yes?"

"Correct."

"Ja, I think this should be doable with the proper organization, time, and funding. But why are you asking this ridiculous question? We work with monkeys, not humans." A pause, "Or are you thinking we do not do this with monkeys? It is impossible with a monkey, yes, impossible," she muttered.

"Again, this is purely hypothetical, but what if we were to try this on a human?"

Another long pause. "Ja . . . from a theoretical standpoint it is possible . . . maybe . . . but this is much more difficult than what we are presently doing." A trace of excitement had snuck into her otherwise level tone. "Do you not agree?"

"I think it might be possible . . . yeah, it'd take some serious work, but maybe . . ." He realized he was no longer sounding hypothetical.

"And when would you want to do this . . . this experiment? You *are* wanting to do it, ja?"

Far from being discreet, he'd blown it. "I don't know for certain if the, ah, opportunity will come up, but I've been talking to some people . . ." He decided to let it hang. "The thing is, if it *does* become a real possibility, we would have to be able to move quickly. Within the next few days."

"Hmmmmm, this is a problem, you see. As you know, I am planning to visit my brother in München. My tickets, they are already purchased and the trip entirely organized. Can this experiment not wait?"

Russell drew a deep breath. "No, I'm afraid it can't."

"Ach, but I have plans. I cannot alter them on a whim."

"Gerda, I'm afraid you and I don't have much choice. There are these people . . . don't ask me who, because I don't know . . . exactly. But they kidnapped Angela and are threatening to kill her if I don't cooperate."

"Mein Gott!"

"Hold on, it gets worse." He found his throat constricting, the words difficult to speak. She was about to feel the same threat he had been dealing with for the past several hours. "They told me if you don't cancel your trip and help me, they'll kill your brother." He tried to swallow but his mouth was dry. He hadn't been able to speak her brother's name; it would make the situation all the more real. "They told me to tell you to check your e-mail, that there was something there that would convince you they are serious."

"Mein Gott! I will check immediately and will call you back," sounding frantic now. "What number are you at?"

"No!" A possibility he hadn't considered hit. Could someone be listening to the conversation? NSA computers monitored all cell phone conversations for key words. Had he said the word terrorist? Would they track him? Sweat sprouted on his brow. "I don't have a way for you to call me. Not until I'm back in Bethesda. I'll contact you later."

"Gerhard! They have him?" She now sounded terrified.

"No, I don't think so. But I don't know for certain. Tell you what . . . check your e-mail and I will call you back in ten minutes."

Gerda hung up.

Hussein held out his hand for the telephone. Russell kept it. "I need to call her back."

Hussein smiled. "She is not believing? Yes, but she will. Still, I will wait with you until you make your next call."

Russell paced in the small dreary room, waiting, watching the Cessna being refueled. Where was Angela? Was she being treated with at least some care? He entered a small one-urinal men's room. Hussein followed him inside.

"Do you mind?"

"You cannot be trusted. I will stay with you until you are finished."

Russell found he couldn't urinate so he simply washed his sweating, trembling hands and reentered the waiting room.

After five minutes, unable to stand the suspense any longer, he dialed Gerda's phone. She picked up immediately.

"Russell?" He heard the phone drop, the scrape of it being picked back up. "They sent pictures. Gerhard." Her voice had a raw edge of panic in it. "There are shots of him in his house with his child. A child, no less. What should I do?"

"I don't see that we have a choice—either of us. If they're going to have any chance, you'll have to postpone your travel plans and work with me on this."

"But we must *do* something! We can't let them do this to us."

"I don't think you understand. These people . . . they aren't ones we can negotiate with."

"I am frightened. When will you be back here?"

"I don't know for certain. I want to say three or four hours, depending on if we go straight there . . ."

"Call me when you get here."

"Then you'll help me?"

"Ach, do I have a choice? No, I do not have a choice, so yes, I will help."

"Thanks for—" For what? "Thanks for being there to help."

Handing Hussein the phone, Russell felt some comfort in the knowledge that he wouldn't be alone in dealing with this mess. Gerda was brilliant. Maybe together they could find a way out.

"We are leaving soon. If you are wanting something to eat, you should get it now," Hussein advised.

Russell popped the top to his can of Mountain Dew. "I'm not really hungry." Mind racing, he headed for the glass door and back out onto the tarmac, trying to figure out where to start.

"Hold it right there, gentlemen."

Russell glanced up. An official-looking man in his forties, wearing a short-sleeve tan shirt with dark epaulets, was striding directly toward them with an officious gait. Russell recognized the round TSA emblem patch on his left shirtsleeve.

The man pointed unmistakably at Russell. "Sir, I'd like to speak with you a moment. Inside."

Russell didn't remember seeing any scanning device in the office. He pointed a thumb at his chest. "Me? Why?" He noticed Ahmed and Raveena standing at the jet's opened door, watching. Hussein slowly moved his hand inside his coat.

The agent glanced from Hussein back to Russell with a flat expression. "Because I want to ask you some questions. That's why."

Hussein was eyeing him now, hand still inside his coat.

"But we're ready to take off."

"Sir, that bird you're riding in ain't going nowhere unless I give the tower your clearance. See what I'm tellin' you? Now, I suggest if y'all are in such a big-ass hurry, you," stabbing a finger at Russell's chest, "better step inside with me." He flashed another dead-eye glance at Hussein. "Alone."

RUSSELL SENT HUSSEIN what he hoped was a pleading look. "I'll make this as short as possible so we can get going. Okay?"

Hussein stared back with ice-cold, determined eyes. After a moment he gave a barely perceptible nod, the entire time his hand stayed near the hidden gun.

Back in the empty charter terminal the TSA agent leaned his bulk against the counter and folded his hairy arms across his chest. "Where y'all headin'?"

Russell gave a slight shrug. "Bethesda. Why?"

"And the reason for the trip?"

Uneasiness increased in Russell's gut.

"Look, I thought you guys were supposed to check passengers to make sure flights aren't in danger. Weapons, things like that. We're in kind of a hurry here. Just check me out and let's get this over with."

The agent wagged his meaty head side to side. "Y'all ain't going nowhere unless I say you are. Now I asked you a question. Why y'all heading to Bethesda?"

All he needed was for some passive-aggressive bureaucrat

to delay or possibly halt takeoff. Russell sighed in resigna-
tion. "I work there. At NIH. Here, let me show you my ID.
Would that help?"

"Since you mentioned it, yeah."

Russell handed over his Public Health Service ID. "See?
I'm a government employee, just like you."

The TSA agent studied the plasticized card. "That may
be, but you don't see me flying around in no private jet."

"I believe it's chartered."

"What happened to you?"

"What do you mean?"

"That's a pretty good bruise you got on your face. Mind
tellin' me how that come about?"

"I fell."

He handed back the ID. "That right?"

"Right."

"Cain't say that I believe you."

The agent looked him over again, fueling Russell's anxiety.
Finally the agent asked, "What the hell's goin' on, podna?"

"What do you mean what's going on?" He took the circular bulge in the man's breast pocket for a tin of chewing
tobacco.

"What I mean is, we got us a heightened security level,
what with that FAA computer thing happenin' a few days
ago. And now you're flyin' through here in the middle of the
night with a group of rag heads. Mind explainin' that to
me?" The man crossed both tanned muscular arms across
his chest and spread his stance a bit.

Russell read the man's name tag: ROBERTSON and figured
he knew the type. He said sternly, "Let me tell you something, Robertson, one government employee to another. The
term "rag head" is not politically correct."

The man's posture stiffened, the corners of his tight lips
curled down.

"That's because," Russell continued, "those really aren't rags they wear. They're actually little sheets."

It took a few beats to register. Suddenly the officer's eyes twinkled, changing the frown into a toothy, tobacco-stained grin. "I git it! Sheet heads. Oooo weeee, that's a good one." He punched Russell's shoulder good-naturedly, but the smile quickly vanished. "So you won't mind if I take a look inside that fancy jet, huh?"

Russell's heart rate accelerated. "No problem, officer."

They exited the small office, the agent leading, heading directly for the Cessna's lowered stairs. Hussein, who had been waiting just outside the door, fell in beside Russell and asked, "What is going on?"

The tone of Hussein's voice froze the lining of Russell's gut. He tried for a casual shrug, but it felt herky jerky. "I don't know."

Hussein studied him a moment before following the agent up the stairs, his hand coming out of his coat with the gun. As the agent stepped into the cabin Hussein raised the black weapon. Before Russell could yell a warning, Hussein shot the agent in the back of the head, turned and frantically waved his free hand, "Get inside. Quick."

Russell stepped into the cabin and around the prone body. "Jesus, you killed him!"

Hussein was already pulling up the stairs and yelling something to the pilots through the open cockpit door. The engine whine began increasing as the plane jerked forward, sending Russell tripping into Raveena as she buckled her seat belt.

Russell pushed off her and dropped into his seat just as he was backhanded across the face, hard. "Keep your filthy hands off her." A wild-eyed Hussein stood next to him, legs spread, gun still in his right hand.

Ahmed yelled something to Hussein.

Russell clenched both fists and tried to ignore his stinging face. "Oh, that was brilliant. Absolutely brilliant. You just shot a federal agent. I wouldn't be surprised if a fucking SWAT team's waiting for us when we land."

Hussein was cracking the knuckles on his free hand, *POP POP POP*. "They will never find us, sha'allah."

"They know the number of this plane so they probably know your flight plan."

Again, Ahmed yelled at Hussein. Reluctantly Hussein put the gun away and dropped into his seat.

Ahmed nodded at the dead TSA agent. "Unfortunate, but perhaps necessary. And as far as tracking us? Our flight plan is for Seattle and our transponder is turned off. Yes, they will eventually discover the plane after we land, but by then we will have disappeared. And as far as he is concerned," with a chin jut toward the body, "his absence may not be noticed for some time. Who knows?" he added with a shrug.

3:05 AM EST, Baltimore International Airport

The whine of the Cessna's jets wound down in front of a small corporate hanger remote from the larger commercial terminal at Baltimore International Airport. Again, Hussein tended to the door while the others unbuckled their seat belts. As Russell waited to deplane, the cockpit door opened and two young pilots appeared, both with the same Middle Eastern looks as his captors: dark skin, black hair, black moustaches. He looked for ID badges clipped to their short-sleeve white shirts, searching for any bit of identifying information he might be able to tell the authorities if he survived this ordeal, but he saw nothing.

"We go now," Ahmed said as Hussein started down the stair. Raveena followed, Russell next, Ahmed taking up the rear. Russell had no idea if the pilots deplaned or what they'd do with the body. Earlier, Hussein had dragged the slain TSA agent to the very back of the plane.

Along the side of the hanger awaited a black minivan, motor running, another young stereotypic Middle Eastern man behind the wheel. Raveena climbed into the front passenger seat. Hussein directed Russell into the rear seat, then climbed in beside him. Ahmed took the entire middle seat for himself.

Thirty minutes later the driver dropped the four of them off at a nondescript parking lot in the Baltimore suburbs where they picked up another SUV, this time without a driver. Hussein, who already had a set of keys, drove, taking a route straight to the freeway.

Ahmed said to Russell, "First, we will drive you to your apartment and leave this van near there. I want you to change into clothes you would normally wear to work. Do you usually wear a uniform?"

Russell thought of the uniforms for Public Health commissioned officers. Like most NIH physicians, he seldom wore his, preferring a blue button-down oxford sans tie, tan Dockers, and topsiders. A tweed sports coat if a more dress-up look was required. "No, not usually."

"I will remind you again before we leave your apartment, just so you won't forget, but we know that you must wear your external ID badge," Ahmed continued. "When we arrive at NIH I want you to appear and act as if nothing is out of the ordinary. We cannot afford to draw any unnecessary attention to us.

"After we all have changed," he continued, "we will ride the Metro to the NIH stop. From there you will lead us to your laboratory. Any questions so far?"

Russell decided to test their knowledge a little more. "My lab's in the basement of Building 31. Or do you already know that?"

Ahmed flashed a quizzical expression. "Yes, we are quite aware which building you are in. But it is Building 10, not 31. Why do you lie about this? It serves neither of us any purpose."

"Sorry, simple mistake. I was thinking about the security building. We'll have to go there, too," quickly changing the topic. "Okay, then you probably also know there's federal security all over the place. They won't allow you building access without a pass. You *do* know this, don't you?"

Without missing a beat, Ahmed nodded confidently. "Yes. We are quite aware of your security, thank you. It is because of this we are relying on you to provide a story sufficient to obtain passes for all of us. If you haven't done so already, I suggest you start devising one that will work without raising suspicion."

During the flight he'd already come up with a reasonable solution. Assuming, of course, the federal cops would buy into the story. And how likely is that going to be? Especially when every one of those bastards except Raveena looked like a certified Iraqi insurgent who just stepped out of a Men's Warehouse store?

Luckily, the guest parking space in the lot for Russell's apartment building was empty, so they dumped the van there. His three captors removed an olive canvas duffel bag from the back of the vehicle and followed Russell inside the building to his first-floor two-bedroom apartment. Russell went directly to Angela's room, intending to close the door to keep anyone from entering it. For a moment, he stood just inside the threshold surveying the dimly lit area, the only light angling in from the street and hall. She was in her "Arts and Crafts" phase; sketch-pad drawings and beads lying around in a general mess, beading being what really engrossed her now. Reading, too. Her stack of Harry Potter books piled in the same cinder-block-and-plank bookcase he had used as a student. Her dress-up blazer haphazardly flung across her unmade bed. The sight triggered a constriction in his throat. He slowly shut the door as his eyes misted.

"You can take turns changing in there." He nodded toward the guest bathroom that served a dual purpose as her bathroom those days she stayed with him.

Russell entered his own bedroom, closed the door, leaned against it, and wiped his eyes. He exhaled, palm-wiped his face, and glanced around at the familiar surroundings, marveling at the comfort they imparted. He wondered how long it might be before he saw them again? If ever.

He'd seen their faces, knew their assumed names. There was no way in hell they would ever let him go free once their mission was complete. They would kill him. He had to work something out. What?

A knock came from the door. He stepped away and opened it. Ahmed looked in. "What are you doing?"

"I'm going to change clothes. Now get the hell out."

Ahmed flashed an angry look before pointing at the phone on the bedside stand. "We have taken the phone off the hook in case you contemplate calling someone."

"Jesus!" Russell pushed the door shut in Ahmed's face but the other man pushed back and stepped into the room. "You will have to change with me here."

Russell shook his head and turned away.

A small silver-framed picture of Angela as an infant stood on the dresser. He picked it up and studied the photo and delicately touched her face. The snapshot was torn in half, the original print having included a smiling Marci kneeling beside her, proudly suspending her upright by raised arms. Where was Angela at this moment? Was she physically and mentally okay? Was she terrified? Probably. And this thought made his heart ache even more.

He removed the back from the frame, slipped out the picture, folded it and placed it in the inside pocket of the worn brown Harris Tweed sports coat that he'd tossed carelessly over the arm of a wingback chair the last time he'd come home from work. He changed into suntans, a white shirt open at the neck, and slipped on the coat. He checked to verify that his plastic laminate ID card was still clipped to the lapel then slipped it on.

He took one last look around the bedroom before saying to Ahmed, "C'mon, let's get this insane show on the road."

With a hiss the door to their Metro car slid open allowing Russell and his captors an exit onto the almost deserted concrete platform. A sign on the tiled wall read: NIH. They rode the long escalator up to street level and out into a cool breeze tinged with car exhaust and the first hints of dawn. Ahead curved South Drive, one of the main roads into the expansive fenced-in campus of green rolling hills crammed full of utilitarian-looking brick, glass, and concrete buildings.

As they crossed to the right side of the road Russell noticed two armed soldiers in full combat fatigues posted outside the guard area usually manned only by federal police. The knot already constricting his gut tightened. This hour of morning was still too early for the majority of employees and visitors to begin arriving, leaving the road free of the usual line of cars and taxis waiting to clear the checkpoint. Not only would they stand out, but the guards would have ample time to question them without being pressured by a long line of cars.

The conversation between the other three ceased.

They continued walking briskly toward the guard station. As they approached, a federal cop stepped from the guard-house to face them as one soldier shifted his automatic rifle into the ready position. "Good morning."

Russell met the police officer's eyes, "Morning, officer."

The officer nodded back, turned a stone-cold serious face to the three Middle Eastern visitors. "Your IDs, please."

Washington, D.C.

Sandra Phillips rolled over on to her left side, reached for the telephone before having to endure another harsh ring. She didn't bother to check the clock radio—if the alarm hadn't gone off, it wasn't 7:00 AM yet. "Yes?"

"Sandy. Ian."

"Don't you ever sleep?" She pushed up onto an elbow, blinked.

"What did you find out over at Georgetown?"

"I was planning on giving you a complete rundown first thing this morning, sir." She told him about the aggravating pushback from hospital personnel and added, "But I took a chance and just walked into the surgical ICU. They do have a patient in there under the name of Mohammed. I managed to get a quick look at him and, believe me, he does look suspicious. I'll need to take another look through the pictures before I can make that statement any stronger."

"Understood." McGowan paused. "The McLean PD has just filed a request for assistance on a potential kidnapping. An eight-year-old, name of Angela Lawton, disappeared from her backyard last evening and is still missing. The mother believes the father is behind it."

"If he is, how can that be kidnapping?"

"Obviously things are a bit more complicated. The couple is divorced and in some sort of extremely bitter custody battle. She lives in Virginia, he lives in Maryland. So, if he's taken her across state lines, we have to get involved. I want you to go interview the mother."

"Right now? With all this terrorist alert?"

"Preferably. They've been up all night on this thing." Another pause. "I know you're working this other angle hard at the moment, but if the trauma patient is still in the ICU, he's not going anywhere anytime soon. In the meantime, I'll hunt down a magistrate who will sign a court order for the medical center to hand over the patient's identifying information. You don't see any need for any of his medical information, do you? If we can skip that and go only for his name and contact information, that should make it a whole lot easier."

Phillips was sitting on the edge of the bed now, finger combing her hair. "Give me a second to grab something to write with."

RUSSELL ANXIOUSLY SHIFTED his weight from one leg to the other and swallowed. "They're visitors. Grad students, actually. A couple months ago I invited them to spend a couple weeks in my lab on a research project. They just arrived." He extended his hand, encouraging the guard to hand him the clipboard. "I'll be happy to sign for them."

Instead of handing over the clipboard, the cop rolled a pen back and forth between thumb and index finger while eyeing the group. Finally, he said, "Sir, since the security office is closed this time of day, I'll allow them to be on campus for a few hours, but soon as the security office opens at eight AM, you're gonna need to obtain a proper pass for each of your guests. We provide that service over at Building 31," glancing off to his left, "in case you haven't had to do it before."

Russell jutted his chin at the armed soldiers watching the interaction. "Why the increased security?"

The cop's eyebrows rose. "You haven't heard? National security threat's been upped a notch to orange ever since that business with the FAA computers. There's huge talk within the Office of Homeland Security about more of the same kind of attacks. Maybe not the FAA this time but against a government agency." He handed Russell the clipboard. "I'll notify the office to be expecting you shortly after eight."

After putting sufficient distance between them and the guards to not be heard, Russell asked Ahmed, "I never asked, but I assume you guys have passports, right?"

"Of course," he replied in a lowered voice, clearly insulted.

Russell glanced back at the guards. One soldier was still eyeing them. "What country are you supposed to be from?"

"Pakistan."

"Which city?"

Russell had met several Indian neurosurgeons—all trained outside of their mother country—but couldn't remember having met a single one from Pakistan. Did they have any high-powered neuroscience programs in that country? Probably. They had nuclear weapons, why not a neurosurgery training program?

"Karachi. Why are you asking these questions?" He sounded annoyed. As if Russell were demeaning their intelligence.

"Because," Russell said, measuring his words carefully, not wanting to upset them any more. "You can bet that with a heightened security alert someone over at security is sure to grill me about every one of these little details. The preferred move, if we don't want to raise suspicion, is for me to give them the same answers you do. Or, at least answers that fit your story." He thought of how Angela's life depended on no careless mistakes being made.

They walked up the circular drive to the main entrance of Building 10 and entered the high-ceiling lobby through a glass front door. Across the marble floor, on a wall of blond wood paneling, hung a sign identifying the Warren G. Magnuson Building. Another federal cop—an imposing linebacker-sized African-American man with a holstered black 9mm

Glock—sat behind a table watching them. A large sign on the table said GUESTS SIGN IN HERE.

Russell explained to the guard, "My friends here are grad students. They're scheduled to spend the next couple weeks working with me in my lab. I need a pass until the security office opens at eight."

The cop gave the group a cursory glance before handing Russell a clipboard. "Have each one of them sign in, then you countersign in the next column over."

Task finished, Russell exchanged the clipboard for three adhesive-backed red and white paper badges identifying them each as Visitor.

The cop said, "I set these passes to expire at noon. Know where to go to get the temporary passes you need?"

"Yeah, Building 31. Thanks, officer."

Russell led the small group around the corner and along a hall to a metal fire door that opened into a bare concrete and metal stairwell, down to the first basement, through a hall to another door. After punching a code into the numeric pad to the right of the door, he pushed it open. The thick heavy door swung in, exposing a copper flange surrounding the door's perimeter. It mated with another flange lining the door-jamb. Inside, Russell opened the gray metal door to a panel of circuit breakers and started clicking them on, turning on lights and racks filled with electronic equipment. He noticed Hussein and Ahmed inspecting the copper flange.

"The entire room is shielded from electromagnetic interference by a layer of copper. Floor, walls, ceiling," Russell explained. "That's because this room was custom-built for experiments that involve recording single neurons . . . eh, nerve cells." He read Hussein and Ravenna's puzzled faces. "You see, nerve cells produce such tiny electrical impulses that if we want to record and analyze them in a computer, we have to amplify the signals thousands of times. When you do that, it's easy for the recording electrodes to pick up static radiating from other electrical appliances in the building, like elevator motors, X-ray machines, MRI scanners."

The three "Pakistanis" stopped a few feet into the lab to glance around. Russell did likewise, experiencing the familiar sights as if for the first time. Immediately to the right of the door was the large battleship-gray panel of circuit breakers for various areas of the room; the overhead lights, the four sections of seven-foot-high "racks" connected together and holding a variety of electronic equipment including several Tektronic oscilloscopes, a Grass dual stimulation unit, multiple computers, printers, a HP scanner, and a number of other analog and digital electronic devices. The back door to one section of racks stood open, exposing countless cables running in neatly bound tracks. A large white board filled most of one wall, various colored felt-tip pens cluttered the bottom tray. A stainless steel counter spanned the length of another wall, a sink in its center. Shelving above and below the counter overflowed with various printed circuit boards and other electronic equipment. Tight rows of black three-ring binders packed several shelves. Russell's imported Italian espresso machine—a postdivorce feel-good present to himself—sat prominently on the counter. The faint scent of old orange peels and coffee beans hung in the air. The room had no windows.

Diagonally, in a corner of the room, stood a large olive drab sound-attenuating chamber with a double-pane window for observing behavior inside. It faced the electronics rack. The interior of this room-within-a-room was lined with battleship-gray acoustical tile.

Raveena glanced into the chamber. "Is this where you record from your monkeys?"

"Yes."

"And this?" she asked. She pointed to a robotic arm with "fingers" about a foot away from a joystick on a small pedestal. The arm extended from a heavy-looking four-foot-high cylinder for stability.

"That is the arm I have my monkeys manipulate using only their brain activity."

"Where does this go?" Ahmed asked, opening the only other door in the lab.

"To the adjoining lab," Russell answered.

The other room was a mirror image of the first lab, except that it lacked the electronics rack and recording booth, making it appear much larger. In the center of the room, one adjustable high-intensity parabolic surgical lamp hung from the ceiling, its beam focused down onto a small metal operating table.

Ahmed stepped in, head swiveling side to side. "Ahhh yes . . . this should serve us well." He stopped at the stainless steel counter, absentmindedly rubbing a chrome suction outlet extending from the wall. "You must also have piped-in oxygen, yes?"

"No, only pressurized air," Russell realized that, sure, you could probably do surgery on a human in there. That was, if you didn't give a rat's ass about antiseptic operating environments.

As if reading his thoughts, Ahmed added, "In Baghdad and Mosel I worked in much worse conditions than these. The dust and sand were insufferable."

Hussein, who stood in the doorway, shot Ahmed a quelling look. For a moment Ahmed seemed to consider what he'd just said, then muttered something back at his accomplice.

Russell powered up one of the rack-mounted computers, dropped into a task chair in front of the desklike work area protruding from the rack and pulled over a wireless keyboard. While the other three continued exploring the lab, Russell called up Internet Explorer, Googled PAKISTANI MEDICAL SCHOOLS then started scrolling through the resulting list. By now Raveena, Hussein, and Ahmed were looking over his shoulder.

Finished, Russell told them, "When we go to get your

passes, we need to have our act together. If anybody asks, you're from the College of Physicians and Surgeons. It's in Karachi. That's the best I can do for now. At least they have a physiology department." He nodded at Ahmed. "You're a neurosurgeon." Then to Raveena and Hussein. "Both of you are neurophysiology postdocs. Got that?"

The three nodded that they did.

He pointed to two additional rolling chairs. "Sit down. We need to have another talk—go over things one more time, just so I have things clear."

The two men took the chairs, Russell noted, leaving Raveena standing. Real gentlemen.

"As I understand it, you want to bring your buddy with severe crush injuries here to my lab," pointing toward the other room, "and keep him alive long enough to finish some task. Correct?"

Ahmed nodded.

"And if it looks like he's going to die before he can finish, you want me to remove his head and keep it alive and communicating. Right?"

Ahmed said, "You understand perfectly."

"You realize, of course, the chances of pulling this off are next to zero, don't you? I mean, no one has ever kept a human head and brain alive before," then muttered, "Christ, why would someone want to?

"Even if, by some miracle, we design an interface that will allow him to talk—which is a huge deal—the problems of keeping the head alive are horrendous."

"Like?" Raveena asked.

"There are several major ones. First, we have the problem of perfusing the brain properly. Next we have the problem of how to remove toxins from the blood. Then there's the issue of how to deal with anticoagulating the blood. That names only three, but each one is a huge problem. To handle each of these we'll need specialists . . . like a nephrologist to handle the dialysis issue." He was talking directly to Ahmed now, hoping as a surgeon he would understand.

"A what?" Raveena again.

"A kidney specialist," Russell answered.

Ahmed stared back, unblinking. "You still do not understand yet, do you? As I said before: For security reasons, no one else can be involved. You and I must handle this entirely by ourselves. Why do you refuse to understand this?"

"Because I don't want our lack of competence on these issues to botch the project and result in my daughter's death."

Ahmed jumped up. "I am not incompetent!" He pointed a finger at Russell. "And you should pray you are not either. Failure is not an option."

Up went both of Russell's hands. "Okay, okay, yes, I understand. Take it easy."

Washington, D.C.

Angela's drift upward into consciousness was driven by a vague awareness of discomfort. The closer her brain became aware of her environment, the more a dull throbbing pain squeezed her forehead. Suddenly she jerked fully awake. Where was she? She was lying on her back, both arms at her sides. Blackness completely surrounded her. But where? Was this a really bad dream?

She blinked, abruptly aware of being encased in darkness more complete than any she'd ever experienced. She blinked again, not yet believing that the absence of light could be so total. Not even a shade of gray existed. She moved her right hand to touch her face, but it hit something soft and silky. Her elbow hit that same softness, too. Suddenly, both hands were groping frantically as her chest constricted with encasing fear. She was submerged in silk and blackness and stale air. She tried to sit up but her head hit more silk with something solid immediately beyond. The unyielding softness began closing in on her from all sides. She was trapped in a small area!

Angela began to scream and scream and scream, but no one came to help.

CHAPTER

10

BUILDING NUMBER 10—known within the National Institutes of Health as the Clinical Center—topped a gentle hill as a massive fourteen-floor brick structure built in typical drab, no-nonsense, utilitarian government architecture. It serves as the campus centerpiece and hospital. On foot, Russell led the group out an east side entrance, through Parking Lot 3 to Memorial Drive, then north, past Building 4 on the right and the clinical research center on the left. From there they turned east across a main campus road to the one-way drive leading to the front door of Building 31. Russell hadn't set foot in the security office since being photographed for his own plasticized ID badge three years ago, but he remembered the route clearly.

It was two minutes past 8:00 AM when they pushed open the pitted aluminum-frame glass door into the small waiting area. Three unremarkable pale blue walls formed a U around a gray Formica counter. To its left ran a passage that emptied straight into a back hall. An overweight middle-aged female uniformed officer sat at a scarred wooden desk behind the counter. Within reach of her right hand a Gary Larson Far

Side mug of steaming coffee rested half off a coaster, tilting precariously toward a computer monitor. She glanced up as they entered and recognized they represented the first business for the day. Pushing out of her creaky wooden chair, she asked, "May I help you?" in a phlegmy smoker's voice.

"I hope so. I'm Doctor Lawton. I work over in Building 10. These are scientists from Pakistan who are scheduled to collaborate with me in my lab for the next month." He figured he better stick with the earlier story—just in case the cop at the main gate filed a verbal report. "When we signed in through the front gate earlier this morning, they were issued temporary passes. We're here to pick up their Special Visitor passes."

"Uh huh. They called over, said you'd be dropping by."

The officer spread her chubby fingers of both hands on the counter and leaned into her palms. She wore a standard black uniform, badge, name tag, and a poker face wrinkled beyond her years from either too much sun or too many Marlboros. She studied Russell's group a moment without expression. Russell didn't like the suspicious look behind her large brown eyes.

"Well now, I believe we can fix you up," she said after a few beats. She withdrew three sets of forms from the counter and handed them to Russell. "Just have them fill these out and I'll be back in a minute to process them."

A clot of uneasiness coalesced in the pit of Russell's gut as he watched her walk slowly into the back area. He handed each terrorist a form and motioned to the government-issue pens chained to the desk. In the far corner, just above the doorjamb, a video camera angled down at them.

The officer knocked on the opened door to her lieutenant's office. "Got a second?"

The lieutenant, a rail-thin African American with a shaved head and wire rim glasses glanced up from his desk. "Sure. What you got?"

"We got us three—" she caught herself before "rag heads" escaped from her lips. Likewise, she rejected the term "camel jockeys" as probably equally politically incorrect. Especially since this particular supervisor disapproved of racial slurs. She settled for, "Middle Eastern–looking types out in the office applying for Special Visitor passes."

The lieutenant's brow wrinkled. "Is that a problem?"

"I don't know. That's what I'm asking about."

"And why's that?"

"Considering the increased terrorist alert, I sort of thought you might want to take a look-see before I issue them passes."

He carefully set down his pen and studied her a moment with a look just north of annoyance. "Do they have a credible sponsor?"

"Yes, sir, that would appear to be the case."

"Well, then?"

When she didn't answer immediately, he added, "Lucile, you know how I feel about racial profiling. It's unacceptable on my watch. Should be on yours, too."

"Oh, alright, then!" She swiped her nose with a knuckle and shifted her weight, getting ready to leave. "Then I guess you won't give a flip when I duly note in the report I plan to write up about them that I notified you of my concerns. 'Specially seeing how we got us a heightened security alert on, and all."

"Point made." Sending her a look of severe annoyance, he pushed out of the chair.

Russell heard footsteps coming his way and turned in time to see the first officer reenter the room followed by another federal cop, this one a man. In her nasal East Tennessee accent, the female officer asked the group, "Y'all done fillin' out them forms?"

The three terrorists nodded and slid the papers into a pile on the counter.

Ignoring the forms, the black officer's eyes settled on Russell. "They friends of yours, huh?"

Hardly. "Yep, grad students. Couple months ago I sent a memo to this office notifying you guys about them," he lied, figuring if they ever checked and found no such form on file, he could claim they simply were misfiled. "It should be on file. Have you checked it?"

"No, not yet, but I certainly will." He quickly glanced at the other officer, then back to Russell. "Say, you don't mind, I ask them a few questions, do you?" Without waiting for an answer, he turned to Hussein. "You. Where you from?"

Hussein fidgeted. "Pakistan."

"What city?"

More fidgeting. "Karachi."

"What do you plan to do here at NIH?"

Hussein shot Ahmed a nervous look.

Russell began to interject, to explain that Hussein's English was very limited, but the cop held up a thin, almost feminine hand. "Sir, if you don't mind, I'd prefer to let your friend answer for himself."

Hussein's face took on a look of mild confusion. "We are wanting to . . ." snapping his fingers and glancing at the ceiling, playing the perfect role of a vocabulary-challenged foreigner. Then, with a slight smile, "A head . . . we are wanting to be making a head talk." He flashed an approving glance to Russell, as if asking, correct?

The cop's brow furrowed as he studied Hussein, "Say what?"

More confidently now, Hussein repeated, "We are wanting to be making a head talk."

The cop turned to Russell. "What the hell is he talking about?"

Russell cleared his throat, took a more professorial stance and decided a confident answer might just squelch more questions. "My research deals with interfacing brain electrical activity to computer-driven robots," figuring that by sticking closely to the truth, the less chance he'd risk of eventually getting tangled in a morass of lies. "You know . . . turning brain activity into computerized signals that drive mechanical devices that are separate from the body. In other words, robots. So far, we've been working on using brain waves to control a robotic arm and hand to do a variety of complicated tasks. What these graduate students are here to help me attempt is to pilot a project whereby we produce speech from human brain waves.

The officer drilled him an unsettling look, leaving Russell mystified whether it represented disbelief or amazement or complete ignorance of what he just explained.

The officer turned to Raveena. "You a postdoc, ma'am?"

She looked him straight in the eye. "Yes, sir."

"What university?"

Without hesitating a beat, she answered, "College of Physicians and Surgeons Pakistan, Karachi."

The second officer straightened up, told the first cop. "Okay, Lucile, issue them each a thirty-day pass." He turned briskly and returned to the back area.

After the group exited the office, the lieutenant stepped back into the reception area. "What's your take, Lucile?"

She stood at the counter, tapping the three forms into precise alignment. "Dunno for sure. You tell me."

He held out his hand for the papers. "You know how I feel about racial profiling. I hate it. On the other hand, I dearly love this country, and I also lost a cousin in the NYFD when the Twin Towers came down." He tapped the papers against his other palm. "These aliens worry me for some reason. Something just doesn't set right. Know what I'm saying?" He turned to head toward the back offices. "Think I'll run this by a buddy of mine over at Hooverville . . . get his take on it."

CHAPTER

11

THEY RETRACED THEIR route to Building 10 in silence, Russell leading, Ahmed on his right, Raveena and Hussein straggling behind.

He looked over his shoulder at Ravenna. "You did okay in there. You didn't hesitate or give the impression you were bullshitting. You just answered him. Boom. End of questions." He really meant the compliment, too. For a moment, the male cop had worried him by giving him the feeling their story didn't wash. But she had answered his questions convincingly.

She just looked at him a moment without acknowledging the compliment. Hussein, he noticed, was talking on his cell phone in a hushed voice.

Back in the lab, Russell closed the door and turned to Ahmed. "How long do we have before you want to transfer your buddy here?"

"I am thinking soon as is possible. Today, perhaps?"

"Today? No way." Astounded at the suggestion, he swept a hand around the lab. "We don't have any of the equipment we need to support him. Why the hurry?"

"As we were walking back to here, Hussein spoke with a colleague at the hospital who is monitoring our friend's condition. It seems as though he is not doing so well. His mygolbinuria appears to be worsening and is making his kidney function show signs of incipient failure."

"Kidney failure? Damn! How bad?"

"I have no gauge of that. My colleague is not a doctor. He just stole a look at the chart and relayed to me what he could."

"So basically, what you're saying is it's getting more and more likely we're going to have to do this insane head . . . head thing after all?"

Ahmed nodded solemnly. "Yes, more and more this appears to be the case."

Russell held up both hands, "Hold up a second." He stopped talking to survey the lab while a feeling of doom hung over him. "With all due respect, there's a huge difference between battlefield trauma surgery and what you're suggesting we try to do here. If we *do* try to keep your buddy's head alive, we're talking about maintaining it for days on a cardiopulmonary bypass machine. Right?"

"Correct."

"And the whole point in doing this ridiculous experiment is because you want his brain functioning and communicating with you. Right?"

Ahmed nodded, this time with a hint of irritation. Raveena stood, arms folded across her chest, listening to the conversation. Meanwhile, Hussein had busied himself—to Russell's mild annoyance—with one of Russell's computers, surfing the Internet.

"Do you have any idea what cardiopulmonary bypass can do to the brain?"

Ahmed's lack of response confirmed Russell's suspicions. Not a clue.

"Well then, let me enlighten you." Russell leaned forward in the chair, elbows on knees. "First of all, what I'm about to describe is what happens when you put a regular run-of-the-mill heart patient on bypass. I have no idea what additional kinds of problems we might run into if we try this with an isolated head." The image that flashed through his mind was barely comprehensible.

"First, you have the purely physical problems like," he held up an index finger, "since you no longer have a beating heart, you obviously no longer have pulsatile flow in the brain's blood vessels. This, in turn, can cause you to lose adequate perfusion through the brain's smaller vessels. In other words, your buddy can wake up with far fewer than fifty-two cards in his deck."

"What does this mean, fewer than fifty-two cards in his deck?" Hussein asked.

"It means he's not going to be too sharp mentally. I assume you want his brain alive because you want him making some major decisions? Maybe planning something?"

Ahmed hesitated and glanced at Hussein before finally nodding agreement.

"Well, his brain might just become totally trashed from the bypass machine. That's what I'm telling you." Before Ahmed could respond, Russell raised his next finger. "And since you're running the entire circulation through an external machine, as an added bonus your buddy will probably become severely hypothermic. We don't have a good way of heating him other than keeping the room temperature in the high nineties . . . as close as possible to body temperature. Or we might have to do something creative like wrapping a heating pad around his head."

And this triggered another argument he hadn't yet considered. "And in your friend's case, since he'll be missing a body—which, as I know you know, heats the blood that normally feeds the brain—the hypothermia will be worse unless we can somehow figure a way to heat the machine, too.

"Then there's the problem of hemodilution."

Raveena asked, "What is that?"

"Diluting the blood. You see, the extra fluid required to prime and run the bypass machine always dilutes a patient's blood. In other words, makes it anemic. And in your friend's case, since we won't have time to drain every drop of blood from his body before we switch him totally to bypass—which we probably couldn't do anyway—we'll be running at an even worse deficit. This, plus the fact that a bypass machine isn't as efficient as the human lung at putting oxygen into red cells means your friend's brain will have a high chance of functioning under hypoxic conditions." And just in case the others didn't understand that word, Russell added, "That means running the brain without enough oxygen, which, I don't need to tell you, is not optimal."

He remembered a bypass case he scrubbed on during his general surgery training. "There was this mitral valve case— the surgeon was required to isolate the heart by cannulating the superior and inferior vena cava," and then to Raveena: "Those are the major veins draining blood to the heart." Back to Ahmed: "In the process, he tore the inferior vena cava right behind where it passes through the diaphragm, which, as you know, is a spot that's almost impossible to see. Man, it was a total bitch to fix." He sighed. "But, I guess working with the heart and great vessels isn't going be an issue here. The carotid arteries, on the other hand, will be a problem.

"And," up went another finger, "you have all sorts of embolism problems. All sorts of them." He paused to organize this part of the argument. "You have the potential of air embolism. We don't pay enough attention to the venous return reservoir in the bypass machine and we could end up with air in the vessels.

"Then you have the potential of particulate emboli from the cannulation site. Since we're going to be dealing with the carotids, if your friend has any cholesterol plaque in his vessels, we run a risk of knocking off particles that will go directly to the brain and cause a bunch of small strokes. But I guess he's young, so that might not be too much of a problem."

He was on such a roll now, with all the information flooding back from his general surgery training that he forgot to raise another finger. "There's also the prothrombotic and inflammatory response everyone gets to bypass." Then, realizing that Ahmed might not know this, said, "Remember endothelial cells—the cells that line the inside of blood vessels? Well, they're the only nonthrombogenic cells in the body, meaning they don't form blood clots. For obvious reasons. But, when they're cannulated, the blood flows against the polyvinyl chloride surface of the cannula tubing. And this triggers a horrendous immune response that can cause additional problems, including forming blood clots. Which you don't really want zipping around his blood vessels since they cause strokes.

"And finally there is the loss of blood cells we're going to be faced with. All of the different blood components—red cells, white cells, platelets, you name it—are all damaged during bypass. All of them. And since he'll have no bone marrow, he can't replace any. And if you lose platelets you risk having a spontaneous hemorrhage. But, of course, we won't have to worry about hemorrhage in the body, because he won't be attached to that anymore." He paused for another thought to form. "That brings up another point: What the hell are you planning to do with this guy's body? Can't just leave it lying around the lab."

Ahmed said, "Not to worry. We will take care of that."

"How?"

Ahmed glowered. "I said we will take care of that."

Russell shrugged. "Whatever. But, the point is he's got an excellent chance of bleeding into his brain if he's on the machine more than, say, twelve hours."

Russell shook his head slowly side to side and muttered,

"Damn! The more I think about it, it's a wonder more folks don't have problems." Then, looking at Ahmed again, "The point is, most brains take a direct hit from being on bypass. And that's even when you have highly qualified technicians taking care of the perfusion machine. You're suggesting we fire up one of those babies without any prior training. Or have you been trained in how to use one of those machines?"

Ahmed stared hard at him a moment. "No," anger obvious in his voice.

"Well then, we're taking a huge risk . . ." he let it hang, continuing with, "What I'm saying is, if what you're expecting is to keep this guy's brain functioning like it was before his accident, think again."

They didn't respond.

"What is it exactly you want him to do?" Russell asked again. "I mean, is he supposed to be advising you? Does he have information you want? What?"

Ahmed glanced up at Hussein as if looking to see if he had been listening. He gave no response.

Sensing that he might finally be getting through to Ahmed, convincing him of the insanity of his plan, Russell pressed the point. "So you see, this plan . . . it's crazy, insane, totally nuts. It's destined to fail."

Ahmed looked back with deadly serious eyes. "Instead of wasting our time trying to convince us we will fail, I suggest you consider that your future patient is deteriorating with each word you speak. Or, put another way, it is risking your daughter's life. What is your choice, complain or start solving the task at hand?"

CHAPTER
12

J Edgar Hoover Building, Washington, D.C.

"You wanted to see me, sir?"

Sandra Phillips stood on the threshold of Ian McGowan's office, right hand on the jamb and leaning into it.

Special Agent in Charge, or SAC, McGowan raised his gray eyes from the computer printout spread over the desktop, smiled, slid off his half-height reading glasses and pushed up off his elbows. "Yes, I did. I've scheduled a meeting you need to attend in about ten minutes, but first, come on in and tell me what you've found out so far."

Settling back in the high-backed leather chair, his right elbow propped on the armrest, the middle-aged career FBI bureaucrat began sucking a stem of the tortoise-shell glasses. He wore a crisp white button-down shirt and a red and blue rep tie. His only daily variable was the colors of the diagonal stripes. With his tie knotted directly under his Adam's apple and cuffs still buttoned at both wrists, she assumed the shit hadn't hit the fan. Yet. But the terrorist threat still remained at a high level.

"Coffee?"

Phillips considered the Starbucks triple Grande she'd downed an hour ago. "No, thanks. I'm caffeined out at the moment. But hey, ask me again this afternoon." She folded her thin frame into the chair across the desk from her boss and crossed her long legs. She wore a cream-colored blouse that contrasted sharply against her flawless ebony skin. It also complemented her dark brown slacks with a white plastic FBI ID card clipped to a matching thin leather belt.

"I assume this is about the Lawton inquiry and not the Georgetown patient?"

The uncharacteristic concern in his voice caught her by surprise. "Yes, sir, but since you brought it up, how you doing with getting a signed order?"

"Lewiston is reviewing the papers as we speak. She should have a ruling for us within the hour. You had a chance to look over the pictures yet?"

"Not yet. Haven't had time. I've been working up a few things after interviewing the mother. Which brings up a point . . . why the interest in the Lawton thing? Considering I haven't been able to confirm it is a kidnapping yet."

"Some recent developments. But before we get to that, what have you been able to dig up?"

"Fair enough." She paused, kicking herself: Should've thought to bring her notes. However, a dead-on memory was one of her strong points. "As you already know, the husband's name is Russell Lawton. There was no problem obtaining an accurate background check on him." She cracked a smile. "He's a federal employee, a commissioned officer in the Public Health Service and he's stationed at the main NIH campus."

McGowan pensively tapped the stem against his lower lip. "A neurosurgeon, isn't he?"

"That is affirmative, sir."

When McGowan did not embellish—which was also

uncharacteristic—she continued. "When trying to track him down, I was informed he was out of town attending a medical convention in San Francisco. He was booked into a Hilton close to the convention center. But when I called I was informed he checked out yesterday, which is three days sooner than his original booking."

McGowan tapped the stem against his front teeth. "Interesting. Do we have any hard evidence he actually set foot in San Francisco yesterday?"

"Apparently he gave a podium presentation at the Moscone Convention Center in front of an estimated 1,500 witnesses."

Sucking the stem, McGowan nodded for her to continue.

"The hotel confirmed that Lawton checked out of his room at exactly four oh seven PM which happens to be the same time he was scheduled to be at the podium giving his presentation."

"Okay, so obviously someone other than Lawton checked him out of the hotel. Either that, or they made a mistake. Did you—"

"—ask how the bill was paid?" she interrupted. "Cash."

McGowan considered this, nodded, and muttered, "Could fit."

"Sir?"

His eyes snapped back to her as he waved his glasses dismissively. "We'll discuss that after you wrap this up. Go on. Finish telling me what you've got."

"A government travel agency is contracted with NIH to handle business travel for all personnel. They were able to send me a copy of Lawton's itinerary. He was booked on a United nonstop from Dulles to San Francisco. According to United, he actually boarded that flight." She held up a finger, cutting off McGowan's next question. "Yeah, yeah, yeah, I know you're about to say . . . someone, not necessarily Lawton, could've boarded that flight with his ticket. But, don't forget, we have witnesses who saw him in San Francisco, so it's safe to assume he was—or still is—out there."

She paused to allow him to answer. He just nodded.

"The date of his scheduled return flight corresponds to his original Hilton checkout date. Thus far his original return ticket hasn't been revised, and there's no record of any person using the name Russell Lawton catching a flight yesterday evening out of any of the airports in the greater San Francisco area. I also checked all the domestic airlines other than United. Same story. Nothing." She figured the implication needed no further explanation. "So, given the facts as stated, the best assumption is he's still in San Francisco attending the meeting, but for whatever reason, changed hotels. If, like the ex-wife claims, he's somehow involved in his daughter's disappearance, it doesn't appear to be a direct involvement."

McGowan nodded that he understood her point. "Agreed. From what you've been able to work up, clearly he wasn't physically involved in her abduction. That is assuming it was an abduction and not just a case of an eight-year-old walking off and getting lost. However, this still doesn't rule out the mother's claim that he's the one *behind* the kidnapping. This could all be very well orchestrated. And, as you've already stated, being seen in San Francisco yesterday gives him a bulletproof alibi."

"How come I keep getting the feeling you know something I don't?"

He grinned. "Because I do." With a nod, "Continue."

"That's about all I've been able to run down."

"What about the wife? What's your take on her?"

Phillips shifted positions and crossed her legs. "Yeah, the wife . . . well, since she's the one who lodged the complaint, I really didn't interview her from the standpoint of a suspect. Not yet, at least. But I can tell you one thing . . . mmmm mmmm, there's one nasty custody dispute going on between her and the husband."

McGowan's eyebrows shot up. "So I'm told.

"They were granted a divorce six months ago. Since then the daughter's been living the majority of the time with the father. The mother is moving back to Toronto, where her parents still live. She wants to take the daughter with her, but the father has petitioned the court for total custody, claiming the mother is mentally unfit to effectively care for her. Apparently, she's had a bit of a substance abuse problem, as well as depression. Alcohol mostly. But some prescription drugs, too. She's on some major medication for the depression. The daughter, by the way, is their only child. As I already mentioned, the maternal grandparents live in Toronto. The paternal grandparents—the mother, that is—lives in California. None of the grandparents claim to know anything about the alleged kidnapping, other than the wife claims it happened."

"Since the daughter lives with the father the majority of the time, how does that fit with a kidnapping?"

"It's hard to put together."

"You check with any other relatives besides the grandparents? Aunts and uncles?"

"She's not with any of them. Now tell me what you have that's just bursting to get out."

McGowan's expression turned somber. "Lawton materialized in Bethesda earlier this morning, accompanied by two males and one female who claim to be Pakistani nationals. Lawton requested visitor passes for all three under the guise that they're visiting grad students who have come to the U.S. to do research with him. From what I've been able to find out, that kind of arrangement is par for the course with the NIH boys."

"From your expression, there's more to it than that."

"Right. A heads-up cop at the security office ran their passport names and numbers on a routine check. The names and numbers are legit, but Pakistani immigration claims those particular passports never cleared their boarders."

"Meaning what? They're forged?"

McGowan shrugged. "That's one possibility. But, as we all know, the Pakistani border is about as tight as the *Titanic*'s hull. The point is, considering the present national security situation, the issue of who these alleged graduate students really are needs to be worked up. I've asked the Pakistani authorities to check to see if the valid holders of those passports are still in the country."

Sandra considered this a moment. "I don't get how this whole thing hangs together. Are you saying that illegal Pakistanis aided Lawton in kidnapping his daughter? Or are the two events completely unrelated?"

McGowan's lips pursed. He tapped the stem against them pensively several times before replying, "I have no idea. The facts are as we presently know them. But I can tell you one thing: The situation doesn't pass *my* sniff test. How about yours?"

Phillips agreed. "So, how do you want to proceed? Bring Lawton in for questioning?"

McGowan shook his head. "Not yet. Let's assume the worst . . . that Lawton is collaborating with, shall we say," miming quotation marks with both hands, " 'people of interest.' If so, we need to move with extreme caution. I want you to run an extensive background check on Lawton and his former wife, and I want it ASAP. I'm assigning Delorenti and Haller to provide any additional help you might need." He glanced at his wristwatch. "I've scheduled a meeting in Conference Room AA for five minutes from now. This will give us a chance to fully brief them on the situation. While we wait for INS to check with the Pakistani authorities for some clarification on our three visitors I want Lawton's home and laboratory under twenty four-seven surveillance. We can't afford another 9/11 to blow up right under our noses."

13

Building 10, NIH Campus

Russell demanded, "I want to talk to my daughter."

Ahmed considered this a moment before shaking his head. "No." He seemed to reconsider. "Not until you have shown me significant progress in acquiring the needed supplies for our patient."

"Significant progress? What the hell's that supposed to mean?" Momentary despair snapped back to anger. "I want to talk with her . . ."

"Or what? What are you going to do?" Ahmed simply looked at him. So did Raveena. Hussein ignored the confrontation by continuing to read the monitor screen.

Russell realized he had no leverage. "Asshole."

Ahmed sighed. "Doctor Lawton, again I must remind you that time is extraordinarily precious to us. I suggest we begin our work. Perhaps a good place to start is by making a list of equipment and medications we need. You agree, yes?"

Russell remembered a point made by a psychiatry professor during locked ward rounds after visiting a patient who had attempted suicide. The point being there's a huge difference between helplessness and hopelessness. "Given two depressed patients, which one is more likely to commit suicide?" he had asked. When none of the medical students answered, he said, "It is the one who sees their life as *hopeless*. The one who sees their life as *helpless* is simply asking for help, and is more likely to make an impotent suicide *gesture* than be successful." Well, things were not yet hopeless.

Russell angrily uncapped a black marker and printed BED in the upper left-hand corner of the white grease board. Without looking at Ahmed, he said to him, "Since you're so used to working under such adverse conditions, help me out here."

"No, you start the list. You need the distraction."

Russell began naming items as he wrote. "You say your buddy has a lot of fractures?"

"Yes. Legs and pelvis. But the leg fractures have already been pinned."

"At least that's a help."

Russell pictured a badly injured patient in bed and decided the best strategy for listing the equipment they would need would be to work from the legs upward, rather than using the standard routine he'd been taught for writing typical orders.

"Okay then, because it will be difficult to move or turn him we'll need an alternating pressure mattress to mitigate pressure sores. Do you know if they've done any fasciotomies on him yet?" Unsure if Ahmed knew the English word, "You know . . . had cuts made in his legs to release the tissue pressure from the edema and hemorrhage that crush injuries typically cause?"

Ahmed rubbed the right side of his jaw. "Yes, yes, I am well aware of the term and the need for that. And yes, they did place some just last evening. In both legs, I might add."

"Okay, and if they've pinned his leg fractures, he's not in any casts, right?"

"This is correct."

"Okay, in that case, we need ACE wraps for his legs—to limit his risk of deep vein thrombosis and embolism." Russell jotted that down. "And a Foley catheter drainage system replacement."

"Add a physiologic monitoring system to the list."

"And where the hell am I supposed to find one?" Russell snapped.

"Wherever you plan to find the other equipment. If all else fails, steal one," Ahmed said matter-of-factly.

Russell remembered seeing two Hewlett Packard units that had been surplused from the surgical ICU. They were stored with other old equipment in another basement area not too far from the lab. They were antiquated by today's standards, but probably still functional enough to do the job.

He added an IV stand and oxygen tanks to the list and said, "We can work on a list of medications once we finish the equipment list." He added a suction trap and hose. They'd need a crash cart nearby, too, but stealing one off a floor would be impossible.

"Think there's any chance we'll need a respirator?" Russell asked.

"I think not. If it comes to that, we can support him on a cardiopulmonary bypass machine."

"Oh right, the cardiopulmonary bypass unit. That's going to be a bitch to find one." He printed it on the white board. Then: "Is that about it? Can you think of anything we've missed?"

Ahmed answered, "No, I think that should about cover the equipment. What thought have you given to pharmaceuticals?"

Russell was already starting to list the generalities: pain, fluids, antibiotics, drugs to control the hypotension that accompanies hypovolemic or septic shock, to say nothing of medications needed to treat the cardiac problems arising from toxic byproducts the massive crush injuries produced.

He stood back and scanned what he'd written. The list seemed overwhelming, to say nothing of the problem of procuring them. It wasn't like you could walk into Walgreen's with a list to fill, especially the intravenous drugs.

Russell asked, "Is he taking oral fluids, or does he have a feeding tube?" thinking, they'd have to provide some form of nutrition until . . .

"He has a J-tube in place."

Russell made a mental note to send Hussein out to pick up some Ensure. He could buy that just about anywhere.

By now, both Raveena and Hussein were silently watching the list grow, a look of real concern on Raveena's face, as if finally realizing the enormity of the task. What was her background—was she really a journalist, or had that been merely a story to entice him?

Ahmed began rubbing the side of his jaw and studied the list. "That looks like an excellent beginning. I am certain we will need to add things as various needs make themselves apparent. And before we begin to collect these items, we must discuss another issue. Since it now seems very likely that we will be forced to remove Mohammed's head, what is your solution to the problem of developing the interface with his brain?"

CHAPTER 14

RUSSELL ASKED, "THAT'S his name? Mohammed?"

Ahmed did a startled double take, as if having committed an error by divulging the injured man's name. Hussein and Raveena shot him a look of admonishment. Ahmed glared back at them as he sheepishly admitted, "Yes, his name is Mohammed. But you have not answered the question."

Russell nodded, thinking the name was probably false, just like all their names. Their identifications, too.

He sucked in a deep breath while organizing and parsing down the complex explanation into one he suspected Ahmed might understand. "Like I said, far as I know, this has never been done before. Probably never even been attempted. So, I can't even begin to imagine if we have any kind of a chance at pulling it off. But yes, for what it's worth, we have a plan. I discussed it briefly with Doctor Fetz last night when we stopped in Omaha." *Last night?* Felt like a lifetime ago. "But not in any detail, and I'm not sure she even agrees it has a snowball's chance in hell to succeed.

"Setting up a brain/machine interface requires a fundamental series of logical steps. First of all, you need to define which brain function you wish to interface with. Obviously, in this case, it's speech. Not written or signed speech like deaf people use, but spoken words. And, as I'm sure you know," addressing Ahmed now, "simplistically, there are two parts to oral speech: Not only do we need the physical means of producing words—vocal cords, tongue, and lips—but we also must be able to listen to and understand what we are saying. A sort of quality-control system. Otherwise, all that would come out of our mouths would be nonsense words."

"Explain that, please," Raveena asked.

"In order to speak intelligibly, we must be able to hear and understand what we're saying. I'm sure you've had the experience of saying the wrong word and the moment it's out of your mouth, you stop and correct yourself. Right?"

"Yes."

"Well, there you go. That's because you're listening to what you're saying and comparing it to what you intended to say. If the parts of the brain that monitor what you are saying become damaged, say from a stroke, you lose the ability to speak intelligibly. When that happens, nonsense comes out. To give another example, people who are born deaf never speak very clearly, or with the proper intonation, because they've never been able to hear how others sound and compare it to themselves." He paused.

"Okay, then. As I was saying, the next step is to figure out which brain area serves the function you want to transfer. In this case, the good news is the area responsible for producing speech—at least the part that deals with physically moving your lips, tongue, and vocal cords—is nothing more than, shall we say, a suburb of the same area that moves your hand. This means we pretty much know the general area in Mohammed's brain where we should implant our recording electrodes. With me so far?"

Ahmed nodded.

"And I'm assuming that since we can use brain activity to

manipulate a robotic hand, we can use the same principle to produce speech. All we need to do is move from the hand area to that speech area." *Sorta.*

"Okay then. The next step is to decide which level of brain activity we need to feed into the computer. Most people know about the brain's electrical activity that can be recorded from the scalp," turning to Raveena now, still unsure of her depth of medical knowledge, "commonly known as the EEG, or brain waves. Because the EEG is recorded from the scalp, it's relatively easy to obtain. But because these weak electric signals have to pass through scalp, skull, spinal fluid, and the membranes surrounding the brain, they become even weaker and prone to interference by electrical signals produced from other tissues within the person's body. The heart and the jaw muscles, for example. The second problem with the EEG is that it is formed by the activity of hundreds—maybe even thousands—of individual nerve cells. And because of this, it lacks the degree of resolution necessary to tease out the information we need to drive a computer interface. It's like trying to listen in on a conversation between two people on the other side of a packed football stadium.

"Using the same example, if we really wanted to hear their conversation, we might use electronics to help us. A highly directional microphone, for example. Better yet, if we could place this highly directional microphone on a boom and move it closer to their conversation, we'd do even better. In other words, the closer you get to the source, the better you can make out the individual words. It's the same with understanding brain activity.

"In Mohammed's case, that's sort of what we'll do. Instead of using EEG, we'll record from individual nerve cells, themselves. We do this by implanting tiny, needlelike electrodes directly into the brain's outer surface, the gray matter—where the neurons are located. This way, each electrode can pick up the activity of only two or three nerve cells, giving us signals that contain much more specific information than the EEG. That's good. But the downside is that we can only sample very limited numbers of neurons out of millions involved with producing speech. This is just barely enough to unravel complex commands.

"The more electrodes we implant, the better off we'll be. Up to the limits of our computer's computational capabilities. I figure we can maybe implant two hundred. Then, with each one recording from maybe two or three neurons, this should give us a yield of three to four hundred signals for decoding speech. You still with me?"

Ahmed and Raveena nodded. Hussein no longer appeared interested.

"But this brings up the most difficult step in the whole process: decoding the brain activity. For this," Russell continued, "we use these computers." His hand swept toward the rack filled with electronics.

"And how do they do that?" Raveena asked.

"The computers have special software . . . it's a form of artificial intelligence called a neural network. It's what we use to translate a monkey's brain activity into the information that controls a robotic arm."

"Explain that, please." Raveena was studying him now, a tinge of concern etched around those beautiful almond-shaped eyes. Eyes that had deceived him.

Her concern momentarily puzzled him. Then an implication hit, forming a kernel of a plan. He decided to return to that idea later. Maybe discuss it with Gerda. Maybe not.

"How much do you know about how computers function?" Hussein tuned back into the conversation.

Sonofabitch! Bastard's been tracking all this time.

"Very little," she answered.

He doubted that. "Know what? I think we're straying from the most important point, which is how we can optimize our chances of making your insane plan work."

Just as Raveena appeared to challenge this statement, Ahmed broke in with, "And so where *is* your colleague, Doctor Fetz? I understood you told her you would contact her as soon as you arrived. Yes?"

Oh shit! "I forgot."

RUSSELL CRADLED THE phone, said to Ahmed, "She's on her way," and quickly consulted his watch. "This time of day, that trip usually takes about a half hour, forty-five minutes, depending on the Beltway traffic." He worried about the stress in her voice and imagined the speed she'd probably push from her prized Mercedes CLK she'd scrimped for years to buy. He hoped she wouldn't wrap it around a bridge abutment or T-bone some unfortunate commuter while barreling through a red light.

"In the meantime," casting a defeated look toward the impossible list of equipment scrawled over the grease board, "why don't we take a walk down the hall?"

"Where to?" Ahmed asked suspiciously.

"There's an area in the subbasement. It's a place where the clinical engineers store surplused equipment."

They stood in the hall, peering beyond a half-opened steel fire door into a vast, dimly lit windowless room of bare cement: walls, floor, and ceiling. It made Russell think of what a World War II German bunker might've looked like, except it smelled of mildew and stale mops. In the hall behind them, lined up in tandem along both pale green walls were strings of adjustable height tables—the kind that slip over patient beds.

"Over there. Look." Ahmed pointed to the far corner of the room.

Following the trajectory of Ahmed's extended finger, Russell squinted through the gloom until he saw the target: four vertically oriented clear plastic cylinders jutting up from behind a series of stripped-down hospital beds. The cylinders looked suspiciously like parts of a cardiopulmonary bypass machine. He nodded and started working his way through a maze of IV stands, beds, bedside tables, portable suctions, and—to his delight—two Hewlett Packard life support monitors, each sitting on stainless steel rolling tables. In passing, he patted one of the monitors and commented to Ahmed, "We're in luck."

Ahmed grunted agreement.

He stopped beside a low rectangular blue and white bypass unit set on four omnidirectional wheels. Attached to each end were stainless steel seven-foot vertical poles, a similar horizontal pole connecting the two about five feet up. This pole, he knew, was frequently used by perfusion techs for hanging plastic bags of blood products and IV fluids when in operation. A clear plastic stay—the kind police use to restrain prisoners' wrists—looped around one pole and through a hole in the upper corner of a tattered instruction manual. Russell flipped open the blue cover and read:

ANN ARBOR, Mich.–March 20, 2003–Terumo Cardiovascular Systems Terumo® Advanced Perfusion System 1, the newest model in the longest commercially available line of heart lung machines. The system is intended for use during procedures requiring cardiopulmonary bypass. Incorporating a variety of technologies, including some developed by the high-end automotive industry,

the system allows heart teams to adopt current trends
that positively affect patient outcomes . . .

"Perfect," he muttered, grateful that someone had the fore-
sight to keep the instruction manual attached to the machine.
"Hussein and Raveena can help move these beds out of the
way so we can roll this back to the lab. And, while they're at it,
have them bring back one of these beds." He glanced at the
label on the bed. "Hill-Rom."

"What?"

"Only the best for the government."

Thirty minutes later, as they positioned the bed and the bypass machine in the room they were converting to a temporary
one-person ICU, Gerda Fetz breathlessly entered the other
lab. She wore black jeans, a man's black Ralph Loren short-
sleeve polo shirt, and black Reeboks. With closely cropped
hair and thin, five-foot five-inch frame, she reminded Russell
of some kind of tightly wound Teutonic pixie.

Russell called to her, "Stay right there, Gerda. I'll be with
you in a second." He turned to Ahmed. "Give us a few minutes. We have to talk," and turned toward the door.

Ahmed grabbed his shoulder, abruptly stopping him.
"No. You cannot talk with her privately."

Russell swatted his hand away. "The hell I won't."

Ahmed replaced his hand on Russell. "I will not allow it.
Whatever you need to say to her, you can say in front of me."

Russell slapped his hand from his shoulder. "Get your
goddamned hand off me."

Hussein, who was standing in the doorway to the hall,
tensed and shot Ahmed a look. Raveena froze, eyes moving
from Russell to Ahmed and back.

Calmly, Ahmed said, "Talking to her in private is simply
not an option, and that is final."

Gerda frowned at the group, "Russell, these are the
pigs? Ja?"

Russell spun around to face her again, a fist of anger constricting his chest. He shouted, "Yes, these are the ones who—"

In the next instant, Russell found himself sitting on the floor, gasping for breath, pain shooting across his rib cage. Hussein, he realized, had hit him with something. Something hard. Gerda squatted next to him, arm on his shoulder, asking, "Russell. Are you okay?"

"Oh, man," he gasped, each breath knifing a sharp pain through his chest. He gently palpated the spot where he'd been hit. The slightest pressure sent another searing jolt around his ribs. "Damn, I think a rib's cracked."

Ahmed scowled. "What does it take to teach you? You wish this to end badly? If so, please continue to draw attention to us by yelling so that the entire building can hear."

Ahmed straightened up, reached out a hand to Gerda, "Allow me to introduce myself and my colleagues," as if they were at a cocktail party instead of their present situation, "I am Ahmed. This is Hussein, and this is Raveena."

Eyes glaring, Gerda fired off a volley of harsh-sounding German invectives at the group.

Hussein hauled off and backhanded her across the face, knocking her off balance, sending her crashing against the wall, effectively silencing her. Before she could respond again, his fist slammed her solar plexus, doubling her over, causing her to gasp for air. Quickly, he grabbed the front of her shirt before she slumped to the ground, pulled her up and slid his right arm around her neck, catching her trachea in the elbow crook. He squeezed and hissed in her ear, "Silence, woman!"

She kicked back blindly, trying for his groin but connected with his kneecap, instead. He squeezed harder as Russell struggled to his feet.

"Dammit, leave her alone!" Russell lunged toward Hussein, but was shoved aside as Ahmed charged past. Off balance, Russell's shoulder slammed the wall.

Ahmed was aiming a gun with a silencer at Gerda now, who was still struggling to loosen Hussein's choke hold.

Ahmed said, "Both of you!" eyes darting to Russell, then back to Gerda, "Silence!"

Gerda stopped kicking.

Ahmed asked Gerda, "Are you quite done with your histrionics now? Or do I have to shoot you?"

Bracing his ribs, Russell struggled to his feet.

Gerda tried to answer but clearly was not getting sufficient air, her face now purple, the neck veins engorged.

"Let go of her," Russell yelled. "You're killing her."

Ahmed said something and Hussein suddenly released her.

With a gasp, Gerda slipped to the floor and leaned back against the wood cabinets, rubbing her neck.

Russell rushed to her, dropped onto his haunches, "You okay?" He checked to make sure she was moving air into her lungs despite the alarming wheezes from her neck. She was. Hussein hadn't fractured her trachea. Only then did he allow his mind to acknowledge the rib pain the movement had caused.

She nodded, managed to shoot Hussein a withering glare and croak, "*Gott verdammte idioten.*"

Gerda continued to rattle off a string of unintelligible words to Russell.

Hands on both her shoulders, he said, "Whoa, slow down. You know I don't speak German. Stick to English!"

She coughed, rubbed her throat again. "Sorry. Sometimes I forget this," and shot Hussein another look. She muttered, "Goddamned idiot."

Russell touched her chin, focusing her attention back to himself. "Gerda, we don't have a lot of time. It sounds like their friend's condition is deteriorating faster than expected, so we better start planning how to make this . . ." searching for the word. Clusterfuck came to mind, but instead he opted for, "How to get ourselves through this . . . this situation."

To Ahmed: "Look, I know you're paranoid as hell, but you see how worked up she is. Just let me get her calmed down, so we can get started." He jutted his chin at the sound attenuation chamber. "In there. That way you can watch us through the window."

Ahmed thought it over. "No."

Gerda shouted, "Assholes."

Russell sliced his palm through the air. "Not now, Gerda."

Her eyes studied him a moment. "Describe to me again, this situation. I cannot believe the words I heard last time."

He explained that Mohammed was in the Georgetown Medical Center ICU with severe crush injuries and that the plan was to transfer him here, to the next room, as soon as possible. That they would care for him without proper medical support, and in all likelihood would need to remove his head.

When he finished, she said, "We cannot allow this to happen. We must refuse to help them."

"We have no choice," Russell answered.

"Nein! We *do* have a choice. These swine are terrorists," pointing directly at Hussein. "We can refuse to help them. We can say to them, go fuck yourself."

"But your brother . . . they won't hesitate to kill him. They have Angela. They'll bury her alive. I can't let them do that."

She drilled Ahmed a defiant look and spat on the floor between his feet. "Then this is very unfortunate for all of us because we cannot let them succeed." She locked eyes with Ahmed and said, "Go ahead, get it over with. Put a bullet through our heads."

Ahmed nodded to Hussein, who was still aiming the gun at Gerda. "This is most unfortunate, but you leave us no choice." Then to Hussein: "Do as they wish. Kill them."

RUSSELL HELD UP both palms at Ahmed. "No, no! Wait. Please just give me a few seconds to talk to her," and jerked a thumb at the sound isolation booth. "In there . . . where you can see us through the window."

"No!"

"Wait. Think about it. You kill us, your mission—whatever the hell it is—goes down the toilet. You let me talk to her, get her to cooperate, and you at least have a chance. How about it?"

Ahmed picked at the side of his jaw a moment with his index finger. "Mmmmm . . . Alright, but I will be watching you closely."

Russell helped Gerda to her feet and with a protective arm draped across her shoulder, led her into the gray acoustical tiled booth interior and pulled the door solidly shut behind them, knowing the double-wall construction would keep their voices from being heard outside. Still taking no chances, he whispered, "Talk to me."

She turned her face away from the double-pane Plexiglas.

"Those oily swine probably cannot lip read, but just the same, turn away."

"Good idea."

He did as she suggested.

"Russell, we cannot let those pigs win. You know that, don't you?"

"Yes, but—"

"No buts." She slapped the wall with her palm. "Do you really believe they will allow us to leave after they force us to help them? If you believe that, you're as insane as they are."

Russell grabbed her wrist. "Whoa. Don't draw any attention to us." He stole a quick glance over his shoulder at Ahmed. The man was watching them closely. Russell took a deep breath. The air was heavy with the smell of monkey fur and the apple juice the little guys loved to work for.

"Calm down and listen to me a second." He paused to look directly into her eyes. "Yes, I know . . . in all probability they do plan on killing us when they're finished. But it's going to take some time to accomplish whatever it is they plan to do."

"How much time is that?"

"Hell, I don't know. The point is, if we let them kill us now we've lost any opportunity to escape or even stop whatever they're trying to do."

She seemed to consider his point.

"Look," he continued, "I have a plan. It's going to take some time to work out all the details but, whatever we do, for right now we have to make them believe we're helping them."

She shot him a suspicious look. "What plan? Tell me."

"No. Not yet."

Her expression melted into pleading, "Do not do this to me. You must tell me."

Russell shook his head. "Look, I think it's better you don't know the details. That way, if something goes wrong, they can't blame you."

Her mouth and eyes tightened. "That is totally insane and you know it." She studied his face a moment. "Please tell me you know it is insane."

"Hell, yes, it's insane, but for right now we have to wait for our chance to do whatever we can to stop it."

"Alright, then. And you also know if something goes wrong, they'll kill both of us without giving it a second thought. So I ask you, what difference does it make if I know this plan of yours? I might even help with the details."

He patted her arm. She jerked it away. "No, I do not need assurance. I need details."

He said, "I know, I know. You're right. It's just that I believe that for now it's best if you don't know very much. Trust me on this."

"I always have, Russell. But this is different. Think of Angela and Gerhard. What about them?"

Russell clamped his jaw shut, afraid to tell her Angela's safety was all he could think about and that he really didn't have a plan. "Just trust me on this. Okay?"

For several seconds she stared at his eyes, judging him. "This is my life I am trusting you with."

"I know." Russell looked away and opened the door.

Russell stood in the doorway between the two laboratories, surveying the mini-intensive care room they'd cobbled together in a few hours of productive scavenging. *Not bad,* he thought with a nudge of self-satisfaction. The Hill-Rom hospital bed occupied the center of the room. To the left of the head of the bed was the Hewlett Packard monitor, to the right sat the Terumo Advanced Perfusion System. To save precious space, they'd decided to use the system's horizontal rod to hang IVs instead of hunting for a separate pole. He glanced at the list of equipment crossed off the grease board. Next item: oxygen.

He thought of the area enclosed in cyclone fencing and

topped with razor wire. It was at the rear of Building 10, off
to the side of a loading dock, where The Gnomes of Gas
stored full-sized steel canisters of various gases.

"Ahmed. Come with me. I need your help." Hussein and
Raveena had taken off ten minutes earlier for the cafeteria to
buy sandwiches and soft drinks for the group. Perched on a
high stool, Gerda hunched over a countertop work area, peering through a tripod-mounted magnifying glass, working on
the first stages of assembling a human-sized electrode array.
She planned to piece it together from three smaller monkey
arrays. The lab now carried the acid-sweet odors of solder
resin and the warm electronics that were driving the temperature toward eighty degrees in the poorly ventilated room.

Russell inspected the heavy brass Yale padlock before letting
it clang back against the three-inch galvanized pipe that supported the high chain-link fence. The lock secured a chain-
link door into an area filled with full-sized tanks of various
gases: Black for nitrogen, green for oxygen, blue for nitrous
oxide, gray for CO_2 each one looking like a miniature tor-
pedo. Mostly, these tanks fed lines that served anesthesia
machines in surgery. The majority were chained together in
upright positions and secured to steel posts embedded in the
concrete floor. Several additional cylinders lay on their
sides. A gray, rust-spotted metal dolly for transporting individual tanks stood just inside the locked door.

Russell studied the area around the loading dock until
spotting what he was looking for. He'd missed it the first
time, but caught it on the second pass: A security video camera mounted just under the eves of the loading dock roof angled down to monitor the gas storage area.

"Damn."

Ahmed asked, "What?"

Hands stuffed in his pockets, Russell started ambling back
toward the loading dock and rear entrance of Building 10.

"Don't look now, but there's a security camera aimed at the storage area. I don't know how we're going to get a tank for the lab." He took the first of three concrete stairs up to the loading dock.

"I doubt it will be a major problem. I will ask Hussein to take care of it tonight, after it becomes dark. Yes, I see it now. Good. At least we know what we are dealing with and can work around it."

We. As if he was part of their sick little team. "If that's the case, while he's at it, have him pick up a tank or two of nitrous oxide. We could use it."

"For?"

Russell stopped, hand on the doorknob. "Are you kidding?" He inspected Ahmed's face. No, he wasn't kidding. And this guy claims to be a surgeon? "To supplement anesthesia, of course." He opened the door and entered the long hallway.

"Anesthesia? For what?"

He stopped again. "What the hell kind of question is that?"

"A simple one. We do not need anesthesia for the surgery we have planned."

Russell glanced up and down the hall, saw no one, but lowered his voice anyway. "Jesus Christ, you're a surgeon. Or, so you say . . . when we have to remove your friend's head, he'll have to be under anesthesia."

"No. That will not work."

"Why the hell not?" He studied Ahmed's face, said, "Oh, no way!" His fingers turned icy cold. "Please don't tell me you're thinking of doing the surgery under local anesthesia."

Ahmed stared back. "Yes, I am. And for good reasons, too."

"Look, doing a surgery like that under general anesthesia is one thing. The patient won't know what the hell's going on. But, doing it while the patient's wide awake . . . Damn!"

Tingling nausea filled his gut, making him gag. He swallowed, sucked a breath to keep the gag suppressed.

"You must not be thinking clearly, my friend. There is no other way to do it."

Russell locked eyes with Ahmed. "First of all, let's get one thing clear: I am *not* your friend. Secondly, it would be inhumane to . . ." Again, he glanced around at the seemingly deserted hall. You never know how far voices carried along these painted concrete corridors. He lowered his voice again. "Dammit, Ahmed, that's sick! Can you imagine what it'd be like to lie there listening to someone detach your body from your head? To say nothing about knowing damn well it was starting the countdown to your immediate death. That's sick!"

"Every one of us is fully prepared to die for this cause."

"Being prepared to die is one thing. Lying there while your head's being permanently and irreparably detached from your body is an entirely different matter."

Ahmed sighed. "You still are not thinking this through clearly. Let me explain. Inhalation anesthetics are eliminated from the body by the lungs. So, yes, perhaps some of those drugs would be removed by the heart-lung machine hours later." He shrugged. "But, neither you nor I know for certain exactly how much would be cleared. And the other drugs . . . the morphine, the ketamine, whatever you might think of using for anesthesia, they are all removed by the liver. And, of course, he will no longer have a liver anymore, so any drug effect will linger an indeterminable amount of time. Think about it. Our entire objective is to keep his brain functioning, and functioning at optimal capacity, for several days. This is the reason that I cannot allow you to use anything but local anesthetic."

Russell found it impossible to agree with Ahmed, even though he was correct. Any agreement, no matter how slight, would be condoning the surgery, and he couldn't bring himself to do that. Instead, he turned and stormed toward the stairs that would take him down to his laboratory, wondering with stomach-churning anxiety what other crucial points he was overlooking.

CHAPTER 17

Hoover Building, District of Columbia

Sandra Phillips led Special Agents Toni Delorenti and Ron Haller into the small crowded conference room of pale blue utilitarian walls, a sensible oval conference table, six matching metal-framed blue-fabric chairs, and color photos of both the director and the president of the United States in simple black frames. McGowan already occupied one of the chairs. His fingers curled around a white ceramic mug, obscuring half the royal blue and gold FBI seal glazed into the side, making the steam rising toward the ceiling appear to emanate from his left hand. In his other hand he held a mechanical pencil and was jotting on a legal-size pad of yellow paper. The room carried a faint scent of metallic air-conditioning.

Sandra folded her thin frame into the chair directly across from McGowan. Delorenti and Haller opted for the chairs to her right, filling in the remaining space between her and her boss. She slapped a manila folder containing several pages of computer printouts and some handwritten notes on the table in front of her, opened it and cleared her throat. "Tony and Ron have been a big help in procuring the intel for this debrief," and with a cursory nod at the folder, withdrew the top page.

"Let me begin by stating that the following information was secured in its entirety from various governmental and private databases and none via direct personal interview. This tactic was specifically elected for the purpose of remaining below our target's radar. We can certainly jettison it if we elevate the inquiry to a higher, more open level, pending your decision after this strategy discussion." She glanced up at McGowan for his approval. He nodded for her to continue.

"The queried databases include the U.S. Public Health employment records, the DOD, DMV, IRS, and the NCIC using a Wanted Person search. Tony also ran a Triple-I through NLETS."

"An Interstate Identification Index." McGowan said offhandedly, nodding another approval. "Excellent."

"For completeness, Ron and I worked up Lawton's visa statements and bank records. Additional financial background was no problem obtaining due to the fact he settles almost one hundred percent of his bills online through his bank." She paused for a breath. "Okay, so much for the prelim. Everybody on board?" She scanned the audience.

"Here goes. Russell Lawton is thirty-eight years old, six foot, one hundred and eighty pounds, Caucasian, male with no known priors. I then searched for arrests without convictions. None there either. I was thinking he is about as clean a citizen as you're likely to come across these days. In fact, almost too clean. And that in itself kind of worried me. So I checked with the local PD."

"Which one?" McGowan asked.

"Rockville. He rents a two-bedroom apartment out there."

"Go on."

"There was one domestic violence call to the residence nine months ago. The wife claimed he beat her fairly badly and demanded to file charges. The responding officer's report states that she showed no evidence of physical trauma. She was taken to a local hospital and examined, but no serious injuries could be documented."

"Were any injuries documented?" McGowan again.

"The report didn't state one way or another, but the next thing you know, the charges were suddenly dropped. A female officer followed up on it and asked around to some of the neighbors. I guess there had been some fairly loud arguments between them for several months before they finally split up."

She withdrew a color printout of a full facial shot and slid it across the table to McGowan, thinking that the guy's face had nice features, one most women would find attractive. "Here's an employment photo. As you see, he has brownish blond hair and hazel eyes. He has no scars, tattoos, or other identifying physical attributes. Okay, so much for the physical description." She didn't bother asking for questions, knowing full well they would've already asked them.

"He was born in Sacramento, California. His mother wasn't married at the time, so Lawton is actually the mother's maiden name. The father, a man named Jesse Hill, was employed as a career correctional officer at the state prison there. The mother taught high school. The two eventually married when Russell was in grade school, but it lasted only five years before the mother filed for divorce on the grounds of incompatibility. For whatever that's worth.

"Russell graduated a public high school with average grades. His school and military records indicate a young man with well above average IQ who apparently didn't apply himself. Immediately after graduation he signed up for a minimum stint in the navy." She glanced up at McGowan, who she knew never served. "That'd be four years."

He eyed her without moving his head. "I knew that."

"He did boot camp at Great Lakes, outside of Chicago,

then was stationed at San Diego for corpsman training. This time he excelled in school. After training, he did one tour of duty aboard an aircraft carrier before serving the remainder of his time at a small naval base in Everett." She smiled at her geographically challenged boss. "That's in Washington State, just north of Seattle." She grinned. "Washington State is just north—"

McGowan pulled off his glasses, said, "Okay Sandra, you can cut the humor."

"Apparently it was during this time he made the decision to try for a career in medicine and made a deal with the navy: If they paid his way through school, and if he was able to make it through premed into med school, he'd pay them back with six years of duty as a physician. This turned out to be a sweet deal for him because he later discovered he could serve those payback years in the U.S. Public Health Service. Assuming, of course, he could wangle a stint at NIH rather than pulling a posting at some godforsaken PHS hospital like Sitka, Alaska." She'd never set foot north of the Canadian boarder, but for some reason pictured Alaska as nothing more than icebergs and polar bears. "Fast forwarding for a moment, apparently that's exactly the course he took.

"Now, backing up a few years, the story continues like this: Immediately after completing his active duty tour with the navy, he entered University of California–Davis where he again excelled—consistently landing on the dean's list. His premed degree was a little out of the mainstream: computer science and artificial intelligence. He applied for medical school at UCSF where he'd previously made some contacts as a corpsman a few years earlier. Obviously, he was accepted. There he also excelled, finishing in the top quarter of his class. He went directly from medical school into neurosurgery training at UC–San Diego. Interestingly, during his residency he began working on brain-computer interfaces."

"Say what?" McGowan asked, now sucking a stem of his glasses.

Phillips grinned. "Yeah, I needed to find out the answer to that one myself. Apparently, it deals with building interfaces between brain and computers so that the brain activity can be used to manipulate robotic devices . . . like robotic arms and such. Least, that's *my* understanding."

"To manipulate robots? Why would they want to do that?" Haller asked.

"Yeah," Phillips responded. "The docs are thinking things like this will help quadriplegics flip hamburgers on a grill. The military types are thinking more along the lines of having soldiers control robots to do their fighting."

"Got it." McGowan nodded, making a note on the pad. "Go on."

"From residency, he went straight to NIH to start his six payback years. Been there ever since. Seems to love the research angle of medicine." She exchanged one sheet of paper for another.

"So much for his professional life. Moving now to his personal life . . ." she surveyed the room. Still no questions. "During freshman year at UCSF he married a woman, name of Marci Dillon. She was also a student at Cal, but was in business school, not medicine. Marketing to be exact. They divorced six months ago and apparently it has not been a very pretty show. More like *War of The Roses*, if you ever saw the film."

"Most divorces are ugly," McGowan commented solemnly, the voice of experience. "We know the reason?"

"I wondered that, too, thinking maybe it has some kind of abuse thing—you know, considering the dropped charges I mentioned earlier . . . something that might have to do with the present situation. But no, we have nothing on that. Not yet, at least. From what I gather, it's a hot button between them. We might want to keep that in mind, case we need to

push a few buttons when it comes time." She judged Mc-
Gowan's reaction. He was jotting a note on the legal pad,
giving her nothing.

She continued, "Next issue: finances. Best we can surmise
from picking through his credit card charges, he's a conservative dresser." She considered how this sounded and decided to clarify the point. "By that, I mean as far as how
much money he spends on clothes. Apparently, he's not into
Armani and Zegna, but couldn't afford those duds even if that
was something he was into. Doesn't smoke. He's a moderate
drinker—mostly beer. The restaurants he frequents appears
to be primarily family places: Applebee's, Starbucks, Out-
back Steak House, places like that. I assume these choices
are dictated by the fact his daughter lives with him most of
the time." Another glance at her boss to see if that registered.
Again, nothing.

"He subscribes to *PC Magazine, Wired,* and the *Washington Post.*" She paused before, "How we doing?"

McGowan nodded. "Very good so far."

"We drilled a little further down into his finances. Want
me to go into that now?"

"Any reason not to?"

"Right." Again, she exchanged papers. "He rents the
Rockville apartment I just mentioned. There's no record of
him ever owning a house, even when he was married. His total bank account, as of the close of business yesterday, was a
grand total of five thousand dollars. There's no record of
him ever owning stocks or bonds and he doesn't appear to
have any other legitimate financial accounts within range of
our tracking ability. But so far I haven't requested a FinCen
rundown on him since he doesn't strike me as the type of
player who'd be squirreling away money in an offshore account. But, you never know for sure until you look." Then,
with a half shrug: "I can trigger an audit on that if you want."

McGowan said, "Not with what you've told me so far.

But we always have that option later for completeness sake. Go on."

"We couldn't find any records of church donations, so, I guess it's fair to assume he's not overly religious. On the other hand, he's made some minor political contributions but not to any groups that'd suggest any terrorist sympathies. Especially Middle Eastern leanings. He contributes a few bucks each year to The Brady Campaign to Prevent Gun Violence and to Mothers Against Drunk Driving. And he contributed to the Kerry campaign during that election.

"He's never been audited by the IRS, but I guess that's not any huge surprise considering his total net worth is probably less than ten K.

"Staying in character with the Mister-Straight-and-Narrow image, there's no record of any disciplinary problems during his active-duty navy stint. And, so far, ditto for the time spent in the Public Health Service. Finally, he hasn't had any disciplinary issues with the state medical society's Quality Assurance board." She stopped speaking and closed the folder.

"Oh yes, I forgot to add, he drives a five-year-old Volvo."

Eyes closed, McGowan dropped chin to chest and made a snoring sound before jerking his head back up, and saying, "Sounds like a pretty boring guy," He turned to Haller and Delorenti. "Either of you have anything to add to what Phillips just said?"

Haller offered, "She gave a very complete download. Nothing from me."

Delorenti nodded affirmation.

"So," asked McGowan, "what's your take? Doesn't sound like he's the type to be kidnapping his daughter. You think?"

Phillips shook her head. "No, sir, I don't," and glanced at the other special agents for their opinion.

Delorenti said, "I agree."

McGowan leaned back in his chair, removed his glasses

and sucked a stem. "Next question: how do you think we should handle him?"

Phillips began straightening the papers in the folder. "Way I see it, we have two agendas here. The kidnapping, of course, but then there's the whole issue of those potential," her fingers mimed quotation mark in the air, "illegal aliens," figuring the others would make the politically incorrect translation, "with him. The kidnapping is the easy one. We interview the wife, make certain the child *is* missing and not just chopped up and stored in her deep freeze. Then we sit back and wait for a ransom demand. Meanwhile, we watch the husband to make sure he really didn't abduct her."

"And the second issue?" McGowan asked.

She grinned, getting to the more interesting part of this inquiry. "Well, sir, sooner or later we're going to have to have a talk with the good doctor. Maybe even interview a couple of his new Pakistani drinking buddies."

CHAPTER

18

Building 10, NIH Campus

Ahmed said to Russell, "I just talked to a colleague who is monitoring the situation at the hospital. It would appear that we should transfer Mohammed here straightaway."

Ahmed's words didn't register with Russell, who was too engrossed in designing the neural network they would use to translate Mohammed's brain activity into speech. He had opted to start with a copy of the basic, untrained network he'd developed for producing robotic hand movements instead of starting from scratch. But it was a huge leap of faith to assume that speech production could be achieved using the equivalent computer approach. Not only that, if one accepted the fact that two human brains never function *exactly* the same, why would one expect two artificial intelligence networks to function similarly. Just as identical twins end up perceiving the world differently because their individual nervous systems have been molded by a lifetime of slightly different experiences, neural networks developed with the exact same data sets could vary somewhat. But he had to start somewhere.

Something shook his shoulder. A voice in his ear said, "We must go now."

He glanced up from the glowing monitor. Ahmed stood next to him with a concerned facial expression, his right index finger picking at a spot on his jaw. He was dressed in the green scrubs Russell had swiped for each of them, thinking the outfits blended into the clinical center better than designer jeans.

"Go? Go where?"

"To the hospital, of course. We must collect Mohammed, now."

"What do you mean, collect Mohammed?"

"His condition has worsened further. It is clear that we must move now. If we wait any longer, the opportunity will be lost."

"Can't you give us just a little more time. A day, maybe?"

"Absolutely not."

Outside the main gate, by the security hut, the three of them—Russell, Ahmed, and Hussein—descended on a powder blue Bethesda cab that was in the process of dropping off a visitor. They climbed in and asked the balding driver to take them to Georgetown University Hospital. The cabbie took I-270 south toward Washington, exited onto Wisconsin Avenue, headed south to Reservoir Road and turned right. He pulled to a stop at the Medical Center front door. Russell climbed out first, figuring to let Ahmed pop for the fare.

Just inside the lobby door, a Middle Eastern man in his thirties stood waiting for them. He wore blue jeans and a tan Ralph Lauren sweatshirt and was nervously rocking back and forth on his heels. After a hushed conversation in their native language, the man turned and led them to a bank of elevators where a small group of visitors and scrub-clad hospital personnel waited. An elevator arrived, the doors opened. They all crowded in and their guide punched a button. The door rattled closed.

They stood to the side of the twin doors leading into the SICU. Mounted across the left-hand door was an engraved red plastic sign warning: SURGICAL INTENSIVE CARE UNIT, Authorized Personnel Only. Visitors Limited to Five Minutes per Visit.

Ahmed leaned in close to Russell, whispered, "Mind you, the transfer has already been negotiated. What is now required from you is to perform the duties of the receiving physician. The treating team has stated quite emphatically that they will not release Mohammed without a written acceptance by a qualified physician. Obviously, that is you."

It dawned on Russell that if these terrorists successfully pulled off an attack against the United States, and if it was traced back to them, his signature would be on the chart. Ergo, it would incriminate him as a willing participant. Then again, he realized, if things got that far, he had little to worry about. He'd be dead.

Russell asked Ahmed, "Aren't you worried about leaving a paper trail?"

"No." Ahmed flashed a what's-your-point? look.

Neither did the pilots who flew into the World Trade Center Towers. They were willing to die for their cause.

"Well, in that case, why not just sign him out AMA?" Unsure if Ahmed knew the term, he added, "Against medical advice."

Ahmed frowned. "We discussed this option already. The trauma team is adamant. They consider Mohammed's condition extremely critical and would never consider releasing him to anything less than to an adequate facility. They also require a family member sign the transfer papers. As it is, we had a devil of a time convincing them Abbas," with a nod at the newest member of the team, "is his brother."

Russell thought of Angela. "Fine, let's get this show on the road."

Mohammed lay on his back under a single white sheet pulled up to midchest. He wore one of those typical sky blue tie-in-the-back hospital gowns stamped with multiple faded gray GEORGETOWN MEDICAL CENTER seals, as if that might be a deterrent to anyone seriously weird enough to want to steal one. The urine in the drainage bag hanging from the bed frame was strongly tinted burgundy, indicating probable presence of blood. One IV fed a vein in the back of his left hand. Small white gauze dressings held in place with two-inch nonallergenic paper tape covered abandoned large-bore IV sites in both antecubital regions of the elbow, artifacts of the initial resuscitation. An arterial line skewered his right wrist, a small red clot inside the coiled tubing danced back and forth in time with the heartbeats from the cardiac monitor. Russell was surprised to see Mohammed wasn't intubated, but realized it probably wasn't necessary. Yet.

Mohammed smiled weakly at Ahmed and mumbled something in his native tongue.

Ahmed replied. Then, in English—probably for the benefit of the nurse who had accompanied them into the room. "This is Doctor Lawton, he is from the NIH. As we have discussed, he will be taking over your care. Do you understand me?"

"Yes."

Russell thought he noticed a silent message flicker between them before Mohammed turned unfocused brown eyes to Russell. Russell couldn't bear to hold eye contact and looked away, wondering if the man knew what was in store for him? Surely he must.

"Doctor Lawton," the nurse chirped in a brisk, professional tone of screaming disapproval, "before we will consider

discharging this patient to your care, you must sign a release
and then write a note in his Georgetown medical record
clearly acknowledging the fact you are aware of the grave
risk you are submitting him to by moving him and that you
assume full clinical and legal responsibility for Mr. Mohammad's very serious medical condition.

"Also," she said with stern accusation, "you should know
that none of the attending staff caring for Mr. Mohammed
approves of this transfer." She shook her head disapprov-
ingly. "Not at all."

He wanted to scream at her, "You think I do?" but simply
nodded, relieved to have an excuse to get the hell out of the
room. "Understood. Just give me a form and his chart."

MOHAMMED WAS QUIETLY transported from Georgetown Medical Center to Bethesda by commercial ambulance, the two attendants suddenly materializing in matching white short-sleeve shirts, pushing a collapsible gurney into the SICU room before Russell had finished his chart note, again impressing him with Ahmed's organizational skills and ability to adapt to adversity.

During the drive Ahmed tried several times to discuss something of apparent importance with Mohammed, but the injured man drifted in and out of shallow-breath clouded consciousness, leaving Russell to wonder if the pissed off but well-intentioned nurse had slipped her ex-patient a bit of narcotic to make the transfer more tolerable. He checked the freshly copied medical records for evidence of that, but found nothing. Most likely the records had been copied before any medication was given, or, equally likely, Mohammed's deteriorated neurologic condition was simply a direct effect of complications from his severe crush injury. Either way, if Ahmed was expecting Mohammed to direct or finish planning any sort of attack, they were presently flat out of luck. He thought about this a moment and decided, *perfect.* All the better to stall their progress until he could figure a way out of this mess.

Russell turned so Ahmed couldn't see the faint smile on his lips.

The ambulance parked in the patient transfer area for Building 10. The driver asked Russell, "You have a room number?"

"Wait here. I'll get a gurney."

The driver frowned. "You don't want us to take him straight up to the ICU?" He sounded astounded.

Russell scrambled for an appropriate lie. "You saw the guards at the gate. The national security threat level's been raised. Do you have a Class Four clearance for entering a federal building?"

"A Class Four clearance? Never heard of that," the second attendant said, looking puzzled, "so no . . . guess we don't."

"Yeah, it's a new requirement. A directive from the Office of Homeland Security. A lot of people haven't heard of it yet, but that'll change."

When neither driver said a word, Russell added, "Okay then," and opened the ambulance's back door, "Wait here," and stepped out onto the concrete sidewalk.

He took the only available stretcher in Patient Transport, this one complete with a small green portable oxygen tank in an angled rack welded to one of the front legs.

Using a white plastic fracture board and a draw sheet, they slid the semiconscious Mohammed from stretcher to gurney. Russell pulled up the stainless steel side rails and locked them in place, hung the IV on a gurney pole and unhooked the EKG leads and arterial line from the battery-powered PhisoControl monitor. The driver handed Ahmed a white plastic garbage bag with the remnants of Mohammed's clothes, the pants and shirt had been cut off with bandage scissors in the Emergency Department to facilitate evaluating his injuries.

After Russell signed the forms to complete the transfer and bid the attendants good-bye, he wheeled Mohammed to a back bank of elevators used specifically for transporting patients and food service carts.

Ahmed asked, "We are taking him downstairs, are we not?"

Russell ignored the question and punched the elevator button.

After several seconds Ahmed said, "Oh, I see," and continued unsuccessfully to try to talk with Mohammed in a foreign language. Hard as he tried, Mohammed could not overcome his lethargy.

With only enough room in the ambulance for Ahmed and Russell as riders, Hussein had been left at the medical center to find another way back.

They had a difficult time squeezing the gurney into the cramped lab. Once in, they positioned the gurney parallel to the hospital bed, leaving barely enough room to stand on each side. The bed had already been prepared with an alternating-pressure air mattress under the bottom sheet.

This time they had no fracture board to expedite the transfer. Ahmed stood on one side, Russell on the other, each holding a rolled-up end of the draw sheet under Mohammed's back and butt. Russell instructed Raveena to be responsible for controlling his head before reaching down to flip the switch activating the air compressors for the mattress. He checked everyone's positions one last time. "Okay, on the count of three. One . . . two . . . three." Lighter than anticipated, Mohammed seemed to levitate from the gurney onto the bed. Even so, the effort triggered a jab of pain from Russell's cracked rib.

"Okay. Ahmed," Russell ordered, "take the gurney back

to the transfer area," and pushed it out into the hall to make more room. "I'm going to need some initial lab work." To Raveena: "Grab me two red-topped tubes and a 10cc syringe," with a nod toward the test tubes with color-coded rubber stoppers.

Obviously not pleased with being delegated such a menial task, Ahmed shoved the stretcher into the hall, saying, "Hussein can dispose of this when he returns. I must stay and help with Mohammed."

"Not a good idea, Ahmed. We don't want someone to see a patient stretcher down here where it doesn't belong. Might draw attention. Also, close that door. I don't want someone walking by to look in here."

Ahmed shot him the glare of a pissed-off teenager, then stormed into the hall.

Screw him, Russell thought and then grabbed the IV bag and hung it from the horizontal crossbar over the perfusion machine. Next, he began hooking up EKG leads to the Hewlett Packard monitor, then the arterial line. Finally, he hung the urinary catheter drainage bag from the lowest bar of the side rails.

Done with the routine tasks, he bent down to Mohammed and shook his shoulder slightly. "How you feeling?" He removed the gray Littman stethoscope from his right coat pocket.

Mohammed's head turned slightly, his mouth cracked open, "My computer . . ." He looked over at Raveena, but couldn't keep his eyes open.

"In a moment, Mohammed," Raveena answered softly. Then to Russell: "We need him more alert. He cannot function like this. Can you give him some caffeine or Ritalin?"

"No."

"Oh? And why is this?"

"Goddamnit, he is what he is," he yelled, making no attempt to mask his anger. "I told you guys this wasn't such a red-hot idea. He should be back in a hospital where they have the facilities to properly care for him."

Russell let the plastic stethoscope earpieces snap into his ear canals, blocking out Raveena's reply. He gently tapped the instrument's diaphragm to determine if he was listening to it or the bell. He found it set for diaphragm, so he switched to bell before leaning over the bed and pressing it against Mohammed's chest, just below the right clavicle. "Deep breath."

Mohammed continued to snore lightly.

He moved the bell lower, then repeated the exam on the left side. Mohammed's breathing sounds were loud, clear of wheezes or the crinkling cellophane sound of rales—from fluid collecting in the lung's small air chamber. Good. Next, he listened to his heart. Slightly rapid, but not alarmingly so. Finally, the abdomen, where weak bowel sounds were present. He replaced the stethoscope in his white coat pocket and started examining Mohammed's cranial nerves.

He glanced up to see Gerda standing in the doorway separating the two labs, watching him work.

Finished, Russell tore open a packet containing an alcohol-soaked sponge and reached for Mohammed's left hand. More awake now, the patient tried to pull away. "Hold still, I'm only going to take a blood sample."

He swabbed the back of the hand, then, letting the alcohol evaporate, encircled the man's forearm with a rubber tourniquet. Russell held up his own hand for Mohammed to see and opened and closed his fist. Mohammed did the same, distending the veins on the back of his hand. Russell popped the needle into a vein and filled the syringe before releasing the tourniquet.

"Gerda, please take these to the lab," handing her the two blood-filled tubes. "Tell them I want a crit, creatinine, liver functions, and myoglobin level." He paused, asking himself if there was anything else he needed, then realized he hadn't squirted blood into a pink-topped tube—which contained chemicals to prevent clotting—making the hematocrit impossible to run now. *Shit!* "Forget the crit, but tell them I need the others stat."

He paused, wiped the back of his wrist across his forehead and wondered, *What other mistakes am I making?* Eyes shut, he squeezed the bridge of his nose, his fingertip placing pressure on his eyes, trying to squeeze out the tacky fatigue coating his brain like heavy oil.

Ahmed returned and said, "Raveena can assume his nursing needs. She has had a great deal of experience in this."

Russell nodded and backed away from the bed. He reminded himself to read up on hemosiderosis, refresh what very little he knew about it. He asked Ahmed, "What do you know about hemosiderosis?"

"Hemosiderosis? Do you not mean myoglobinuria?"

Russell considered trying to cover up his error by asking if hemosiderosis—the chronic buildup of iron deposits in the lungs and other tissues—could be a byproduct of myoglobinuria, but dropped it. He simply shook his head at the stupid mistake, said, "Yes, of course. Just tired, I guess."

Ahmed studied him a moment. "You look it. Perhaps we should go for coffee and take a short break. We can talk about it in the cafeteria."

"Good idea," he answered, grudgingly feeling gratitude for Ahmed's help. "I could use some caffeine."

They sat at a burnt orange Formica table for four in one corner of the large cafeteria, as far away from others as possible, Ahmed across from Russell, two white Styrofoam cups wafting steam between them. Russell peeled the cap from a small cream container and started dripping the white liquid in drop by drop while stirring a red plastic swizzle stick. He watched the coffee transition from black through infinite shades of brown until becoming light tan. He tapped out the remaining drop, before setting the spent container on the table. The room smelled of steam and boiled cabbage and the chunks of Swiss steak swimming in thick brown gravy in a stainless steel serving tray.

Ahmed said, "In my view, from a general surgery standpoint, the most important thing we must watch for right now is compartment syndrome."

Russell remembered the condition from his required year of general surgery before entering neurosurgery residency. Or, to be more precise, his three-month rotation on Orthopedics. "Right. When the injured muscles begin to swell, the fascia," meaning the tough connective tissue encasing the muscle groups, "can't expand and becomes a tight compartment. If the tissue pressure within the compartment gets too high, it squeezes off the blood flow to the muscles and the muscles begin to die and become necrotic. This, in turn, causes more swelling and a vicious cycle starts that, if allowed to continue, literally rots away the limb."

Ahmed nodded. "He has already had fasciotomies in both legs to relieve the pressure and help prevent this from happening. Mind you, that sometimes is not enough."

Russell realized he'd forgotten to examine Mohammed's legs and mentally visualized the pressure-relieving incisions the Georgetown orthopedic surgeons must have made through the fascia.

Ahmed continued, "You were spot on in ordering the creatinine. The kidneys are one of the first organs to be damaged from myoglobin."

Russell reached deep into his memory for information about the small bright red protein, myoglobin. And didn't come up with much of anything other than it is very common in muscle cells and gives meat much of its red color. And the protein's job is to store oxygen for use when muscles work hard. Crush injuries can release it into the bloodstream. Unfortunately, when it accumulates in organs other than muscles, it is toxic to the cells and damages their function. The kidneys and heart being prime examples.

Russell said, "Yeah. The one thing I *do* remember about myoglobin kidney toxicity is it causes acute tubular necrosis," referring to the renal tubules that filter impurities from blood to form urine. "And the treatment for it is volume expansion. Not more red cells, but just more blood volume, right?"

"Yes, you are quite correct. We must treat it with Mannitol or normal saline."

"And shoot for what? A urine output of two to three hundred cc's per hour?"

"Yes, very good." Ahmed smiled. "You must have had good surgical training. Calcium gluconate can also be helpful."

Russell knew he could've looked all this up online, but figured involving Ahmed would remove some of the blame from his own shoulders if—or more likely when—Mohammed's condition crashed and burned.

"Hypotension can also be a problem," Ahmed added.

"Which is easily treated with vasopressors. But, as you know, the problem is compounded by the fact those drugs themselves can be toxic to the kidneys."

"Yes, this why we must watch closely for crystal formation," Ahmed stated. "But this is easily being treated by alkalinizing the urine with sodium bicarbonate."

With all these effects on the kidneys, Mohammed's fluid balance would be a major problem. Although most surgeons were skilled at dealing with routine post-op fluid balance problems, they were not skilled enough to handle someone heading into complete renal shutdown. Under normal circumstances that would be the point you called in a highly skilled kidney specialist. "Damn! So we're looking at having to manage a rising potassium and dropping calcium."

"Yes, but only until Mohammed finishes his task. Once he had done that, we can let him die," Ahmed said without the slightest trace of emotion.

CHAPTER

20

RAIN BEAT A tattoo on the Tote umbrella, cascading rivulets onto the ground, splashing, soaking his black socks, filling his wingtips. Russell listened numbly as the priest spoke insincere words describing an eight-year-old girl he had never known. Marci stood glaring at him from the other side of the excavated ground. The backhoe operator smoked under partial protection of a Douglas Fir, waiting patiently for the service wrap-up so he could finish the job. A royal blue canopy protected the small coffin from the downpour.

"You bastard," Marci yelled, "it's your fault she's dead!"

Someone next to him placed a hand on his shoulder.

"Russell, wake up."

Russell became aware that Angela's funeral really didn't exist, that he was actually slumped forward in the task chair, chin on chest, tongue desert dry from mouth breathing, a sheen of sweat covering both hands. How long had he been snoozing? He tried to move, but his neck muscles cried foul. He reached back and began massaging the aching chords, before straightening in the chair and sucking moisture into his mouth. With the tips of both index fingers, he massaged granules of dried protein from the nasal corners of both eyes and blinked.

Gerda stood next to him, the lab now thick with soporific warmth from heated electronics. The room's poor ventilation didn't help, either. And that was a result of the copper shielding surrounding the entire room. She handed him a computer printout. Lab results. Curious, he glanced at the patient's name and hospital number, wondering how the hell she'd managed to finesse the blood specimens through the lab when Mohammed was not registered as an in-patient.

He read the report header and chuckled. Gerda Fetz, Ms. Ingenuity. Instead of submitting Mohammed's blood to the clinical lab, she'd run it through the veterinary lab, logging him in as one of their registered rhesus monkeys. Made perfect sense. He was so accustomed to just ordering lab studies on humans, he hadn't thought about this possibility when handing her the tubes of blood. But they could only do this once or twice before the veterinarian would become alarmed and come to see what was wrong.

"Very clever, Gerda, running this under Adam's name."

Ahmed moved closer to them, obviously listening to their conversation while craning his neck to see the paper. Hussein was sitting back in a task chair, feet propped up on a desk, reading what appeared to be an Arabic newspaper. Raveena, he decided, was probably in the other room caring for Mohammed.

"Ach, I told them we have a very sick animal. I only hope they do not notify the veterinarian. This is not good, ja?" she said, as her fingertip flicked against the paper.

"No."

"Give it to me!" Ahmed reached for the printout, but not far enough to span the distance.

Instead of leaning forward, Russell tossed the report to him, forcing Ahmed to grab for it and miss. It fluttered to the concrete floor. Seeing this, Hussein dropped both feet to the floor and straightened up, preparing for a physical confrontation.

Russell said, "His myoglobin level's worse than the last Georgetown draw eight hours ago." He and Gerda both looked at Ahmed.

Ahmed picked up the paper and frowned at the result. "He cannot function in his present state. He needs to be more alert. You must be giving him pain medication. I want that to stop." He balled up the lab result and tossed it at the wastebasket. It missed, bouncing along the floor a few feet. "He will be given no medicines at all. For any indication."

"I haven't given him a damned thing," Russell lied. "I wanted to see if his mental status would improve on its own."

Ahmed shook his head. "I do not believe this. I suspect you are trying to keep him from doing his job. You do realize, do you not, that by keeping him sedated you risk the lives of your daughter and," pointing a finger at Gerda, "Gerhard. Yes?"

"Look," Russell said, keeping his voice down so Mohammed couldn't hear from the other room—assuming, of course, he was alert enough to understand. "I know you've treated very sick patients in less than optimal conditions, but his injuries," pointing toward the other door, "are not your run-of-the-mill battlefield trauma. This is way more complicated now. The kind of trauma surgery you're used to is relatively easy. You just stop any bleeding, patch up what you can, and ship the victim off to a real hospital. This isn't quite that simple. Here, we're dealing with the *secondary* effects of trauma. There's no way we—you and I—can treat him optimally. We're both surgeons. He needs an internist. An intensivist, for sure. Probably a nephrologist, too, the way his kidneys are slipping down the drain."

Ahmed scowled. "No. We cannot risk anyone knowing what we are doing here."

"Look, if it were just you and your friend's life on the line I would say fine, have it your way. But by denying him proper care, you're gambling the life of my daughter and Gerda's brother. I can't let you do that."

Ahmed's eyes narrowed almost to slits. "You need to understand. *You* have no choice in the matter. I do not really care if your daughter lives or dies. And be assured that we are all of us willing to die for what we need to do. It goes without saying that you will die, too, if you try to obstruct us, or have you forgotten that already?"

The door to the lab scraped open. Ed Ogilvy, the head of the Surgical Neurology branch and Russell's boss, stepped into the room and glanced from Russell to Ahmed to Hussein to Gerda and back to Russell with a bemused expression. "What the heck are you doing here? You're supposed to be in San Francisco."

Russell found himself at a complete loss for words.

Ogilvy demanded, "Well? I want an explanation."

"Ed, these are friends of mine . . . Ahmed and Hussein. And, of course," he stammered, "you know Gerda." To his horror he noticed the door to the other room stood half open.

Frowning, Ogilvy ignored the introductions. "You haven't answered my question. Why aren't you in San Francisco?"

"Well, I—" Move and close the door to Mohammed's mini-ICU? Or would that only draw his attention to it?

"Who is this man?" asked Ahmed, his face a mask.

"Who the heck are *you*? That's the more germane question," countered Ogilvy, taking another step into the room. "And what the heck's going on in here?" He glanced toward the other room, did a double take. "What the hell!"

On his feet now, Hussein moved quickly. He slammed shut the door to the hall, whipped the gun from behind his back and aimed the silencer point blank at Ogilvy's forehead. "You! Over there. Move!" and flicked the barrel toward the sound attenuation chamber.

Ogilvy shook a finger at Hussein. "The hell I will. This is federal—"

Hussein quickly squeezed off two shots directly into Ogilvy's forehead, dropping the senior neurosurgeon onto the floor.

Hussein pointed the gun at Russell. "Quick! Move him into the chamber."

CHAPTER

21

RUSSELL SUDDENLY BECAME aware of an unnerving stillness shrouding the laboratory and glanced up from the computer monitor. The tiny hairs on the back of his neck became erect and his heart accelerated. He began feeling light-headed and realized he was hyperventilating. *Christ!* He'd never done that before.

He watched the clock and held his breath for thirty seconds. By about thirty-five seconds his fingers stopped tingling. *A panic attack,* he realized.

He blew out a long breath through pursed lips and looked around the lab, but everything appeared exactly as it had for the past several hours since Hussein had dragged Ed Ogilvy's dead body into the sound attenuation chamber and closed the door. Gerda was going through the motions of working, but accomplishing next to nothing. Raveena was in the other room, caring for Mohammed. Hussein had been gone for several hours now. How long? He didn't have a clue. One moment the sonofabitch was there, the next moment you'd realize he'd been gone for an indeterminable time without ever knowing exactly when he'd left. Nor did

Russell have any idea what the bastard might be up to. Ahmed was spending his time camped out in front of the other computer, surfing Arabic Web sites or reading.

Russell straightened his arm and studied the tremor in his fingers with amazement. He made a fist, then extended his fingers and made a fist again. It didn't help. He shook his hands. The tightness and shakiness remained. He leaned forward again and tried to type another command into the computer. Three times in a row he hit the wrong key.

He sat back, his arms hanging limply by his side, and sucked another deep breath.

Ahmed turned toward him. Russell could see he'd been scanning the Al Jazeera Web site. "Are you finished?"

Russell glanced down at the floor, at the path to the booth that had been smeared with Ed's blood. Someone had wiped it up, but he couldn't remember that happening.

"Christ, is he still in there?" He turned and peeked through the window into the booth. He could barely make out the crumpled body in the shadows by the far corner.

"Yes." Ahmed stood and, hands on hips, arched his back, saying, "I think I will visit the cafeteria. Do you wish me to bring something back for you? A coffee, perhaps?"

"What are you going to do about him?" Russell asked, unable to actually say Ed's name. "Sooner or later someone else is going to come by. We can't just leave him there."

"That is not something you need to concern yourself with. Focus on your work. Let us handle those details. I asked about food. Do you want me to bring you some?"

Russell stared back at Ahmed.

"Yes? No?"

He knew he should try to eat something, but wasn't really hungry. Not after all that had happened. He pushed out of the chair, knowing he'd be unable to eat here in the lab next to Ed's body. Besides, he needed to get out of the room for a while. "I'll get it." He asked Gerda, "Want something?"

Ahmed put his hand on Russell's chest. "No. Stay. Work on programming the computer. This is more important than running errands. But be warned, I will have told Raveena to keep an eye on you. She is armed and has killed before when it was needed."

Russell slapped his hand away. "Don't touch me, god-damn it."

Ahmed glared back, his muscles coiled, ready to strike. He seemed to battle a series of emotions before finally saying, "No, you stay and work. He," stabbing an index finger toward the other room, "cannot finish his job until you finish yours." He hesitated before adding, "Need I remind you your daughter is not returning until you finish?"

Russell relaxed his fist. "A sandwich and Coke." He re-considered. "Wait . . . make it a Mountain Dew," figuring the extra caffeine would help. Then, to Gerda who was sitting at her workbench watching, "How about you?"

"Ja, a sandwich and a Coke would be lovely," obviously relieved that emotions hadn't escalated into something more serious.

Ahmed leaned into the other room, spoke sharply at Raveena before storming out into the hallway, slamming the heavy shielded door behind him.

Russell muttered, "Asshole," knowing it sounded juvenile.

Gerda nudged the door to the other room partially closed then scurried back to him.

She whispered, "Quickly. Tell me. Your plan. What is it?"

Russell sighed and massaged the back of his neck and sighed. "I'm sorry, Gerda."

"Sorry? What means this, sorry?"

Her English deteriorated when she was mad or excited. Which was it, he wondered? Probably both.

"Sorry I got you involved in this," figuring it was his fault. Sure, they knew her name before he'd mentioned it, but the fact remained that she wouldn't be part of this if they hadn't kidnapped him.

"Ach, we can do nothing to change that now." She glanced at the partially open door, lowered her voice another notch. "So tell me, what is your plan?"

He tried to act pensive, as if weighing what to tell her when actually his mind was scurrying for something—anything—to say. Finally, "Look, I know you want to know, but what if they suspect something and start to question you? If I tell you, they could get it out of you." This sounded good, so he pressed the point before she could answer. "I know you wouldn't want to tell them anything, but what if they tortured you?" It sounded melodramatic. Then again, it *was* possible.

She thought about this a moment. "I will tell them nothing."

"Look, I know you're strong. But stronger people than you have yielded to pentothal. Remember, Ahmed's a surgeon. He knows exactly what drugs to use. I don't want to take a chance."

Again, she considered this, nodded, said, "But you do have a plan. Yes?"

22

"DOCTOR, MOHAMMED IS getting much worse, I think."

Raveena stood in the doorway separating the labs, left hand on the doorjamb, Russell's gray Littman stethoscope draped around her neck in the fashion popularized by TV medical dramas. Loose, damp strands of long black hair clung to both cheeks now, her forehead glistening with a patina of sweat, her scrubs rumpled. For the umpteenth time, Russell wished the room had air-conditioning, especially with Ed Ogilvy still slumped in the recording booth. But it didn't, and with the electronics running full tilt the temperature probably maxed at close to 80 degrees several hours ago, filling the room with essence of hot circuit board, stale breath, and the faint smell of Ed's urine.

"Worse? In what way?" Russell pushed up out of his chair, the movement shooting a stabbing pain from the base of his skull straight down his spine in a reminder of the beating Hussein had given him. The knuckles of his left hand knocked a crumpled cellophane sandwich wrapper off the workstation counter onto the floor. As he stooped to pick it up and toss it into the yellow plastic wastebasket, the move triggered a jolt of pain from his rib. He purposely avoided looking at the window of the booth and Ed's body still slumped in the corner.

"His chest is beginning to fill with fluid, I think."

Mohammed lay on his back, his right hand was still trying to type, his left hand fumbling to hold the computer.

Russell leaned over the bed's side rails and pushed the computer toward Mohammed's feet. He pulled aside the white sheet clinging to Mohammed's damp chest and raised the thin patient gown. He pressed the stethoscope bell under the right nipple and listened to a few breathing sounds before sliding it lower and around toward the back, comparing the loudness of the two areas. Clearly his breathing sounds were less distinct at the base of the lungs, meaning fluid was accumulating where gravity pulled it.

"Deep breath."

Mohammed tried, but the effort triggered a series of phlegmy, racking coughs.

Russell grimaced at the man's pain and waited for the spasm to calm before repeating the process on the left. Correct. Score one for Raveena. Fluid was accumulating at the base of both lungs. Most likely the first signs of heart failure. More precisely, left heart failure. Probably a direct effect of myoglobin toxicity to the heart muscle.

"What is happening?" Raveena asked. Her tone struck Russell as strange—more detached clinical curiosity than actual regard for Mohammed as a person.

Russell asked Mohammed, "Feeling a bit short of breath?" and, placing both hands, fingers spread, across his own chest, took an exaggerated deep breath, pantomiming the question, just in case he didn't understand.

Mohammed nodded yes and drew another labored breath.

Russell could hear soft, wet crackles from his lungs—like phlegm in a smoker's cough—even without the stethoscope.

"Here." Russell leaned over, placed the tong of the green nasal oxygen tubing over Mohammed's head, directing the jets into both nares, and then dialed the control valve to a five-liter flow rate. A musty, yeasty, fruity scent registered in his consciousness. He muttered, "Dammit! Just what I need."

"What?"

"Pseudomonas. That's what."

"Explain that, please."

He stripped the sheet further down, the move wafting the distinctive odor up into his face. Before exploring any further, he dropped the sheet and pulled on a pair of latex exam gloves. Movement in his far right peripheral vision caught his attention. He turned. Ahmed stood in the doorway watching, eyebrows raised questioningly.

Russell gave a slight head shake, silently signaling him to say nothing. He returned his attention to the fasciotomy wounds in Mohammed's legs.

Gently, he peeled back a bulky white ABD dressing from one wound. As expected, greenish pus stuck to the dressing and a thin layer covered the raw edges of the incision. Without a word he replaced the dressing and thought back to what he knew about the bacteria. *Pseudomonas aeruginosa,* the epitome of an aggressive opportunistic pathogen. Opportunistic, because the damn bug always infected compromised tissues. Yet there was hardly any tissue it could not infect if the body's defenses were damaged to some extent. Crushed thigh muscle provided a perfect medium for the bug to thrive. Even so, it didn't need much in the way of nutrition, having been observed to grow in nothing more than distilled water.

He gave Mohammed a reassuring doctor's pat on the arm before turning and motioning Raveena into the other room. Ahmed stepped aside to let her pass. Gerda watched from her lab stool, a fresh Diet Coke in her right hand.

Russell closed the door so Mohammed couldn't hear what he was about to say. He addressed Ahmed directly. "I told you we shouldn't have discharged him from the hospital. Now we're totally fucked."

"No. This is not true." Ahmed shook his head. "Consider the odds, the prognosis. Given the severity of his injuries, he was doomed regardless of whether he is in or out of that hospital. And I need him here."

"So you say. But at least in a real hospital they have the specialists, equipment, and facilities to treat him. You've condemned him to death by bringing him here."

Ahmed's posture stiffened. "Enough of your bloody philosophy, damn it. It's boring and counterproductive. Besides, we have work to do."

"What is wrong with him?" asked Raveena.

He turned to her. "What's wrong with him? Christ! What isn't wrong with him is a better question. Every damn bone in his pelvis and thighs has been crushed and we're trying to treat him in what amounts to a third world environment. And now he has a bad infection."

"Russell."

He looked at Gerda, his frustration boiling over. "Well, it's true, goddamnit."

Gerda said, "Ja, this may be true, but I am thinking about my brother. You should be thinking about Angela." She glanced at the door shielding Mohammed from the discussion. "How serious is his condition?"

"You mean how much time do we have before . . ." he couldn't bring himself to say it. He sucked a deep breath, held it a few beats before blowing it out slowly in an attempt to quell his frustration and anger. "To start with, his lungs are filling up with fluid because he's developing left heart failure."

"Left heart failure? Is that different from heart failure?" Raveena asked.

Gerda leaned against the wall to listen. Ahmed remained strangely silent.

Russell explained, "The right heart pumps blood through the lungs. The left heart pumps it to the rest of the body after it returns from the lungs. If either side works less efficiently than the other, you develop problems. In this case, since the left side is at fault, blood backs up in the lungs, forcing fluid across the membranes and into the little air spaces. I believe that's what's happening to him now." He surprised himself with his lack of sarcasm. "He's literally slowly drowning in his own edema."

Ahmed nodded agreement. Gerda popped the tab on her Coke.

Raveena appeared fascinated. "Why is it happening?"

"Probably because the myoglobin—the protein released by the crushed muscle—is damaging his heart muscle, making it weaker. But there could be another cause, and I'll get to that in a moment."

"How do you treat it?" Gerda asked, before taking a deep pull of Coke, her voice uncharacteristically flat.

"With a drug primarily. Digoxin, for example. We can use the drugs to whip the heart muscle into working harder. But it can't go on like that forever. Not with a toxin destroying it. The other thing we can do is to give diuretics, which force the kidneys to dump extra fluid—hopefully from the lungs." He paused, ran his hand over his head. "But he's also got the other problem now, and it's bad—the pseudomonas infection."

Ahmed frowned. "Are you quite certain it is pseudomonas?"

"Yes, dammit. Can't you smell it? I sure as hell can." Once learned, you never forget the scent.

Ahmed shook his head woefully. "Here," handing Russell a slip of paper.

It contained lab results. The creatinine and BUN. Both measures of kidney function elevated from the last values, signifying Mohammed's kidneys were deteriorating further.

Russell wadded the slip into a tight little ball and threw it at the wastepaper basket. It hit the wall and bounced across the floor, landing next to a wheel of Gerda's task chair. He made no effort to pick it up.

"What?" Gerda again.

"The problem is he's slipping into kidney failure and now he's got an infection in his legs that, even under optimal conditions, is a real bitch to treat. And to treat it we're forced to sock it to him with some serious antibiotics . . . I mean the kind that can easily rot your kidneys out under normal conditions. God knows what's going to happen with his kidneys already compromised. And we don't even have a choice. If we don't treat it, the infection is going to spread throughout his body."

Ahmed shrugged. "Right. The point is, we must move more quickly to the next phase."

"The next phase," Russell muttered. The words carried a clinical detachment that blunted their full implication.

"Meaning?" Gerda asked.

Russell looked at her for a long moment.

She asked, "Oh. Detaching his head?"

Ahmed shot Russell a hard look. "Yes, this is exactly what I mean. Time is running out, so I suggest you explain in very precise terms how you and Doctor Fetz," with an angry glance at Gerda, "plan to accomplish that task. You've had sufficient time to plan for this moment. The time is now here."

Suddenly overcome by fatigue, Russell sighed, dropped into his chair and scanned the three faces staring back at him.

He addressed Ahmed directly, saying, "Okay, here's the plan. This needs to be done in three very separate stages. The first stage is to implant the set of electrodes over the speech area of Mohammed's brain. How we define that exact location is going to be tricky. Yeah, we know in general anatomical terms where it is, but to pull off a stunt like this, we need to know exactly where it is *functionally*. If we were to do something like this with any other patient, God forbid, we'd simply take him over to imaging and do an *f*MRI." Seeing Ravenna's confused expression, he said, "That means a functional MRI."

She still didn't get it.

"See, a regular MRI only shows the brain's anatomy. A functional MRI shows the function that's associated with the anatomy."

Well sort of. He decided not to elaborate.

Then back to Ahmed: "First, we implant the electrodes and record from the nerve cells in his speech cortex. Then the second phase is to train the computer to translate those signals into speech. Only after we've made absolutely certain the computer is trained to an acceptable accuracy will we be able to . . . you know . . . ah, do the final dissection."

"How long will this step take?" Ahmed asked, sounding more like a midlevel accounting firm manager than a terrorist.

"Dammit, Ahmed, how should I know how long it'll take? I've never done anything like this before."

Ahmed smirked, turned to open the door into the adjacent room. "With Mohammed's condition slipping away, I suggest you find a solution to that question, and do it very quickly."

McLean, Virginia

Sandra Phillips caught a quick visual on the two-lane road ahead, saw a strip mall off to the right, and said into the cell phone, "Hold on a second. Let me pull over." She slowed, turned the motor pool Crown Vic into the asphalt lot and braked, replaced the clamshell Motorola against her ear. "Okay, I'm back." She fumbled in her purse for the wireless earphone/microphone.

McGowan asked her, "Where are you now?"

"McLean, Virginia. Just finished interviewing the ex-Mrs. Lawton," figuring he wanted her back in the office; otherwise, he wouldn't have asked. "Why?"

"The kidnapping angle is now taking a backseat on the Lawton inquiry. Something else just popped up. I need you back in the office pronto for a debriefing. Can you be back here within, say, half hour, forty-five minutes?"

She considered the traffic. "More like on the forty-five-minute side, but yep, I'll kick in the afterburners."

Hoover Building, District of Columbia

Phillips entered the conference room. McGowan, Delorenti, and Haller were already sitting around the oval table chatting, waiting for her. She said, "Sorry. The Beltway was a phenomenal mess. Total gridlock. Which, I guess, shouldn't come as any big surprise to any of you."

McGowan motioned for her to take a seat, which was unnecessary since she was already dropping into one of the metal and fabric chairs. She asked, "Whassup?" using her sixteen-year-old nephew's vernacular.

McGowan asked her, "Ever hear of a guy, name of Jamal Azzam?"

"The terrorist? Oh, hell, yes. Who hasn't?"

"Right." He tossed an 8" by 10" glossy color photo across the table to her. "Does this look anything like the man you checked out at Georgetown?"

She picked it up, saw a man she estimated for late twenties or early thirties. Black hair, pockmarked dark skin, about a "5" in the looks department. From the grain and depth of focus, she could tell the close-up was shot through a high-powered telephoto lens in strong sunlight, then enlarged and cropped to target the man's face. She studied it a moment. The patient's face she remembered was fatter, but the aftermath of trauma could contribute to that. "This is a closer match than any of the other photos I looked at." She passed it to Haller. "You seen this yet?"

He accepted it without a word.

McGowan said, "It just arrived from Israeli intelligence. I wanted you to check it out to see if he's our mystery patient. So what are you telling me; is it or isn't a possible match?"

She pulled the photo back from Haller to double check. "I'd have to categorize it as highly probable."

Her boss leaned back in the chair and nodded. "Good." He scanned the other agents present. "Just so we're all on the same page here, I'll review his history. Azzam was born in Palestine but grew up in Trenton, New Jersey, after his parents immigrated to the States when he was only one year old. His school records show a brilliant kid with a natural talent for computers. In fact, he got into big trouble during high school for hacking. He graduated from Rutgers with a MS with honors in computer science. Starting in high school, he took an openly strong anti-American position on our Middle Eastern policies and was very active in a campus fundamentalist Muslim sect that criticized the U.S. stance there. After graduation, he left the States to return to the Middle East. But he had already been targeted by most intelligence agencies as someone to keep under surveillance. And that they did. The CIA has very strong evidence that he became an active al Qaeda sympathizer and quite possibly received actual terrorist training at one of their training camps in Afghanistan."

McGowan addressed the group; "Any of you remember the Vengeance virus that hit last year?"

Delorenti answered, "Hell, yes. Who could forget that one? That little turd took down the Pentagon's intranet for four days."

Haller asked, "They ever figure out how the coder targeted it so precisely?"

McGowan: "All I know is it had something to do with specifically infecting computers using e-mail addresses ending in dot-mil and then worked its way up the food chain. Never did understand much more than that."

Delorenti: "They ever find the piece of shit who did it?"

McGowan: "No, but they strongly suspect Azzam."

Delorenti: "Based on?"

McGowan: "Something to do with the coding style."

Delorenti, the techie of the group, said, "I understand the guy's supposed to be nothing short of brilliant."

Haller: "If that's the case, why's he al Qaeda?"

All laughed.

McGowan said, "Let's stay on point, here folks." He removed his reading glasses and hooked a stem in the corner of his mouth. "There is every indication that the worm that took down the FAA system for forty-eight hours was his work, too."

"Man! What a frigging disaster that turned out to be," muttered Haller.

McGowan continued, "The day after that attack, a man of apparent Middle Eastern ethnicity was struck by a vehicle and pinned against a brick wall. He sustained severe crush injuries to his pelvis and legs and was taken to—and treated at—Georgetown Trauma Center. His condition was critical. Apparently he didn't have health insurance, but a friend signed an agreement to cover expenses. Because of the seriousness of the injuries and the need for intensive care, the hospital requested a payment of fifty thousand up front. Amazingly, the friend coughed up the retainer in cash."

"Jesus, how stupid," muttered Delorenti. "Let me guess. The bills were marked."

McGowan shook his head. "Close, but not quite. What it did do, obviously, was draw attention to them. The sum was reported to our office and we ran a routine check on the patient. The name on his identification was Mohammed Mahfouz but, interestingly enough—"

"He's a dead ringer for Azzam," Phillips finished for him.

McGowan grinned at her, "You tell me. You're the only one who's actually seen him," and slipped his glasses back on.

She shrugged. "He wasn't looking his best, and I wasn't able to get a long look at him. They kicked me out. Which brings up another point. How are we coming on getting a magistrate's order to get access to him?"

McGowan pulled a paper from a manila envelope. "Funny you should ask. The order was signed by Schniederman about four hours ago. But when I sent Delorenti down to

Georgetown to obtain a direct visual confirmation, well, Tony, you tell them."

Delorenti cleared his throat. "Seems some of his buddies checked him out of intensive care against medical advice." He paused to scan the group. He had their attention.

McGowan said, "Now this is where it gets *really* interesting." Off came the glasses again. "Because of the seriousness of his injuries, the medical staff wouldn't allow him to be signed out without a written agreement for a physician to assume direct responsibility for his transfer. Guess who that turned out to be?"

"Let me guess . . . the good Doctor Lawton," Haller offered.

"Bingo. But it gets even weirder." McGowan nodded for Delorenti to continue.

"Soon as it became apparent the target was linked to our ongoing inquiry, the task force punted responsibility for identifying the target to us. So, first thing I do is make a routine call to NIH to inquire about Mahfouz's condition. Guess what?"

"He died in transfer?" Haller offered.

"Well this is the weird part. They wouldn't confirm or deny that Mahfouz was even checked into the hospital. Claimed that HIPAA laws don't allow information of that nature to be given out, even to law enforcement agencies and *especially* over the phone."

"What the hell's HIPAA?" Haller asked.

"The Health Insurance Portability Accountability Act," Delorenti continued. "I looked it up. The only part relevant here is a series of administrative, technical, and physical security procedures to assure the confidentiality of health information. In other words, they can't give out anything to anybody. Not even a spouse."

"Wife abuse," noted Phillips.

"Say what?"

"Especially the spouse. That part was set up to protect battered women. So husbands can't be calling to find out where their wives are after beating the snot out of them."

"But that's crazy. We're trying to conduct an investigation. And we now have an order from a federal magistrate."

"Yeah," Delorenti said. "Well, tell that to the people over at NIH. Anyway, so I go over there and show them the court order. Now they start cooperating. Guess what? Mahfouz isn't even in the hospital. In fact, there's no patient presently admitted there under Lawton's name."

"So, maybe he's got Mahfouz at another hospital," Phillips suggested.

Delorenti shook his head. "Nope. Lawton doesn't have medical privileges at any other hospital in the area. I checked with the local medical society. He's at NIH, and that's it."

"So you're saying Mohfouz vanished into thin air?"

"Looks that way."

"You have a talk with the good doctor?"

"No," interjected McGowan. "In fact, this new wrinkle's elevated the sensitivity of this inquiry right up to the top. As such, the brass has discussed in detail how they think we should proceed with the investigation. They decided they want us to back off until we acquire a better assessment of the situation. If this Mahfouz truly is Azzam, then this might be an opportunity to take down an entire cell. If we can do that, and get enough members to talk, we might be able to work our way up to an even higher level." He glanced from one agent to the other, then nodded.

McGowan continued, "There's good news and bad news. What I just gave you was the good news . . . that this could end up being a conduit right in to a major al Qaeda arm. The bad news is that from what little information we could obtain about Mahfouz's injuries, he's either dead or dying. I guess if we can't bring down an entire cell, just knowing he's dead is a reasonable consolation prize. But until we can get our hands on the body, we can't positively ID him.

"Obviously, Lawton is where we start looking. But before we get to that, there's a few more facts we need to consider." McGowan finally glanced at the paper in his hand. "Our first reply from the Pakistani intelligence agencies has been less than rewarding. I pushed back, but it remains to be seen just how cooperative they'll be on this one. In the meantime, I've filed a query with Interpol as well as requested more information from all our intelligence resources, including the CIA. Once we've had a chance to evaluate this information we'll bring Russell in for questioning. But for that initial interview, I want us to home in on nothing more than the kidnapping angle. I don't want him getting the slightest hint our primary interest is his friends." He scanned the group again. "Any questions?"

Phillips asked, "We have any idea where he might be?"

McGowan pulled the stem from between his lips. "We called his apartment numerous times. If he's there, he isn't answering the phone. We asked the NIH operator to page him on his beeper, but she shows him signed out until day after tomorrow—when he's due back from San Francisco. She beeped him anyway. He didn't answer. So Tony asked around. No one seems to think he's even back from San Francisco."

"Hold on," Phillips interjected glancing through her notes. "His ex said he has a research laboratory in the basement of the hospital. And since he claimed his Pakistani buddies are supposedly there to do research with him, that seems like a logical place to start looking for him."

Building 10, NIH Campus

Russell yawned, rubbed his burning eyes and considered the bug he just found while reviewing the speech-synthesizing neural network he was building. A stupid mistake, one he wouldn't have made if he wasn't shrouded in bone-aching fatigue. Yes, time was their enemy now, but so were mistakes. How long had it been since he slept, other than nodding off in the chair? He wasn't even sure what time of day it was. Hell, he hadn't even stepped out of the lab in hours or looked at the clock. The hours just rolled past without any windows to clue him into the time of day. He glanced at the cot Hussein had brought into the lab. They were all using it in shifts now, Ahmed lying on his side, snoring softly, completely relaxed, sleeping not five feet from a dead body. Russell wondered when Ed would begin to smell worse.

He said to Hussein, "I'm going up to one of the call rooms and catch a couple hours of sleep, then take a nice long shower. Got a problem with that?"

Hussein considered this a few beats. "I will go with you."

Russell was just about to tell him to go fuck himself when he heard a pounding from the door to the lab. A glance at the CCTV monitor, showed a heavyset man in the black federal cop uniform standing at the door.

Hussein told Raveena, "Police. You stay with him," with a nod toward Mohammed, before quickly closing the door between the labs. Then to Russell: "They have keys to this room?" He shook Ahmed awake.

Russell nodded.

"Well then, I suggest you open the door and talk to the man."

Russell shot a glance at the sound attenuation booth, where Ed Ogilvy's body still lay crumpled on the rubber floor mat. "Jesus Christ. But what about . . ."

Hussein nodded at the thick door. "Do as I say." He said something to Ahmed, who was wide awake now.

Russell opened the door only enough to talk to the cop. "May I help you?"

"Yes, sir. Are you Doctor Lawton?"

"Yes."

"Then I need to ask you a few questions about Doctor Ogilvy."

Russell's heartbeat accelerated again. "Doctor Ogilvy?"

"Yes, sir. He's gone missing. May I come in?"

CHAPTER

24

RUSSELL SAID, "GONE missing?"

The federal officer laid a heavy dose of cop eye on him. "Yes, sir. Gone missing," and let it hang.

Russell cleared his throat and wiped both hands on his thighs. "Know what? I have been out of town for a couple days. I just returned. I don't have a clue what Doctor Ogilvy's schedule is supposed to be."

The cop adjusted the thick black leather belt holding a pistol, a radio, and other paraphernalia. "Is that right?"

"Yes."

"That's funny. Ogilvy's secretary says he was heading down here last time she saw him, and so far she's the last one to see him."

"I don't know what to tell you, Officer. I haven't seen Ed since I left town and that was days ago."

The officer scratched the back of his neck while studying Russell a moment, "What happened to you?" and pointed toward his temple.

"Oh, that?" Russell gingerly touched the side of his head. "I got hit playing racquetball. It's sore as hell, too."

The cop eyed him suspiciously a moment longer. "Okay. Thanks for your time." He turned and headed back down the hall.

Russell shut the door and slumped against the painted metal surface, his heart racing. He sucked a deep breath and tried to calm his caffeine-frayed nerves. He shook his head and said to Ahmed, "Look, I can't take much more of this. I need a break. I'm going to find a call room and try to calm down and, if possible, catch a nap."

Ahmed studied him a moment. "Yes, perhaps it would be wise for you to rest a bit." Then, to Hussein: "Go with him."

Hussein nodded and slid the gun under his waistband and covered it with the scrub shirt.

"Oh, for christsake . . ." Russell turned and walked away.

Russell found a vacant on-call room and changed the attached door sign from VACANT to IN USE, then opened it. The room was not much larger than a walk-in closet. It contained one single bed with a wall-mounted reading light above the pillow and one straight-back wooden chair. "Make yourself at home. I'm going to the bathroom."

"I come with you."

Hussein followed him inside the one-urinal, one-stall toilet. Russell decided on the stall just to get away from the bastard. As he started to open the door Hussein stopped him to check inside first. Apparently satisfied, he stepped aside and allowed Russell to enter. Russell closed and locked the door and sat for a moment trying to calm his anger before undoing the ties to his scrub pants.

Russell slid between the sheets and reached up to pull the string to turn off the small reading light. Hussein sat in the chair, gun in his right hand, watching him. Russell shook his head in angry disgust, turned out the light and settled down on his right side. For a moment he stared through the darkness at the band of light slipping between the floor and the bottom edge of the door and listened to Hussein's soft nasal breathing.

Four hours later

Russell stood at the heavy, copper-shielded door to his lab, left hand clutching a fresh Mountain Dew, right hand gripping the steel door handle.

After a few beats, Hussein asked, "Is there a problem?"

Russell glanced at him, fear choking back a knee-jerk sarcastic reply.

Hussein pushed against the door. "It is not good we stand out here in the hall."

"Right." Russell pushed the door open. He felt slightly refreshed after the nap, a shower, a change into fresh scrubs and a break from this overheated room he now considered a facsimile of hell. Fatigue still clung to his brain like a sticky cobweb. But at least it had been a break. He entered the laboratory's warm, stale air. Hussein followed and closed the door.

The door to the adjoining lab stood half open. Gerda was napping on the cot now. Ahmed was scrolling through the Al Jazeera Web page. Raveena was presumably in the other room tending to Mohammed. Hussein said something to Ahmed, then turned and left the room.

Ahmed said, "You look better."

Russell pressed the cold can against his forehead and went directly to his workspace. He set the can next to his keyboard then gently touched Angela's picture. He allowed only a couple seconds of self-pity before refocusing on work.

He asked Ahmed, "When was the last time you checked him?"

Ahmed glanced at the watch on his left wrist. He wore the dial on the palmer side. "Fifteen minutes ago."

"And?"

"His lungs are slightly better, but his urine output continues to slow down."

Russell contemplated checking Mohammed himself, but figured Ahmed was a general surgeon and could probably evaluate his lungs competently. Probably better.

He settled into the task chair and turned his attention to the glowing monitor. The artificial intelligence system was probably as good as it was going to get until it had a chance to chew on some real data. Later, once they began training it to recognize the particular nuances of Mohammed's brain activity, he would start tweaking it, improving its accuracy.

At that moment, a thought hit him. It had occurred to him just before nodding off but he'd forgotten it during sleep. It was a crucial one and concerned the difference between the options that filter through a person's brain milliseconds before they choose which thought to verbalize. A rush of excitement flooded his chest. A real plan began to take form.

He sat back in the chair and considered it.

He asked Ahmed, "How well does Mohammed speak English?"

Ahmed cocked his head and scrutinized Russell. "Why do you ask?"

Russell took a pull on the Mountain Dew and let the cold liquid run over the back of his tongue. "Think about it, Ahmed. I'm supposed to make an interface between his brain and synthesized speech. Right?"

Ahmed nodded.

"Okay, then. To make it work with any reasonable degree of accuracy, I'm going to have to do a lot of fine-tuning. Right?"

Ahmed half shrugged. "I suppose so."

"Believe me, I do." He took another pull of Dew, hoping

168

Allen Wyler

the caffeine would wipe some of the cobwebs off his brain. "The point is, how am I going to be able to tweak the network if he doesn't speak a language I understand? It's a quality control issue. See? If I can't tell if the computer is interpreting his thoughts correctly or not, how can I optimize the program?"

Ahmed took a moment to formulate a reply. "You do not necessarily have to speak the language, so long as I do. I will tell you how correctly the computer interprets his thoughts."

"The thing you have to understand is that designing neural networks is as much art as science. The more accuracy you want from one, the more tweaking it's going to need. If he can't communicate in English, I can't evaluate nuances in his speech. That happens and I won't be able to guarantee the results. It's like the old saw, garbage in, garbage out. And I assume, since he's crucial to your plans, that you want the best interpretation possible. Am I right?"

Ahmed frowned. "Perhaps the degree of accuracy you wish to achieve is too high. Maybe we do not need that degree of finesse?"

"That doesn't make any sense. If that's the case . . . if you don't need accurate output from him, why is it so important to keep him alive and communicating?"

"His role is no longer crucial. But it is very important. And that, my friend, is all I will share with you."

"So, what role does he play in your plans?" Russell thought of the laptop Mohammed was trying to operate. "It has to do with a computer, right?"

"How many times need I tell you? That is none of your concern. Stop asking."

"Why? Because you're terrorists?"

Ahmed's eyes flashed anger. "You say terrorist, I say freedom fighter. I ask you this . . . what did the English think of this country's heroes, your Paul Revere, your George Washington? Your heroes fought to free your colony from oppression. That colony eventually became the United States. I am certain the British viewed your leaders in the same light as you view us; terrorists. I ask you, what difference is there between what we are doing now and what your ancestors did then? Answer me that."

Anger ignited in Russell's heart. "Way I understand it, we fought to free ourselves from economic oppression and in the process gain religious freedom. And we did it in an area that was remote from our origins. You're fighting to inflict a fundamentalist Islamic oppression on everyone in the world. I have nothing against your religion but I do have a problem with any extreme fundamentalist religion of any kind, Christian, Jewish, Muslim, or whatever."

Realizing the discussion was only riling up his frustrations, he muttered, "Damn!" and pushed out of the chair to walk into the other room.

Russell leaned over Mohammed. "Let me ask you a few questions."

Curled up in a chair, chin on chest, legs tucked under her, Raveena stirred and awoke.

Mohammed's right hand fumbled, weakly closing the laptop lid enough so that Russell could not view the screen.

"How well do you speak English?"

Eyes half open, voice weak, he answered, "Why do you want to know?"

Raveena pushed out of the chair, knuckled both eyes, and approached the bedside.

Russell realized he hadn't really talked to Mohammed in any depth other than to ask how he felt. He realized the man lacked any foreign accent.

"Because . . ." Russell paused, wondering how much Mohammed knew of the plan to decapitate him. Then again, in actuality—in the greater scheme of things—did it really matter? Probably not.

Russell cleared his throat. "Because, if I am to operate on you . . . to . . ." still unable to bring himself to say the words. "To implant a brain-computer interface . . ." There! That should help determine his English vocabulary. "You will need to communicate in English. Fluently."

"What?" Mohammed's voice came out slurred by the metabolic lethargy sapping his brain. "You think I'm some rag head who grew up in a desert rock pile hovel humping camels on Saturday nights?"

Speechless, Russell stared down at his patient.

From the doorway came, "Does that satisfy your curiosity, Doctor Lawton?"

The phone rang in the other room, giving him a perfect excuse to walk away from the situation. Russell pushed past Ahmed to answer it. Just as he was reaching to pick up, Ahmed leaned over and punched the button labeled SPEAKERPHONE.

The phone rang again.

Ahmed said, "Anything you need to say to anybody can be said with all of us listening."

"Don't worry. This is an unlisted line. Anybody who'd call me on this number thinks I'm still in San Francisco. It's probably a wrong number."

"Perhaps. Perhaps not." Ahmed tapped Angela's photograph, smirked. As if to say, "Remember what is at risk."

Determined not to show Ahmed how much he aggravated him, Russell pushed CONNECT and said, "Hello," fully expecting a wrong number.

A female voice screamed. "Goddamnit, you prick, what have you done with her?"

STUNNED, RUSSELL ANSWERED, "Marci?"

"You self-centered jerk. You couldn't be satisfied letting the court decide, could you! No, you had to go do it your way, didn't you! Just like you always do. Bastard."

Even over the phone he could tell she was screaming, her words rounded into the Chardonnay slur so characteristic of the way she dealt with the day-to-day stresses of life and their marital problems, which, from her point of view, focused on the fact he was stuck in the military instead of in a more lucrative form of practice.

"What the hell are you talking about?" Face hot with embarrassment, he glanced at his audience. *Goddamn her!* Ahmed was obviously listening, the corners of his lips turning up in a bemused expression. Gerda sat up on the cot now, stretching.

"What the hell you talking about? The hell you talking about?" she taunted. "You know exactly what I'm talking about. You kidnapped her, you son of a bitch."

"Who? Angela?"

"Oh, puullleeezzzz . . . don't try that brain-dead routine on me, Russell. I'm not some nurse bimbo you can boss around playing mister brainiac neurosurgeon, lord of the frigging manor."

Russell gave Ahmed an I-don't-know-what-the-hell's-going-on shrug as he mentally tried to grapple with the situation.

"And you know what else? They were right," Marci screamed.

A sinking sensation settled in the pit of his stomach. "What? Who was right?"

"You *are* here instead of San Francisco. And that doesn't make a frigging bit of sense if you're trying to act innocent. If you didn't kidnap her, Russell, what are you doing back in Bethesda in your lab when you're not supposed to be back for another two days?"

Panic twisted his intestines. "Whoa, whoa, whoa . . . back up a second. This who . . . who are we talking about?"

"Who do you think I'm talking about, you prick? The frigging FBI. That's who. Who else do you call when your daughter's been kidnapped and transported across state lines?"

Your daughter? There it was; their marriage distilled into one word. He would've said "our baby" or "our only child." Not, "your daughter."

"You talked to the FBI?" Panic squeezed his stomach harder this time, shooting foul-tasting bile up into the back of his throat. He choked, swallowed it back down and felt the acidic after-burn. "When did that happen?"

"Why? What the hell difference does it make?"

"Please, Marci. When did you talk with them?"

Ahmed was staring at the phone, the bemused expression from a moment ago replaced with thin-lipped anger.

"Please, Marci. Please, Marci. When you want something, it's 'Please, Marci.' Well fuck you, Russell."

"Please, it's important. When did you talk with them?"

He heard heavy breathing come over the line, as if she'd exerted herself.

"A couple of hours ago. What? You honestly believe you can pull off a chicken-shit stunt like this and just walk along your merry way? Ha! Think again, buster, because in no way am I letting you get away with this."

Ahmed was at the connecting door now, waving Raveena into the room. Gerda stood off to his right, staring at him in horror.

What to do? Admit Angela was kidnapped? Deny any knowledge of it? "Whoa . . . slow down . . . let's talk about this a moment."

The rasp of her sloppy, wine-laden breathing slid over the telephone line again, triggering the memory of the stale alcoholic stench of her snores as she lay next to him in bed those all-too-frequent nights she drank too much. "There's nothing to talk about. They're going to arrest you, you prick."

"What if I were to tell you Angela will be all right?"

"Jesusfriggingchrist, Russell! What's that supposed to mean! I mean, where the frigging hell do you get off. S'that mean you actually admit having her?"

Russell cut his retort short, suddenly aware the call might be recorded by the FBI. Could he be incriminating himself?

He drew a breath and rethought his reply. "No, it doesn't mean that. And I don't have her. All I'm asking is to let me handle this, okay?"

Soon as the words were out, he knew he'd made a mistake.

Marci emitted a sarcastic snort. "Just like you handled our marriage? Well, fuck you!"

CLICK.

Dial tone.

"Ahhhh, Russell?"

He'd been staring at the rack of electronics, too embarrassed to face the others in the room. He turned to see what

Gerda wanted. Ahmed and Hussein stood shoulder to shoulder five feet way, aiming guns directly at Russell and Gerda's hearts.

Ahmed jabbed a finger at their chairs. "Sit. Both of you."

CHAPTER
26

RUSSELL AND GERDA sank slowly into their respective chairs, Russell thinking, *Jesus Christ, this is it. It's over.*

Ahmed barked a sharp blast of staccato words at Raveena. Her eyes darted back and forth between Ahmed and Russell twice before sending Ahmed a defiant frown. She spun around, took two quick steps into Mohammed's room and slammed the door, isolating the four of them in the main lab. The air suddenly seemed thicker, making Russell acutely aware of the sweet, nauseating stench of Ogilvy's decaying body seeping through the sound attenuation chamber vents. The only sound he heard was the soft, white noise from the power supply cooling fans.

A drop of sweat slithered into Russell's right eye. He massaged the sting away, and blinked at the gun barrel pointing at his heart. Was it worth trying to rush Ahmed and wrestle the gun away? Did he have a chance?

Ahmed told Hussein, "Do not speak English. Stay with our own tongue. They must not understand what we are saying."

Hussein answered, "It does not matter anyway. The mission

is now doomed. We must kill them immediately and escape while we still have a chance. There is no other choice."

"I do not agree. There is still a chance. There is always a chance. Do not lose faith. God is good and God will watch over us. We will carry out our mission and then kill them."

"Why do you say we will succeed? Can you not see? Open your eyes and look around at what is happening. It is pointless to continue on. Look at Jamal. He hovers near death. How can he possibly complete our mission?"

"You underestimate God's will and Jamal's will, too. Like all of us, Jamal is a true believer even if he was born American. He will rally and we *will* complete our mission. Then we will kill these two infidels and his sniveling daughter. But for the time being we must let him salvage the information in Jamal's brain."

Hussein flashed him a look of disbelief but said nothing.

Ahmed told Russell, "This FBI business . . . it adds a very serious complication to what we are doing here."

"What the hell did you expect? You kidnapped my daughter, for christsake. Like that's not going to draw some attention? Damn!" He shook his head, uncertain whether to be thankful or angry with Marci for fingering him as the kidnapper. For the first time since this ordeal started, his captors no longer held total control over the situation. Then again, Marci's actions had just increased the risk to Angela.

"What you say is true, but I think it is not all that common for a parent to be the target of suspicion. You see, this now causes us the huge problem because as we both know, the FBI will eventually come here to ask questions. What will we do then?"

"You can't be sure of that."

Ahmed slowly shook his head. "Oh but I am. I am quite certain they will come here to pay you a visit. Did you not listen to what your wife just said? They know you are in

Bethesda, now. And this brings up an interesting point; how do they know this?" He eyed Russell suspiciously. "Did you somehow send them a message?"

"Are you out of your mind? Why would I do that?"

"I can think of several reasons. Maybe you believe they can help you find your Angela. Or maybe you feel a strong sense of patriotism and believe you can do something good by sacrificing yourself to stop an attack? There are even more reasons. Do you want me to continue listing them?"

Russell nervously watched Hussein grip his gun, studying his trigger finger to see if it tightened. "But you've been with me every minute since San Francisco. How could I have had the chance to tell anyone?"

Ahmed waved an admonishing finger at him. "This is not true. Not true at all. You have had multiple opportunities, starting with the telephone calls you made when we refueled the jet. And then there was the security officer."

"The security officer? You got to be kidding. Hussein killed him before he could do anything. Remember?"

Ahmed waved away the statement. "Regardless, we now are presented with a dilemma: Should we kill you and leave or should we attempt to salvage our mission? Hussein . . . well, I think you can guess what his vote is. Me? I believe we should press on. What do you think, Doctor Lawton?"

"But why on earth would I tell anyone and risk Angela's and Gerhard's lives?" Russell asked.

"That is not an answer to my question. People do irrational things when stressed. And you are obviously stressed. Now answer the question. What should we do?"

"Far as I'm concerned I want you to leave and give Angela back to me."

The door to the other room flew open. Raveena said, "Doctor Lawton, come quickly. Mohammed is no longer putting out urine."

Ahmed glanced at Hussein and then toward the other

room, then back at Russell. He muttered a few words to Hussein. Instead of an answer, Hussein shook his head and looked away in obvious disagreement.

Ahmed said to Russell, "Go. Have a look at him. See what you think." Then, to Hussein, "I know what you are thinking but I am in charge here. We will wait and see what happens." Back to Russell, "Remember, if anything goes wrong I will kill you and Doctor Fetz. Do we have an understanding?"

A wave of relief swept through Russell, "Understood. Thank you." He pushed out of the chair toward the other room.

Ahmed held up his hand to stop him. "Wait."

Russell halted.

Ahmed said, "From this point on, since sooner or later we can expect the FBI to come here, we must keep the door to Mohammed's room closed at all times. Above all, whatever happens, they must not find him. If they do discover him, everyone will die. Are we absolutely clear on this?"

Raveena stood next to the bed, pointing down at the Foley catheter. "I have been measuring his urine output every hour, just as you instructed. He has put out no urine for the past two hours."

Russell nodded a hello to Mohammed who looked back at him intensely. Russell picked up the clipboard that held the vital sign sheets he'd swiped from the ICU. As instructed, Raveena had kept a meticulous record of blood pressure, pulse, temperature, urine output, and specific gravity. Mohammed's urine output had been tapering off over the past six hours, dropping to zero for the past two hours. There could be a couple reasons for this, but renal shutdown secondary to myoglobin toxicity headed the list. Especially considering the potential kidney toxicity of the IV antibiotic Mohammed was receiving to combat the *pseudomonas* infection.

Or, the low output simply could be due to a low blood volume. Without sufficient fluids on board, the kidneys stop dumping water. He checked the total amount of IV solutions given during the past twenty-four hours. It added up to two liters; one liter of half normal saline and one liter of lactated Ringers. Mohammad's oral intake had added another liter, making a grand total of three liters in. During the same time, Mohammed's kidneys had dumped one liter of urine. Three liters in. One liter out. Not particularly rocket science. More like plumbing 101.

Okay, so other causes could account for additional fluid loss? Sweating was a process that continuously lost water and could be accelerated with fever. Mohammed was running a low-grade temp of 99.1 degrees, but that wasn't high enough to accelerate losses. Also, we constantly lose fluid from the moisture in our breath. That would be minimal. He also had an unknown amount of fluid trapped as edema around his badly fractured legs and pelvis. Add this to the extra fluid the Mannitol squeezed out of his system earlier and the bottom line was he could very well have a low blood volume—a possibility supported by the fact that over the past three hours his urine concentration had been nudging higher.

He shook Mohammed's shoulder. "How are you feeling?"

Mohammed's eyes refocused on Russell. He licked dry lips and croaked, "How do you think I feel in this situation?" The laptop computer rested on his chest.

"Thirsty?"

He forced a slight nod. "A little."

The problem was not having rapid access to the kind of lab data available in an actual ICU. There was only so much monkey lab work he could request without raising suspicion. To treat Mohammed correctly, he needed to know, among other things, the concentration of sodium and potassium in his blood. As it was, he was flying blind.

Lab test or not, he had to do something.

"What do you think?" Ahmed asked.

"It's pretty basic medicine. He's either in renal shutdown

or he's volume depleted. Could be a combination of both."
Russell shrugged. "Take your pick."

"I agree. How do you plan to treat him? Dialysis?"

"Not with that raging infection going on," with a nod toward Mohammed's legs. "I figure the safest thing would be to
give him a fluid challenge, see if he starts putting out urine."

"I agree with your logic, but the risk, of course is, if it *is*
renal failure a fluid challenge could worsen his congestive
failure and kill him."

Russell cringed and glanced at Mohammed out of the
corner of his eye to see if he had heard. He appeared to have
nodded off.

Russell lowered his voice. "Yes, it's a definite risk, but the
way I see it, we have to do something. Or perhaps you'd prefer to manage his care. If so, be my guest."

Ahmed raised both hands. "No, no. Do as you wish."

"Okay, then . . ."

He shook Mohammed awake. "I want you to try drinking a
liter of fluid over the next half hour. Think you can do that?"

Mohammed licked his lips. "I'll give it a try."

To Raveena: "Get me an IV bag of normal saline, please."
Then, to Mohammed, "I need to check your catheter, make
sure it isn't obstructed." It would be a disaster to mistake renal shutdown for nothing more than a blocked Foley.

With a 50cc syringe and a sterile basin, Russell irrigated
Mohammed's bladder through the Foley catheter. Nothing
more than the irrigating solution returned, indicating the
drainage tube wasn't blocked. So much for an easy diagnosis.
He was back to either renal shutdown or volume depletion.
Well, they would have part of the answer within the hour.

Before returning to the other room, he reminded Ahmed:
"If it is renal shutdown we'll be forced to . . . take it to the
next stage."

"Indeed. I suggest we begin making preparations, immediately."

CHAPTER

27

RUSSELL STEPPED WEARILY back into the laboratory and folded himself into his task chair. With a sigh, he leaned back and stared at the acoustical tile ceiling. He slowly palm-wiped his face and asked himself why he was so worried about the ethics of decapitating Mohammed? The man was circling the drain faster than he could possibly keep up with. Sooner or later he was going to die regardless of what anyone did to or for him. It wasn't his fault a car had nailed Mohammed against a brick wall.

Gerda was lying on the cot, also staring up at the acoustical tile ceiling.

He turned to see Ahmed quietly studying him,

"What? What the hell you looking at?" he asked, not giving a damn whether or not he pissed Ahmed off.

"I am thinking that you are a very skillful physician. Take it as a compliment."

Gerda turned to look at him also.

Physician, not surgeon. Did Ahmed realize the difference or was his choice of words meant as a weird compliment. "You mean, for a neurosurgeon?"

"See? You look for disrespect. I meant it as a sincere compliment. You are good."

When Russell said nothing, Ahmed continued, "You are betting on fluid depletion as the cause of the renal problem. That is probably the smartest diagnosis."

Russell resented being forced into a collegial conversation but answered, "Maybe, but, my gut tells me he's probably heading straight into renal shutdown regardless of his blood volume. Like most docs, I play the odds. Common things are common. That's why they're called common. I needn't tell you he's set up for a renal disaster. He's got four-plus myoglobin floating around his bloodstream. If that weren't enough, we're shooting him full of megadoses of a renal-toxic antibiotic. I mean, what could be a worse setup than this? So, the way I see it, if this present situation isn't signaling the end of his tubules and glomeruli, then it's just around the corner. It's only a matter of time. Which brings up our next major problem."

"Yes?"

"Sooner or later we're going to have to find ourselves a dialysis machine. I suspect it has to be sooner."

"Indeed. I was thinking precisely the same thing."

"Well, it was coming . . . sooner or later . . . if we were really forced into detaching his head." He surprised himself at being able to verbalize it so easily. "This just speeds up that part of the game plan,"

He glanced at the computer screen. Before the distraction he'd been reading copies of White's original articles, the ones describing his attempts to transplant the heads of dogs and monkeys. He had downloaded them from the *Journal of Neurosurgery* archives.

Russell sighed wearily at what a totally fucked-up situation he was mired in. He glanced at the time in the lower right-hand corner of the screen. 12:05 AM. "Jesus, is it morning, again?"

Gerda answered, "Yes."

He looked around vacantly. "Which day?" but wasn't really asking anyone.

He turned to Gerda. "This dialysis thing, it forces our hand."

"What do you mean?"

"It means sooner or later we're going to have to decapitate him. And it's looking like sooner than later. This, in turn, means we're going to have to implant the interface straightaway and start training the network."

"So soon? Do you really think we're ready for that?" Gerda asked.

"We don't have much choice. Point is we have to do it before he goes on dialysis. Which means tomorrow." He thought about what he'd just said and corrected it, "Excuse me. Since it's officially past midnight that really means later today."

"Ach, I am ready."

Russell sat forward, slapped both thighs and wearily stood. "I'll be back."

Ahmed took a step toward the door, blocking it. "Where are you going?"

"To steal a dialysis machine. Now, if you don't mind," he reached for the door handle.

"No. I cannot let you go alone. I will go with you."

"Think about it, Ahmed," he said, exasperated. "I'll be sneaking into a restricted area. If I get caught I can spin some story that might get me nothing more than a slap on the hand. But if you're with me it will really raise suspicions. Yes, you're worried about me, but I'm equally worried about you blowing our little charade down here. Get what I'm saying?"

Before Ahmed came back with an answer, Russell added, "Believe me, I'm not going to do anything to risk Angela's life."

"Just make certain you keep that in mind."

* * *

Russell moved silently down the long dark empty hall, thankful he'd thought of changing into the old pair of Nike Airs he kept in his locker for surgery. Street shoes would make too much noise. The last thing he needed right now was to draw the attention of another federal cop. Sure, he was a staff surgeon and that was enough to explain his presence in Building 10, but no way could he explain sneaking around the outpatient clinics when the area was supposed to be completely buttoned up and off limits this time of night.

His right hand squeezed a ring of keys tightly together to keep them from jangling. He'd borrowed them from the in-house surgeon on the flimsy excuse of having left a book in the neurosurgery outpatient clinic. Ten minutes was all he needed, he claimed. The surgeon had offered to accompany him, since the keys supposedly were not to physically leave the surgeon's possession until turned over to the next poor soul pulling duty, but she'd been totally occupied tending to an open-heart patient who'd been coded and was easily talked out of them. A pang of guilt flicked his heart. What if he got caught? What kind of grief would that cause her? No, he decided, he had to keep focused. He couldn't afford to worry about that right now.

"Hey you! What are you doing up here?"

Russell jumped, the voice catching him totally by surprise. He froze. The shadow on the floor streaking out in front of him indicated that a high-powered flashlight was shining on him from behind.

Without exposing his face, Russell turned slightly, said, "Oh, man! You scared the bejesus out of me. Who's there?"

"Security. The bigger question is who are you and what are you doing here? This area is closed and off limits."

"Yes, I know." Russell could hear the soft clanking of metal against metal as the cop started toward him. Since the only way into this area required keys, how the hell was he going to explain the set in his hands without implicating the surgeon? Worse yet, it would just put him squarely in security's radar again.

Russell took off running down the long dark hall toward the green EXIT sign high on the wall at the far end. Although he seldom set foot on this particular floor, the floors in this tower all had the same general plan: one central hall with various small clinics to either side.

"Stop! Or I'll shoot."

The *slap slap slap* of running feet followed as he sped toward the metal fire door below the glowing EXIT sign. He turned and lunged, hitting the horizontal push bar with his hip, throwing open the heavy door. He started racing up the stairs two at a time, figuring the cop's first inclination would be to head down. Luckily, he'd kept the master key separated from the others on the ring with his index finger. He hit the landing where the stairs switched back, heard the door bang open below, and shot up, two stairs at a time, his lungs already burning from oxygen debt.

Sure enough, it sounded like the cop headed down. This gave him enough time to twist on the small AAA powered Mag-Lite, illuminate the fire door lock, insert the key, open the door, and slip through into the hall.

He ran to another stairway, flew through the door and dropped back down to the original floor. He dropped into a crouch at the fire door and waited, listening for footsteps but heard nothing but his own labored breathing.

He waited three minutes before opening the door and slipping into the deserted darkened hall, and headed toward his original destination.

He clicked on the small Mag-Lite in his left hand and played it across the wall signage, verifying that he was now standing in front of the glass door to the outpatient dialysis clinic.

Crouching, he tried ten different keys before finding the

one that opened the deadbolt. He unlocked it, stepped inside, closed the door, and swept the tiny beam around the rectangular room. Along the far wall was a string of recliner chairs alternating with dialysis machines. *Perfect.* He moved to the machine on the far end, figuring a missing end unit would not be as readily noticeable as one in the middle of the row if a guard glanced in. He studied it a moment, a Baxter 1550— for whatever that was worth. He was leaning over, searching for the 110-volt cord to unplug when the door handle rattled.

He dropped into a crouch just as a flashlight beam swept the room.

Silently, he crab-walked sideways, using the five-foot-high dialysis machine as a shield. He slowly edged it away from the wall, hoping the wheels on the base wouldn't squeak.

"Anyone in here?" called a gravely male voice.

A smoker. Sounds African American, Russell thought.

Keys jangled. Hard leather soles slapped linoleum. He heard the forced breathing of a person who was either obese or flirting with chronic obstructive pulmonary disease. The flashlight beam swung past again, moved on, stopped, came back around to the machine he was hiding behind. The beam slowly moved up and down the unit.

Damn! It was now obviously out of line with the other units. If the guard came over to push it back, he'd be screwed.

Footsteps started in his direction but then Russell heard a ring, like a Nextel walkie talkie. The cop said, "Yeah? . . . Roger that. I'll be right down."

The light moved on, followed by more footsteps, then, the metallic click that could only be a lock snapping into place.

Knees aching, Russell remained squatting behind the dialysis unit.

Had the guard really left or was this just a ploy to trick him into moving?

He listened for labored breathing, the jangle of keys, and heard nothing.

He counted off two minutes in seconds before edging around the machine, turning on the Mag-Lite and sweeping the room.

Carefully, he moved to the door and glanced out into the dimly lit hall.

Was it clear?

Or was it a trap?

CHAPTER
28

AN HOUR LATER, Russell propped open the door to the room housing Mohammed's slowly disintegrating body and pushed in the Baxter 1550. After plugging in the unit, he crossed over to the other section of the lab. Ahmed was sitting in front of the computer but had obviously nodded off. Gerda was gone, probably up to one of the call rooms to catch some sleep, Hussein standing guard and making sure she didn't tip off the authorities. The cot was empty. This time of early morning, he was unlikely to find an on-call room available, so he curled up on the cot without a word to Ahmed and closed his eyes.

Russell was awakened by a muted *thump thump thump* reverberating off the thick door, as if someone were pounding it with their palm—which, was the only way one could really knock on it. He looked at Ahmed, who raised his eyebrows questioningly and tensed.

"Think maybe it's Hussein?" Russell asked hopefully.

Ahmed jumped up from his chair, patted the gun hidden under his scrub shirt, checking to be certain it was still there and shook his head. "That is highly doubtful. Hussein would not knock. He would simply enter. I think we may be receiving a visit from agents of your FBI," and nodded at the CCTV security monitor in the rack. On the screen he could see an African-American female and a taller Caucasian male standing in front of the door eyeing the video camera.

Heart racing, Russell glanced at the sound attenuation chamber. "Jesus Christ! Ed's body is still there. We can't let them in. They'll see it."

"Keep your voice down!" Ahmed whispered harshly.

The banging came again.

"Fuck!"

"Open the door. You must deal with this sooner or later."

"But, the body!" His pulse was racing, his mouth dry. "After that deal with the campus cop . . . goddamn it, you assholes should've done something with him. Somehow . . ."

Russell glanced around frantically, thinking, *Gerda, where is she?* Then he remembered she had probably gone to catch a quick nap in one of the call rooms.

Ahmed held up an index finger, "Give me one moment to lock this door," as he moved to the door between labs, "and then answer it. But, my friend, keep in your mind the cost of making a mistake. Remember, I will be standing right here and I am armed and I am not afraid to do what I have to."

The phone rang. *Shit! What now?*

Rather than open the door, he picked up the phone. "Hello."

"Doctor Lawton?"

He didn't recognize the voice. "Yes?"

"Special Agent Sandra Phillips. FBI. I'm standing outside your door. Will you please open it for us?"

"Oh, yeah, sorry. Right away."

He punched off, said to Ahmed. "It's the FBI. We're totally screwed."

At the door now Russell straightened his posture, drew a deep breath, then tugged the heavy door open. A slender, attractive African-American female and a taller, heavier framed Caucasian male stood in the hall facing him.

The woman asked, "Doctor Russell Lawton?"

He judged her to be five-foot-eight and the guy to be the same as his own six feet. She wore a tailored light brown pant suit, no jewelry, and a serious expression. The guy wore khakis, a light blue short sleeve polo shirt, and an equally serious expression.

"Yes." His heart rate accelerated further. His mouth turned dryer. He stood with one hand on the door, the other on the jamb.

She opened a wallet, displaying official-looking credentials. "Special Agent, Sandra Phillips," and with a nod at the man to her right, "and this is Special Agent Tony Delorenti. We're with the District FBI office. May we come in and talk to you?"

"You want to come in?"

"Yes. You mind?"

"Ah . . . no." He stepped away from blocking the doorway.

Agent Phillips entered first, swiveling her head side to side, taking in the lab, a look of awe on her face, which was typical for first-time visitors. "This is your lab, huh?"

Russell wiped his palms on his scrubs. "Yes."

"What kind of work you do here?" She eyed Ahmed but said nothing.

"Ah—" fear that he might give a wrong answer—something that would raise their suspicions—blanked his mind.

The FBI agent stood watching, waiting for an answer.

He swallowed and said, "Brain computer interfaces," and let it go at that, figuring it was her problem if she didn't understand.

Butt propped against a below-counter drawer, Phillips cupped both elbows in her hands and eyed him, the pose reminding Russell of a grade-school teacher he once had. Sort of the same look, too, like she was sizing things up. Delorenti remained just inside the door, leaning casually against the wall, intense eyes staring at Ahmed, apparently satisfied with letting Phillips lead the interview.

Phillips asked, "Have any idea why we're here?"

Russell swallowed but there was no saliva in his mouth. What to say? Stick as closely to the truth as possible, an internal voice warned.

"Because of my daughter?"

"What about your daughter?"

Russell knew the interviewing technique all too well. It was exactly the same as he'd been taught during a medical school psychiatry rotation: Use open-ended questions, sit back, see where they take you. Knowing this buoyed his confidence. Slightly. He realized he was standing next to the booth and moved a few steps away from it.

"Well, you see, my ex-wife called a few hours ago all hysterical, as she's prone to do . . . and claimed our daughter has been kidnapped. She said she'd notified you guys, and here you are." He shrugged, as if that explained everything. "I assume it's about that."

Phillips asked, "And that news didn't upset you?"

He realized his error. Any parent would be upset if their child disappeared. Mentally, he scrambled for an appeasing answer.

He licked his lips. "No, not really."

Phillips seemed surprised. "And why's that?"

Russell shrugged again, "Guess you'd have to know my ex to understand. She has a nasty tendency to exaggerate at times. Not only that, but she can be overly melodramatic when doing it. In fact, that's the way she is most of the time. You know . . . the drama queen? Exaggerates things?"

He licked his lips and realized he was breaking the rule of how to deal with these kinds of questions. Supplying too much additional information always got you into trouble.

"Especially when she's been drinking."

"And had she been drinking?"

He shifted weight to the other foot and swallowed again. "Sure sounded like it to me. I lived with the woman too many years to not pick up on it when it's there. And it was definitely there."

Phillips's eyes wandered the room for several seconds before returning to Russell.

"So what are you trying to tell me, Doctor Lawton? You don't believe your daughter's been kidnapped?"

He knitted both hands together and cracked his knuckles. "Look, if I seriously believed Marci, I'd be very worried, but, like I just said, you'd have to know her to understand."

"That right? Huh!" Phillips paused a beat, eyeing him even more closely. "Then how do you explain the fact she's gone missing?"

Russell sucked a deep breath. "Do you know for a fact she's missing? I mean, how certain are you that my ex hasn't sent her off someplace?"

"Like?"

"Like to her parents. She could very easily have her stay with them a week or two. Angela's grandparents love to have her around."

Phillips's eyes zeroed in on his pupils. "Let me ask you flat out, Doctor. Did you have your daughter removed from her mother's backyard?"

Confidence growing, he drilled the look straight back at her. "No, I didn't."

"And for the record, you state that you have no idea where your daughter might be at this time?"

"I wish I knew." Then: "Like I just said, I assume she's with her mother or that her mother has her safely hidden some place."

Phillips cocked her head. "Don't *you* usually have custody of your daughter?"

"Angela."

"What?"

"Her name's Angela."

"Right. So, back to my question." Her brow furrowed as she eyed him. "Don't you usually have custody of Angela?"

Russell fought the urge to look to Ahmed for an assessment of how things were going. "Usually. But she's staying with Marci for a few days."

"I see." Phillips considered this a moment. "Help me out here. See if I can summarize this correctly. Your daughter's staying with your ex-wife but your ex-wife claims your daughter's been kidnapped. And you claim you don't believe her. Is this how it plays?"

The dryness in Russell's mouth intensified. His fingers began to tingle. "That's correct."

"I see." Phillips looked down at her shoes a moment. "Then where is she?"

"Excuse me?"

Phillips eyed him. "Your daughter . . . Angela. Where is she?"

"Like I just said, I'd bet you anything she's with Marci, my ex."

Phillips suddenly turned to Ahmed, "And you are?"

Ahmed straightened slightly and extended his hand. "I am Doctor Ahmed Khan, from Karachi. I am collaborating on a research project with Doctor Lawton." A heavy trace of English prep school accent threaded through his voice.

Ignoring Ahmed's proffered hand, Phillips returned her attention to Russell. "Mind coming down to Ninth Avenue for a more formal interview?"

Russell's peripheral vision caught Ahmed's head move and felt both eyes boring in on him. "As a matter of fact, yes, I would mind."

"Oh? Then, for the record, mind explaining to us why you refuse to cooperate with an investigation into your daughter's disappearance?"

Russell wrung his hands together. "I'm not refusing to cooperate. This just isn't a good time."

"Let me get this straight. I just told you your daughter's been kidnapped and you're telling me it's not a good time? What kind of parent are you?"

"I resent your implication, Agent Phillips. Exactly what are you saying? That you believe I kidnapped my own daughter? And now that I think about it . . . how would that work? Legally, I mean. Way I see it, Angela's my daughter. For the moment, the court has granted me legal custody of her. Given these facts, and assuming you are right—that I've hidden her someplace—how could that be considered kidnapping?"

Phillips just kept eyeing him with that intimidating expression.

Finally, she asked, "What's in there?" and jutted her chin toward the door to the other lab.

Russell's heart accelerated. "Another lab's in there. It's not mine. That door's been locked for years."

"Uh huh." She stopped looking at Russell and glanced around again. "Man! What's that smell?"

Russell cleared his throat. "What smell?"

"Don't tell me you don't smell it. Man, that is ugly."

"We ah, this room . . . we work with monkeys in here . . . they sometimes aren't the cleanest animals, you know? And this room has poor ventilation."

Phillips was back eyeing him again.

Finally, Russell said, "Look, unless you have something else to say, I'm very busy here."

She continued to stand there, eyeing him, jaw muscles tight, lips pressed thin.

She finally said, "It's a common assumption neurosurgeons are smart. Are you smart, Lawton?"

Before he could answer, she said, "I don't think you are. Believe me. We'll be back." Then, to her partner, "C'mon, Tony."

She spun around and marched off.

CHAPTER
29

RUSSELL ASKED MOHAMMED, "Do you understand what I am about to do to you? The surgery, I mean."

Mohammed answered, "I think so. You're going to implant something in my brain."

"Right. We're going to implant this electrode," holding it up, dangling it by the cable so that he could see the actual part that would contact his brain. Mohammed reached up. Russell moved it away. "No. You can't touch it. The electrodes are very delicate. You might damage it if you don't know exactly how to handle it." He carefully set it down.

"Sorry."

"We're going to make an incision here," Russell said, using Gerda's head to demonstrate as his straightened index finger drew a line that started behind her left eye and arched backward and then down to stop in front of the left ear, forming a question mark. "Do you have any questions about it we haven't already discussed?"

Mohammed glanced away, then used the heel of his palm to brush away a tear. "How long will it take?"

Russell hesitated. Did he mean how long did he have to
live?

Mohammed swallowed and seemed to gather his compo-
sure. "The operation, I mean. How long will it take?"

Russell had to think about that. He was so used to operating on patients under general anesthesia, that he couldn't
really estimate the time it would take to do Mohammed's
craniotomy under only local anesthesia. Once they opened
the skull, it'd go relatively quickly since the brain has no
pain fibers. Then again, he would not have to spend the time
it took to put a patient under general anesthesia. And when
people asked "how long," they usually meant the time between entering and exiting the operating room and not the
actual skin-to-skin time frame. "My best guess would be
about four hours."

"That long, huh?"

He realized Mohammed had a slight East Coast accent
and wanted to ask him how he'd picked it up? School?

"I don't think you want me to rush this, right?"

Mohammed gave a brave laugh. "Right."

For the first time in his career, Russell was going to start
a case without a signed consent and it made him uneasy.
*Then again, what is al Queda going to do if he gets a major
complication? Sue me?*

He glanced at Gerda, Ahmed, and Raveena, said, "Okay,
let's get started."

Angela was awakened by the sound of scraping above her
head. She yelled, "Daddy?" believing her father had finally
come to rescue her. A moment later the ceiling of her prison
opened up, blinding her with light. Reflexively, she scrunched
her eyelids tightly closed. "Daddy? Is that you?" and reached
out both hands, expecting his gentle touch.

An unfamiliar voice said, "You may get up now." Fingers

roughly gripped her right hand and pulled up. She jerked her hand away. "Leave me alone."

"Come now. Up. You must eat and drink something. And you may need to go to the bathroom." The fingers regained their grip and pulled upright.

For a moment she sat there, eyes closed, head spinning. "I want to go home. I don't like it here."

"You cannot go home. Not yet."

"But wheeeeeen?" She started to cry.

"Stop that!" Hands gripped both shoulders and shook her, making her cry harder. The hands slid under her armpits and lifted her up, letting her legs dangle. Then she was being lowered, her feet hitting the floor. She stood there for a moment cracking her eyelids, trying to see. She sniffed and swiped at her nose with the back of her index finger but couldn't stop whimpering.

A thin man in a black suit stood before her in a room with a metal table and counters with sinks. Behind her was a large wooden box that sat on sawhorses, its top open. This is where she must have been.

"Here. Maybe this will quiet you down." He held up Cloe, her Bratz doll in her Rock Angels outfit.

"Cloe!" She grabbed the doll and hugged her. She remembered now. Cloe was with her in the backyard. . . .

"You need to go to the bathroom?"

"Yes."

"In there." He pointed to a door.

It was a plain, small room with a sink and toilet. No windows.

When she came out of the bathroom the man offered her a sandwich and glass of water. She didn't want to accept anything from him but was thirsty so she drank the water. When she finished, he said, "Now you must go back in the box."

"No! I don't want to."

"You have no choice." He picked her up and sat her back in the box, then pushed her down. She screamed as the lid was closed, encasing her once again in blackness. But this time she had Cloe with her so it wasn't as bad as before. She held Cloe against her heart and murmured, "Don't cry, Cloe. Please, don't. We have to be strong. That's what daddy would want. I'll protect you."

Parking Lot P-3, NIH Campus

Delorenti drove while Phillips sat in the passenger seat, a Bluetooth earpiece in her right ear canal, a Motorola cell phone in her right hand. She thumbed SEND. While listening to the connection being made she turned to Tony, "The good doctor was nervous as hell. Sure as hell, he's hiding something, isn't he," saying it as more statement than question. She started drumming her ballpoint pen against the clipboard on her lap and watched Delorenti back the baby-shit-brown Crown Vic out the parking space in the P-3 short-term lot, just to the west of Building 30's front door. The car interior smelled of old coffee and orange peel and someone had used the ashtray. That sucked.

Looking over his shoulder, Delorenti answered, "Yeah, that's for sure. That's for damned sure."

"And what's your make on Doctor Ahmed Khan from Karachi?" She exaggerated rolling the *r* in Karachi.

The phone connected. "McGowan."

Her hand shot up, cutting off Delorenti's answer.

"Sir, it's Phillips. We just finished up our interview with Lawton. He was in his lab, alright. Just like his wife said he'd be. We're heading back to the barn now. Should be back in, oh . . . forty minutes give or take."

"He's with you?"

"No, sir, he declined to be interviewed. Said he was too busy."

"Interesting." A few beats passed. "Your impression?"

Delorenti turned the Crown Vic onto the long, curving road that would take them over a couple of low rolling hills on the way back to South Drive and the main NIH entrance.

"He's definitely hiding something, sir," falling back into her old habit of calling McGowan "sir."

"You referring to the kidnapping or the terrorist angle?"

"Could be either one. The man's nervous as hell." She explained Lawton's lame suggestion that his ex-wife had sent their daughter somewhere.

"Agreed. Sound's like a weak excuse to me, too. What about his visitors. Get a good look at any of them?"

"Affirmative on that. I got a full face visual on the one going by the name Ahmed Khan. He's a male, late thirties, early forties. Didn't see any of the others. Khan's face didn't ring a bell, but my gut says he's a definite suspect. I suggest you bring out what's available from intelligence so Tony and I can examine them again. But even if we can't make a positive or even tentative ID, I'd categorize him as warranting a more in-depth evaluation—"

Delorenti had waved his hand at her.

"Ah, hold on a sec." She turned to Delorenti. "What?"

"Elevate that. I'm fairly confident I've seen his face before and it wasn't in *People* magazine."

She nodded. "Good." Then, into the phone, "Strike that last comment, sir. Tony believes the suspect is a definite possible."

"How possible?"

She repeated the question to Delorenti.

"I'm fairly certain of it, but we better wait until I can look at some pictures."

She relayed Tony's answer.

McGowan asked, "And Lawton?"

"Well, that's the thing . . . I don't exactly know what's going on there. But he's one hell of a nervous surgeon." She waited to see if McGowan would acknowledge the lame joke. He didn't.

She continued, "He strikes me as a person who's trying to cover up something."

The car slowed. Up ahead was the security station, beyond that the red stop light at the intersection that would allow them to turn right onto Rockville Pike and head back toward the District.

"I'm getting confused here. What do you mean when you say cover up something? You referring to the kidnapping or terrorist angle."

"It means he's hard to read. Like I just said, could be either or both. We can't tell with the limited information we presently have. But one thing for sure, we need to bring him in for more conversation than we just had. He got a little too surly. If we can get him on our turf and away from his friends, I believe we can have a real Come To Jesus Meeting with him."

The stoplight changed to green and Delorenti accelerated, turning onto the main street.

McGowan asked, "How do you want to proceed?"

He knows exactly how he wants us to proceed, she thought. *He's testing my judgment again.* She wondered if McGowan had her annual performance evaluation form in front of him, ready to grade her answer.

"There are a couple thoughts I've been kicking around. The thing that bothers me the most is how this whole story doesn't much hang together. We got him leaving the daughter with his ex while he attends a meeting in San Francisco. He leaves that same meeting early on the same day his daughter disappears from her backyard. Coincidence? Maybe, but you know how we both feel about coincidences like that. Point is, that stays a hot issue that needs to be followed up until proven otherwise. Then we got his Pakistani buddies showing up. Hey, explain to me why they suddenly appear here in Bethesda at a time when he's supposed to be in San Francisco? That doesn't make a hell of a lot of sense and we didn't even bother delving into that one. And that story about them being graduate students? That doesn't wash, either. Unless I'm wrong, I would think that kind of arrangement takes planning. And I'm talking about the kind of planning that doesn't have them arriving at the same time you're scheduled to be out of town at a convention. Again, doesn't make a whole hell of a lot of sense. Does it to you?"

"Nope."

She watched Delorenti turn into traffic, driving with both hands now but listening with one ear.

"To top it off, when I asked him about his daughter, he totally blew it off. I gotta tell you, the whole thing stinks."

"Okay then, how you want to handle this?"

"Like I said earlier, I want to split him off from his Karachi pal, put a little pressure on him and see if he changes his attitude and story. When I asked him to come in for an interview, he flat out told me to take a hike. Looks to me, the only way we're going to get a real chance to have that conversation is to arrest him."

"On what charge?"

"Probable cause, kidnapping his daughter. Can you think of anything better?"

"Why not go after the terrorist angle?"

The question convinced her McGowan was testing her judgment, getting a feel for her capabilities after having been transferred to his command from New York four months ago.

"Well, sir, let's make the wild-ass guess they *are* terrorists and we bring them in. Then what? We don't have enough to hold them, other than we've got a heightened security situation underway. Unless, of course, something shakes out on the passport angle. Wrong or right, some ultraliberal reporter gets wind of it and teams up with some ACLU supporter and we're off to the races.

"On the other hand, in Lawton's case, we have every reason to bring him in and question him on the kidnapping angle. That shouldn't raise too many suspicions with the Pakistanis. After all, his daughter is missing.

"Oh, yeah . . . I almost forgot. Say we *are* dealing with an al Qaeda cell . . . we bring one or more of his Pakistani buddies in, we tip our hand and *poof*—the rest of them vanish. If they are even marginally involved with an al Qaeda cell, I want the whole bunch of them, not just one or two of those assholes."

"I concur. Where you now?"

She caught a glimpse at the passing street sign.

"We're still in Bethesda. We should be back in, say, thirty minutes, depending on traffic," which, looking out the front window ahead of them, was thick.

"Alright. I'll get hold of Wilenski—"

"The prosecutor?" she asked, remembering the short, thin pit bull federal prosecutor from a prior case.

"Right. I'll explain the situation, see if she can finesse a grand jury indictment against Lawton within the next couple hours. I have to be honest with you, she'll probably be able to get you an arrest on exigent circumstances, but we all know it isn't likely to withstand a magistrate's opinion. Unless, of course, something shakes out between now and then. Bottom line is you won't be able to hold him more than seventy-two hours."

"Understood. My gut says I don't need to hold him more than seventy-two hours. If he's got something to say, we'll get it out of him within twenty-four. Thirty-six, tops."

"In the meantime, I'll touch bases with the spooks, see if there are any updated photos to run by you and Tony when you get back."

CHAPTER

31

Building 10, NIH Campus

"You sure you're ready for this?"

Mohammed looked straight into Russell's eyes. "Yes."

What he really wanted to ask was, "Do you really realize what this means? That this will be the first step in detaching your head?" However, another voice in Russell's mind reminded him that Mohammed had probably been a dead man as soon as the SUV crushed his pelvis and upper legs against the brick wall. Probably. Who knew? Maybe he would have survived had he been allowed to remain at Georgetown Medical Center? Regardless, the route they were now about to embark upon guaranteed his death.

"Got the donut?" Russell asked Ahmed. Earlier, he'd sent Hussein out to Walgreen's to buy a donut-shaped cushion, the type hemorrhoid sufferers rely on for comfort. He rotated Mohammed's head until he was looking over his right shoulder then shimmied up his left shoulder with a rolled-up blanket so his neck wouldn't be strained and uncomfortable during the long surgery. This done, he positioned the donut under his head to keep any pressure off his right ear because the cartilage can become painful after even a few minutes of compression.

"Comfortable?"

"Yes."

Earlier, they had detached the headboard and raised the bed to an easier height for Russell to operate from. One that would minimize leaning into awkward positions that would strain his back. But still, the major problem with working on patients in a hospital bed instead of a much narrower operating table is that beds forced you to operate from some gawdawful angles. If his back didn't ache by the time this case was over, his neck sure as hell would.

"I'm going to give you several injections now."

He lifted a syringe filled with Marcaine, a local anesthetic having a much longer effect than Novocain. Then, to Ahmed: "I'm going to infiltrate the major nerves to the scalp. The reason I'm doing this now, before I prep him, is because Marcaine takes several minutes to take effect."

Russell used his left index finger to probe the bony ridge above Mohammed's left eye, searching for a slight indentation in the bone. This is where a nerve exited the skull to supply the forehead.

He told Ahmed, "The supraorbital nerve comes out the skull through a foramen you can palpate. It's right here." To Mohammed: "Okay, here comes the first injection."

After swabbing the skin with an alcohol sponge, he injected a wheal over the foramen. Next, he gently palpated just in front of the patient's left ear. "As you know," which he assumed Ahmed really didn't, "the nerves run next to the blood vessels. I'm feeling for the superficial temporal artery. If I inject right next to it, I'll block the nerve."

His fingertip sensed the small artery's faint pulsations beneath the skin. Keeping his finger on the spot as a guide, he injected this second site. Finally, his fingertip explored the back of Mohammed's head for the occipital artery. He injected it, too. With all three nerves now infiltrated with local anesthetic, he'd effectively blocked the area of scalp he would be opening.

He stepped back from the bed to study Mohammed's left side, picturing the underlying anatomy, visualizing the temporal lobe as it sat on bone over the inner ear, the tip hiding just behind the eye. Next, he placed two fingers against Mohammed's head, the bottom one running from his ear canal to the corner of his orbit. Thus, the top finger approximated the Sylvian fissure, the large indentation that divides frontal from temporal lobe. He drew a line straight up from just in front of the ear. The spot where this line intersected the second finger gave him an approximate location of Broca's area; a brain area named after Paul Broca, the neurologist who first described this frontal lobe area as essential for producing speech. He noticed a small skin mole just behind this area. Good. He could use this as a landmark to guide him to the site after prepping and draping.

Next, he scrubbed the operative site with Betadine, a dark brown, antibacterial liquid. After patting the scalp dry with sterile towels, he drew the incision with a sterile felt-tipped pen. Finally, he infiltrated the skin directly under the blue line with additional local anesthetic.

Russell and Ahmed scrubbed at the stainless steel sink in the lab then gowned and gloved. They had given Raveena a crash course on how to function as circulating nurse. After draping Mohammed's head they were ready to start.

He said to Mohammed, "Tell me if you feel any pain." Russell probed the incision with a hypodermic needle. When finished, he asked, "Did you feel that at all?"

"Feel what?"

"Perfect. That's exactly what I was hoping to hear."

With the scalpel, Russell started the incision, cutting from skin to bone in one slice, meticulously coagulating any bleeders with each enlargement. Once the incision was fully open, he peeled the scalp away from the ivory-colored skull and the muscle that clenched the jaw. If he were performing this operation in a real operating room, he would use human-sized power tools for the next step. But he'd not been able to scrounge any. His only options were to either use old-fashioned hand tools or power instruments from the animal surgery. For various reasons, he'd elected the latter. Using an electric drill with a round burr attached, similar to a dental instrument, he cut a groove into the skull outlining the bone flap he intended to raise. With the drill rotating at maximum RPM, he gently worked the burr back and forth in one spot while Ahmed squirted saline irrigation over the area to wash away the accumulating bone dust and cool the drill. Every few millimeters of depth he'd pause to probe the thickness of the remaining skull until he eventually broke through to the dura, the thick membrane attached to the underside of the skull. With this vital landmark clearly identified, he could work faster, bringing the rest of the skull incision down to the same level. This step finished, he was able to carefully pry the oval bone flap off the dura. The smell of burnt bone filled the room. The odor reminded him of his dentist's office.

He straightened his back and rocked side-to-side loosening up the muscles. He asked Mohammed, "How you doing?"

"No problem. You?"

"I've seen better operating conditions, but fine so far."

Using a small hook, he snagged the dura and elevated it off the underlying brain. Then, with a different scalpel, he carefully slit the membrane for a centimeter. Clear spinal fluid spilled out, providing a glimpse at the underlying, glistening brain. Russell used blunt-tip scissors to open the remaining tissue circumferentially, about a centimeter from the bony edge, leaving one small section intact.

For a moment he stood, watching the overhead lights

reflect off the brain surface as it pulsated in synch with the
bleeping heart monitor. As routine as opening a head had become, he never lost the sense of awe when seeing and touching
a living, functioning brain. As it turned out, he'd positioned the
flap well, for along the lower edge was the Sylvian fissure,
identified by the emerging branches of the middle cerebral
artery. The only question remaining was, had he targeted
correctly in the front-to-back dimension?

He picked up a sterilized wand about the size of a felt-tip
pen. A long electrical cord exited the end of the wand to termi-
nate in a plug. Two silver wires, each ending as a small metal
ball, extended from the wand's other end. Russell passed the
electrical cord to Gerda, who had been watching from the connecting doorway. She pushed the plug into the output jack of
the stimulator—the instrument that would provide electric current to the probe.

"I assume you want it set for fifty Hertz, ja?" referring to
the stimulation frequency.

"Correct."

"What current?"

"Let's start at four milliamps."

She adjusted the stimulator output to be precisely four
milliamps and flipped the toggle switch to the ON position,
providing electric current to the wand in Russell's hand.
"You are now active," she warned.

Russell told Mohammed, "Start counting slowly."

Mohammed started counting, "One, two, three . . ." Russell touched the probe to Mohammed's brain. Mohammed
was only able to mumble, "fooo . . ." before the last number
slurred to a stop.

Russell removed the two silver balls of the probe from his
patient's brain. "What happened? You stopped counting."

"I don't know . . . it was really strange. I wanted to keep
going, but I couldn't get the words to come out. It was like
my mouth froze up . . . my jaw and tongue."

"You did fine. Let's try that again. Start counting."

"One, two," Russell touched the probe against the brain surface again, "th . . th . . ."

Russell turned to Gerda. "Lucked out." Then to Mohammed, "Same thing?"

"Yes. Did you do that to me?"

"Uh huh. We just found our target." He picked up the delicate sterilized electrode array and gently positioned it on the cortex. To Russell, the electrodes resembled a miniaturized "frog" used to impale flower stems in a vase. Once he began closing the dura, the pressure of the pulsating brain would drive the needlelike electrode tips a few millimeters into the brain's outer surface.

He told Raveena, "Open me a pack of dura silk," with a nod toward several unopened suture packs he'd set along one of the stainless steel countertops.

As he started to suture the dura closed, he told Ahmed, "In the 1940s a neurosurgeon named Wilder Penfield mapped the brain's surface using pretty much the same technique as I just did. Much of our understanding of the brain's functional surface anatomy comes directly from that work. Even today his observations are being refined with more modern imaging techniques like PET and MRI scans."

Ahmed asked, "It is possible for you to now start training your neural network as soon as you close up?"

"Yes. Why do you ask?"

"Because, my friend, his kidneys," pointing to Mohammed, "have produced no urine in four hours now. This time I suspect he's certainly has gone into renal shutdown for good. In which case, I suggest you hurry."

CHAPTER
32

RUSSELL FED THE delicate ribbon cable that Gerda had spent countless hours constructing, directly out the craniotomy incision. He would've preferred "tunneling" it between scalp and skull to exit from a small stab wound inches away from the main closure because doing so would decrease the risk of infection, but the extra length of the thin wire would increase its signal loss. Better yet, would be to have the output from each electrode transmitted by radio waves to a receiver, but they hadn't had time to obtain the electronics to do it. There just wasn't enough time to do anything right, Russell thought angrily. As it was, Gerda would have to spend hours crimping a tiny gold connector at the end of each wire into individual silicon amplifiers that would goose up the signal enough to send microvolt neural signals to the computers.

With the cable now in place, he secured the bone flap back in its original position by screwing three bridging titanium struts into the bone. This step completed, he began closing the scalp in two layers: 2–0 absorbable Vicryl sutures to approximate the deep fascia, inverting each stitch so that the knot ended up the deeper than the loop—a trick to

keep the "tails," those little residual suture lengths that remain after cutting it free from the parent fiber, from sticking
up through the wound and causing infection—then stapling
the outer layer shut. These were meticulous details that some
surgeons ignored, but eventually paid for with above average
infection rates.

Finished, he dabbed residual blood from the wound with
a saline dampened four-by-four cotton sponge before dressing it with a strip of Telfa. This he held in place with paper
surgical tape. He stood back to admire the job.

"Nice job," Ahmed said, as if reading his thoughts.

"Doctor Lawton," a voice whispered urgently.

Raveena stood in the connecting doorway, waving frantically at the other room. "Someone is knocking on the door."

"Oh, Jesus Christ! The FBI," he muttered without knowing exactly why. *Hell yes, you know why. That insane line of
bullshit you fed them last time was totally unbelievable.*

Russell stripped off his gloves and gown and said to
Raveena, "Stay here with Mohammed and lock the door behind me." To Ahmed, "Come with me," and glanced around
to see where Hussein was. He figured Hussein was the least
stable of the three and the most likely to act on emotional
impulse rather than rational choice. If there were going to be
a problem, he'd provoke it.

Russell rushed into the other lab. Gerda jumped out of the
way and then shoved the door closed behind Ahmed, who had
followed right behind him. He stopped, smoothed his pitted-
out scrub shirt, palm-wiped his face, took a deep breath before
reaching the door.

His arm stopped just before exerting any force on the
door pull. It hit him: the door to the sound attenuation
chamber—where Ed Ogilvy still laid, rotting—was closed.
Hussein had to be in there. Damn it, why hadn't they taken
care of Ed's body? Especially considering the close call the
last time those two FBI agents were here.

More pounding came from the door.

Russell shot Ahmed a questioning look. They could simply not answer the door. Then again, if the FBI was back with a search warrant they could just as easily ask security to open the door anyway. To both labs. If that happened, they'd be totally screwed.

Russell jerked the door open.

Correct. The same two, serious-faced, FBI agents stood in the hallway, the woman—he thought he remembered her name being something like Phillips—in front of the man, who, he wanted to say, had an Italian-sounding name.

Phillips said, "Doctor Russell Lawton, you're under arrest for the kidnapping of Angela Lawton. Collect a coat if you want to, but this time you're coming with us. Now."

Russell flashed on Angela and on all the things that needed to be completed before Mohammed's kidneys and heart completely shut down. He held up both hands, palms out, signaling surrender. "Please, I'll come with you. I just can't come at this very moment. I'm in the middle of a crucial experiment. You have to believe me, I can't leave here now."

"You got a problem hearing, Lawton?" Phillips asked. "You're under arrest. Coming with us is not negotiable. If necessary we will use force. Now what's it going to be?"

He stepped further into the lab, over to where his windbreaker remained draped over the back of his task chair. "I'm telling you, I haven't kidnapped Angela. I'll even take a polygraph to prove it, if you want. Just give me some extra time here. I'm begging you." He was back far enough now to casually glimpse through the double-paned Plexiglas into the shadowy booth interior. Enough light from the overhead fluorescents angled in to make out the shadow of Hussein. The terrorist raised a straightened left index finger to pursed lips. His right hand held an automatic pistol with sound suppressor attached, aimed toward the chamber's door.

Awww Jesus, all he needed was for Hussein to start blasting away at a couple federal agents.

"Okay, look . . ." Russell continued, both hands still held up. "I'll come answer your questions, but give me one second to leave my colleagues a few instructions."

He pulled his jacket off the chair, said to Gerda, "Go ahead and hook up the cable." Then, to Ahmed: "I'm sorry, but this involves my daughter. She's the most important thing in my life right now," hoping he understood the veiled message those words carried. "I'll take care of this as quickly as possible and then get back as fast as I can. Okay?"

Ahmed eyes locked into his. "Yes, I am certain you want to do everything possible to insure her safety. Yes?"

"Count on it."

Phillips held up her hand, asked. "Lord have mercy! What *is* that smell? Man, I'm telling you that sure ain't monkey piss I'm smelling."

Russell's heart seemed to stop and then accelerate. "What smell?"

Phillips glanced at her partner. "Don't tell me you don't smell it. You got a nose."

Delorenti was scanning the lab. "Holy Mary, Mother of God! Did something die in here?"

Russell swallowed hard, turned to Phillips. "Oh, *that* smell . . . Yes, you're right. Something did die. We think a rat chewed through some wires and got fried up there in one of the light fixtures," pointing up at the recessed fluorescents. "I just haven't had time to find out which one yet." Russell turned and walked into the hall, saying, "Hey, you guys coming or not?"

CHAPTER

33

Hoover Building, District of Columbia

Phillips pulled open a solidly constructed metal door. In its center, about shoulder height, was a small square window reinforced with chicken wire. Phillips stepped aside in an obvious gesture for him to enter a bleak rectangular interrogation room. A metal table jutted from the wall at the opposite end with three mismatched metal and vinyl chairs scattered to either side. A wall-to-wall mirror extended from just above table level to the ceiling. Undoubtedly it allowed unobstructed observation and videotaping of interviews from a room beyond. The walls and ceiling were painted a depressing gray blue, a color that, for some reason, reminded Russell of weathered clapboards dotting the coast of Maine.

The room carried a residual trace of body odor and nicotine even without an ashtray in sight. He glanced around for a microphone and didn't see one. There had to be one. He figured it was probably concealed in the recessed overhead lights, to make the interviewee more relaxed.

Russell entered the room, but made no move to sit or to

say a word. He'd received the cold shoulder throughout the entire ride into D.C. Fortunately, again he recognized the interviewing technique; let your silence increase the detainee's nervousness to the point of spontaneously offering information. Well, it wasn't going to work. He would wait until they initiated conversation. Still, anxiety churned his stomach. He should be back in the lab working. More importantly, what was Ahmed thinking? Did he take the opportunity to escape, taking with him any chance for Angela's survival? He had to get back. And soon.

From the doorway Phillips asked, "Want something to drink? Water, coffee, a soda?" Delorenti stood slightly behind her and to the right.

His irritation spiked. "How about a phone call to my lawyer?" *My divorce lawyer*, he thought with a note of bitterness. At least she'd probably be able to refer him to a criminal lawyer.

Phillips didn't look pleased with his answer.

"You get one more chance, Lawton. You want something? Yes or no? Your choice."

He could hear a definite shrug in her voice.

"Mountain Dew, if you have one. Otherwise Coke or Pepsi."

Phillips told Delorenti, "Coffee. Black. Thanks."

She entered the room, pulling the door shut behind her.

"Might as well take a chair, Lawton. I have a feeling this could take a while. More like seventy-two hours to be exact. Which, I might point out, is the amount of time we can hold you without officially arresting you."

Sitting was the last thing he felt like doing. "Thought you said I was arrested."

"You're here on a seventy-two-hour hold for starters. We'll see how this plays. Go ahead, sit down."

"I'll stand."

"Suit yourself." She rotated a chair out from the table,

dropped onto it sidesaddle, right arm draped casually over the curved metal top, legs crossed. After a beat: "Want some advice, Lawton?"

"I didn't kidnap my daughter. How more clearly can I say it?"

"You look like shit," she continued. "Those ain't bags under your eyes, man, those are Samsonites. You'd need an army of Sherpas to lug those beauties around. But, I got to tell you this, bad as you look, it's not the look of someone who's gone without sleep from putting in too many hours on call. I know that look and that ain't you. Nooo nooo. Nuh uh. You got the look of someone who's hiding something." A pause. "You hiding something, Lawton?"

Russell turned his back to the mirrored glass and the person on the other side, in what his TV-imprinted mind visualized as a darkened room heavily scented from overcooked coffee. Maybe Delorenti was in there watching. Maybe some hot shot FBI psychologist. Then again, maybe he only rated a video recorder. He stared at the closed door, waiting for something cold to drink to help settle his stomach. He avoided looking at Sigmund Freud Phillips, the Good Cop. Delorenti must be setting up for the Bad Cop role.

"You'll feel a hell of a lot better if you unburden yourself, doc. Believe me. And I can't say I blame you none, either, if you did take her. What with that custody battle you got going and all. After all, you're the one deserves to keep her. Right?"

Good cop for sure.

Part of him wanted desperately to explain the entire nightmare and beg for help. After all, these are highly trained FBI agents. The best. Who better to help him? He flashed on Hussein calmly gunning down the cop outside the Moscone convention center and then Ed Ogilvy. He thought of Ahmed, the paranoid sonofabitch who thought nothing of decapitating Mohammed. Even if he told the feds nothing and even if they were still there when he returned, would they believe him?

He thought of their threats against Angela.

An icy fist grabbed his gut and squeezed the breath from his lungs. Was it already too late? Had Ahmed deemed their mission blown and pulled out the team? If so, was Angela already dead?

Sweat beaded up on his forehead. He shifted weight.

Phillips continued studying him as seconds ticked away. Seconds better spent in the lab.

He swallowed, wiped both palms on his thighs and looked away.

"From what I understand," Phillips finally said, "it's getting pretty ugly, this battle between you and Marci. It *is* Marci . . . her name, right?"

He turned to the mirror so there would be no mistaking his next comment. "Don't I have a constitutional right to contact a lawyer?" figuring it didn't hurt to get it on the record as many times as possible.

"Maybe. Maybe not. We'll see how things play out here. How forthcoming you are. Right now we're just getting ourselves comfortable. You know . . . getting to know one another. So you can find out we're not bad guys. In fact, we're on your side. After all, our only concern in this case is exactly the same as yours is, you agree?"

"And what concern is that?"

"Finding where Angela is. Isn't that what this is all about?"

"What's that supposed to mean?" He shifted weight from one leg to the other, the movement making him aware of how damp the back of his scrub shirt had become.

The door latch clicked. Can wedged between arm and chest, white Styrofoam cup in his right hand, Delorenti used his left hand to manage the doorknob. He handed Phillips the cup, then offered Russell a silver and red can of Diet Coke.

Russell eagerly took it. The can was room temperature. He wondered if Delorenti had to go out of his way to find a warm one.

"Sorry it's not cold," Delorenti muttered, unable to suppress a grin.

"Hey, I love warm Diet Coke," Russell shot back. He pulled the tab. Amber fizz exploded out the top, spraying his face and chest. Froth bubbled over the can edge and dripped down over his hand and onto his scrubs.

Delorenti smirked. "My, my, didn't anyone tell you—you shouldn't shake those things up before opening them."

Blinking, Russell slowly set the can on the table and flicked both wrists, flinging Diet Coke from his hands. He asked Phillips. "Is there a place where I can rinse off?" He'd be damned if that son of a bitch Delorenti was going to get the best of him.

Leaning over, water dripping from face and hands, Russell studied the pale blue American Standard logo on the white porcelain as Delorenti continued ranting in his heavy Bronx accent, "Think you're one smart sonofabitch, don't ya huh? Just cause you're a neurosurgeon? Well, let me tell you something else, Lawton; we know you're involved in this and you better believe we're going to prove it. Might as well save yourself a shitload a grief and let us know where she is. Least that way we can say you cooperated."

Russell jerked a paper towel from an inlaid stainless steel wall dispenser, dried his face and hands, looked back into the mirror and brushed lint off his cheeks where it clung to dark stubble. He hadn't realized how much he needed a shave.

"Have it your way," Delorenti continued, "Refuse to cooperate. And when we find her, you can rot in a federal pen. It's not worth it, man. Believe me."

Russell picked his scrub shirt off the counter and shook it out, "I'm ready to go back," and slipped it over his head.

* * *

Sitting across from Phillips now in the interrogation room, she asked, "Explain to me, again, why you don't believe your daughter's been kidnapped." Delorenti hadn't bothered entering into the warm cramped room after escorting him back.

"Because it just feels like something Marci might come up with."

Phillips wagged a finger at him. "See, now that's the part I'm having trouble buying into. Explain that to me, again."

The gnawing fear that Ahmed had panicked and fled intensified. Russell shifted positions in the chair.

"Well, the thing is, you have to know how she thinks. As you already seem to know, we have a custody battle over Angela coming up in a few weeks." He paused, choosing words carefully. "Like I told you before, Marci has had problems with depression and substance abuse. That's the reason Angela stays with me the majority of the time. Marci probably thinks the judge will weigh this heavily during the hearing and probably figures it puts her at risk to lose the case. But . . . and here's the thing . . . if she makes it look like I kidnapped Angela, she probably thinks it will help her win custody. See? Easy. Problem solved."

"Yeah? Then explain to me what's supposed to happen to Angela? Is she suddenly going to turn up when the hearing's over? She think the kidnapping angle is just going to go away? Huh? How's that work into this plan?"

"I don't know. Ask her." Russell checked his watch.

Phillips regarded him a moment. "Really? I can't believe a man as smart as you'd marry a woman that stupid."

"We all make mistakes." Again Russell wiped his palms on his thighs and tried once more to find a comfortable position.

Phillips tapped her pursed lips once, twice. "Well see, there's a problem with your explanation and here it is: There's no evidence to make us believe she kidnapped your daughter." She was looking at him hard now.

"What evidence would that be?"

"Her daughter's gone."

"All I can say to that is *I* didn't do it."

"Oh, so does that mean you admit she has been kidnapped?"

He stood up, turned a tight circle.

Phillips waited for a response.

He dropped back into the chair. "I didn't say that."

Phillips shot back, "Then what did you say?"

Russell raked his fingers over his head, and then checked the time again. Another two minutes had flown by since last check. "If Angela was kidnapped, it wasn't me."

"That right? Then why'd you leave San Francisco at least three days ahead of schedule?"

He saw where this was headed. "You tell me, since you seem to know so much about it."

Phillips eyed him suspiciously.

"We checked with the NIH travel office. According to them, you were booked into the San Francisco Hilton for a full four days. The same four days the meeting was taking place. Also, according to the AANS office in Chicago, when you registered for the meeting, you signed up for the whole enchilada. The full four days. I got a copy of your registration forms. You want to see them?"

She didn't wait for an answer. "You even signed up for four breakfast seminars. On top of all this, your United Airlines ticket didn't have you returning to Dulles until the same evening the meeting ended. We also know you made arrangements for Angela to stay with Marci while you were to be out of town. Having said all this, you showed up at the NIH security office the second day of the meeting. My conclusion: You left the meeting early. You going to deny any of this?"

Russell's intestines knotted. It seemed they knew everything. "No."

"Okay, then." She nodded agreement, as if that issue had

finally been settled. "Next hot topic: How'd you managed to get back to Bethesda without using your return ticket? See, we checked that, too. Mind explaining that one?"

He stared back, his mind blanking out the lie he'd concocted during the drive here.

"Well?"

He swallowed and looked down and realized he had knitted his fingers tightly together. He released them. "I flew."

"Yeah? Well, surprise. We sort of assumed that might've happened, given the timeline. What I'm asking is, what airline?"

"A private jet."

Phillips shot a glance at the window without moving her head. "Really! What are we talking about here: A private charter? A personal jet? What?"

Russell shrugged. "I don't know the details. I didn't arrange it. Some friends did. A small corporate-type jet. That's all I know."

"Whose jet?"

"I don't know. I didn't ask." He sucked a deep breath. At least, that was one he could answer.

"Then I assume it wasn't yours and you didn't charter it. Correct?"

Russell saw no way out of the enlarging hole he was digging himself into. "Yes."

"I assume you were a passenger and not the pilot. Correct?"

"Yes." More sweat sprouted above his eyebrows but Russell refused to wipe it away, fearing that would only draw attention to it.

"Then tell me what you *do* know about this jet. Let's start with these friends you flew with. Who are they?"

He tried for it's-no-big-deal tone. "Just some friends I met in San Francisco. They offered me a trip on a corporate jet. I'd never flown in one before and thought it'd be sort of cool, so I took them up on it."

She nodded thoughtfully. "You thought it'd be sort of cool . . ." Phillips echoed with a clear edge of doubt.

Silence.

"These friends of yours . . . they wouldn't happen to be your Pakistani buddies, would they?"

The intestinal knot tightened. He saw no way to avoid it. "Yes, actually, they were."

Phillips raised her eyebrows. "I didn't realize medicine paid so well in Pakistan. Especially for doctors so young."

Russell didn't answer.

"How long have you known these Pakistanis?"

He shrugged meekly, trying to remember what they had written on the NIH visitor pass request. His mind blanked.

CHAPTER
34

"**TELL YOU WHAT,** Lawton, let's cut the foreplay and get down to business." Phillips leaned over, arm on the small table, her lips pressed into a thin line that she held for a moment. "We're in possession of a few disturbing facts about your new buddies. Hey! Are you listening to me?"

"Yes."

"Good, because you might want to hear some of these things, just in case you haven't been paying attention to what's been going on in the world." She stopped a moment to adjust the watch on her wrist. "We requested passport verifications on each of your friends from Pakistani immigration. And guess what? They haven't responded."

Russell looked down at the floor.

"Does that bother you at all?"

Russell licked his dry lips and studied the linoleum a moment. "Should it?"

"Yeah, it most definitely should. And you know why? Because when something like that happens there's usually something funky going on."

Russell heard the overhead fluorescent lighting humming softly.

"Like what, you might ask? Like maybe they're using false passports. Did that thought ever cross your mind?"

"No. Why should it?"

"How long have you known each one of these people?"

Russell checked his watch again and tried to ignore the corkscrew skewering his abdomen. "I thought this was only going to take a few minutes. I need to get back to work."

Phillips cleared her throat. "Let me tell you something Lawton. Hey! You listening?"

He shot her a look.

"News flash! Your buddies are suspected terrorists, Lawton. Wake up."

A crushing silence settled on Russell's shoulders. He swallowed.

She continued, "What this means is, we're now obliged to investigate them in very great detail. In fact, you might even say excruciating detail. And you know what? Since you're kindly hosting their visitor passes—passes that allow them to access a government building—you are now an accomplice. You're now on record as a terrorist, Lawton. Think about it."

Russell swallowed and looked away.

"Here's the deal, Lawton. We were brought into this investigation on the assumption you kidnapped your daughter. But now, without any evidence to link you to your daughter's disappearance—other than your embittered ex-wife's allegation—we're no longer considering her disappearance a kidnapping. Instead, we're going to treat it as nothing more than another missing person investigation. That means we're tossing it back into the McLean PD's lap. So guess what? Where does this leave you?

Phillips paused to sip coffee.

Russell stood. He pressed both hands against the cinderblock wall and leaned into it, feeling the muscles tighten across his back. "If you're so convinced that my visitors are terrorists, why not interrogate them? Better yet, why not arrest them?"

"Bear with me a moment and let me finish." She took another sip. "Here's where things start looking particularly grim for you. See, since you're now considered a potential terrorist, a whole new set of rules apply to how we're going to deal with you. And as far as you're concerned . . . the thing most important to you, since you're in such a hurry to get back, is we can hold you here . . . right here in this building," pointing at the floor, "for a long, long time. I'm talking months. I'm talking a lot of months."

The room fell silent again.

"And you know what? There's not a damn thing you can do about it. Not a damned thing. Call a lawyer?" Phillips shrugged. "Sure. *If* you were being detained on kidnapping charges. But now? As a terrorist? No way you're going to make a call to anyone. You just lost every one of your rights as an American citizen. The moment you walked through that door you simply disappeared off the face of the earth. And you're going to stay that way for, oh, say, a year? Yeah," nodding in appreciation, "a year. Twelve months sounds like a good round number."

Silence.

"Think about it. Think about all the repercussions that's going to have on your life. Your job? Forget about it. It's history. That nasty custody suit with your ex? Forget about that, too. You're going to lose all of it. And for what?"

Wearily, Russell dropped into one of the remaining chairs, leaned forward, elbows on thighs, and pressed his forehead against both palms. Where was Ahmed now? And Angela?

Phillips continued, "Think I'm making this up? Think this is all a crock of shit? Well, think again. And when you do, think about all those al Qaeda prisoners who vanished from Afghanistan after the Taliban fell. They weren't prisoners of war. They were classified as terrorists. There's no Geneva convention for what we do to terrorists. And you know what? The same thing's going to happen to you. Like to fly around in private jets? Hey, that's part of the deal. We'll stuff you away in one of those fancy CIA Lears and airmail your ass straight out of the country to a place where no one will ever know who the hell you are. Picture it: tomorrow morning you wake up in Afghanistan in a CIA prisoner of war camp. Does that appeal to you?"

Silence.

"And while you're thinking that over, ask yourself this: Besides your wife, who knows you're here in the District?"

The thought of Ed Ogilvy surfaced again. No one else knew except Marci.

"Ever since you returned from San Francisco, you've been keeping a low profile, Lawton. We know because we had a hard time tracking you down. Far as your colleagues are concerned, you're still at a meeting in San Francisco. It was your wife who told us where to look." She studied him a moment before.

"Fast forward a few days. Next week you're supposed to be back at work but you don't show up. Same thing the week after. Anyone know where you are? Someone, let's say a secretary starts checking, calls the travel office. Travel office gives her your itinerary . . . well, you see how it goes? Far as anyone knows, you simply disappeared during a meeting in San Francisco. Hey, maybe you're down on Mission Street with the homeless? Who knows?"

A hollowness opened in Russell's chest. "My wife knows."

"Your ex?" She let out a sarcastic laugh. "Think she cares what happens to you?" Phillips raised her hands in a for-what-it's-worth gesture. "Besides, from what you just told me, no one in their right mind's going to believe her, what with her problems and all . . .

"Not only that," Phillips continued, "but you don't show

up in court and guess what? She wins custody of Angela. No problem. Especially if the judge hears about your history of spousal abuse."

"Spousal abuse!" Russell was on his feet now, a growing burn on his face.

Phillips met his glare. "Cut the righteous indignation. I'm not buying it. I got the story straight from the Rockville PD. Bet you didn't know that in cases like yours they always investigate to make sure the wife isn't being intimidated into dropping the charges."

Russell jabbed an index finger at her. "That's a damn lie!"

The chair legs screeched as Phillips jumped up and backed two steps toward the door. "Stay clear of me, Lawton, or the entire building's going to come crashing down on your head."

Russell turned toward the wall, drew a deep breath and leaned into it again. Mind churning, he held that position several seconds. Finally, he muttered, "It didn't happen like that."

"Doesn't make any difference what happened, Lawton. It's on the record and I can drag it up for the judge."

Russell wiped both eyes with his palms, drew another breath. "She'd been locking Angela in a small closet."

"What?"

He pressed both palms against his forehead. "Marci couldn't handle parenting very well . . . especially right after Angela started walking. If she did something Marci didn't like, she'd lock her in a small closet until . . ." he threw up both arms in frustration. "We argued about it several times and finally, after I first threatened to file for divorce and a custody hearing, she agreed to stop. I thought she had. But then one day I came home shortly after noon with a case of stomach flu and found Marci drunk and Angela locked in the closet . . ."

"And?"

"Marci started mouthing off at me. About how I was such

a loser for not going into private practice . . . how . . ." He turned to face Phillips. "I slapped her."

Phillips continued standing. "That's it? You slapped her? I mean, what do you consider a slap? How hard is that?"

"Hard enough to redden her cheek but not hard enough to bruise her. That's why when the police came to the apartment there wasn't . . ." He felt drained. "To this day Angela is still damaged, she's afraid of the dark . . . and terribly claustrophobic . . ."

"My heart goes out to you, Lawton, but that still doesn't change things. The point is, you're abetting terrorists. Until we sort this out, you're going nowhere but here."

Russell heard himself say, "You're right. They *are* terrorists . . ." Engulfed in a mixture of relief and despair, he dropped wearily into the chair, pressed his forehead with the heels of both palms, and started through the entire story from meeting Raveena at the Moscone Convention Center until Phillips and Delorenti showed up in the lab.

NIH, Building 10

The pounding on the thick door startled Ahmed. He spun around in the chair to check the video monitor, his hand already on the gun. He squinted at the image, and then relaxed his grip on the pistol. Hussein and Yusef were standing outside the door looking at the small camera, Yusef's left hand holding the chrome end of the narrow collapsible mortician's gurney that served as a tool of his trade. Raveena poked a worried face in from Mohammed's room. "Who is that?"

He sliced a palm through the air, "Mind your patient, woman," and, ignoring her frown, pulled open the heavy door. "Come, come." After waving his two comrades inside, he leaned into the hallway to glance in both directions. To his relief, the drab cement corridor remained empty. He quickly shut the door and threw home the deadbolt.

Yusef began to say something but Ahmed cut him off by asking Hussein, "The guards? Did they give you much problem?"

Yusef, a slight man dressed in an impeccable black suit, starched white dress shirt, and dark gray tie, kept fidgeting, mouth open, index finger raised to catch Ahmed's attention.

Hussein grinned. "The business of death, it would appear, is the perfect disguise. They asked very few questions. Perhaps it is not too uncommon for a hearse to come to this building."

"Did anybody notice you when you entered the building?"

Hussein nodded without hesitation. "Yes, I am certain we were seen. As we agreed, we parked at the same loading dock as where the oxygen tanks are stored . . . where they have a security camera. But I am told this is where all hearses park, so I am hoping this will look like a routine pickup."

"Ahmed!" Yusef finally broke in, "Is it true the FBI was here?"

Ahmed shot Hussein an admonishing look before turning to him. "Yes, they were here." That small area to the right of his chin began itching again as if something was burrowing just below the surface of the skin. He began scratching it with his thumbnail but the irritation remained unsatisfied.

"And they have taken the doctor? For questioning?"

He studied the undertaker's agitation a moment, sizing it up as mostly fear. The same fear he's seen in some patients as they realized death was near. Maybe he was not as committed to the jihad as Hussein. Or even Raveena, who, for a woman, seemed a true believer. Perhaps it was a manifestation of the corruption living in the United States caused. It had happened before to those who had been planted here for years to establish credible identities and await their call.

"What is the problem, Yusef?"

"What is the problem? You have to ask?" Yusef flashed a look of incredulity. "You," sweeping a palm at the three of them, "have been found out. Discovered. They will come for all of us. We must leave the country immediately or risk imprisonment."

"And if we do, what will we accomplish?" He spit out the word, "Nothing!"

"And if every one of us ends up in prison camp what will that accomplish? On the other hand, if we escape now, we will still be able to carry on. Maybe return under new identities."

And I will fail as a leader. "And by running away like little rabbits, we will admit to the FBI our true identities. They will know who we are and this will make it impossible to ever return to this country for a second attempt."

Yusef sighed in exasperation. "Yes, yes, but what are our chances of succeeding with—" he shot a cringing glance toward the other room and lowered his voice, "Jamal in such a bad condition?"

Ahmed clenched both fists. "Are you questioning my ability to care of him?"

"Ahmed, he is correct," Raveena cut in. "Mohammed's condition is critical. His chances of survival, slim."

Ahmed stabbed an index finger at the open door. "Back in your room. You have no place in this discussion." Then to Yusef: "You forget the American legal system. The FBI will not be allowed to do a thing until they have gathered sufficient proof that we are a clear and present threat. By that time we will have succeeded and, God willing, we will disappear from this miserable country."

"But—"

"Besides," Ahmed continued, "the doctor is unwilling to gamble the life of his daughter. I am confident he will tell them nothing."

Yusef did not look convinced. "So *you* think. I do not

share your conviction. The FBI has every means of prying that information from him."

"That, my friend, is the gamble I am willing to take for the sake of completing our mission. In the meantime, I suggest you pick up that body," with a nod toward the booth, "and be gone before you raise too much attention from being parked out there too long."

Then, as a concession to the man he relied on for help, Ahmed placed a hand on his shoulder and added, "Rest assured, from this point on, we will watch the doctor even more closely than before." The hint of a smile crept into Ahmed's lips. "Jamal discovered a wireless network in here," with a sweep of his hand around the room. "It is encrypted. But Jamal is breaking the encryption as we speak. He will not be able to communicate with the outside without us knowing exactly what is said."

Hoover Building, Washington, D.C.

"You believe his story?" McGowan asked Phillips.

They were sitting in the darkened observation room on the other side of the mirrored window from Lawton. Through the thick one-way glass she could see him pacing the room and stealing repeated glances at his watch.

Phillips was still nursing her coffee and had the cup to her lips. She lowered it to respond when Delorenti opened the door to their room. She and McGowan turned toward him.

Delorenti said, "Story about the SFPD cop getting capped checked out. Not a hell of a lot of details but like he said, the shooting took place right out in front of the convention center with about a hundred people walking by. But, of course, no one really saw much of what happened. That supports his claim about using a suppressor. Ron checked out the part about the Omaha airport. They confirmed a refueling took place that night just about the same time Lawton claims it happened, so that part seems to confirm. And finally, a TSA agent *did* disappear that evening. They haven't found a trace of him either, so that checks out, too. Ron's on the horn right now with the FAA trying to run down the aircraft."

Phillips nodded at McGowan. "There's your answer. Story checks out. What's not to believe?"

McGowan sat, drumming his fingers on the table. He scrutinized Lawton a moment before shaking his head. "Know what bothers me? The thing that really gets me? It's the part about removing the guy's head. Man! The visual on that one gives me a serious case of the hebbie jebbies." He shivered and shuttered, as if shaking an evil spirit off his back. "And Lord knows, I've seen my fair share of mind-blowing, heart-stopping crazy-ass weirdo hoo-ha shit in this job, but that . . . God Almighty!"

Phillips asked, "That's got to be Jamal Azzam he's got squirreled away in that basement over at NIH."

"One would assume so," McGowan agreed. "We were pretty certain of it when they had him at Georgetown, but we need a solid confirmation."

"Got a suggestion," Delorenti offered.

They both turned to him.

"Assuming we buy Lawton's story, his next step is to train the computer. If that's the case, then it should be a chip shot for him to send us the guy's voiceprint. It wouldn't be conclusive, but for the time being it'd be more than we have right now. Agreed?"

McGowan nodded. "That'll work."

Delorenti added, "Another thought occurred to me. Since his buddies are taking such extreme measures to keep him communicating, you think it means they haven't finished plans for the next attack?"

McGowan answered, "That's one possibility. But the one thing I think we can all agree on is we don't know. Until proven otherwise, we should assume they're moving ahead with plans already in place. Clearly, the more information we can capture, the better."

Phillips anticipated what was coming. "And you want Lawton to get it for us?"

"Right."

"What are you suggesting he do, bug the lab?" Delorenti asked.

Phillips jumped in before her boss answered. "Hell, no. Just look at him." She jerked a thumb toward the window. "He's so nervous you can read him like the *Washington Post*. They'd know right away what was happening. If we're going to use him, we have to do it without him knowing."

She looked directly at McGowan.

He said, "You're absolutely correct, Sandra," then checked the round-faced wall clock. "As it is, too much time has passed since we extracted him. I suggest we return him before the Pakistanis become any more suspicious than they probably already are."

Phillips turned to leave, but McGowan touched her shoulder. "Hold up, Sandra. We haven't discussed any terms with him. What were you going to offer him?"

She saw Delorenti watching and wondered if this had been agreed upon before she got in the room. "Immunity from federal charges."

McGowan nodded approval. "And the daughter?"

She shot Delorenti another look. He broke eye contact. "We do all we can to bring her home alive."

McGowan cocked his head to one side. "And will we?"

Now she saw where this was going. "Far as I'm concerned we will."

"And that is exactly the reason we're clarifying this particular point. I want no confusion on this." He locked eyes with her. "I suspect you're right on one point. He'll refuse to cooperate if we don't agree to do everything we can to save his daughter. I'm a parent. I can relate to that. But our primary mission in this case—and I want you perfectly clear on this point—is to take down those terrorists and take them down before they cause any more damage to this country." His face hardened. "His daughter's safety is clearly a much lower priority. Do we have a clear understanding on this point?"

She stared right into his eyes but said nothing.

McGowan nodded. "This isn't about your brother, Phillips. Now, do we have an understanding or not?"

"Yes, sir."

NIH Building 10

Ahmed entered Jamal's room and looked at his injured comrade. He was sleeping. Raveena folded her arms across her chest and turned away. Rather than wake him, Ahmed moved close to Raveena. Her posture stiffened. He whispered, "How is he doing?"

She ignored his eyes. "He is too sleepy to be able to work."

"How is he progressing with breaking Lawton's encryption?"

"The computer is working on that while he sleeps. He said it was problematic. It may take," she shrugged, "minutes or hours. We will know only when it breaks it."

Ahmed nodded and left the room.

Hoover Building

Phillips said to Russell, "Here's the deal. You help us nail those assholes, we wipe the slate clean, meaning we drop all terrorism charges against you."

"What about Angela?"

"What about her?"

"The deal has to include finding her or I won't help."

"Yes, of course, . . . sorry. That goes without saying. We'll do everything possible to return her to you." Phillips dropped her eyes and pinched her lower lip. "Assuming of course, she is still alive.

Silence.

"She's alive," he said with conviction, then paused, sensing an opportunity. "If I were to help you guys, could you do anything to . . . ah . . . affect the outcome of the custody hearing?"

She impatiently checked her watch. "Only in the sense I can put in a good word with the judge when I explain you had nothing to do with her kidnapping." She paused. "Let me ask you something that's been bothering me. Am I to assume your split with your wife was primarily due to alcohol abuse and parenting issues?"

"Yes."

"In that case, why did you leave Angela with her?"

Russell's shoulders sagged. "It wasn't really planned that way. Angie has a play friend in the same building where I live. They are a real solid family. I'd arranged for her to stay over there while I was gone. But her grandfather died unexpectedly and so the family had to fly out to Ohio for the funeral. I had no other choice."

"Sure you did. You could've cancelled your trip."

"Easy for you to say."

She shook her head ever so slightly. "The deal . . . you in or out?"

"I'm in."

"In that case, we better get you back to the lab. I'll explain the particulars of what we want from you while we drive."

"We need a recording of Mohammed's voice ASAP. Think you can get that for us?" Phillips asked from the front passenger seat. Delorenti was driving the same shitty Crown Vic they used during the trip into the District. Russell sat in the back, directly behind her, listening to her instructions.

Delorenti had uttered a minimal number of words and no apology for the ones in the men's room. Not that Russell expected one.

"Getting one shouldn't be too hard . . . assuming he's conscious enough to talk when I get back. Problem is how do I get it to you?"

"Know how to FTP files?"

File Transfer Protocol. He knew it was a way of transferring large digital files from one computer to another. Especially files large enough to choke most e-mail servers and not be allowed through. "Sure."

She passed him a scrap of paper. "Here's a URL, but be careful. If your buddy, Mohammed, is who we suspect he is, he's a computer expert. A world-class hacker, in fact. Although my techie associates assure me this address is supposedly safe, I wouldn't want to have him hacking into it or, worse yet, catching you sending me something. Understand?"

"Yes, but for what it's worth, his brain isn't in the greatest shape to do much serious hacking."

"Excellent. Oh, and one more thing. The other e-mail address on the paper? That goes to my Blackberry. I keep it on twenty-four seven. You find out anything about these assholes . . . anything about what they're up to, where they have contacts . . . any bit of information, no matter how insignificant you think it might be, pass it on immediately. Understand?"

CHAPTER 36

Building 10, NIH Campus

Russell curled his fingers around the burnished steel handle but stopped short of pushing open the heavy door. Soon as he stepped inside he would know if Ahmed had panicked and fled, killing Angela in the process. Part of him feared the answer. The other part sought resolution. Russell steadied his resolve and blew a deep breath between pursed lips. With his free hand he pounded three warning blows against the heavy door before unlocking and pushing it in a few inches.

Mouth to the crack he warned, "It's me, Russell," before opening it far enough to step into the all-too-familiar warmth and smell of heated electronics. A vivid contrast to the stark cold interrogation room he'd left forty-five minutes ago.

He thought, thank God, they're still here until seeing Ahmed and Hussein aiming guns at him and the look Ahmed was giving him.

"What?" Russell asked.

Gerda sat tightlipped at her workstation. He shot her a questioning glance. She looked past him, toward the door.

Ahmed waved the gun to the left. "Move away from the door."

He did as directed but Ahmed continued aiming at the partially open door. "Did anyone accompany you?"

Russell glanced at the door, then back to Ahmed. "No, no one. They dropped me off at the front of the building. Check the security camera if you doubt me."

Ahmed said something to Hussein. Hussein leaned into the hall and looked left and right before shutting the door and driving home the deadbolt.

Russell asked, "What? You think I'd do something stupid to jeopardize Angela?"

Ahmed aimed the gun at Russell's head. "Your clothes, take them off. All of them."

Russell didn't understand the command. "What?"

Ahmed repeated the instruction. Gerda turned her head.

It dawned on him. "Jesus Christ! You think I'm wearing a transmitter?"

"Your clothes!"

Speechless, Russell pulled the scrub shirt over his head, untied and dropped the cotton pants. "Satisfied?"

"Shoes, socks, and shorts."

"Jesus!"

He heard a familiar snap, turned to see Hussein smooth a surgical glove over his right hand.

Hussein said, "Open your mouth."

Hussein jabbed his finger inside and probed along his cheeks and under his tongue.

Ahmed said, "Bend over."

"Hell, no. You're not—"

Something hard crashed into the side of his temple just above his left ear, sending scintillating pinheads of light across his vision. A hand grabbed his neck, slammed his head against the wall and held it as a finger forced itself into his rectum.

Russell yelped in pain and tried to straighten up his weak

knees, but the finger vanished along with the hand holding his neck. Dizzy, he straightened up. The left side of his head stung and he felt a drop of fluid slide down behind his ear then down his neck. He touched it knowing it was blood before his eyes appreciated the red smear across his fingertips.

Ahmed tossed him a pack of four by four gauze bandages. "Here."

Hussein was quickly inspecting Russell's discarded clothes. Finished, he threw them at Russell.

Totally humiliated, Russell tore open the package and pressed the entire wad of dressings against the stinging pain.

Ahmed asked, "What did the FBI discuss with you?"

Left hand holding pressure on the dressing, he used his right hand to step into his shorts and then scrub pants. "What the hell do you think they wanted from me?"

When he got no reaction, he said, "My daughter's been kidnapped. They're investigating it. They wanted to know where I was and every damn thing I did the day she disappeared. They pressed me for every little detail because, as you damn well know, my ex-wife told them I did it."

"And what exactly did you tell them?"

"The truth. That I was in San Francisco when it happened." He lowered his left hand, inspected the amount of blood on the dressing. "Damn."

"It is only a small cut," Ahmed said. "It does not require stitches."

Russell glared at him before slipping on his scrub shirt then reapplied the dressing and pressure. Gerda was watching again.

"And did they inquire about us? Anything at all?" Ahmed asked.

"No."

Ahmed and Hussein exchanged a nonverbal message.

"Do you believe they suspect us?"

"How should I know since you never came up in the conversation?"

Ahmed and Hussein were studying him closely, looking, Russell knew, for signs of lying. Hussein's right hand still clutched the automatic pistol, kneading the handle like a wad of pizza dough, his free hand cracking knuckles, *pop, pop, pop.*

Russell drew a deep breath and tried to subdue the anger and humiliation over what had just happened. He spoke directly to Ahmed, "I don't know. They never asked about you and I didn't offer. Like I told you, I'm not about to do anything to jeopardize Angela's life." He looked down and retied his scrubs tighter.

He could feel Ahmed's eyes on him. He looked back at him again. "What?"

Hussein muttered something to Ahmed.

Russell nodded at the door to the other room and asked Ahmed, "How's he doing?" in an attempt to distract his rage.

Ahmed studied Russell a moment longer before answering, "He is about the same as when you left. I started the dialysis in hopes it might clear up his mental status some. But more than that, I did it because one of us has to familiarize ourselves with the machine. Especially since you need to begin training the computer."

Russell nodded to Gerda, "Come on, let's get started."

During Russell's absence, Gerda had meticulously connected the wires from each electrode in Mohammed's brain to a tiny amplifier. In actuality, the implanted wafer held five hundred electrodes but they had only two-hundred-fifty amplifiers available for sending brain signals to the computer. From past experience, Russell knew not every electrode would successfully record a neuron. To stack the odds in favor of succeeding, he'd implanted twice the number of electrodes than could possibly be used. This way he could maximize the chances of coming away with two hundred and fifty good recordings.

The job of these tiny amplifiers was to give the tiny signals enough oomph to be transmitted from Mohammed's head to the electronics in Russell's main laboratory. Once there, the signals would be amplified and be inspected for the presence of neural activity. If an electrode was recording activity from one or more nerve cells, it would be added as one digital channel of the computer. This task would be repeated over and over until they were feeding activity from two hundred and fifty separate electrodes into the computer's artificial intelligence software.

Russell dropped into the chair at the main console and adjusted the angle of the gooselecked microphone extending from the rack. "Can you hear me okay?"

"Ja!" Gerda's voice issued from a rack-mounted speaker. She was in the other room with Mohammed. The door was closed.

"The first step," Russell explained to Ahmed who stood next to him watching closely, "is to test each electrode to determine if it's picking up any activity."

He pressed the intercom button, activating the microphone. "Okay, Gerda. Have Mohammed begin talking and keep him going until I say stop."

"I am trying to have him read a magazine, but he keeps falling asleep."

"Do the best you can."

"I don't think he can do it well enough."

"Hold on." He opened an above sink cabinet, withdrew a vial and syringe.

Ahmed jumped up, hand out signaling stop. "Wait! What are you planning to give him?"

"Some caffeine. If that doesn't work I'll try some amphetamine. You have a problem with this?"

Ahmed held out his hand. "First, let me inspect the vial."

* * *

When Mohammed was finally alert enough to talk, Russell began to build a digitized record of his speech. Once this was established, he could then start refining the neural network.

First, he needed to isolate the electrical activity of as many nerve cells—up to a maximum of two hundred and fifty—as possible. He pressed the intercom button and told Gerda, "Have him start talking."

"Anything in particular?"

"No. Just have him speak. If he can't think of anything, have him read something."

He typed a command that would switch whatever was being recorded from the first electrode into the oscilloscope. A wavy line flashed across the amber screen. He adjusted the triggering level so that each trace would begin only if the signal rose above the level of random "noise." Sure enough, vertical blips representing individual bursts of electrical activity from a neuron—called action potentials—rose out of the noise.

"There we go. Each one of these lines represents the little packet of electricity that neurons use to send information to other neurons." He tapped a ballpoint pen against the trace.

"Fascinating," Ahmed muttered, with a note of genuine awe.

Russell remembered experiencing that same awe the first time he saw a neuron's action potentials flash across an oscilloscope screen with a corresponding pop from the audio amplifier.

Within a half hour, Russell and Gerda were able to select two hundred and fifty excellent signals from the first three hundred and fifty electrodes tested, a yield far exceeding his conservative estimates.

"How's he doing? He ready for the next phase?" he asked her over the intercom.

Gerda said, "Hold on."

He explained to Ahmed, who by this time appeared slightly bored, "Now that we have isolated enough signals to feed into the network, the next step is to start training it to recognize the activity from all the signals simultaneously as sounds."

Gerda came back over the intercom, "He needs to rest before he can do any more work. We can give him thirty minutes, ja?"

Without thinking, Russell glanced at his watch. He sighed. Then again, what did it matter? Either Mohammed was up to the task or he wasn't. He couldn't continue to whip his brain with drugs forever. Do that too much and he'd run the risk of perverting the very system he was trying to decode.

"Okay, take a break. We'll start again in thirty minutes." To Ahmed, "After I close this down I'm taking a shower. Okay?"

"Fine, but I will accompany you."

"Damnit! I can't even . . ." he didn't want to overplay the role. "Fine. Whatever," and returned to the keyboard. Then it flashed on him. The smell was gone. He glanced through the booth's double-paned glass. "What happened to Ed?"

"He has been moved." Without more explanation, Ahmed scooted the task chair to the other computer, the one used to monitor Al Jazeera.com.

Quickly, Russell dropped into command-line mode and uploaded Mohammed's voice file to the Internet site Phillips had given him. Task done, he double-checked to make certain no record of the key strokes remained in the computer.

"Come on, Ahmed, let's go shower." He was looking forward to climbing into a fresh set of scrubs, ones that didn't have dried tacky Coke on them.

Ahmed eyed him suspiciously. "What did you just do with the computer?"

Russell's heart seemed to stop and then accelerate. "Just checked on how we're doing so far, why?"

Ahmed didn't look convinced. He held up a finger. "One moment. I have something I need to discuss with Mohammed."

Ahmed closed the door between labs, leaned over his comrade and shook the man's shoulder. "Jamal, wake up."

Jamal opened his eyes. "What is it?"

"Have you broken the encryption yet?"

Jamal blinked and stared back. "Oh, yes, the encryption. Just a minute." He licked dry lips and blinked both eyes, then slid the laptop back onto his chest and focused on the screen. "Yes, we have it. The computer must have cracked it a few minutes ago."

"Perfect. Begin monitoring everything Lawton does with the computer. Immediately. I do not trust him."

Hussein exited the plate glass front door to Building 10 and stood under the high roof that protected the loading zone from the occasional driving Maryland rain. He looked out at the oncoming dusk. He wore a pair of black Ralph Lauren jeans, an olive polo shirt, and black windbreaker against the slight chill in the air.

After a moment, he walked briskly along the left arm of the circular driveway to South Drive where he turned right, heading toward the main entrance and the Metro stop beyond. He rode the escalator down to the loading platform and positioned himself on the Glenmount side, waiting for the Red Line train's arrival. Three minutes later, the train squealed to a stop and the doors shushed open for the exchange of passengers. He purposely chose to board the last car.

Although the car was not full, he chose to stand in the center of the isle, left hand clinging to a metal overhead stay. This way he could casually glance both up and down the car without being obvious. If someone from the FBI were tailing him, he wouldn't be stupid enough to ride the same section, but you never know, these Americans were so arrogant.

At Metro Central he detrained, caught the escalator up to the main station and stood to get his bearing amidst the flow of people moving in all directions. For a moment he considered the irony of a terrorist being only a few blocks from FBI headquarters.

He chose the 12th Street exit.

Out on the sidewalk now, he paused a moment before crossing 12th to the Grand Hyatt Washington. There he entered the lobby, walked slowly through the gift shop apparently looking at trinkets. Satisfied, he exited the building by a different door and proceeded south along 12th for a block and a half to F, where he turned west to 14th, and then walked south again to Pennsylvania.

In a few minutes he entered the plush lobby of the Willard, a venerable D.C. hotel. There he found a pay phone, stepped into the booth and shut the oak and glass door. He dialed the number for Lawton's lab. After three rings the German woman answered.

"This is Hussein. Let me speak to Ahmed."

A moment later. "I'm, here."

Hussein switched from English, just in case the line was tapped, and said, "You are right. I am being followed." He hung up.

Hoover Building, Washington, D.C.

Sandra Phillips pushed open the glass door to McGowan's office and waited. He glanced up from his desk and said into the telephone, "Hold on a moment," before covering the mouthpiece. He flashed her an expectant look. "Yes?"

"Sorry to interrupt your conversation, sir, but I thought you might want to know. The voice print from Lawton confirms that Jamal Azzam *is* Lawton's patient."

McGowan nodded, said into the telephone, "Something vitally important just broke. I'll call you back," and hung up.

Building 10, NIH Campus

Russell pressed the intercom button. "Ready?"

"Ja."

They had replaced Mohammed's laptop with their own, which was linked, through the lab's wireless network, to the master computer in the rack. Training would begin by Russell flashing letters on the laptop screen. As soon as each letter appeared, Mohammed would pronounce it into the microphone.

They began. An A flashed onto the screen. Russell heard Mohammed say, "A." Milliseconds before he produced the sound the nerve cells in the speech section of his brain began firing. The activity of all two hundred and fifty neurons being recorded was then swallowed by the computer and fed into the artificial intelligence software.

"Each time he speaks a designated sound," Russell explained to Ahmed, "the network will modify itself until it will be able to recognize the neural pattern that produces that sound. We'll start with simple letters and then progress to more complicated sounds. By doing this, in a way, it simulates the way we learn from experience."

"But this process is so slow."

"Yes, but consider how long it takes a child to learn to talk."

The letter A was repeated five times before advancing to B and then on through the alphabet.

When this initial phase was completed Russell said, "Let's find out how we've done."

This time, the computer flashed each letter of the alphabet at Mohammad just as they had last time, but, as Mohammed's brain prepared to respond, Russell let the computer use the brain activity to predict the response and produce the sound through a voice synthesizer. In doing this, Russell heard how the computer interpreted Mohammed's brain activity rather than his actual voice. Each time Mohammad and the computer responded, he compared the two.

Gerda opened the door and stepped into the lab. "And what did you discover?"

Russell could not suppress a grin. "Amazing. One hundred percent correct."

Beaming, Gerda raised her hand for high fives. "Ja!"

"Let's not be too hasty," he warned. "There's a huge difference between single letters and words." Caution aside, he couldn't help but savor a small sense of victory.

Gerda said, "He is asking for another period of rest before any more training."

"I guess we can afford a break." Russell wondered how long it'd been since he'd eaten anything. "Want a sandwich?"

"Ja, but Russell, it is eleven o'clock at night. The cafeteria is closed."

Ahmed offered, "I'll call Hussein. He can be bring us something. How does Chinese food sound to you?"

Strange. He couldn't remember his last meal. "I'm starved." He stood to stretch.

When they resumed training the network it was twenty-five minutes past midnight. This time, instead of individual letters, they used a list of fifty simple words that had been carefully chosen to reinforce phonetic distinctions between similar sounds like *show* and *chow*.

By 1:30 AM Russell decided he'd pushed everyone to their maximum endurance and it wouldn't benefit the system to train further. Russell told Gerda and Ahmed, "Take a break. Four hours, everybody. We'll begin again at 5:30." Then to Ahmed, "After I check on Mohammed I'm going to sack out in the call room. You have any problem with that?"

Ahmed flashed him a look of annoyance but said nothing.

Russell entered Mohammed's room and closed the door.

Raveena appeared to be sleeping soundly in the chair next to the bed. Russell bent close to his ear, trying to not disturb her. "You're doing well, Mohammed."

The man studied Russell a moment before licking his lips and whispering, "Maybe when this is over, you will have learned what true commitment is."

"Don't start preaching that crap to me. I don't want to

hear it. How are your lungs?" He picked up the stethoscope from the counter. Raveena began to stir.

"Getting harder to breathe. Or maybe it's just all the talk is tiring me."

Russell listened to the man's lungs. Breathing sounds in the lower, posterior segments were becoming more muffled, meaning the lung bases were filling with fluid again, probably as a result of losing ground in their battle with congestive heart failure. If they were in a hospital Russell would have a respiratory therapist giving him regularly spaced treatments. Instead, he was laying here in a basement laboratory sliding down the drain.

Russell picked up the clipboard and checked his vital signs. Nothing jumped out to cause any more concern than already present. But, of course, the problems would not necessarily show up here. A rapid dive in vital signs would show itself only if his condition reached catastrophic proportions. Nonetheless, he was definitely deteriorating.

"Get some sleep. We have more work to do in a few hours."

"My laptop. Please hand it to me." Mohammed's laptop sat on the black composite counter, its power cord plugged into the counterhigh wall outlet, the green light in the transformer pack glowing.

"Really, you need to rest."

"Yes, but I also need to work."

Russell reluctantly reached for the computer. "What kind of work?"

"That doesn't concern you."

As Russell handed him the computer, he flashed on Phillips's warning—that Mohammed was an excellent hacker. "Do you understand neural networks?"

Mohammed shot him a glance of irritation. "See, here is your problem. You think because I'm Palestinian, I'm stupid. Stop trying to sucker me into telling you what I am doing. Fuck off, Russell."

"Just make sure you're able to work first thing in the morning."

Russell entered the lab a few minutes before 6 AM, having freshly showered, shaved, eaten a breakfast of bacon, eggs, and coffee. Most importantly, he'd crashed for three hours. Not enough to begin paying back the REM debt owed his brainstem, but sufficiently revived to begin work. Per their established routine, Hussein had watched over him the entire time. Now, with Russell back in the lab, Hussein left. Probably to get some sleep of his own.

Gerda was sipping coffee fresh from the lab espresso maker. Ahmed lay on his left side on the cot, snoring softly. Russell placed a finger to his lips and silently closed the door. He lowered himself into his task chair, slid the mouse to awaken the computer from sleep mode, then, as quietly as possible began typing an e-mail informing Phillips that Mohammed let slip he was Palestinian. In addition, he included his suspicion that Mohammed may be using the computer in some way to orchestrate an attack they were planning.

Ahmed awoke abruptly and sat up rubbing his eyes. "What are you doing?"

Russell hit the button to cancel the e-mail instead of sending it. "Ready to start again?" Gerda was watching him with apparent interest.

"Go ahead. I am going to the restroom and wash up." He eyed the computer again.

Gerda headed to the other room. A moment later her voice came over the intercom, "Ready."

"Hold on a second." He glanced around. For the first time since the ordeal started he was completely alone with the computer. He looked at the glowing screen again, his fingers hovering over the keys. He scanned the lab once more to make sure. Yes, he was completely alone. Retype and send Phillips the information? A strong gut feeling warned him not to.

Instead, he leaned forward and pressed the TALK key for the intercom. "Okay, Gerda, let's start."

They began the next level of training. One in which they would now show Mohammed a series of novel words. After speaking each one, Russell would compare the response the computer predicted based on Mohammed's neural activity against the words he actually spoke.

One hour into this session Russell suddenly realized that the network was functioning to a higher level of accuracy than he initially expected. More than that, he saw a possible way to learn where Angela might be hidden.

Russell leaned back in his chair, stretched, and let all his muscles relax for a blessed moment. Fingers laced behind his head, he asked Gerda, "What do you think? We ready to put it to the test?"

She was leaning against the rack of warm electrical equipment. "After only eight hours of training?"

Ahmed sat in his task chair, watching, listening.

Russell smiled at her cynicism. "Ah, but you're basing your estimate on how long it takes to train arm and hand movements, a situation with an almost infinite number of degrees of freedom." He turned to Ahmed. "What I mean by that is that in three-dimensional space, if you execute the same intended movement, such as reaching for a cup, but you start it from any number of different positions, each starting position requires the computer to derive a slightly different solution even if many physical elements as angular velocity and trajectory are held exactly similar. It's not quite the same for speech."

"Ahh, yes, but when a child is born—" Gerda started.

"That child has the ability to make any sound required for any known language," Russell finished the thought for her. "A Chinese baby, for example, is capable of making a perfect L sound, a skill that's lost as he begins to acquire his native language. And, as that child grows older, if he speaks only one language, the range of sounds he's capable of producing narrows to those required only for that language." Again, to Ahmed, "This is why children who learn a second language can do so with little or no accent whereas very few adults can do the same."

Gerda pushed off the rack. "And what are we doing to test this network?"

Russell assumed she knew the answer and was only asking for Ahmed's sake.

"Up to this point we've only had Mohammed pronounce letters and words that appeared on the laptop in a predetermined order. It obviously was a prescribed order, one our computer knew and anticipated. We did this pairing," he patted the mouse next to his hand, "of brain activity to his verbal response. So far, so good. The computer can now recognize every letter of the alphabet and put them together to synthesize common sounds and even some words. And, yes, these results are very encouraging. But, we haven't gone far enough. We need to take it up to a higher level of functioning."

Russell paused, concerned about how to set the stage. On the surface, Ahmed appeared to know little about computers and artificial intelligence. On the other hand he was smart and paranoid; a dangerous combination. He might even be smart enough to figure out his plan.

"We've only validated the computer's performance by changing the *order* of what it's been trained to learn. We've never tested its performance handling *novel* content. So what we need to do in this next step is to ask Mohammed a few questions and see how accurately the computer interprets his brain activity. Get it?"

The question seemed to puzzle Ahmed.

"Okay, let me walk you through it again. If we plan on detaching his head, he will immediately lose the ability to talk. Right? I mean, that's what this whole training thing is about. You follow?"

Ahmed flashed an exasperated look. "Yes, this much is perfectly clear."

Russell held up both hands. "Hey, take it easy. I'm just trying to walk you through it."

"Proceed."

"I assume you want to have pretty good confidence that the computer is accurate—that what Mohammed *intends* to say is the same as what the computer produces. With me?"

"Yes."

"Okay, then. Do you understand that there is a difference between *spontaneous* speech and *prompted* speech? What I mean is that when you read something out loud slightly different areas of the brain are involved than when you speak spontaneously."

"Yes, now I follow you. So far you have only tested the system's accuracy with prompted speech. What we need to do now, is test how well it translates spontaneous speech. Yes?"

"So, what we're going to do now is have him answer questions that are entirely different from anything the computer's been trained to recognize. Still with me?"

Gerda's eyes twinkled. "Do you want me here with you or in there?"

Her reaction told him she'd figured out what he was doing. He would have to be careful and not let her slip up.

"I need you in the other room with Mohammed."

Now came the gamble. He asked Ahmed, "You want to be in here or with Mohammed?" He wanted him out of the room, unable to read the computer's response.

Ahmed seemed to weigh the possibilities. "Is there some reason I should be in the room with him?"

"This time the door is going to be closed and I'll ask the questions over the intercom. With Raveena sleeping, I'd like someone in the room with him in case he doesn't hear the question clearly."

Ahmed nodded thoughtfully. "Yes, perhaps it is better if I

am with him." He looked from Russell to Gerda and back to Russell. "But you be with me?"

"Ja."

Ahmed thought about it a moment. "No. I cannot trust you. How will I know if the computer is translating his thoughts correctly?"

Russell said, "Shouldn't be a problem. I'll play them back over the intercom. That way you can validate the responses."

Ahmed stood. "Maybe we should wait until Hussein returns so I can stay here and make certain you are truthful."

Russell shrugged. "Have it your way. But you're the one who's been pushing this."

Ahmed thought about it. "No, you are right. Time is our enemy now. We must use every minute possible."

As Ahmed and Gerda began to leave, Russell said, "Be sure to close the door tightly."

Ahmed shot him a suspicious look. "Why? What does it matter?"

"Simple. The voice recognition software will be picking up words from Mohammed's microphone. I can't afford to have any cross talk or feedback occurring between it and the speaker in here."

Ahmed's brow furrowed, but he said nothing. He wavered a moment, then followed Gerda into the other room and shut the door.

Computer readied, Russell held up both hands, fingers crossed, and muttered, "Here goes." He adjusted the threshold sensitivity of the system so that it would only activate the voice synthesizer if the intensity of the nerve cells response exceeded a certain level while still recording more subtle activity.

He pressed the intercom button. "Ready?"

He heard Mohammed reply, "Yes."

"Remember, only Mohammed should answer the questions. If he doesn't understand, then Ahmed, you whisper it in his ear. Okay? Once I ask a question, neither of you say a word until after Mohammed has spoken. Is this clear?"

"Yes."

"Here goes." Russell typed a keyboard command, hit EN-TER. Into the microphone he asked, "What country is this?"

A line appeared on the monitor:

LAWTON: WHAT COUNTRY IS THIS?

Two lines appeared on the screen:

MOHAMMED:
CONSIDERED REPLY: UNITED STATES
ACTUAL REPLY: UNITED STATES

Russell pressed the intercom, "Here's the computer's answer."

From the speaker the voice synthesizer said, "United States."

Russell shuddered. The computer sounded exactly like Mohammed.

Gerda's voice came over the intercom. "That was correct."

Russell pressed the intercom. "Next question. What is your first name?"

The screen refreshed to:

LAWTON: NEXT QUESTION. WHAT IS YOUR FIRST NAME?

MOHAMMED:
CONSIDERED REPLY: JAMAL
ACTUAL REPLY: MOHAMMED

Russell pumped a fist in the air, whispered, "Yes!"

CHAPTER

38

RUSSELL WAS ABOUT to press the intercom switch to ask another question when the door to the lab flew open and Ahmed rushed in. "Come, I need your help. Something has happened to him."

Russell pushed out of the chair. "What do you mean?" and followed Ahmed, the surgeon, back into the other room.

Mohammed lay on his back, jaw hanging slack, short, labored gasps sending off fetid breath. His lids hung half open, his eyes showing mostly white. Russell prodded the man's shoulder and shouted, "Mohammed!"

He gave no response.

"What happened," he asked Ahmed. The only things that could devastate the man's brain so abruptly would be a cataclysmic event like a seizure or massive hemorrhage.

"I have no idea." Ahmed's voice carried a tinge of desperation.

Typical general surgeon. Totally confident until something goes wrong with the brain. Then total panic. Same thing with the eye. Something bad happens with the eye and no one knows how to deal with it other than run in circles screaming for an ophthalmologist.

He looked at Mohammed's pupils. Round and regular. "Did he have a seizure?"

Ahmed was picking at the edge of his jaw again. He stopped and started wringing his hands. "No, no. No seizure. He just," he threw both arms apart, "collapsed."

"You mean he became unconscious?"

"Yes, yes. That is it." Ahmed was fidgeting with the tie on his scrub pants now, wrapping it and unwrapping it around his index finger.

Russell gently picked up Mohammed's head. It moved easily, meaning the neck was supple, which helped rule out a subarachnoid hemorrhage or meningitis. He replaced his head on the pillow. Using his left thumb and index finger he held open Mohammed's eyelids and rocked his head back and forth, causing the eyes to move side to side in their sockets. This was a finding termed "doll's eyes" and named after the moveable eyes used in dolls in the thirties. This signaled that the midbrain was effectively detached from the cortex, which in turn, helped Russell localize which part of the nervous system was malfunctioning.

Russell turned off the overhead lights, picked up a penlight and pointed the intense beam into Mohammed's eyes one at a time. Both pupils reacted sluggishly. Although not a great sign, it was better than no reaction at all. Next, he pulled one end of a Q-tip into a cotton wisp to gently brush against his corneas. Both eyes responded by blinking although sluggishly. He pinched the skin over each hand. Both times Mohammed's hand slowly withdrew from the pain.

"Without a CT or MRI I can't be absolutely certain of the diagnosis, but with his exam so symmetrical, I put my money on a metabolic coma rather than something like a hemorrhage. Probably from a combination of liver and kidney failure."

Ahmed rubbed both hands together and let out a long breath. "This is not good. He cannot complete his work in this condition."

Russell saw an opportunity. "What exactly is he trying to do?"

Ahmed slammed his palm against the stainless steel counter. "Damn it, man! How many times need I tell you, this is no bloody concern to you." He started picking at his jaw again, at a spot that now stayed red constantly.

"The hell it isn't," Russell yelled. "I'm trying to get my daughter out of this mess. I need to know what we're trying to do here."

Ahmed's eyes turned angry. "If that is your main objective, then all you really need to do is keep him," pointing at Mohammed's still body, "functioning until . . . until we finish what we have set out to do. Otherwise you are only going to get yourself killed." He blew out a long breath through pursed lips, glanced at his comrade, paused, returned his eyes back to Russell. "Let me understand. You are saying he is unresponsive because of metabolic problems, yes?"

"Yes."

Ahmed nodded thoughtfully. "Then the solution appears to be quite simple. If what you say is true, then if we remove his head from his body, we will remove the source of his coma."

"Guess that's one way of looking at it."

"Does this mean you agree? That if we remove his head he will wake up?"

Russell shrugged. "Christ, how should I know? No one's ever done anything like this before."

"But it *should* work, should it not?"

Russell massaged the corded muscles in the back of his neck in an attempt to relieve some of the tension. "I guess . . . I guess it all depends upon how well we can dialyze the toxins out of his blood."

"But I see no other option. If we just stand here and do nothing, he will most certainly die. Is this not what you Americans like to call a sure thing?"

Russell decided the answer was obvious and didn't need his endorsement.

Ahmed stood, looking at the floor, tapping a knuckle against his upper teeth for several seconds. "Yes. We must begin at once . . ."

"Whoa. Hold on a minute. There are a lot of details we haven't discussed yet. There's probably a ton more we haven't even considered. We have a lot of planning to do before we plunge ahead."

"No. The decision is simple. The longer we procrastinate with him in this condition—"

Russell's control evaporated. "Jesusfuckingchrist! What did you expect? Your buddy here," with a thumb jerk at Mohammed, "sustained a major crush injury. You're a trauma surgeon . . ." He thought of Angela and let his frustration over the medical situation die. He sighed and dropped into the chair Raveena routinely used.

Ahmed asked, "These details? What are they exactly?"

Russell grunted a sarcastic laugh. "Details? That seems to trivialize them." He leaned forward, elbows on knees, palms pressing against his forehead. "Okay, first one. What do we do with the head?"

Ahmed looked puzzled. "What do you mean, what do we do with the head?"

Russell ran his palm over his scalp. "What do we do with the head once we detach the body? We can't just let it roll around on a pillow."

Ahmed picked harder at the spot on his jaw. "Oh. Yes, yes, of course. I see your point."

"Yeah? Well, it gets worse than that. I assume you want him looking at his laptop. How do we handle the head so he can read it and still stabilize the tubes running from his carotids to the perfusion pump? Because, if we don't stabilize them, I guarantee you they'll pull apart and then we'll have a real mess on our hands."

Before Ahmed could answer, Russell continued, "Next question: What the hell do we do with the vertebral arteries? Huh? We can't canulate them. Remember, they're encased in the bones of the vertebrae. So what do you want to do with them? Tie them off? Sure, we can do that. Probably will. But if we do and he doesn't have good collateral circulation to the brainstem, he'll end up with a lethal stroke." He stood up and paced a tight circle, the corkscrew skewering his stomach again. "Shit! We're gambling the entire outcome on that one."

"Stop it. You made your point." Ahmed slapped his hand against the counter. "That is the chance we must take. I knew this was risky when we started down this path. It is all a gamble. You are telling me nothing new. Now back up a step. Let me suggest a solution to our first problem. Can we use tongs?"

"Tongs?" Russell asked incredulously.

"Yes. The kind used to put neck fractures in traction."

"I don't get it. What are you suggesting? Hang him from the ceiling like a mobile? So he'll rotate in the breeze?" Russell let out a sarcastic laugh.

"Stop mocking me. I made a suggestion. Do you have something better in mind?"

Ahmed glared at him with an intensity he hadn't seen before. Russell's intestines chilled. He held up both hands in surrender. "Okay. I'm sorry. Calm down. I just got a little crazy."

Ahmed started in on the scrub ties again, twirling them around his finger. "God is great and he is smiling upon us. But if you refuse to help us we will be happy to simply kill your daughter," a shrug, "and then vanish. But mind you, if we do, then we will return another time. So you will have accomplished nothing."

Ahmed opened the door. "We asked for your help and you agreed, but now you are ready to give up. Fine, I will collect the others and go. How unfortunate that you will never see your only child again. Ever."

"No. Wait. Please."

Ahmed's eyebrows arched. "Yes?"

"I was thinking along the same lines, but differently. I was thinking halo. You know what I mean?"

Ahmed shook his head but closed the door instead of leaving.

Russell explained, "You know . . . one of those metal rings used to treat neck fractures with. You secure it to the head with four screws? They're usually stabilized by embedding four rods into an upper body cast. Only in this case we could build a plaster base to keep it upright."

A faint smile flitted across Ahmed's lips. "Yes, yes . . . good. Now, what are some of the other details we should be considering?"

"Just little things," relieved they were talking again, yet still seething inside. "Like the skin flap. How are we going to close off the bottom of the neck? This is where I'll need your help," purposely playing into Ahmed's ego.

"See? Even a neurosurgeon needs a general surgeon's help occasionally."

Russell bit his lip.

"We will make a simple flap like we do for an amputation."

"Okay, that helps." He paused long enough to change subjects, "And what level of the neck do you suggest we detach?"

"That decision I will leave to the neurosurgeon."

Russell nodded thoughtfully. "Then there's the problem of the spinal fluid—especially because he's going to be upright. I've got to figure out a way to close off the dura so that all the CSF doesn't drain out. If it does and we put him upright his brain will sink down in his skull, giving him, among other things, the mother of all headaches. If that happens he won't be able to do much of anything with the computer. See? There are all these little details we need to think through before we actually do the surgery."

"Yes. But for each one of them there is an answer. There! It is decided. We will move ahead with the surgery, immediately."

CHAPTER

39

RUSSELL SURVEYED THE operating room they had transformed to a miniature ICU. The hospital bed had been replaced with an operating table swiped from animal surgery. The surface was too small, of course, but it didn't matter if Mohammed's legs hung limply over the end. Also, Russell hadn't bothered to pad the sheet metal surface with an alternating pressure mattress as was customary. What did it matter if Mohammed developed a pressure ulcer during surgery? His body would be discarded afterward anyway.

Discarded. Russell shivered at the thought.

This time, Raveena—already scrubbing at the sink in the other room—would serve as scrub nurse while Gerda functioned as the circulator. Ahmed, of course, would assist.

Standing at the sink, he adjusted the water to a steady, warm flow. Not like the cold water that seemed the only option at the scrub sinks outside the real operating rooms upstairs. Why even bother with scrubbing, he wondered with a trace of bitterness. He knew the answer: Because they still had to minimize the risk of infecting the electrode or causing meningitis.

He turned to Ahmed. "What do you plan to do with the body? We can't just leave it lying around."

"There is a . . . mmm, how would I best say it? A person who is sympathetic with our cause who is also a mortician. He will retrieve the body and take it to a crematorium. There should be no problems."

"So that's what happened to Ed?" He'd been wondering how they had managed to make Ogilvy's body disappear.

"Yes."

"Okay, tell me something. How do they get rid of the ashes?" Russell wasn't quite certain, but believed morticians had to abide by strict accounting procedures for disposing ashes.

"Indeed. That is quite simple, actually. He will mix them in with others. Not all at once, mind you—that would be too obvious—but little by little. Over time Mohammad's ashes will simply vanish."

"Sweet Jesus."

Russell stole a quick glance over his shoulder at Mohammed and wondered why he felt so guilty for not having discussed surgery with him? It was more than ingrained routine that bothered him. There was also a bit of morbid curiosity . . . a fascination to probe if behind all the political rhetoric Mohammed harbored a fear of the certain death awaiting him? Suicide bombing was one thing. You pulled a cord or pushed a button and BOOM, it ended in a blink. No pain. No suffering. You didn't have to think about what was happening one second past detonation. Seeing your head detached from your body was quite another matter, Russell imagined. Perhaps the situation was more humane as things stood right this moment, with his brain living in coma. Then again, if he awoke . . .

A wave of nausea washed through his gut.

* * *

Arms and hands scrubbed, Russell removed the sterile towel from the opened wrapping and dried his hands and forearms. He picked up the surgical gown by its interior side and slipped both arms into the sleeves. With Gerda holding the back of the gown approximately closed, keeping both hands within the sleeves, his left hand picked up the right glove by its cuff and slipped his right hand inside without skin touching and contaminating the exterior. He repeated the process with his left hand. With him now sterilely gloved, Gerda jerked the back of the gown tight, eliminating excess sleeve. She then secured the Velcro stays.

Gerda had already prepped Mohammed's neck and upper chest, allowing the thick, brown, Betadine solution to drip onto the metal table and puddle. Russell scanned the room, running through one final presurgery checklist. The cardiopulmonary bypass machine was primed and ready. So was the kidney dialysis unit. Earlier, they had connected the dialysis unit into the venous return of the bypass machine so a portion of the circulating blood would be continuously dialyzed.

"One problem we haven't discussed is," Russell said, examining Mohammed's neck while planning the incision, "once we've detached the head," unable to say "*his* head," "except for a few lymph nodes in the neck, he'll have no immune system at all. He'll be set up for an immediate infection. So, to compensate, we'll have to pump him full of broad-spectrum antibiotics. And, of course, in spite of that, sooner or later he's going to develop an infection. And believe me it's going to be a beauty, too. Either a fungus or a drug-resistant bacteria. Take your pick, they'll both probably end up being lethal."

Ahmed grunted agreement while smoothing the glove tight over his right hand. "Just as long as he finishes his task."

"You're all heart, Ahmed."

"Did I ask for your opinion?"

Russell used a blue felt-tip pen to draw out the incision. It curved around the base of the neck and down over the front of the chest, forming a sort of bib. He pointed to the bib. "This should give us enough skin to close off the stump with."

Next, Russell infiltrated a mixture of Lidocaine and epinephrine along the proposed incision, not so much for the local anesthesia effect, but so the blood vessel's constricting effect of epinephrine would reduce oozing and total blood loss. He figured they would lose enough blood when connecting Mohammed's carotids to the bypass unit that he needed to do everything possible to conserve what he could.

He asked Ahmed and Raveena, "Ready?"

Both nodded.

God, forgive me for what I'm about to do.

"Okay then." Russell held out his hand. "Scalpel."

With the frontal skin flap elevated and the incision extending around as much neck as possible without rolling Mohammed onto his side, Russell turned his attention to exposing the carotid arteries and jugular veins on both sides. This dissection would be relatively easy, one he'd done numerous times during operations to remove a cervical disk.

"See here," he pointed a retractor at the large muscle attaching to the clavicle just it joins the sternum or breast bone. "The carotid is right through here." With his left hand he placed the right-angled end of the steel retractor over the muscle and pulled it away from midline. Sweeping his right index finger back and forth, he easily dissected a plane down between the trachea and the retracted muscle until his fingertip touched the warm pulsations of the large artery.

"Hold this."

After handing the retractor off to Ahmed, he sorted through the instruments until he found a self-retaining retractor to replace the handheld one.

Now, at the depth of the wound he could see the pulsating artery and, just a little to the left, the large glistening jugular vein. Using an angled vascular clamp, he dissected a plane around both vessels as far as he could go up and down the neck, freeing them. Next, he used the same clamp to thread two white vascular ties around the artery and vein. By pulling gently on each tie, he could elevate each vessel within the wound and move it side to side. Perfect.

He repeated this process on the left side.

"Now the tricky part," he muttered more to himself than his assistants. "We have the bypass ready?"

"Yes, it is." Ahmed answered.

Carefully, they laid out the four clear plastic tubes: two for the jugular veins, two for the carotids and filled them with saline, being careful to remove any air bubbles.

Using two ties per vessel and starting with the right jugular vein, Russell moved the ties apart, one above and one below the point where he would cut to slide the cannula into the vessel. One tie would be used to stop blood from flowing out of the vessel, the other to prevent air from being sucked into the bloodstream. Quickly, now, he slit the right jugular vein, inserted the cannula then deftly slipped another tie around the incision to close it over the tube. This move completed, he released the other two ties, letting the blood flow into the diversion. This sent all blood returning from the brain into the bypass machine and out of Mohammed's circulation. Quickly he worked on the two arteries, placing in each one the cannula that would send the output of the bypass machine and send it to the brain. In this manner, he was effectively draining blood from Mohammed's body directly into the bypass machine. Once there it would be oxygenated and returned to the brain.

"Okay, pull his legs up and crank the head of the table down."

Anticipating this move preoperatively, Russell had rigged

pulleys and ropes to the ceiling so that Mohammed's legs could be elevated above the level of his heart.

"Why are we doing this?" asked Raveena.

"This will allow gravity to help drain as much blood as possible from his body into the bypass machine before we isolate his body from his circulation," replied Ahmed.

Russell watched the oxygen-carrying liquid drain out, turning the skin on Mohammed's legs to the translucent pale of a dead man. The nagging nausea curling in his gut intensified. It would grow worse, he knew, and flashed on the part he dreaded most—cutting the spinal cord.

The beeps from the cardiac monitor grew faster as Mohammed's failing heart fought desperately to maintain a blood pressure in the face of an increasingly diminishingly volume to pump against. Russell listened, gruesomely fascinated with witnessing the heart's losing battle. Even in coma, the most primitive, deep-seated areas of the brainstem battled to maintain equilibrium in the body as a response to reflexive danger signals triggered by sensors in the chest and abdomen. Finally convinced he'd drained as much blood as possible from Mohammed's body, Russell quickly tied off both carotids just below each cannula.

"Scissors."

Raveena placed a pair of heavy Mayo scissors in his hand.

He lifted the first jugular vein with a pair of vascular pickups and slid the open jaws over the vessel. He hesitated, momentarily incapable of actually severing it. Up to this point the operation was reversible. The cannuli could be removed, the arteries and veins repaired, the wounds closed.

"Do it!" Ahmed said harshly.

"Do it for your daughter," Ahmed added more softly.

Russell snapped the scissors closed, transecting the vein. As he repeated this with the remaining major vessels, the increasing nausea almost gagged him.

He found the next stage—cutting the long strap muscles

of the neck—less emotionally draining. This he did easily with cautery, filling the room with the sickly odor of burnt steak. This step finished, he paused to inspect their progress. The muscles and vessels had been moved aside in the depths of the wound, exposing the trachea and esophagus and fibrous thick connective tissue covering the vertebra.

There was no turning back now.

"I figure on taking the trachea with a knife and the esophagus with the cautery. You agree with that?" He asked this with clinical detachment that sounded as if it came from someone else.

Ahmed nodded and said, "That is exactly how I would proceed," with no trace of emotion.

With both structures severed, Russell inserted the ends of two two-foot clear plastic tubes in each and sutured them into place. He draped these over the opposite side of the neck from the blood-filled tubes to the bypass machine, the presence of all these tubes now making the exposure more cumbersome.

"What are those tubes for?" Raveena asked.

"They're essentially exhaust pipes. He'll still have saliva forming in his mouth and he'll reflexively swallow. It needs to drain someplace."

With a sickened expression in her eyes, she looked away from Mohammed and began straightening instruments on her draped Mayo stand. "Yes, I guess that makes sense."

Russell glanced at the clock. They'd been working for two hours already. It felt more like ten.

"Okay, time to turn him on his side."

Knowing they would have to rotate him to sever the muscles in the back of the neck, they had not bothered to sterilely drape his torso. They had simply draped the table instead. With Gerda helping, Russell and Ahmed turned Mohammed onto his left side, giving Russell enough room to complete the skin incision around the back of the neck, connecting the left and right sides. He used the cautery to sever the remaining muscles, leaving the head attached to the body by only the vertebral column and spinal cord.

"How you doing?" He asked Ahmed and Gerda.

"He is becoming very heavy," she answered.

"Okay, roll him back. I'll finish this part with him flat on his back."

They did as instructed, giving Russell a straight-on view of the vertebral column. Again using the cautery, Russell burnt through the disk between the sixth and seventh vertebrae. Then he cut apart the tan fibrous capsule holding the facets—the joints of the spine—together, leaving only the ligaments as the sole connections between the neck and body.

"Okay, back up on his side."

With Mohammad repositioned, he finished cutting these ligaments. This left only the dura and spinal cord connecting head to body.

"Crank the head of the table down, please. I don't want to drain out any more spinal fluid than necessary during this last step." The last step: the part he'd dreaded so much.

Working from right to left with a long-handle scalpel and a #15 blade, he gently began opening the dura, entering the spinal canal itself. Then using a bipolar cautery, he cut through the delicate blood vessels that fed the spinal cord and the cord itself. Suddenly, he was out the other side, having completely transected the structure. As he did, a bolus of bile and gastric juice shot up from his stomach to the back of his mouth. He stopped and forced a swallow to push the burning fluid back down into his gut and gasped for air.

"Something wrong?" Gerda asked.

"No." He coughed from the irritation in the back of his throat, barely getting the word out. "Pull on his legs."

The gap between torso and neck expanded in surreal slow motion. He heard a loud thump but forced himself to look away, knowing full well what had just happened: The body had fallen off the short table onto the cement floor.

Forcing his concentration back on task, he used a 0-0 Vicryl suture to tie off the dura like the end of a sausage. It seemed as if he was working in a dream state now, the moves running on automatic pilot.

After repositioning the tubes to either side of the stump of the neck, he used the flap of skin from the chest to close the skin in layers; first an inverted suture through the deep layer, then staples through the outer layer, the dermis. Extra skin he trimmed away with the cautery.

Surgery completed, he attached the halo device to the skull, being careful to avoid the craniotomy wound and wires from the electrodes. Next he secured the struts to the metal table with C-clamps.

Finished.

He stood back to take his first real look at what he'd done.

The halo suspended Mohammed's head upright in space. The tubes—six in all—exited the base of the neck. The bundles of recording wires emanating from the craniotomy wound were fed into the amplifiers and then to the computers in the other room.

Mohammed's eyes were closed, a strangely peaceful expression on his face.

Russell ripped off his gloves and tore apart the ties holding the back of the gown together and wadded them into a large blue bundle.

Ahmed asked, "How long do you think it will take for him to come around?"

Exhausted, Russell threw the bunch into the corner. "Look at him! What makes you think he'll ever wake up?"

PHILLIPS USED THE flat of her palm to bang on the thick, electromagnetically shielded door to Lawton's lab. Delorenti stood, feet slightly apart, right thumbnail nervously tapping the butt of the flat black Glock holstered on his belt. Ever since the voiceprint Lawton had sent confirmed that the Georgetown trauma victim was probably Jamal Azzam, the risk associated with this investigation had ratcheted up several notches, making them both on edge.

"What do you think?" Phillips asked.

"I say try the door. It's either locked or unlocked. Either way, we're going in. Want me to open it?"

"No, I can handle it. But back me up."

Mentally, she quickly reviewed Lawton's story. She knew from the prior visits that this was the lab holding the computers. The adjoining room, the one to their right, held Jamal Azzam's damaged body—assuming, of course, they hadn't attempted to detach his head yet. God only knew how that debacle would end up.

Heart pounding with the anxiety of entering a potentially dangerous situation, she gripped the brushed-aluminum

handle and pushed the door. After a soft *whoosh*, as if breaking a seal, it swung noiselessly inward, exposing a wedge of
laboratory. Warm, stuffy, electronics-scented air wafted out.
Phillips held up her hand, signaling Delorenti to remain
silent. For a few beats she waited, watched, and listened intently for a response. She saw no movement and heard no
sounds other than the white-noise hum of the computers'
cooling fans.

She had two options: call "hello" or walk in. Maybe this
was turning out to be an unanticipated opportunity. She
pushed the door's arc wider, exposing more of the warm
stuffy room. She saw a body and looked closer. Over against
the far wall was a cot with a woman curled up on her side. It
took a second, but she recognized her as . . . what was her
name? German. Fetz? Yes, Fetz. Gerda Fetz. Was she dead?
A moment later she noticed her chest rise and fall with deep
slow breaths. Lips pressed tightly shut, she pointed, drawing
Delorenti's attention to the still figure and signaled him to
stay silent before sending him a questioning glance.

He nodded, confirming what she'd just transmitted.

She stood motionless, watching the woman breathe. Apparently Fetz was sleeping soundly. Phillips stepped further
into the lab and checked behind the door, making certain she
wasn't leading Delorenti into a trap. So far it did not appear
to be.

She raised an index finger to her lips and then waved Delorenti in. Without a sound, he stepped in, quickly did a 360-
survey of the area before tiptoeing to an electrical wall outlet
just above one stainless steel countertop. He pulled a small
black transformer with a length of black insulated twin wire
from his coat pocket and plugged it into the outlet, then coiled
the wire and set it on the counter, making the voice-activated
transmitter appear like a common cell phone charger.

Phillips heard the rustle of fabric and instinctively gripped
the stock of her Glock. She turned toward the sound. Fetz

changed positions slightly, drew in a deep breath and exhaled.

Phillips nodded at Delorenti. He also was gripping his weapon in anticipation. He returned the acknowledgment, pulled a second transformer from his other blazer pocket. In two quick long steps he was at the opposite wall, inserting the prongs into the 120-volt AC outlet.

Satisfied, they backed out into the hallway, silently pulling the door tightly closed behind them. They said nothing until stepping into bright sunlight as they exited the elevator four floors above the lab where the federal police had discreetly secured a small conference room for setting up their listening and recording devices.

Phillips asked Delorenti, "Tell me something. If that room's electromagnetically shielded, how the hell are those things supposed to work?"

He shot her his techie grin. "They don't transmit through the air like most devices. They transmit through the AC power lines. That's where we'll pick it up from."

"Sweet!"

"Wake up!"

Russell's consciousness began ascending from a void so deep and black that he'd been unaware of time. Something was rocking his shoulder back and forth. He realized he was on his left side curled tightly into the fetal position. He wanted to ignore the intrusion and return to the warm weightless void he was being dragged from.

"Russell, wake up!"

When he tried to stir a lightening bolt jabbed the muscles in the back of his neck, making him acutely aware his head was no longer supported by a pillow. He tried moving again, this time more gingerly, his right hand massaging the stiff neck muscles. The inside of his mouth felt like a dusty country road in August.

"What?" he croaked milliseconds before the memory of the operation flooded his mind. "Mohammed died?" then wondered if a detached head could really be considered alive? Now there was a question for the philosophers and medical ethicists.

He blinked, knuckled dried protein from both eyes, blinked again, and willed his squinting eyes to focus in the blinding light. Gerda stood beside the single bed in the call room, a cup of dreadful vending machine coffee in hand—the kind that assimilated the taste of the cardboard cup the moment it was dispensed. Hussein was also standing there, just as he had been when Russell had curled up to sleep.

"No, no, no . . . this is the really incredible thing . . . he is awake!"

Russell pushed up, swung his legs over the side of the bed and leaned forward, elbows on knees, "Awake?" He continued massaging the sore neck muscles.

She shoved the steaming coffee toward him. "Ja! And he and Ahmed are talking to each other."

He gratefully accepted her offering, not so much for the awful, watery coffee facsimile, but because of needing to wet his mouth. He ignored the taste and sipped the hot liquid before setting down the cup. He finger-combed his short brown hair and inhaled deeply. For a moment he sat rigidly upright, letting his brain acclimate to being fully awake and his body vertical.

He was shocked to admit to himself a perverse curiosity in witnessing Mohammad's decapitated head functioning—a revelation he found simultaneously disgusting yet motivating. He pushed off the bed and headed for the showers, Hussein in tow.

Russell entered the lab. Gerda sat at the main computer watching the monitor. Over the speaker came a disembodied voice he recognized as the speech-synthesized interpretation of Mohammed's brain activity.

Gerda glanced up at him. "*Mein Gott*, have you been in there yet?" with a nod at the door between the labs.

"No. I wanted to stop by here first." Soon as the words were out, he realized the real reason for the detour—to delay coming face-to-face with the man he'd decapitated.

"He is programming."

"Huh?" Russell's attention snapped back to Gerda.

"Ja. Mohammed. He is programming a computer."

"How the hell can he do that without hands?"

Russell wasn't paying any attention to Mohammed's words. Instead he was studying the main computer monitor. It looked as if Mohammed was apparently telling Ahmed what to type into his laptop.

"But look at this," Gerda continued, pointing at the screen, "there is a problem. Your computer is interpreting more words than makes sense. What does this mean?"

He studied the screen a few seconds, trying to make sense of what he saw. Then he realized what she was referring to. "Yes, uh huh, I see that."

"Does this mean it is not functioning properly?"

He snuck a glance over his right shoulder. Hussein was watching and listening from the far corner, right hand holding his pistol.

"Probably means we didn't have enough time to train the network correctly," he lied. "It's just random noise."

As Russell opened the door to the adjoining room the voices inside stopped immediately. Ahmed and Raveena turned quickly to look, fear momentarily flashing across their eyes until they recognized him.

"Damn it! Knock first! Do that again and you bloody well might get yourself killed," Ahmed said, relief in his eyes.

Only then did Russell look directly at Mohammed's head. It was suspended in the halo, just as he'd left it. Unable to make direct eye contact, Russell looked past him at the wall. He realized Mohammed was ignoring him, too, preferring to study the laptop on the table in front of him. Or maybe he was simply engrossed in his work. Did it really matter? Ahmed was typing into another computer on his lap.

Mohammed spoke a computer command to Ahmed. But instead of coming from his mouth, the synthesized voice came from the ceiling-mounted speaker. What made it even more surreal was that Mohammed's minor jaw and lip movements were out of synch with the synthesized voice, like you sometimes see in translated foreign films. Mohammed's eyes darted back and forth across the screen as he watched Ahmed type in the command.

The sight sent a chill burrowing between Russell's shoulder blades.

The voice said, "Ahmed! You are not paying attention."

Ahmed held up a hand. "Wait. We can wait a moment." He glared at Russell. "Stop listening to what is being said. This is none of your business. The less you know, the better your chances of surviving."

Russell's gut tightened, his palms suddenly needing to be wiped. He resisted the urge, knowing it would give him away. "I just wanted to see for myself. Gerda woke me up to tell me the good news."

"Now that you are here, there is a problem. Listen." Then to Ahmed: "Please repeat the last command."

Russell listened to the command and shrugged. "Since I don't know what he's intending to say, I can't comment."

"You don't appreciate the extra words being said?" Ahmed asked incredulously.

Russell shrugged, trying for his most innocent expression. "If you say the computer is inserting extra words, I believe you. But, as I just said, without a frame of reference, I can't tell you how bad the problem is. You want me to spend time tweaking the network?"

"No! We do not have any extra time. The end of our task is drawing near."

Russell took a step backward, toward the lab. "Fine by me, but remember, we never really finished training the network. So maybe there are some bugs in it. What can I say?"

Ahmed eyed him suspiciously for several seconds before waving his hand toward the opened door. "Get out! Close that door!" Then, with lips curled into a curiously cunning smile, he told Hussein, "Stay a moment."

Russell paused, afraid of what might be taking place.

Ahmed turned to him. "You did not hear me? Out!"

CHAPTER

41

RUSSELL SLOWLY CLOSED the door separating the two laboratories, then stood still, looking at the deadbolt, waiting to see if it would turn from the other side. Something was brewing. He'd seen it in the look Ahmed gave Hussein and immediately thought of Angela and worried. Were they done and ready to launch their attack?

He warned himself to not give up hope and reminded himself that at least part of his plan was working. But was he already out of time?

Something brushed his arm. Russell jerked it away, spun around, ready to strike out. Gerda stepped back in self-defense. "It is just me."

He lowered his arm. "Sorry, I . . ."

"They do not need us so much now that Mohammed is working for them again, Ja?"

"What are you saying? We're expendable? Is that just sinking in? I thought we both knew that from the get-go."

She nodded agreement. "Yes. All the more reason we must do something to save ourselves and we must do it quickly."

"Yes, but what? Contact the FBI? The police? We do that and we lose everything."

"We must do *something*."

"I'm open to suggestions."

"I have none, but there has to be a solution to our problem. We must brainstorm, like we do during our projects."

But Russell couldn't brainstorm. His mind kept snapping back to Angela, and with Gerda now standing next to him, Gerhard.

"Gerhard," he muttered.

"What?"

He snapped his fingers a couple times, thinking. "Hold on a second."

An idea began germinating. He glanced around the overheated room, just to make certain they were really alone. Strange, they had been left alone together without one of the terrorists standing guard. A trap of some sort? He tapped her shoulder and motioned for her to follow him into the sound isolation chamber. Once inside, he closed the door and positioned himself to see through the double-paned Plexiglas into the room just in case Ahmed or Hussein came looking for them.

He whispered quickly, "The e-mails. Do you still have them?"

"What e-mails?"

"The ones they sent you when this first started. The ones with Gerhard's pictures."

She thought a beat. "Ja. They are still intact."

He eyed the door and licked his lips. "Here's the deal," and lowered his voice even further. He told her about his FBI interrogation, about the e-mail address Phillips had supplied for sending information.

"What I'm thinking is, we forward the actual e-mail he sent you to the FBI. They have computer specialists who might be able to trace the address back to the person in Germany who sent it. From there they might be able to work their way back to this group."

She nodded. "Ja, that sounds like a reasonable idea. Good for Gerhard, but this does not help find Angela, I think."

"Yes, but at least it's *something*. It's a start. You think you can retrieve them?"

"I think so." She reached for the door handle, her eyes showing the first glimmer of real hope since the nightmare began. "I will do it now."

Russell dropped into the chair in front of the computer, kicking himself for not having thought of this earlier. How much time had he wasted by overlooking this obvious lead? He quickly composed an e-mail to Phillips explaining the logic behind forwarding Gerda's e-mail. He asked Gerda, "What's your password?" It took her only seconds to move the deleted files into her e-mail in-box.

After including her e-mail address and password in the message, he hit SEND and watched to make certain the message had actually been sent before backing out of Outlook. Next, he wiped out any trace of the e-mail on his own computer.

A moment later, the door to the other lab banged open. Gun in hand, Hussein burst into the room. Ahmed followed. Hussein pressed the suppressor barrel against Gerda's temple, yelled at Russell, "Hands off the keyboard!"

Ahmed asked, "Just how stupid do you believe we are?"

RUSSELL TRIED FRANTICALLY to think of a possible reason for their anger other than the obvious. He came up blank while slowly withdrawing his trembling fingers from the keyboard. If this was about the e-mail, how could they possibly know? He'd sent it only a minute or so ago.

Ahmed barked something at Hussein who withdrew the gun a few inches from Gerda's forehead but did not step back or lower it.

Ahmed then said to Russell, "It was a stupid attempt you just made. But it does tell us some important pieces of information. When you were questioned by the FBI you obviously told them about us."

"What the hell are you talking about?" Russell asked, trying to feign innocence.

"What do you think I am talking about? The e-mail you just sent your friend Agent Phillips."

Fighting the urge to glance at Gerda, he kept his eyes on Ahmed. How the hell did they know? Then it hit: the two labs were set up for wireless networking. They were monitoring his e-mail. But how did they crack the encryption?

"The address?" Ahmed continued with a tone of barely controlled anger, "do you really think we are so stupid as to leave an address that can be traced?"

Russell knew the question was better left unanswered. The anxiety freezing his gut intensified. He thought of Angela. What would happen to her now? "Look . . ." he started to say but found no words readily came.

"You have now broken the rules and so now one of you must pay the price."

"No, wait!" Russell raised his hands, without any idea what he could possibly bargain with.

Gerda sat motionless, her face painted in grim stoicism, eyes fixed on the gun in Hussein's hand.

Ahmed pointed to the sound attenuation chamber. "In there."

"What? What are you going to do?"

"I said, in there. Now, go!"

"No. I refuse to move unless you tell us what you're planning to do."

Jaw muscles rippling, eyes narrowed to slits, Ahmed jabbed a straightened finger directly at Russell. "I will tell you this. If you do not move into that chamber with Fetz right now, I will have Hussein shoot her immediately. It will be your doing."

Russell turned, held out a hand to Gerda. "Come on Gerda. Let's go."

After stepping into the chamber, Ahmed closed and locked the door from the outside. Russell watched as Ahmed and Hussein moved out of sight. He sat down on the ribbed rubber floor mat, back against acoustical tiles and hugged his knees. Gerda did likewise but in the opposite direction so they were side by side, facing each other.

"Oh, Gerda, . . . I'm so sorry."

Her eyes had that ten-thousand-yard stare he'd seen all too often in patients to whom he'd just broken bad news.

"Gerda?"

"I am a dead woman," she said after a few beats, her voice trembling with fear.

"No, don't say that. I don't think they know what they want to do yet."

"Yes they do. They want revenge. They want blood. What is there to do but to kill one of us? They cannot afford to kill you yet because they may still need you. But me? Ach, they can put a bullet in my head and, in so doing, teach you an important lesson. No, I am dead."

"Gerda, please don't talk like that. There's still hope."

She looked at him, shook her head. "You will never learn. Always the optimist. You are wrong, Russell. You will see."

Russell wanted to put his hand on her arm and tell her again how sorry he was for having provoked this situation, but knew that this small act would only serve to further reinforce her fear. Instead, he closed both eyes and rested his forehead against both knees and tried to blank his mind from thoughts of the horror that would surely come.

With the door to the chamber locked, Ahmed paused to calm himself.

"We should simply kill them and leave," Hussein said flatly.

Raveena stood in the doorway between the labs, saying nothing.

Ahmed touched an index finger to his lips, then swept it around the room, conveying his suspicions. "I believe we should go for coffee now. You," pointing at Raveena. "Stay with Mohammed."

Four floors above the lab, in a conference room she had procured for the surveillance, Phillips shot Delorenti and a technician a questioning look as they listened to Ahmed and Hussein's conversation. She pulled out her Blackberry.

"Damnit, I had the ring muted." She pressed a button and eyed it. "Oh, my god. He sent a text message and they caught him at it!"

Ahmed and Hussein each carried a mug of steaming coffee to a relatively isolated table at the far end of the noisy cafeteria. Ahmed set down his coffee on the cream-colored Formica tabletop and held out his hand to Hussein. "The cell phone."

Several minutes later, after two calls, he set the phone on the table between them. "Now we wait."

Hussein sat cracking his knuckles, eyeing Ahmed with contempt.

"You disagree with my actions?" Ahmed asked, already suspecting the answer.

"I do not understand," Hussein whispered harshly in their native language, "why we do not simply kill them and continue with our plan . . . the one we agreed to use if Jamal became incapable of completing his part. We discussed this thoroughly the day he was injured."

Ahmed glared at Hussein's hand a beat before answering. He hated the sound, that *pop pop pop* of knuckles cracking. Was the bastard doing it simply to annoy him or did anxiety compel him to do it?

"Because, my friend, we know our work's effect will be much more potent if Jamal can paralyze their emergency communications."

"Yes, yes," Hussein waved an impatient hand, "we have been through all that. It is obvious. But that was the plan before we were certain Lawton betrayed us. The situation is completely different now. We have no idea how much the FBI knows. They may arrest us at any moment. Then all will be lost. I say kill them all and accelerate the attack before they have their chance to ruin it."

Ahmed nodded appreciatively, as if considering the suggestion. Instead, he was relishing his own plan for finally

dealing with Hussein. "You are right, of course. But hear me
out first and then, if you do not agree with what I am doing,
we will proceed as you suggest."

"You will really honor that?"

Ahmed nodded.

Hussein smiled relief, his hand relaxing. "Then tell me."

Russell's mind was jarred back to reality by a bang on the
door. How long had his consciousness been drifting in and out
of a dreamlike state? He glanced at Gerda then up to see the
door swing open.

Ahmed said, "Get out," with a hand wave.

Russell slowly pushed up on sore knees and a numb butt
and followed Gerda into the overheated room. Gerda kept
her head up, her fiery eyes locked onto Ahmed. If they were
going to shoot her, she was not giving them the satisfaction
of seeing her fear.

Hussein handed her his cell phone. "Here. See for yourself."

Russell put his hand gently on her left shoulder and
looked over her right shoulder at the digital photo. It showed
a full facial close-up of Gerhard, a bullet hole through his
forehead, eyes swollen with "raccoon eye" bruises typical of
basal skull fractures.

From deep within Gerda a crescendoing wail culminated
in a shriek as she threw the camera at Ahmed then lunged
at him.

CHAPTER 43

"IHR ARSCHLÖCHER!" GERDA'S fingers clawed for Ahmed's neck.

Russell heard *thump*, saw Gerda's body stiffen as both arms flexed at the elbows and wrists. Her hands clenched as her knees buckled, sending her crashing onto the concrete floor, a pulsating stream of bright red arterial blood spurting from her right temple.

Russell screamed, "Gerda," and dropped to his knees beside her. He cradled her head in both hands, clinically aware of her neck stiffness and that both her arms were slowly transitioning from tightly flexed to rigidly fully extended in a rapid progression through the obvious phases of brainstem herniation. There was nothing he could do to save her from dying in his arms.

He squinted through tear-distorted vision at Hussein. The bastard still stood spread-legged, the gun in a two-handed grip but now trained on Russell's head. "Asshole," he said, finishing Gerda's last thought. "You didn't have to kill her."

* * *

Phillips muttered, "Sweet Jesus! They just capped Fetz."

Delorenti gave a woeful headshake. "Man, oh, man! Sure sounds like it."

Both technicians looked from Phillips to Delorenti, then back again as if waiting for instructions. One offered, "We were rolling the entire time. That entire scene's been totally documented, just in case you think you might want to move on them."

Delorenti's right eyebrow rose, silently asking Phillips, "Well?"

Phillips ran her right palm from her forehead back over her closely cropped hair, thinking, *Shit!*

She shot him a hard look. "Damn it, Delorenti. You know better than that," hoping he'd read just how pissed she was for siding with them, thereby dumping the whole responsibility for saying no in her lap.

She added, "Too soon."

She thought about how that sounded and turned to the tech who'd asked the unstated question. "Do that and we take down two, maybe three members of a cell." She shook her head. "Not nearly good enough. On the other hand, we wait and stay on them, we have the possibility of taking down the entire cell."

The technician just stared back. He didn't have to say a thing, the look said it all: Heartless bitch.

Delorenti kicked in, "Very true, Sandra, but the thing is, this isn't just two or three low-level soldiers we're talking about here. That's Jamal Azzam down there," pointing at the floor as if sending a laser ray four flights down to Lawton's basement laboratory.

"Point taken. But from what we know, no matter what, Azzam is not getting out of there alive, so that particular point is moot." Fists clenched, she thought of Tyrell, what it

must've been like trapped on the 71st floor of Tower One of
the World Trade Center, knowing there was no way out of
the burning, crumbling building.

"I'm just saying—"

"I don't want to hear it, Tony." Her hand sliced the air.
"Who's running this op, you or me?"

"Don't start that shit with me, Sandra."

"Then stop fucking with me, *Tony*," throwing the first-
name bullshit right back at him. "You knew our game plan
from the start. We're not changing now because one goddamned hostage gets wasted. You know as well as I do, collateral damage is a risk inherent in every hostage situation.
That's why they're called hostages. So back the hell off and
stay focused."

"But this isn't a typical hostage situation."

She hated to pull rank, but with two techs sizing them up
she felt forced to. "I said back the hell off and I mean it!"

CHAPTER
44

RUSSELL THOUGHT, *CHRIST* Almighty, *it's unraveling* as a bolt of fear skewered his gut. Was Angela next? No. If they had killed her, they would've showed him a picture like they had Gerda. Then again, not necessarily. Not if they weren't done with him, yet. But what was there left to do? Frantically he tried to think through his options. He came up with only one thing: somehow he needed to get a call or message to the FBI to ask for help. Call Special Agent . . . Phillips? Yeah, Phillips's her name. Yes, he had to somehow reach a phone.

Russell gently rested Gerda's lifeless head on the liver-colored linoleum before releasing her. The bleeding had stopped when her blood pressure zeroed out. He held up his palms and inspected them. Both hands were painted with her blood, front and back. In fact, so were the thighs of his scrubs. Giving him a perfectly reasonable excuse to leave for a few minutes.

"I need to go wash up . . ." holding out his hand for Hussein to see, as if he were totally unaware of the fact, "you know . . . change scrubs."

Ahmed dialed his cell phone, listened, pulled it away from

his ear to look at the screen, then put it back against his head. He paused and then he barked sharp words at Hussein before shoving the useless phone back in his pocket. He'd obviously forgotten the lab was a cellular dead zone. He grabbed the laboratory landline and dialed, his free hand picking more vigorously at his jaw again. Pick, pick, pick. He glanced around the lab, shifted weight between feet like a fighter ready for round one and began rubbing at the spot again.

Hussein remained silent, still aiming the gun at Russell, eyes dancing with the urge to shoot.

Russell kept his hands held above his head, believing Hussein would use any quick move as reason enough to shoot him. "I'm getting up now," and slowly stood up. "Look, I need to wash up."

Neither Ahmed or Hussein answered.

Russell made direct eye contact with Hussein and shouted, "Hey, take it easy Hussein . . . I'm talking to you and I'm not going to make any fast moves, see?" He waved his palms like a gospel singer. "Ahmed, tell your buddy I need to go wash up. Look . . . see . . . blood." He reached down, pulled up his pant leg a couple inches. "Even my scrubs are soaked. I need to change. Understand?" He took one slow, tentative step toward the door.

Hussein stepped directly in front of him and waved him away with the gun. "You are staying here and not moving from this room."

"For godsake, Hussein, look at me. I need to get this blood off. Jesus, Ahmed, will you please tell Hussein I need to go wash up."

"Use that sink." Hussein waved the gun at the counter.

Talking excitedly on the phone now, Ahmed frowned at Russell while jabbing an index finger at the floor in a clear signal to stay put.

"But, my scrubs . . ."

Ahmed slammed the phone back into the cradle. Eyes

wide, pupils dilated like a meth addict, he said, "Do as Hussein says. You are not leaving this room. Not until we finish. That should not be too long now. In the meantime," he glanced at his wristwatch, "I have an important meeting to attend."

Russell pleaded, "Five minutes, that's all I need. Come on, Ahmed. Look, I have to take a leak. Just let me run up to the dressing room, take a leak and put on new scrubs."

Ahmed's eyes grew harder. "No! That's final. You need to urinate, use the bloody sink," his English accent stronger now.

"But—"

"No!" Ahmed shouted again. "I have given Hussein permission to kill you should you try to leave. And I am certain he will make good use of that order. In the meantime I will fetch you a fresh pair of scrubs." Then, to Hussein: "Yusuf will be coming for the body. Let him and *only* him in. When I return I will help Mohammed finish. We're almost there."

Strange, Russell thought, give Hussein orders in English? Until now, they had always communicated in what he presumed was their native language.

"Is that the mortician?" Russell asked, remembering that someone came for Mohammed's body. The thought of Gerda's remains being cremated and then discarded piecemeal by the terrorists was completely unacceptable.

"Yes." Ahmed held out his hand at Hussein. "Car keys, please."

"No. I don't want you do it that way. Please. Let me make the arrangements for her."

"No. It is out of the question." Ahmed shook his head.

Ahmed cracked the door and stole a look into the hallway. Then, to Hussein he said, "Do not . . . I repeat do *not* open this door for anyone but Yusef. I will return as soon as I can and when I do, we will finish our task."

Sandra Phillips pressed the black rubber transmit button on a walkie talkie. "Hamilton?"

The squelch broke. "Roger."

"Target number one is moving. I believe he might be planning on using the rental we spotted in P3."

"Affirmative. I'm on it."

Shawn Hamilton sat in the nondescript unmarked pursuit car and watched the burgundy Toyota rental exit the parking garage and head for the Rockville Pike exit. As the car drove past, he got a clear look at the driver and identified him as the one Lawton had called Ahmed. He picked up the hand-held transceiver. "Phillips?"

"Affirmative."

"I have a visual confirmation on our target. You are correct. He is suspect number one and he is driving the rental."

"Excellent. We'll have the second and third cars within two to three blocks if you need them."

Hamilton rapidly clicked the transmit button twice to confirm receipt of the message before shifting the transmission into drive and pulling onto the same road.

After a right turn onto Rockville Pike traffic the Toyota continued straight toward D.C. Traffic was thick enough to convince Hamilton he could tail the target without being noticed. After several miles the road transitioned into Wisconsin Avenue. The Toyota continued straight ahead.

The radio squelch broke. "Hamilton, you have a copy?"

Hamilton picked up the handheld with his right hand, his left remaining on the steering wheel. "Affirmative."

"You in need of assistance?"

"Negatory. This guy has no idea he's being followed."

"You absolutely certain?"

"Affirmatory."

They were approaching the intersection of Wisconsin with Massachusetts Avenue now, in the shadow of the National Cathedral. The Toyota turned left onto Massachusetts, heading into the heart of the District. For a moment, Hamilton thought he'd lost the car but then noticed it had moved into the left-hand lane. He switched lanes just before a gap in traffic closed and would have forced him to stay in the non-turn lane.

As they passed Union Station the Toyota's left turn signal began blinking and the car slowed to wait for a break in traffic to open up. It came. He then turned onto 2nd Street NE but the streetlight changed before Hamilton could cross the intersection, freezing him on Massachusetts.

"Damn it!" Hamilton slapped the steering wheel and watched helplessly as his target's car turned left and continued on. He considered radioing the other two cars and requesting assistance but felt comfortable with the GPS tracking device they had planted on the car's undersurface. As long as the suspect didn't move too far ahead, he would be able to track and catch up with him.

Soon as the light changed, Hamilton punched the gas and turned, inserting his vehicle into the oncoming lane and stopping traffic. Several horns blew in protest. He accelerated. Union Station was now on his left, the confluence of train tracks stretching out beyond that as he entered an area of mostly warehouses and industrial buildings, the streets now only sparsely populated with traffic. Using the GPS system for directions, he made a turn, then another into a narrow street. He hit the brakes and stopped. A half block ahead a truck completely blocked the street.

"Shit, shit, shit." He slammed the steering wheel with his palm again. The area was getting dicey. Better ask for assistance from the backup. He reached for the radio. Just then a man, face hidden by a black ski mask, appeared at the driver side window aiming a gun at his head. Before Hamilton could press the transmit button to request help, the passenger door was jerked open. Another hooded figure ordered, "Out of the car."

CHAPTER

45

RUSSELL SAT IN the task chair in front of the work area looking at the nineteen-inch Samsung. Hussein sat in Gerda's chair watching him. Between them Gerda remained sprawled on the floor where he'd left her after placing her head on a seat cushion and covering her face with her jacket.

A heavy foreboding had congealed in his gut, making each second that ticked by move even more slowly than the previous one. He needed to find a way to make the phone call to Phillips. "Come on, Hussein, let me change. You can watch everything I do."

Hussein did not even consider his request. "No. And no using the computer, either."

Russell sucked a deep breath, stretched both arms over his head with his fingers interlaced and started to stand.

"Sit!" Hussein aimed the gun at his head again.

Russell sank back into the chair. "Where did Ahmed go?"

Hussein smiled vaguely but said nothing.

Through the open door to the adjoining lab, Russell could see Mohammed's suspended head, eyes closed, apparently sleeping. The angle gave his face an almost peaceful appearance. Raveena was curled up in the chair, legs tucked under her, both eyes also closed. Given any other circumstance, the setting might even seem tranquil.

Phillips answered her cell phone before it had a second chance to ring. "Phillips."

She listened, nodding a couple times, then punched off and folded the phone shut. "Goddamn him. I told him to be careful!"

Both technicians and Delorenti stared at her, their expressions ones of thin-lipped concern. Delorenti asked, "What?"

"They found Shawn's car a couple blocks from the train station."

Delorenti cringed. "And Shawn?"

She shook her head. "His cell phone was in the front seat."

"Any witnesses?"

"They're working on that now, but so far nobody saw nothing."

Three thumps came from the door to the hall. Russell and Hussein jerked bolt upright in unison. Hussein shot him a questioning glance and nodded at the CCTV. "Yusef?"

Russell leaned forward to inspect the screen. He shook his head. "No. It's Ahmed."

Hussein threw the deadbolt and pulled open the heavy door. Ahmed quickly stepped inside the warm lab and closed it before Hussein had the chance to do so. He ordered, "Lock it," and then started for the other room. He suddenly stopped moving and glared at Russell a moment, a similar vague smile on his lips.

Russell asked, "What?"

Ahmed then scowled at Gerda's body and nodded, as if realizing something. He muttered, "Yusef has not come yet," before storming off to Mohammed's room.

Hussein called after him but Ahmed slammed the door before letting out a curt retort.

The feeling of doom occupying the pit of Russell's stomach intensified. He turned to stare at the nineteen-inch flatscreen Samsung. He had to reach a phone. His frustration and feeling of helplessness grew with every second that ticked past. Gerda had been right. They should have simply refused to help. Yes, they probably would've been killed outright, but Gerda was now dead. He and Angela would be next. He had failed before getting a chance to carry out his plan. The first part of it—overtraining the computer—had gone beautifully. The second part—tricking Mohammed—had failed.

His strategy was elegantly simple and relied on how we speak. As we decide what we intend to say, the speech area in our brain begins sending signals "downstream" to those structures that actually form the sounds; our lips, tongue, and larynx. If we suddenly change a word before uttering it, those signal are replaced with new ones. But those signals—or thoughts, as they are—actually exist in our brain milliseconds before being replaced by the corrected thought. And this means the computer should be able to interpret these "neural traces" before they vanish.

Put another way, when asked a question our automatic first response is the truthful answer. To lie requires an active act of deception. And as far as what happens in our brain, the truthful response exists fleetingly in our neural circuits before being replaced by the fabrication. Russell had hoped to discover where they had Angela hidden by exploiting this phenomenon. But he hadn't had the chance. And right now it didn't look like he would get another chance.

Time had run out. He was a dead man. What did he have to lose at this point? Why not do something to stop their attack? The only thing he could think to do is cut off Mohammed's ability to speak. It would mean, however, his and Angela's life.

He sucked a deep breath and confirmed the decision to

move ahead. He asked Hussein, "Hey, did someone just knock at the door?"

Hussein glanced up from the newspaper he was reading. "I did not hear any knock."

"Yeah, sure. I heard it."

"I am not opening the door unless I have to. Check your video monitor to see if someone is out there."

"I did, but they could be standing off to the side. You're still expecting Yusef, aren't you? Maybe it's him."

Hussein pulled the gun from his waistband and shot Russell a look. "Stay in your chair. If you attempt to get up I will shoot you." He moved to the door.

"Understood."

Hussein eyed him a moment longer before throwing the deadbolt. He opened the door and leaned into the hall. As he did this, Russell quickly typed a command into the computer, disabling the speech synthesizer and silencing any words Mohammed might think.

Hussein closed the door and stood for a moment looking at Russell, his left hand working through the knuckles again, *pop pop pop.*

Russell shrugged. "Sorry. Guess I was mistaken."

Russell heard the door to the other lab scrape open and saw Hussein straighten up. Ahmed rushed into view, panic etched into his face, Raveena behind him, stretching to peer over his shoulder.

"We are having problems, I need you to come see Mohammed," Ahmed said, nervously wringing both hands together.

Russell stood up slowly, as if concerned. "What kind of problems?"

Ahmed glanced toward the room where Mohammed's head hung suspended in the air by a halo brace, tubes running in and out of the neck stump. His tongue flicked over his lips. "He stopped talking."

"Stopped talking? How? What happened?"

"He was talking normally and then just seemed to stop." Ahmed cocked his head and studied Russell a moment. "You! Did you do something to disable the system?"

Hussein started to say something but Ahmed silenced him with a glare. Hussein sat back, crossed both arms across his chest and shot Ahmed an equally defiant expression.

"Well?" Ahmed asked.

"What could I possibly do?" Russell looked at Hussein. "He's been watching me the whole time."

Hussein nodded agreement.

Ahmed asked, "Then what is causing Mohammed to not speak?"

Russell made like he was checking something on the monitor. "Could be a lot of things."

"Then you must diagnose and fix the problem. We are so close to being done . . . we only need a few more minutes."

"Forget it. I'm done helping you. Go ahead and kill me. That's what you've been planning to do all along anyway, isn't it." It wasn't a question.

Ahmed's expression hardened. "Bloody hell! Get in here right now and solve the problem!"

Hussein grinned and watched the interaction. His knuckle cracking picked up tempo.

Ahmed: "Is that what you wish? For me to have Hussein shoot you now?"

"Like I just said, you've been planning on killing me anyway. What the hell difference does it make if I die now or later? At least this way I get the pleasure of knowing you can't finish your plans. Right?"

Ahmed nodded slowly. "Yes, we can kill you but what about Angela? Do you wish her to die by being buried alive? Because that is exactly what we will do."

"Yeah? How do I know you haven't killed her already?"

Russell held Ahmed's glare, determined to not flinch or look away.

Ahmed said, "I believe you did something to stop him speaking. So, you can fix it. Yes?"

"Why would I do that? Why do you not think it is something to do with Mohammed?"

"Like?"

"Could be a lot of things. A hemorrhage, for example. Right where the electrodes touch the brain. He's probably lost all his platelets by now and can't clot anymore. Which was a problem I warned you about at the very beginning."

"If it were that, could you do something about it?"

Russell shrugged. "Guess we'll never know."

Seconds ticked past.

Ahmed spoke to Hussein in a language Russell didn't understand.

Hussein muttered a reply.

"Angela is still alive." Ahmed paused. "I will trade with you; your life for Mohammed's speech."

"Where is she?"

Ahmed wagged a finger at him. "I will not tell you this."

"In that case, no deal. Where is she?"

Ahmed shook his head. "Presently we are at what you Americans like to call a stalemate. If I tell you, you might attempt to find a way to pass this on to your FBI friends no matter what happens to you. You are willing to die to save her, I believe. So your only chance to save her is by telling me and you must decide quickly."

Russell said nothing.

Ahmed said, "Time is running out. You have nothing to gain by stalling. If you do not help us we will simply use our alternate plan. Your silence will have gained you nothing but your death. At this point nothing you can do will alter the ultimate outcome."

"That's right, but since you already killed Gerda and will eventually kill me, how can I be sure you haven't already killed Angela? No. I will not help you unless I can speak with her. That's the only way I can be assured she is okay."

Ahmed stood motionless, Raveena behind him said nothing while Hussein watched the interchange with a bemused expression, cracking his knuckles one by one.

Frantically, Russell scanned the room for a weapon of some sorts, figuring it was better to go out fighting than do nothing. But with what? He needed something other than bare hands. He came up blank.

Ahmed finally said, "If I let you speak with her you will set things right so Mohammed can finish his work?"

"You are assuming I can fix things. What if I can't?"

"I believe you know the answer."

The telephone on the counter rang.

CHAPTER

46

RUSSELL FLASHED AHMED a questioning look. Ahmed said, "Answer it, but do so on speakerphone."

Russell punched the button. "Hello."

An accented voice came out of the speaker. "I must speak with Ahmed."

Quickly Ahmed picked up the receiver and disconnected the speaker. "Yes?"

Ahmed listened a moment, nodded, and hung up. He said to Hussein, "I need to leave the building to take care of some business. I will return shortly. See that he is not allowed to touch the computer."

Out in the circular drive to Building 10 Ahmed stood next to an idling diesel bus to help mask his voice in case someone with a parabolic microphone attempted to monitor him. He dialed his cell phone and listened to the call connect. Using his mother tongue and cupping the phone with his other hand, he whispered, "What is it?"

"We are finished with the FBI agent. It took several hours, but we were able to finally obtain what we needed from him.

You are correct but you have also failed in your security. Somehow they managed to plant a monitoring device in one of the rooms."

Rage seemed to squeeze the blood from his heart. "Which room?"

"Not the room where Jamal is kept."

The computer lab. For one paralyzing moment, Ahmed tried to remember every word he uttered in that room. Had he said anything to allow the FBI to learn their plan? What exactly had he divulged? He quickly realized it was a futile task, so he gave up trying.

"Then we have nothing more to discuss. Activate the timer. We must proceed with the alternate plan."

"And the little girl?"

His rage focused on Lawton. If they failed, he would be the reason. "Seal the casket and leave her be. They will never find her in time."

CHAPTER
47

RUSSELL SAT IN the task chair frustrated at his inability to do anything to save himself or help Angela. He wondered if this was the same emotion Gerda experienced during those agonizing interminable moments of waiting in the booth before they shot her in the head.

Do something!

What?

Anything. Anything but sit here waiting to die.

The hall door swooshed open. Ahmed filled the doorway, face red, lips pressed into a thin determined line, hands clenched into white-knuckle fists.

Hussein said something to him but Ahmed shook his head "no" without verbally answering.

Russell swallowed and wiped both palms on his thighs. *This is it.*

Ahmed closed the door to the hall and stood motionless, glaring at Russell. He absentmindedly picked a scab off his jaw, causing a droop of blood to fall to the floor. For a moment he studied the red smear on the tip of his index finger with mild curiosity before turning and opening the door to Mohammed's room.

Russell heard Ahmed shout at Raveena. A moment later she scurried into the lab, fear in her eyes. The door separating the two rooms slammed shut.

Ahmed pulled up a chair and sat leaning forward, his face only about a foot from Jamal's ear, their eyes horizontal to each other. His friend's eyes glowed more intensely than he had ever seen before, as if needing desperately to communicate something.

In his native language Ahmed whispered, "Jamal, can you hear me? Do you understand me? If so, blink twice."

Jamal Azzam shot back two hard, rapid blinks.

"Good. I have much to tell you." He paused to corral his anger. "My friend, a very grave situation has developed." Ahmed paused to scan the room one more time, searching for another listening device the captured FBI agent may have purposely neglected to divulge. He admitted to two having been planted in the other room before he died. But what if he realized his life was about to end and in a last-ditch act of revenge, had purposely misled them? What if a listening device had been planted here, too? But how could that have happened?

But it had happened!

"Our security has been breached." Rage constricted his throat, making words difficult to speak. "The FBI knows about us. They know about you and the condition you are in. They know that you are being kept alive here. Their only reason for not acting before now is they hope to discover who all of us are and what our plan of attack is.

"I know for a fact—" He caught himself. "No, that is not true. I do not know this for the whole truth, but we captured an FBI agent. And although I am telling you what we learned from him, he may have purposely fed us false information. Some of it, however, is most certainly true. We believe the other room has somehow had a listening device planted in it.

We know that they are using this listening device to monitor what we are doing. I believe this room is still secure, but I cannot be certain beyond doubt that it is, so this is why I am whispering." He paused to glance around him once more and held up a finger. "Just a minute."

Half-heartedly he stood and scanned the room again, resigned to not being able to find the bugs. Given sufficient time, he most assuredly would. He would rip every wire from the walls, unplug every piece of electrical equipment, unscrew every lightbulb. But no time remained. Instead, he moved to the sink and turned on the water full force against the metal sink then he started a music file playing from the laptop. Satisfied that enough noise was being generated to effectively mask his words, he resumed his position in front of Jamal. "Are you still able to hear and understand me?"

The suspended head blinked twice.

"I realize just how much you desperately wanted to witness your contribution to the attack. It is brilliant. And being able to include it would have added your special touch of genius . . . the touch that has become your trademark. But, you see, my dear friend, time has run out for us. We must act immediately or risk the loss of everything we have worked so hard to achieve. I hope you understand this."

Again, Jamal blinked twice.

"Good. I had faith you would." The bitter emotional knot forming in the base of Ahmed's throat forced a choice; either pause or lose control of his voice and emotions. He looked away as if having heard something and blinked, then blinked again, squelching the fluid accumulating along his lower lids. A moment later he had his emotions sufficiently in check to meet his dear colleague's eyes again.

"You have fought the jihad courageously and will die a martyr, a true soldier and disciple of Islam. For this you should be very proud. But before you go, you must be able to bask in the glory of the damage we will inflict upon the infidels."

Ahmed stood and moved a small TV set as far as the cable connection would allow and turned Jamal's table so that he could easily watch the screen. He changed the channel to CNN Headline News and then bent at the waist so that his lips were less than an inch from his comrade's ears. "You can see the screen clearly?"

Two blinks.

"Good. Then you will be able to enjoy the results of our attack. But because of the circumstances, I have altered the plan to something I believe you will find befitting the situation. Once again we will use the Americans' arrogance to help destroy them.

"From our FBI agent we learned that they have a rapid response team organized and ready to attack the moment they learn the location of our safe house. So what must we do?" He smiled at the thought. "We must let them believe they have indeed learned that location. But when their arrogant soldiers enter the building this will become the trigger for our bomb. The explosion will take all of them with it. Do you like this?"

Jamal Azzam blinked twice.

"Excellent. But I have added a special benefit to the plan. I will not allow you to die without taking a few of the infidels with you." Ahmed walked to the counter where an old model black Sony portable stereo system sat on the stainless steel counter next to the sink.

"As you know, Americans call this a boombox." He smiled at the joke that would be apparent in his next sentence. "It is filled with C4 plastic explosive. Enough to cause serious damage to this entire building. It is set to detonate in two hours. By then, you should have witnessed the effect of our attack on CNN. The timer activates as soon as I plug it into the wall outlet. Do you find this an appropriate way to leave this life and to move to the next one?"

Jamal blinked twice.

CHAPTER

48

RUSSELL AND HUSSEIN were silently glaring at each other when the door to Mohammed's room whooshed open and Ahmed stepped back into the overheated room. Raveena stood in the corner diagonally across from Russell watching them intently as if waiting to see if Ahmed would explode.

The minutes Ahmed spent with Mohammed had transformed Ahmed's face from fist-clenching rage to placidity. The unexplained change caused the icy cloud filling Russell's chest to grow colder.

Ahmed pointed at the computer and said offhandedly to Russell, "There is no need to worry about Mohammed's—" He stopped abruptly and held up a finger. "Correction. It is time to answer all your questions. His name is, as you probably suspected, not really Mohammed. It is Jamal Azzam. Are you surprised?"

Ahmed's strange change in demeanor sounded an alarm in Russell's brain. "What's going on, Ahmed?" The feeling of impending doom in his gut intensified.

"Oh? Now you are concerned? Now you wish to be helpful?" He flipped a dismissive wave. "Too late, Doctor Lawton.

You see, we are quite finished with our work here. We will be leaving. And, of course, that means your services are no longer required."

Ahmed turned to Raveena and said with clear annoyance, "You and I will return to Yamal's grocery store immediately."

She frowned at him and said, "You know you should not say his name or mention the store aloud. You have made that point several times. Very strongly."

"And why not? The rules no longer apply." He shrugged. "There is nothing he can do now. The die is cast, as these Americans like to say."

"That may be, but you warned us repeatedly to never mention that name. It can endanger more than just us."

Ahmed's eyes narrowed. "Enough!" He turned to Hussein. "But, you, my friend, have a special job. One I know you will appreciate. You must wait until I call you. That will be in," he glanced at his watch, "perhaps a little over two hours from now. Then you may finish the job here," with an almost imperceptible nod at Russell.

Hussein grinned and glanced at the gun in his hand.

Ahmed added, "But kill him only after he can witness the fruits of our labors. He must see what he helped us accomplish. Do you understand?"

Hussein's grin widened.

Russell glanced at the counters once again for something to use as a weapon. Just like all the other times he had done this, he saw nothing.

Ahmed turned toward the door, hesitated, turned back to face Russell. "Oh that's right. I said I would finally answer your questions. Yes?"

Russell wiped both palms on his hips and licked dry lips. "Not really. My only question at this point is what happens to Angela?"

"Oh yes . . . Angela." Ahmed stroked his chin and rolled his eyes toward the ceiling in mimed consternation. "Let me think, what should we do with her? Should we show her mercy and release her? Or should we slaughter her in cold blood like your soldiers have done to the Iraqi children when you invaded Baghdad?" With an exaggerated flourish, he stroked his chin again. Then, after a contemplative nod, "Yes, I think slaughter her is the equitable alternative. An eye for an eye. But rest assured, we will not kill her quickly. We will let her suffocate. In fact, the order has already been given to start the process."

Ahmed's fingers absentmindedly began picking at the same spot on his jaw, knocking off the freshly clotted scab. Annoyed, he glanced at his fingers and shook off the scab. "Now for the other question that has seemed to intrigue you so much. What have we been working on all this time? Yes?"

The air felt sucked from Russell's chest. "Please . . . kill me, just let Angela go. She has done nothing to you."

Ahmed's eyes narrowed. "Do you want to hear this or not?"

"I don't care what you're planning. I just want my daughter safe. Just do what you plan to do, but let her go. Please."

"No, I cannot do that. You betrayed us, you see. And for that you must pay. And you must pay dearly. But first you must see what you have helped us accomplish. And then you must remain alive while your daughter suffocates, knowing full well what is happening to her. Then? Well, then Hussein may mercifully put you out of your misery.

"You will learn what we have been working on by watching the news. CNN, of course. I would not think it would be considered appropriate for you to witness it on Al Jazeera." He laughed at the little joke.

"Please let her go."

"You must listen! Repeatedly you attempted to learn what we were doing so you could feed this information to the FBI. Now you must hear it!" Ahmed wiped the side of his jaw where another drop of blood had formed. "Mohammed is a brilliant computer programmer. What you Americans term a hacker. Yes?"

With a dismissive wave, Ahmed said, "It does not matter. The point being that he has written a computer virus. Not just any virus, mind you," wagging an index finger at him. He paused and cocked his head. "Do you know what the biggest computer system in the United States is?"

"I have no idea."

"Guess."

"Jesus, Ahmed—"

"Guess!" Ahmed shouted, his face darkening in rage.

Russell wiped his palms again, his eyes still searching the room for something to use as a weapon. "Probably some government supercomputer. A Cray or something like that. Why is this so important?"

"You are not even close. The biggest computer is the telephone system. Think about it."

"I don't get it."

"The telephone system is nothing more than a huge computer system. It runs just like your computers here. The only real difference is its operating system is Unix, not Windows." Ahmed sighed, impatiently shifting weight. "Jamal was developing a virus to bring down the entire phone system along the Eastern seaboard. Why, you ask? Because the effectiveness of our attack would have been tremendously enhanced if all telephone communication was disrupted for several hours immediately before and after the attack. If you do not believe me, just remember what the lack of emergency communication did for the effectiveness of the 9-11 attacks."

All Russell could think about was Angela. He glanced around the lab again in frustration. Once again he saw nothing that might be of use.

"We have what your military likes to refer to as a dirty bomb. We plan to detonate it in the very heart of your government." Ahmed smiled broadly. Then abruptly the smile vanished. "Unfortunately, Jamal could not complete his part of the attack. Nonetheless, I think merely detonating a nuclear device in the District of Columbia should prove to be quite effective. Even if it is less effective than originally planned, it will prove that we can strike at any time and any place in your country. That nothing is sacred."

Russell did not respond.

Hussein raised the gun and aimed the barrel directly at Russell's head.

Ahmed nodded at Raveena and then the door.

"Now it is time for us to go." Ahmed turned, opened the door to the hall and let Raveena exit before he turned back to Russell.

"I have a better idea of what to do with Angela. I think we will take her home with us to be sold to a Muslim . . . perhaps some wealthy man in Afghanistan. Yes, I think this is what would be best done with her."

Ahmed then told Hussein. "After I shut this door no one should enter before you leave. Should anyone . . . *anyone* attempt to enter this room, shoot him first. Do you understand?"

With his free hand, Hussein tossed him a two-finger salute. "I am prepared to die if that is what is needed."

Ahmed said, "Allah Akhbar," before closing the door behind him.

CHAPTER 49

Building 10, NIH Campus

Special Agent Sandra Phillips was on the telephone saying, "It's a grocery store. Yamal is either part of the store's name or the name of the owner. Probably D.C. but check all the surrounding suburbs also. Delorenti and I will be in the car ready to roll. Just get us a location." She punched off, folded the cell phone and said to the techs, "You guys can break this stuff down and get it loaded up," pointing to the electronics. "We're done here. Tony and I'll retrieve the bugs in the lab later."

Delorenti was already out the door. Phillips had to hurry to catch up with him.

Four floors below Russell pleaded with Hussein, "Just one phone call, please."

Hussein shook his head and waved the gun barrel at him. "No phone calls. No computer. Nothing. Turn on the TV to CNN. We will watch our little fun. Yes?"

Visitors Parking Lot, NIH Campus

Special Agent Sandra Phillips sat tapping a white BIC ballpoint against a partially used pad of yellow, lined legal paper; a Bluetooth earphone/microphone headset lodged in her right ear canel, wirelessly connecting her to the silver Motorola clamshell phone wedged between her thighs. To her left, Special Agent Anthony Delorenti sat drumming both index fingers on the Crown Vic's steering wheel to a tune playing only in his brain. They were parked in the visitors lot sandwiched between NIH Buildings 2 and 4. A place where they were unlikely to be spotted by anyone entering or leaving Building 10. Ready to roll, just no idea where. Not yet. Soon, however.

Phillips glanced at the Seiko on her wrist and remarked, "Man, you'd think they'd be able to locate that fucking store by now."

Delorenti executed a quick drum roll. "Yeah, you'd think so." He twisted in his seat slightly, asked, "Mind if I ask you something?"

"Depends."

"That thing about your brother McGowan's mentioned a couple times. What's that all about?"

Her hand froze, the ballpoint a half-inch off the paper. She dropped her eyes. "He was an investment banker. First one in our family. He was working for Merrill Lynch. Mergers and Acquisitions. He was in the second tower on September 11th. Ninety-second floor."

Delorenti glanced away. "Sorry."

"Yeah, so am I. We were close. Like brother and sister should be."

Her cellular rang. She punched the SEND button. "Phillips."

A gravelly male voice on the other end of the line said, "We've narrowed it down to two possibilities. One out on

Seventh Road North and one out on Nebraska Avenue. Don't have a clear idea which one yet, but we're working it hard as we can."

Phillips noticed Delorenti watching her, his fingers no longer drumming. Mentally she pictured a map of D.C. and the suburbs. "That's just great! Opposite directions."

The voice answered testily, "It's the best we've been able to do so far."

"You run the property tax records for an owner, name of Yamal. Either first or last?"

"You know, thanks for mentioning it," he said, each word dripping with disdain. "Never would of thought of doing that."

"Cut the fucking sarcasm, Lloyd. This is important."

"Yeah, Phillips, we are fully aware just how important it is and we're running the records. If you'd given us more to work with we might have had it ten minutes ago. As it is, we'll have something for you in, say, five minutes, maybe a bit longer."

She considered having Delorenti start driving toward the main office. At least that way they'd be able to cut the distance some, be able to respond more quickly. "The HRT team scrambled?"

"They're ready to lock and load the moment you say the word and we have a place."

"Fine." She nodded at the ignition so Delorenti would fire it up. "We'll roll toward the District. Call us as soon as you get a hit." She reconsidered what she just said. "Call even if it comes up negative, you hear? One way or the other I want to know. But if you get a hit on the names of those property owners, run them through every database we have. I want everything known about them soon as you can get it."

Building 10, NIH Campus

Russell stared blankly at the monitor, his mind frantically
searching a mental list of the contents in the various draw-
ers. There had to be something he could use as a weapon.
Something. Simply attack Hussein bare-handed and hope
for the best? The man was quick. Probably too quick. He remembered trying to attack him in the backseat of the car and
how Hussein had reacted. He had to make an opportunity, to
do something. There was no other choice. Not if he wanted
to ever see Angela again.

Russell swallowed hard, letting his eyes wander familiar
shelves one more time.

Wait a minute!

He focused in on the one above the counter and settled on
a beige Microsoft mouse. The kind with a cord.

His heart accelerated and his mind started racing as he
palm-wiped his mouth. Would it work?

Don't think. Just do it! Now!

Hussein was leaning against the stainless steel counter

now, scraping debris from underneath his fingernails with the pick on one of those cheap chrome-plated nail clippers that seemed to always be displayed next to the batteries, gum, and *National Enquirer* at Walgreen's checkout stands.

Russell stood, yelled, "Fucking mouse!" and picked up the wireless Logitech mouse off the desk and hurled it against the floor, shattering the plastic case, sending two AA batteries, plastic shards, and a gray-brown track ball flying in as many directions.

Hussein's eyes fixed on him, his free hand instinctively reaching for the gun on the counter while his other hand put down the clippers.

Russell pushed back the chair, walked toward Hussein, eyes on the shelf. "You mind!"

Gun in hand, Hussein took a step to his right, allowing Russell access to the shelf. "What? What are you looking for?"

Russell reached out, picked up the mouse. Then froze, heart pounding his sternum, fingers tingling as his mind rehearsed the next move.

He thought of Angela's scream on the phone.

"Only this mouse." He spun left, looping the sturdy cord around Hussein's neck, jerking the man's back against his chest. He pulled with all his strength, tightening the cord. Instinctively anticipating Hussein's next move, Russell tucked in his chin in self-defense. As he did, Hussein thrust his head back hard. But instead of crushing the cartilage in Russell's nose, his skull slammed Russell's forehead with a solid WHACK, sending scintillating fireflies across Russell's vision.

Russell used the change in position Hussein's move provided to jerk the cable even tighter, eliminating the few millimeters of slack, his forehead now pushing solidly against the back of Hussein's head and filling his nose with the flowery scent of the sonofabitch's oily black hair.

Right hand clawing at the cord, Hussein seemed unable to

decide what to do next. Put down the gun and use two hands? Fire the gun left-handed? Change hands and fire?

Seconds decelerated as movements slowed and Russell strained the cord as tightly as possible, his palms feeling as if it were cutting into them. Was he effectively cutting off Hussein's airway? If so, how long before the bastard lost consciousness?

Hussein squirmed right. Russell used the movement to cinch the cord even tighter, his arm muscles now aching in protest against the strain.

The gun clattered against the linoleum floor as Hussein clawed at the cord. Russell grunted, straining, pulling tighter, coaxing every muscle fiber to contract with even more force than a moment ago, knowing he had to either crush the man's larynx or he would die.

Hussein's fist struck at Russell's face, but only a glancing blow. His fingers returned, probing. Russell shook his head back and forth keeping the terrorist's fingers from gouging his eyes.

An elbow slammed his ribs but not hard enough to inflict severe pain. A heel connected solidly against his right shin, sending a bolt of pain up his leg, but Russell pushed through it and clung to the cord, focusing, willing his quivering arm muscles to not relax. His fingers tingled from the pressure of the cord cutting off circulation to them.

In the next moment, Hussein's struggle began to show the signs of weakening, the continued blows losing strength as his body grew heavier. Russell held the tension, never slackening, not trusting the bastard for a moment.

Seconds later, Hussein's body went limp.

Drops of sweat ran into both eyes and down the sides of Russell's chest. His breaths came in sharp gasps. His heart raced. He maintained tension on the mouse cord, feeling as if it was now supporting Hussein's entire weight. How long should he hold? Was the bastard really dead or just faking it?

Russell slowly lowered Hussein's limp body to the floor, stretching it out belly down, his right knee pressed squarely into the middle of his back, both hands holding the cord like reins to a horse. He waited even longer, purposely watching the second hand of the wall clock circle once, then twice as the skin above the ligature remained ghastly purple from venous congestion. Surely he was dead by now.

Quickly, he dropped the mouse cord and scooped up the gun, darting away from Hussein's body while aiming the gun at his head, waiting to see if he would move. He watched the terrorist's chest for another minute but saw no hint of a respiratory effort. Keeping out of arm's reach, he studied his neck veins for pulsations. Nothing. Both Hussein's eyes remained wide open and slightly bulging, both pupils dilated. Still . . .

Russell's hands began to tremble, his breaths came in gasps. Both knees weakened. He dropped into his chair and started to shake uncontrollably but did not stop aiming the gun at Hussein's head.

"Move you bastard and I'll shoot, so help me God," all the while wondering, *What now?*

Rockville Pike, Bethesda MD

"Okay, Phillips, we have a confirmation. The store of interest is the one located on Seventh Road North. You ready for the complete address?"

"Stand by a moment." She said to Delorenti, "Head for Seventh Road North." Delorenti nodded and hit the turn indicator. Then, intending the next words for the telephone, Phillip said, "We're on our way."

Now Delorenti was placing the blue flasher on the dashboard.

After reciting the exact address, the agent on the other end of the line said, "HRT's already deployed. You will be advised of the staging area soon as it has been established by the team leader. Is that affirmative?"

"That is affirmative."

Building 10, NIH Campus

After several minutes Russell could push upright and remain standing on shaky legs. Still aiming the gun at Hussein's lifeless head, he approached the body and squatted down and reached for his neck. His finger probed for a carotid pulse. None was present.

Still squatting, he turned, glanced over his left shoulder and through the open door into the other room. Head suspended by the Halo brace, tubes exiting from the neck stump, Mohammed watched.

Russell called out, "Time to have a little talk, you asshole. We need to figure out who's lying to me. You or Ahmed." He typed a few commands, scrolled through the last several minutes of conversation Ahmed had with Mohammed or Jamal or whatever his name was. What he saw shocked him.

He switched the voice synthesizer onto external speakers and walked toward Mohammed's room.

District of Columbia

Delorenti pulled the Crown Vic into a parking lot already crammed with haphazardly parked federal-motor-pool-looking cars, two black Suburbans with darkly tinted windows and a black minivan of a make Phillips didn't recognize. A dozen or so members of the Hostage Rescue Team were milling around in black paramilitary uniforms with Kevlar vests and communication gear in their ears. She didn't recognize any of them. However, she did recognize Larry Knopp, the agent coordinating the assault on the grocery store several blocks away. He appeared to be giving instructions to two HRT members.

When he saw her step out of the car he waved her over, yelled, "Didn't waste much time getting here, did you?"

Building 10, NIH Campus

"Where is she? Where are they hiding Angela? The mortuary or the grocery store?"

Mohammed smirked as his disembodied voice came over the speaker. "If I told you it wouldn't be a secret anymore would it?"

Russell's fists tightened into knots of white knuckles. "Goddamnit, tell me."

"Or?"

Russell's eyes fell on the humming heart-lung machine. "Or I pull the plug on this machine."

"And what will that accomplish? You will, of course, get some sense of satisfaction from killing me, but you still won't know the location of your daughter, will you?" Another smirk.

"You're good as dead now. It's just a question of how many hours are left until everything gives out. Your clotting factors are heading down the toilet. You've got the start of a yeast infection in your wound." Russell shook his head to underscore the pathos of the situation. "You're finished. Game's over. Why not save an innocent girl from . . ." The words stuck in his throat.

"Oh, so suddenly you are deeply concerned about the killing of innocent children? This sudden compassion, where does it come from?"

Russell picked up the drainage tube from the stump of Mohammed's esophagus. "Don't start with the rhetoric. I don't want to hear it and you don't have time to waste on it. Tell me or this tube comes out."

Mohammed's smirk vanished. "You see? We have nothing more to discuss because there will never be a meeting of our views. You dismiss our beloved Islamic religion as the ranting of fanatics. On the other hand, I despise your morally corrupt, sinful Western lifestyle. That, by the way, is a good example of one of the reasons I rejected the United States and returned to my roots. So there you have it; stalemate. Besides, your fate is cast. Yes, having killed Hussein means you may very well survive *this* little misadventure, but in the final analysis you will lose. And you know why? Because Angela is already dead."

"What!" A breath-stealing chill paralyzed Russell's chest. He jerked the tube from Mohammed's neck stump and threw it across the room. "Bullshit!"

"Oh yes," Mohammed smiled. "They killed her two days ago."

District of Columbia

Knopp told Phillips, "I just received the word. All traffic within a three-block radius of the store is now shut down. The assault team has been fully briefed on the layout of the store's interior. You sure the kid is most likely being held on the second floor?"

She couldn't be certain, but since the two-story building was a functional retail establishment, that was the only thing that made sense. "That's what we believe. Yes."

"Give us ten more minutes to secure the immediate area and then we're ready to rock and roll."

Ahmed studied his only remaining comrades; Yusef, Raveena, and the two who had stood watch over Jamal Azzam during his days at Georgetown Medical Center. The other three had already slipped out of the country during the past twenty-four hours. "You must leave at once. Do not bother to pack your belongings. It is time."

One asked, "And you? Will you be leaving now?"

Ahmed nodded. "Yes, but only after I make certain every-thing goes as planned."

Yusef glanced toward the other room. "What about the girl?"

"What about her? We leave her."

"But she will surely die if left in there. As it is, she might not have sufficient air to survive another thirty minutes." He caught Ahmed's look. "Yes, yes, of course. We will leave her. I understand."

Ahmed glanced from one comrade to another, proud of the job each had done. "Travel safely. God willing, I will see each of you back home. Allah Akhbar."

NIH Building 10

It's a lie. He's playing mind games with you, Russell told himself.

Russell inhaled deeply, trying to squelch the panic that could easily cause him a stupid mistake. He had one shot at finding out the answer and he would be working on nothing more than a hunch. Besides Ahmed, Hussein, and Raveena he had met only two other members of the group: The man who drove the van the night they landed at the Baltimore airport, who, it turned out, was the one watching over Jamal at the hospital. There was also Yusef, the mortician. What better place to have a safe house than a mortuary? He checked the computer, made certain it was recording Mo-hammed's words before approaching the decapitated head again.

"Know what Mohammed? I don't believe you. I think

you're just trying to fuck with my mind. And you know why? Because Ahmed let me talk to Angela less than ten hours ago," he lied. "And you know what else? You and Ahmed purposely tried to feed me wrong information, didn't you?"

Mohammed's emotionless face just stared back.

"She's really at the mortuary, isn't she!"

Mohammed hesitated a beat. "No, she is at the grocery store."

Russell spun around to look at the computer monitor.

Building 10, NIH Campus

Russell checked the clock. Time was evaporating too quickly. Yet, to rush might result in a disastrous mistake. He paused to organize his thoughts before moving to the adjoining lab.

From the speaker Mohammed's synthesized disembodied voice was saying, "What are you doing?"

Perversely, it reminded him of the huge computer, HAL, in Kubrick's *2001, Space Odyssey*.

Russell stood up, his right hand holding the black 110 volt cord to the cardiac bypass machine for Mohammed to see. "What the hell does it look like I'm doing, you asshole?"

"No, wait, don't unplug me." The voice paused. "I can help you recover your daughter. Yes, you are correct. She is still alive. But you won't be able to get her back safely without my help."

"Guess what, Mohammad, Jamal or whatever the hell your real name is?" He held up the power cord to the bypass machine. "See this? This is from Angela." He jerked the cord, whipping the three-prong plug from the wall outlet, sending it banging against the machine's sheet-metal rear panel.

"Wait! If you plug it back in I'll personally guarantee Angela's safe release."

Russell hesitated.

Jamal said, "Let me prove it to you. The boombox over there on the counter. It's a bomb."

"A bomb?" Russell spun around on his heels and grabbed it. He ripped the electrical cord out of the socket, picked the case up and held it above his hand. "First you say they killed her two days ago, now it's she's still alive. You expect me to believe anything you say?"

Mohammad yelled, "No, don't. I'm telling you—"

Russell threw the Sony player across the room, shattering the plastic case into shards of black plastic, electronics, and something else he didn't recognize.

"Are you fucking crazy! That is explosive," Mohammed said. Then, "Please, I beg of you."

"You caught on to me, didn't you!"

"What do you mean?"

"The extra words the computer was picking up . . . they were words you thought but never said, right?"

"Yes, but—"

"But you missed the implication. See, I could tell you just lied to me. She's not at the store, she's at the mortuary."

"Yes. So, please—"

Russell slammed the door to Mohammed's room then ran his fingers down the panel of circuit breakers, cutting off every bit of the power to both rooms except the overhead lights. He picked up Hussein's gun, riffled through the dead man's pockets until he found another full clip of ammunition, opened the desk drawer and rummaged through Gerda's black leather purse for the key to her Mercedes Benz and her cell phone.

Then he flipped the final circuit breaker, darkening the overhead lights and cutting the last of the electricity to both labs. He stepped into the hall and locked the door.

Russell punched in his location on the NIH campus and then the address for the mortuary into the console GPS system. He dropped the transmission into reverse and eased the silver CLK-320 out of the parking space and onto Center Drive. Using his left hand, he punched 411 into the cell phone, hit SEND and pressed it to his ear. A moment later a computer-synthesized female voice answered: "What city?"

"Washington, D.C."

"What name?"

"The Federal Bureau of Investigation."

After a few seconds the computer responded with the number and the option of being connected directly to it. He opted to let the computer make the connection for him.

A female answered. "FBI."

"I need to reach Special Agent Sandra Phillips immediately. It's an emergency."

She gave a reassuring, "I'll connect you," and clicked off. After several rings the line switched over to, "This is Special Agent Sandra Phillips. I'm either on another call or out of the office. Please leave a message at the sound of the beep and I'll return your call as soon as possible."

"Damn!"

At that moment a computer-generated female voice instructed, "Turn right onto Rockville Pike." He glanced at the GPS system and waited for a break in traffic to make the turn.

He glanced at the dashboard clock. Time now seemed to be flying by. He dialed directory information again, was greeted by the same computer-synthesized voice, and again requested it to ring the FBI. After a series of clicks, another recording answered with, "All of our lines are presently busy. If you know your party's extension, you may dial it at any time. Otherwise please remain on the line and an operator will assist you at the earliest available opportunity."

"Jesus!" Russell slammed his palm against the steering wheel. "Can't I talk to someone other than a fucking computer?"

"FBI, how may I help you?"

The car was moving now, accelerating through traffic, Russell coming up behind a UPS truck.

"Look, this is matter of life and death. I need to speak with Special Agent Sandra Phillips but apparently she's not in her office because I just called and was connected to her voicemail. I need to speak with someone now! Preferably whomever she directly reports to."

He swerved into the inside lane and shot around the truck. Several horns blared in protest.

"Hold, please."

Russell braked the Benz for a red light and watched cars speed past in front of him. Time distorted with every second splitting into milliseconds. "Come on! Come on!" He pounded the steering wheel again.

"McGowan here."

"You work with Agent Phillips?"

"Who is this?"

"My name's Russell Lawton, I'm—"

"Yes, Doctor Lawton," McGowan interrupted. "I know exactly who you are. Where are you?"

"On Rockville Pike. Look, I need to speak with Agent Phillips immediately."

"Why? What's wrong?"

"Two things. I know where they're holding my daughter and I know where they're planning to detonate a bomb."

"Calm down. She's there right now."

"Who? Phillips? She's at the mortuary?" he asked, dismayed.

McGowan paused. When he finally answered, he asked "Mortuary? What mortuary?"

District of Columbia

Knopp thumbed the transmit button to the Motorola earphone/mike combination, asked, "Alpha team?"

The squelch broke on the encrypted, spread-spectrum transmitting frequency: "Affirmative."

He keyed the radio again, "Bravo?"

"Affirmative."

He glanced at Phillips. "All entry teams ready. Just say the word."

Her cell phone rang. Annoyed at an interruption at such a crucial moment, she considered whether to answer it or just let it roll over to voicemail.

"**No, no! Don't** go in there!" Russell screamed into the phone. "You got the wrong place. There's a bomb in that building. It's a trap."

Phillips' voice came pounding back over the connection. "The hell you talking about, we got the wrong place? We had your lab bugged. I heard Ahmed tell you about it."

Russell curbed the Benz. Across the street and down a half block a circular asphalt drive led to the front door of the mortuary. He'd driven past once just to scope it out. There were no cars in the drive and no hearse in sight.

"It's a trap. A setup. You go in there, you'll trigger their attack."

"How do you know this?"

Not having the time to explain about the trick with the computer, he settled for a simple, "They told me."

"They told you? And then just let you waltz out of there? Just like that?" Phillips sounded skeptical.

"Look, I don't have the time right now. I'll explain later. The point is, there's this mortuary. One of their buddies is a mortician. It's a perfect place for them to work and not be detected. I just pulled up outside the place. I'm parked across the street."

"You're what!"

"Angela's inside. I've got to go get her out of there before—"

"For christsake, Lawton, stay put. Let us—" Phillips realized the connection had dropped. She turned to the technician on her right. "Please tell me you got a GPS fix on that call before he disconnected." She hadn't thought to ask him to do that when the call came in. Had she known it was going to be Lawton, she certainly would have.

"Yes, ma'am."

"You're an absolute genius. Thanks." She told Knopp, "Have the teams stand down immediately. You need to re-deploy."

Russell ejected the clip from Hussein's gun and checked the number of bullets. Nine. Ten, counting one in the chamber. Good. And he had another clip in the pocket of his jacket. He slapped the clip back into the stock and clicked off the safety before sliding the gun under the waistband of his scrubs, then pulling his scrub shirt over it.

Out of the car now, he crossed the street, heading straight for the asphalt drive leading up to the front door of the white, two-story, Georgian structure, figuring his best offensive asset would be surprise and his second best would be the gun.

The front door opened noiselessly into a hardwood floor foyer with Persian runner, side tables along the opposite walls, interior walls painted rich burgundy with cream-colored crown molding and the faint scents of incense, air-conditioning, and white Mourning Lilies. On either side of him, opened double doors exposed waiting/viewing rooms. Straight down the hall, a staircase ascended to the second floor while a narrower hall paralleling the stairs continued toward the very back of the building.

Before doing anything else Russell slid the gun from his bloody scrubs and double-checked the safety to make certain it was in the off position. He listened for sounds of voices or footsteps but heard none. Had they left the country already? Was Angela still alive?

Suddenly, the slender man Russell recognized as the mortician, the one who had come to the lab to dispose of Mohammed's body, entered from the room on the right asking, "May I help you?" then froze, his eyes growing large. "You! What are you doing here?" He reached around toward his back, a second later a gun appeared in his hand.

Without thinking, Russell raised his gun, aimed dead center at the man's forehead and pulled the trigger. The mortician's head jerked and his legs buckled, sending him crashing onto the floor.

Moving quickly, Russell checked the rooms to either side of the foyer. They appeared to be viewing rooms, sparsely furnished with chairs and a few side tables. Both were devoid of people.

Next he hurried to the back of the building. Since there was no slope to the driveway, he assumed the embalming and preparation area was either back here or that an elevator serviced a basement. At the end of the hall, to the right was a set of double doors, wide enough to allow a casket to pass. He paused to listen but heard no voices or movement from the other side.

Tentatively, he slowly pushed one door open. Yes, here was a room for preparing bodies. He stepped in for a better look at a white tile floor and stainless steel countertops. Off to one side stood a slightly sloped stainless steel table for embalming customers. A coffin sat atop two sawhorses at the other end of the room. There was no sign of Angela.

One back door opened to the outside. Through a window

in the door he could see a garage at the end of a driveway paralleling the side of the house. To his right was the only other door in the large room. He suspected it opened either to a closet or to a set of basement stairs. He opened it. Correct: stairs went down into a gloomy set of shadows. On the wall to the left of the stairs was a switch. He thumbed it on. Sure enough lights came on in the basement. Again, he listened. Again, nothing.

The stairs were open at the sides except for a thin railing. Anyone down there would see him before he ever saw them. He would be totally exposed. But there was no other way to know if Angela was being held down there.

Gun held at ready, he slowly lowered his right foot onto the first step. The stair creaked. He continued down, muscles tense, ears intently scanning for a sound from either above or below him. At the bottom, he stepped onto a solid concrete floor and turned 360 degrees with the gun held in a two-handed grip like he'd been taught to use it. His eyes took in an unfinished basement with furnace, a workbench with various tools scattered over its surface, a heavy-duty washer and dryer, and a door. He tried to open it but found it locked.

He quickly surveyed the room for a tool and saw a sledge-hammer leaning against the workbench. One swing splintered the door's center panel. A second swing took out the entire door. Inside was an empty room about five by eight feet. There was still no sign of Angela or that she'd been kept here.

Had Mohammed tricked him? Was she really at the store Ahmed mentioned? The uneasiness in the pit of his gut worsened. She had to be here in the house. Mohammed couldn't have been able to manipulate the interface. Or did he?

There was still the second floor of the house. Perhaps even an attic.

She had to be here.

He turned and took the stairs two at a time but stopped at

the top of the landing, gun in hand to listen again. If anyone else were in the house, the noise from bashing in the door certainly would attract the attention.

That's when he noticed the casket again. A simple rectangular oak box with three oval metal handles along the side for pallbearers. But something didn't look right. He looked more closely before realizing what exactly bothered him about it. A chain was wrapped around the center of the coffin, an open padlock securing it into place. Why use a chain to house a dead body? Unless . . .

He shoved the gun under his waistband and pulled the padlock from the links and threw the chain off the wood and opened the box. Angela scrunched her eyelids closed from the light.

"Oh, my God. Angie!"

"Daddy?"

"Oh, God, are you all right?" He reached down to lift her from the coffin.

"Daddy!"

"It's me, baby. I told you I'd come." He had her in his arms now, hugging her.

"Daddy!" she wailed and started to sob.

"Shhhh. Everything's going to be okay, honey," he gently set her down, feet on the floor. "Please, don't make a sound. We don't want the bad men to hear you."

Angela reached up and clung to his neck, making it impossible to move or stand.

He tried to pull her hands from his neck. "Honey, let go. We need to get out of here."

"Daddy, behind you!"

Her arms still clinging to him, Russell glanced over his shoulder. Ahmed stood in the doorway, a gun similar to Hussein's in his right hand aimed at him.

"Bloody hell, aren't you an industrious little fellow. Hussein would never have let you out of that room alive. Tell me, please, what happened to him?" Ahmed asked with surprising lack of emotion.

"He was a bad boy, so I grounded him for the week. I told him to stay in his room." Without looking at Angela, he gently pulled her arms from his neck and whispered, "Angie, honey, you need to let go so I can take care of some business with this man." Reluctantly, she released his neck but grabbed his biceps and stood, sniffing tears from her nose.

Ahmed's eyebrows knitted. "I really do not find that at all amusing. Did you kill him?"

Gently Russell took hold of Angela's wrists and pulled her arms free from his arm. He remained on his haunches, his arm around her shoulders, holding her close. "Tell me something. How many virgins is it he's supposed to be rewarded with? Thirty seven? Or is it seventy three? I can't keep that one straight. And do you chauvinists really believe all that crap?"

Ahmed's jaw clenched. He waved the gun barrel to the right as if instructing Angela to move away. "Raveena," he called.

Raveena appeared behind him.

Ahmed said to Russell. "It will be best if you release her now." Then, "Come here, Angela."

Russell did not let go of her. "I've come this far. I'm not going to let her go now."

Ahmed shrugged. "You still have total control. You may continue to hold her, as you wish, but if you do, I will be forced to shoot through her to kill you."

Russell considered the gun beneath his scrub shirt, safety off, and visualized the move: Shove Angela out of the way and try to squeeze off a couple shots before they killed him. Problem was, that kind of move worked in movies, but here? Who else was in the house besides Raveena? And what about Angela? She'd be caught in the crossfire.

Russell glanced from Raveena back to Ahmed. "She won't go to you unless I ask her to. Give me a second."

Without waiting for an answer, Russell turned to face Angela and wrapped her in his arms, hugging her trembling body, pressing her wet cheeks firmly against his stubble. He buried his nose in her hair and inhaled her fragrance, figuring if he were to die right now, her memory would be thoroughly embedded as his last thought.

He whispered, "Baby, you've got to go with these people for just a little bit longer. I have some things to take care of with this man. Once I'm done with them I'll come and take you home for good."

"But I don't want to go with him," she wailed.

"I know, baby. I don't want you to either, but sometimes there are things in life that we have to do that we don't want to do. Understand?"

"I don't want to go! I hate them, I hate them! I want to stay with you!"

"Please, baby, just do as I ask this one time. Okay? Do it for me. Please?"

Gently, he unwrapped her arms from around his neck and stood her on the floor and turned her around to face Ahmed.

Raveena stepped forward, arm out. "Come here, Angela."

Angela started to sob. "I don't want to go with those stupid idiots."

Russell pushed her gently toward Raveena who took hold of her hand and began to pull her in the direction of the doorway.

Angela started screaming, "I don't want to!" over and over.

Still aiming the gun at Russell, Ahmed reached out, grabbed Angela's other hand, stretching her arms out between Raveena and him.

Ahmed said, "One question before we resolve this messy

situation. Out of curiosity, how did you know we were here?"

"Mental telepathy."

"Seriously."

"Seriously. I'm a mind reader."

Ahmed pointed the gun at Angela. "It is your decision. Answer me immediately or I blow her head off right here in front of you. Is this is what you want?"

"No! Wait. I'll tell you." Russell explained it.

Ahmed nodded at the explanation, seemingly appreciative of Russell's resourcefulness. Then he grinned, placed the gun barrel to Angela's temple. "And now you will have the pleasure of witnessing Angela's execution."

"No!" Raveena screamed.

Ahmed looked at her with the same surprise as if she'd just slapped him. He barked a string of harsh words back at her. Glaring, she released Angela's hand and slapped him.

Ahmed raised the gun and fired directly into Raveena's forehead.

Without thinking, Russell pulled Hussein's gun from beneath his scrubs and began firing dead center at Ahmed's chest, squeezing off round after round as he dropped to the floor until the firing pin clicked with each trigger pull. He threw down the empty gun, swept Angela into his arms and started running for the front door.

From the front of the house a voice shouted. "FBI! Freeze!"

CHAPTER
53

Three Weeks Later

"Agent Phillips, hold on a second."

Phillips stopped on the concrete sidewalk and turned to see who just called. Cars were zipping past on the street behind her, the afternoon sun turning the cloudless sky a deep azure.

With Angela in tow, Russell hurried down the remaining three granite steps of the courthouse to catch up with the FBI agent while making certain his daughter didn't stumble. When he finally reached Phillips, he gasped, "Hold on a sec," gulped air and checked Angela, still marveling at the fact she was safely back with him.

Satisfied, he addressed the FBI agent. "Listen, I want to thank you for just about everything. Your testimony today . . . well, I don't think I could've won without it."

"You won because the court ruled in your favor. All I did was explain what really happened with the kidnapping thing."

"Yes, but . . ." he saw by her facial expression he would not win the point. "The other thing is going to bat for me about . . ." he found himself torn between thanking her and Angela hearing the details.

Phillips nodded knowingly. "You did what had to be done. It was nothing more than self-defense. Any grand jury would see that. Way I see it, you should be getting a medal for what you did." She paused as if to change subjects. "Long as we're doing this mutual admiration thing, I want to thank you for taking care of notifying Ed Ogilvy's wife."

Russell swallowed. "I don't know . . . I just felt it should come from me. Thing is, Gerda's folks are all gone. All she had was Gerhard. So . . ."

Phillips put a hand on his shoulder. "Still wasn't easy. Thanks for taking that one from me." She looked down at Angela. "You happy with the court's decision, little lady?"

Angela, both arms wrapped around Russell's waist, beamed up at her.

READERS OF EARLY drafts asked me if the plot premise was science fiction or could the events described really happen? Although this novel is clearly a work of fiction, many of its biological concepts are quite real. For starters, patent number 4,666,425 really was issued on May 19, 1987, to an unidentified inventor using the fictitious name of Chet Fleming. The downloaded copy from the U.S. Patent office makes for interesting reading. As the story points out, the inventor did not use his real name because he realized the controversial nature of the patent and the disruption it potentially might bring to his private life unless he remained hidden. The actual title of the patent is A DEVICE FOR PERFUSING AN ANIMAL HEAD.

The experiments conducted by Robert White, M.D., a neurosurgeon practicing at Case Western Reserve University and the Cleveland Metro Hospital in the sixties and seventies are also very real and can be found in the archived copies of *Surgery* and *The Journal of Neurosurgery* at any major medical school library. The thrust of his work was to actually transplant the head of one animal onto the body of another of the same species, perhaps replacing the recipient animal's head. The real question is why? As a neurosurgeon I find this difficult to understand. If the intent was to allow quadriplegics with high neck fractures to live, one must ask what benefit would be gained by a successful transplant? Since the severed spinal cord cannot be made to reestablish its damaged connections, the quadriplegic would remain a quadriplegic even after such a difficult surgery.

Neural Networks are a form of artificial intelligence used by researchers in various scientific disciplines, including medicine. Commercially available neural network software can be purchased to run on your home PC with astonishingly good results. Just Google *neural network* to find a list of available products.

Finally, there are medical device companies presently implanting electrodes on or in human brains for the purpose of developing brain/computer interfaces. One of the first is Neural Signals (www.neuralsignals.com). This company aims to generate speech from the brains of people suffering from a variety of neurologic disease—such as stroke—that renders them unable to speak. Cyberkinetics is a company that has received FDA clearance to implant arrays of tiny electrodes into the brains of quadriplegic humans with the intent of using their neural signals to manipulate robotic arms. I see these as valid applications that holds real potential to provide some relief to patients with major disabilities.

Readers should realize this ongoing work has its roots in the 1970s' pioneering work of motor control physiologists such as Eberhard Fetz and Edward Evarts at a time when laboratory computers were such clunky behemoths as the venerable PDP 8, the LINC 9, and finally the PDP 12. These old beauties were manufactured by the now-defunct Digital Equipment Company.

Thank you for reading this novel.

Allen Wyler, M.D.
Seattle, Washington